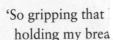 

THE
BONE
FIELDS

THE
BONE
FIELDS

C.F. BARRINGTON

An Aries Book

First published in the UK in 2023 by Head of Zeus,
part of Bloomsbury Publishing Plc

9 7 5 3 1 2 4 6 8

A catalogue record for this book is available from the British Library.

ISBN (PB): 9781804545720
ISBN (E): 9781804545706

Cover design: Matt Bray

Typeset by Siliconchips Services Ltd UK

Printed and bound in Great Britain by
CPI Group (UK) Ltd, Croydon CRO 4YY

Head of Zeus
First Floor East
5–8 Hardwick Street
London EC1R 4RG

WWW.HEADOFZEUS.COM

To Natasha, Christopher, Isla, Henry and Mae-Mae.
I hope, one day, you may love the adventures
of Tyler and Lana too.

THE PANTHEON

THE CAELESTIA (THE SEVEN)

The Legion ~ Lord High Jupiter ~ Marcella Ballantyne
The Titans ~ Lord Zeus ~ Nikolas Petrou
The Horde ~ Lord Odin ~ Raymond J Pearlman (deceased)
The Sultanate ~ Lord Kyzaghan ~ Hakan Reis
The Warring States ~ Lord Xian ~ Zhang Huateng
The Kheshig ~ Lord Tengri ~ Jacob Steinberg
The Huns ~ Lord Ördög ~ Mikhail Malutin

THE PALATINATES

The Legion ~ Caesar Imperator ~ HQ: Rome
The Titans ~ Alexander of Macedon ~ HQ: Edinburgh
The Horde (dissolved) ~ Sveinn the Red ~ HQ: Edinburgh
The Sultanate ~ Mehmed the Conqueror ~ HQ: Istanbul
The Warring States ~ Zheng, Lord of Qin ~ HQ: Beijing
The Kheshig ~ Genghis, Great Khan ~ HQ: Khan Khenti
The Huns ~ Attila, Scourge of God ~ HQ: Pannonian Plain

THE ORBAT (Order of Battle)

The Legion

The Huns v. The Sultanate

The Kheshig v. The Warring
States

The Titans v. The Horde
(dissolved)

THE TITAN SKY-GODS

Strength: 399 troops

Zeus ~ Caelestis of the Titan Palatinate

Hera ~ Wife of Zeus

Alexander, Lion of Macedon ~ High King of the Titans

Simmius ~ Adjutant of the Palatinate, Paymaster,
Custodian of the Day Books

Nicanor ~ Colonel, Brigade of Hoplite Heavy Infantry
Phalanx: 9 rows of 12.
Total: 108

Menes ~ Colonel, Brigade of Light Infantry and
Captain of Companions
Total: 62

Agape ~ Captain of Sacred Band
Total: 14

Parmenion ~ Captain of Peltasts, Archers & Scouts
Total: 43

Hephaestion ~ Captain of Companion Cavalry
Total: 11

The Hellenic Regiment
Total: 161

Other Dramatis Personae

Titan
Diogenes (formerly Brante) ~ Forbes Urquhart
Lenore (Companion Cavalry)
Spyro (Companion Cavalry)

Valhalla
Calder (former Thegn) ~ Lana Cameron
Skarde (former Housecarl)
Bjarke (former Jarl)
Ulf (former Hammer)
Ingvar (former Berserker)
Ake (former Wolf)
Stigr (former Wolf)
Sassa (former Raven)
Geir (former Raven)
Estrid (former Raven)

Legion
Caesar Imperator ~ Julian Ballantyne
Augustus (Prefect of the Praetorian Guard) ~ Fabian Ballantyne
Valerius (Consul)
Flavius (Legate of First Cohort)
Cassia (Legate of Second Cohort)
Domna (Praetorian Guard)

Hun
Bleda (Colonel of the Black Cloaks)
Uptar (Colonel of the First Horn)
Ellac (Colonel of the Second Horn)

Other

Oliver Muir (former Initiate in Valhalla Schola)

Atilius (Praetor of the Pantheon)

Kustaa (former Thane of Valhalla and Paymaster)

Aurora (former Head of Valhalla Operations Support Unit)

Elliott Greaves (tutor at Valhalla Schola)

Meghan (former Initiate in Valhalla Schola)

What Has Come Before

1. The Pantheon is a secret game bankrolled by the world's wealthy elite.

2. Two of the Pantheon's seven teams are located in Edinburgh: Alexander's Titan Palatinate are masters of the rooftops of the Old Town; Sveinn's Valhalla Horde are stationed beneath the Royal Mile.

3. In the Eighteenth Year of the Games, Timanthes (a Titan Colonel) and Olena (a Titan Captain) lead their troops into the subterranean tunnels of the Horde, but they are betrayed. Timanthes is killed, Olena disappears, and the cream of the Titan Palatinate is wiped out. It will change everything.

4. So begins the Nineteenth Year. Tyler Maitland and Lana Cameron are recruited into the Horde and are schooled by Housecarls Freyja and Halvar.

5. Their training complete, the final seven recruits are sworn into the Horde and given Pantheon names: Tyler becomes Punnr; Lana becomes Calder; and they are joined by Brante.

6. Tyler is convinced his sister – Morgan – is also in the Horde, but she has disappeared. Unwisely, he makes his search known to those who wish her harm and he is

thrown into his first Raiding Season against the Titans with as many enemies in his own lines.

7. He learns that Halvar was once Morgan's lover and he also learns he has joined the wrong Palatinate. Morgan was Olena of the Titans and it was she who betrayed her own troops before she disappeared.

8. Tyler asks his neighbour, thirteen-year-old Oliver, to help him search for his lost sister, Morgan. Oliver is a skilled online hacker and sets about his search with gusto.

9. The Nineteenth Blood Season begins. Punnr and Brante and their Wolf litters take part in the first three Blood Nights. Punnr's lack of Bloodmarks on his armour mark him out and he has to fight for his life on the rooftops of Edinburgh.

10. After these Nights, Tyler is whisked away to a distant Hebridean island to prepare for the Grand Battle, the culmination of the Nineteenth Year.

11. Meanwhile, Lord Odin, the Caelestis of Valhalla, knows he must stamp out Tyler's search for his sister and organises the release of a man from Erebus, the Pantheon Prison. This is Skarde, who becomes Odin's trusted killer and joins the Wolf units to seek out Tyler (Punnr).

12. Odin organises the murders of Oliver's parents and oversees the kidnapping of Oliver, who is taken into the dark subterranean world of the Pantheon.

13. On the final Blood Night, Skarde accosts Calder and she realises he is the man who raped her many years ago. Her world falls apart.

14. The rival Palatinates meet in a momentous Grand Battle on white Hebridean sands. At the critical moment in the Battle, Punnr makes a mad attempt to get to the Titan lines. Brante follows him and they surrender to Agape, a Titan Captain.

15. Punnr and Brante must fight for their places in the Titan Palatinate. They receive new Titan names. Punnr becomes Heph; Brante becomes Diogenes.

16. The summer Interregnum arrives and the Pantheon ceases until winter. Tyler goes north to see his friend Forbes (who is Brante/Diogenes) and has his first taste of riding a horse. Lana stays at Freyja's house in Edinburgh.

17. Zeus, the Titan Caelestis, offers Heph the chance to create a small Titan cavalry. Heph accepts and joins Diogenes in training this small group to ride bareback like the ancient Macedonian Companion Cavalry.

18. The Twentieth Season begins. Calder and Freyja oversee the development of a new cadre of Valhalla recruits, then take part in the Twentieth Raiding Season. The Palatinates battle it out at Edinburgh Zoo and Waverley Station.

19. The Season ends with another Grand Battle in the far north of Scotland. The Horde are the stronger Palatinate, and they kill Alexander with a thrown spear.

20. Heph leads his small cavalry unit onto the Field at the critical moment and charges upfield to kill King Sveinn with a sword.

21. Two Kings die. Valhalla falls. And the Pantheon is on the brink of collapse.

Prologue

Before a Titan cavalry captain left his blade in the belly of a King; before the first Seasons had been contested; before the forging of the Rules; before the Pantheon was even an inkling – Raymond J Pearlman, who would one day take the name of a god, scowled over his glass.

Trust Ballantyne to force vintage champagne on them. Fizz had never been to Pearlman's taste, and now the stuff had soured his innards.

It was 1997, Hallowe'en, and somewhere above their heads in the reception rooms of Julian Ballantyne's Hampshire mansion, there was a party going on. Rivers of champagne, mountains of cocaine, serving staff dressed like Celtic chieftains. Marcella – Ballantyne's formidable wife – had decided that her gathering should have *none of that nonsense American import* and had instead based it on the ancient Gaelic celebration of Samhain, which had once marked the end of the harvest season and the beginning of the dark half of the year. Her theming was haphazard. The Celts had been joined by security guards in Roman robes and girls dressed as princesses of the Orient, but Marcella always carried off these events with such diligent panache that everyone was too busy having a good time to notice.

Everyone except Pearlman.

Parties were not his thing, and Ballantyne's jamborees tested his endurance to the limit. But each year, whenever their calendars allowed, Pearlman, Ballantyne and three others got together somewhere in the world to talk business, weigh the odds, shape plans – and Ballantyne invariably ensured the day's discussions were followed by a night of debauchery.

'Goddamn pantomime,' had been Pearlman's opinion as he perched on the cushioned sill of a vast bay window, his back to the Hampshire night, watching the party ebb and flow around an ornate drawing room.

Beside him a small, neat man had smiled. Zhang Huateng was also in his forties, startlingly handsome and attired in a grey designer polo neck. 'I think, perhaps, you're old before your time, my friend.'

'Bollocks. I just wish that one year we could meet without the accompanying showbiz.'

Mercifully, Ballantyne had disengaged himself from the throng, gathered Mikhail Malutin and Jacob Steinberg, and approached the other two men by the window. Six foot three, blond, ramrod straight and oozing charm, Ballantyne looked every bit the lord of the land, although there had been times when the other four had seen him mad with fury, manic with joy and black with gloom. The secret mess of the man.

'Come,' he had said softly, drawing them to their feet. 'I've something special I want to show you downstairs.'

So now the five of them sat in a darkened cinema in the basement – except there was no screen, just a large circle of sand below their tiered seating.

'What the hell?' growled Malutin. It was almost twenty years since Pearlman had first met the Russian. Back then, the man had been a broad-shouldered giant, with a smile and a physique to blow the ladies away, but two decades of high living had run him to fat, and his flushed face now glistened in the lights.

The men had splintered themselves across the seating to give them room to stretch and eye one another. They had been friends once. High-flying lads done good. But in recent years they had sparred too many times over market assets – competed too hard for the best kills, outbid each other too shamelessly and gloated too much when one of them cocked up. Now their annual meetings were frosted with rivalries, but it still suited them to get face to face, look each other in the eye and weigh up their competition.

Ballantyne had placed himself in the power position towards the back, forcing the others to turn to engage him. He smiled at their surprise. 'I've organised a little theatre just for us. A bit of sport. I thought perhaps you'd enjoy a private wager away from the antics upstairs.'

He clicked his fingers and there was movement in the shadows. Four men strode onto the floodlit sand. Two of them were bound and led by the others using leather thongs around their necks. They were positioned next to each other, facing the audience.

'Ah,' said Steinberg with an agreeable nod. 'A fight. Always a pleasant diversion.'

'Gloved or bare knuckle?' demanded Malutin.

Ballantyne allowed a playful pause. 'Just place your bets on what you see.'

Pearlman pondered the figures on the sand, his innards

and his black mood temporarily forgotten. One of them was significantly taller than the other, with powerful legs and a longer reach, but his adversary looked sharp and agile, like he could handle himself.

'A hundred on the bigger one,' said Huateng softly.

Steinberg raised a finger. 'I'll put another hundred on him.'

Pearlman snorted. 'Then I guess I'd better put two on the little guy, just to make things more interesting.'

Ballantyne grinned. 'A good choice. That's the one Marcella chose, and eight out of ten times she gets it right. My wife is a woman who knows her fighters. So, boys, we have two hundred thousand sterling from our dear Raymond. Let's keep it coming.'

Raymond J Pearlman had first crossed paths with Julian Ballantyne in 1973, when he had returned to the Chicago School of Economics after his Rhodes Scholarship year at Balliol College, Oxford. Ballantyne – a Corpus Christi man – was a couple of years older, but already a growing legend in the world of high finance. The two men had been chalk and cheese, but their Oxford experiences bound them, and gradually Ballantyne took the other man under his wing and showed him how real money was made. With the Englishman's guidance, Pearlman soon found he had a talent for spotting and buying undervalued companies and making alpha returns. He loved the thrill, the paranoia, the sheer adrenaline rush of living and dying by immediate choices. He became one of a fledgling group of Chicago graduates that Ballantyne coined the Young Eagles. They were the new kids, smashing barriers, breaking rules, toying with a fresh field of finance that would later be called 'hedge funding'.

But that was only the start.

On 24 March 1976, Pearlman was running his fund accounts from a growing Manhattan office when Ballantyne's call came through.

'Switch on your TV.'

Pearlman watched grainy black-and-white news footage of helicopter flights and explosions blossoming across a blackened city. 'What am I seeing?'

'Videla's junta is taking Argentina. Peron was detained last night.' Ballantyne's voice was smooth, but there was no hiding his excitement.

The images changed to a high-ranking officer, sagging under the weight of his medals. 'People are advised that as of today the country is under the operational control of the Joint Chiefs General of the Armed Forces.'

'Why're you bothering me about this, Julian?'

'Because it's a disaster! Full-blown, off-the-Richter-scale disaster. And don't we just love it!'

'You're going to have to wind back on this one. Who's behind the coup?'

'We are, Pearlman. We are.'

And it was true. Fellow Chicago Boys were flown into Buenos Aires and given top economic posts – secretary of finance, president of the central bank, research director for the treasury. They oversaw the junta's dismantling of Argentina's prosperous public sector. They removed workers' rights, banned strikes, lifted price controls and removed all restrictions on foreign ownership. Over the next few months, amidst the terror, the despair, the disappearances and thirty thousand deaths, Ballantyne led his Young Eagles into the fray – and they took everything. Pearlman had never realised such riches could be made.

Argentina was just the start. Over the succeeding decades, they used their networks to ensure they were always ready to help foment the next economic disaster. When a revolution was initiated, the suddenness of the violence and the collapse of security placed a population in such shock that it was unable to react logically in its own defence – it was utterly malleable. That was when the Eagles swooped. Bolivia, Uruguay, Poland, Sri Lanka, even Russia. From the jaws of disaster, countless fortunes had sprung.

Now, in the little cinema in the bowels of the mansion, the Eagles placed their bets and watched while the two figures were led away. When they returned, their hands were free and one held a short sword, while the other gripped a three-pronged trident and a net.

'What the hell?' Malutin said again, and all heads turned to Ballantyne at the rear.

He shrugged. 'I thought we'd make it more interesting.'

Pearlman felt a frisson of excitement as the adversaries began to circle each other. Suddenly the party upstairs meant nothing. Here was something new, something wrong. Dangerous. What had he just wagered two hundred grand on?

The figures exploded towards each other, all muscle and power. The taller man evaded the steel points of the trident and shouldered into the other, taking him backwards and thrusting with his sword. Somehow his foe kept on his feet and twisted beyond the blow, and the taller man had to leap back as the trident came raking towards his chest.

The audience was entranced. No one shifted or looked away.

The taller man attacked again, but this time he had

misjudged. His adversary possessed the weapon with the longer reach, and he jerked it forward into the path of the swordsman. The prongs caught him in the shoulder, twisting him backwards with a howl. He pulled himself free. Now the room was hot; heavy with the fug of sweat and the metallic tang of blood.

'What are you doing, Ballantyne?' Pearlman said slowly, his eyes not shifting from the fight.

'Do you have a problem? You hunt, Raymond. You shoot.'

'Not bloody humans, I don't.'

'Well what do you expect for nigh on a quarter of a million?' Ballantyne sounded peeved in the back row.

The fighters were gasping now, their eyes wide, their faces creased with terror. They attacked again. Steel prodded. Flesh tore.

'Fuck,' said Steinberg, almost to himself.

The sand was blotched with crimson. Both men were becoming sheeted with blood, so no one could tell who was most grievously wounded.

'Are we really going to let this go on?' asked Pearlman.

'Shut up,' Malutin retorted, his eyes glued.

And then it happened. The smaller man kicked a spray of sand at his opponent, flung his net out and watched as the eyes of the swordsman followed the net. Then he stepped low and impaled the man on the end of his trident. There was a momentary silence, all motion gone, and then the tall man shuddered and vomited blood. Creasing into himself and pawing at the steel in his gut, his coughing became a mewing and the blood kept coming. He stumbled to his knees, raised himself briefly to look at the victor and collapsed on the sand.

'Christ!' swore Pearlman, and he turned on Ballantyne, but their host was already rising and applauding the winner.

'Bravo. What a performance.'

'Looked more like murder to me.'

Ballantyne ceased his clapping and his face darkened. 'It's only murder, my friend, if you get caught. Besides, our performers knew the risk. They accepted the terms. They understood only one of them would receive the victor's ample rewards.'

There was a thorny silence as the remaining fighter bowed and disappeared, and his fallen adversary was dragged away by his heels.

'An unexpected change to your usual entertainments, Julian,' said Huateng eventually.

'And what is your verdict?'

Huateng considered this. 'I've witnessed governments fall, countries burn and no doubt many people die, all for the sake of wealth. But this was different. Death and money entwined and distilled into something so simple. A wager. A reward. A weapon. A fight. An outcome. I admit it was stimulating while it lasted.'

'Exactly,' hissed Ballantyne, his eyes hard. 'Tell me truthfully, is there anything more stimulating than holding a human life in your hands? Just like the emperors of Rome. The thumb up or the thumb down. That, gentlemen, is power.'

Steinberg voiced his agreement, but the others were silent and Ballantyne, still rankled by Pearlman's criticism, let the moment die and heaved a self-indulgent sigh.

'Oh well, I suppose it was too much to expect unanimous enthusiasm for such ancient art,' he concluded tartly. 'My banker will sort your wagers and meantime we should return to the fray. Marcella will be missing us.'

Malutin hauled his bulk upright and raised his glass. 'Well, I say bravo to you, Julian. I'm a hundred grand down for five minutes of entertainment, but I'd pay twice as much to see it again.'

Steinberg concurred. 'Although it would need to last longer and play much more to the gallery.'

Pearlman was still grim when he exited the cinema. He had expected a normal, run-of-the-mill party. A bit of letting off steam after their business meeting. But bloody Ballantyne had decided they should witness a man get butchered. And yet... And yet, somewhere beneath his indignation, he could feel his heart pumping and the adrenaline sneaking through his veins. He had wagered on a man's life. For sport. And, in the moments before the poor bastard's death, the spectacle had been consuming.

'Tell me, Raymond,' said Huateng, coming close. 'You, the man who shoots lions, yet who protests the loudest, surely you felt a prickle of excitement?'

Pearlman was damned if he was going to speak openly in this company. Rule number one: keep your cards close. 'What we witnessed in there bears no resemblance to the exhilaration of a hunt. The planning, the tracking, the chase. The battle of wits between prey and predator. That? That was just—'

'Another goddamn pantomime?' Huateng interrupted archly.

'Exactly. Bloody Julian.'

They wound their way back to the celebrations and the night evaporated in decadence. The next morning, they boarded their jets and went their separate ways. And that should have been that for another year.

But this time, the weekend in Hampshire would linger long in the minds of the Eagles. Not the business meeting or Marcella's stupid party. No, it was Julian's piece of theatre that haunted them. Money and death. Risk and reward.

One day, in the not-too-distant future, the goddamn pantomime would return to claim them all.

For the gods were calling.

PART ONE

REPERCUSSIONS

I

Pantheon Year – Twenty

Season – Blood

'Drink this.'

'I'm okay.'

'Just drink it.' Dio's eyes were diamond hard in the recesses of his helmet as he held out a leather canteen of sweetened wine. 'All hell's about to break loose, so you'd better get some fire in your belly.'

Heph was slumped on a rock at the far eastern end of a glen hidden deep in the folds of Scotland's remote Knoydart peninsula, his body emptied of adrenalin, his mind a bewildered mess. Before him, scattered across the Field, was spread the detritus of battle. Blades, sarissas, spears, arrows, shields, helmets, grass trampled to mud, blood pooling into tinkling Highland streams. Bodies too. The dead and dying. Some crying out for help, some howling to the wounded skies, most silent as the hills themselves.

And flies. So many damn flies. Even as a klaxon had sounded to mark the end of the Grand Battle in the Pantheon's Twentieth Season and the violence between the rival Titan and Valhalla Palatinates had leeched away into the ground, the insects had risen in their thousands from the grasses and danced in clouds above every scrap of bloodied flesh. Their hum accompanied the clack-clack of helicopters and the whine of drones, because the struggle on the Field might have ended, but the cameras were still feeding every last detail to the Caelestia, the Curiate and the other privileged punters across the world.

And, riding on the back of this footage, panic would be spreading like wildfire.

Because Hephaestion, Captain of Companion Cavalry in the Titan Palatinate, had triggered the Pantheon's nuclear button, the one Rule in this game of games that was never supposed to have been activated. He had led his six mounted Titans from out of nowhere and thundered onto the Field just as the Vikings of the Valhalla Palatinate were surrounding the Titan banners and cutting bloody paths to Alexander. Now the bodies piled at the western end of the valley were testament to the desperation of the Titan defence. It had been a cursing, snarling, stabbing, slicing struggle of death and Alexander had been felled by a thrown spear which pierced his femoral artery and left him to bleed out into the mud as Heph's cavalry wheeled away from the melee and swung upfield towards the one remaining King.

Sveinn the Red. King of Valhalla. Screened by only the thinnest line of Raven archers. The Companion riders had torn through that defence, snapped them like cotton thread, and Heph had used the momentum of his mount to bury his shortsword in Sveinn's gut. Kill the King. With a sword in hand. Skewer him like that and his Palatinate must fall. That was the Rule – and until this muggy, greying, fly-infested afternoon in faraway Knoydart, it had never been called upon.

'I said drink the bloody stuff,' Dio said gruffly.

Heph reached for the canteen with an impatient groan and pushed his helm up to get at it, but once the sweet liquid touched his lips he knew Dio was right. He gulped at the wine and felt his insides warm and his senses invigorate.

'Shit,' said Dio above him. 'Here comes trouble.'

Striding towards them, breathing heavily up the grassy slope, came fat Cleitus, Colonel of Light Infantry. Heph's eyes drifted beyond the approaching Titan to Maia, poor dead Maia, spread-eagled in the mud. Spyro had removed the spear embedded in her chest and closed her eyes, then grimly used the weapon to silence Pallas' screaming horse. Now he and Zephyr were holding Pallas still as he whimpered from the livid pain of his snapped arm. Heph allowed his eyes to wander further and meet those of Lenore. She too had pushed her helm back on her head and her flame-red hair hung dank around her shell-shocked face; one hand remained on the reins of her mount and a trampled Raven was sprawled beneath.

Cleitus arrived and blocked Heph's view. He was gasping and rumbling from within his bronze helmet like a cauldron of boiling stew and it took him several attempts to get his words out.

'Just... just who the bloody hell are you?'

The man was sheeted in Alexander's lifeblood. He had been stupid enough to tug the spear from his King's thigh and the punctured femoral had pumped blood high into the Highland air.

'I am seventy Blood Credits,' Heph responded evenly. 'Zeus' secret.'

'What's that supposed to mean?'

Heph tugged his helmet fully from his head and Cleitus gasped. 'You!'

'Yes, me. The Valhalla traitor, now Hephaestion, Captain of Companion Cavalry. And you remember Horsemaster Diogenes too?'

Wary of the cameras, Dio kept his helmet in place, but the eyes of the Titan colonel bulged nonetheless.

'You're supposed to be—'

'Gone?' interrupted Heph. 'Thrown from the Pantheon? Perhaps killed by the Vigiles? Is that what you thought? Well, Zeus made his own plans. He spent those seventy Credits in secret. He bought seven wonderful horses and collected five experienced riders from the ranks to join us. Then we trained and trained, far from conniving eyes, until he released us today onto this Field.'

'And we just changed the game,' growled Dio.

Cleitus mastered his bluster and lapsed into scrutiny, taking the measure of both men. Then he shifted and stared around at the remnants of this new Titan cavalry. Upfield, two helicopters were landing and disgorging Vigiles and *libitinarii*. More would be on their way, scooped up by a flabbergasted Atilius and flown post-haste to this wild corner of Scotland, which had suddenly become the epicentre of all the wealth and all the power of the Pantheon.

Sveinn still lay where he had fallen. Heph had unclipped his cloak and placed it across the corpse, although he had left his sword buried in the belly of the King for all to see. Now two Vigiles were examining the remains and taking photos. At the opposite end of the Field, beneath the colours of Macedon, another group of Vigiles were gathered around the crimson body of Alexander. They were lifting it onto a makeshift stretcher to carry to a waiting chopper.

Agape was there. Heph could see her quietly overseeing the departure of the late King. Parmenion too. He led a group of peltasts across the corpse-littered ground where the Titans had made their last-ditch defence. They knelt and checked each prone figure – Viking and Titan alike – signalling to the approaching *libitinarii* when they found one still breathing. In the centre of the Field, a couple of weak fires were just starting to smoulder, coaxed by older hoplites experienced in the need for sustenance after battle. They had elicited stashes of tinder and matches from beneath their armour, but only the gods knew how they found anything flammable in this mud-soaked land.

And then Heph looked to the northern slopes, where the grass steepened towards the mountains. Nicanor, Colonel of the Heavy Phalanx, had martialled thirty of his troops into a wide circle, shortswords drawn, helmets down and scalloped shields on forearms. Inside this ragged circle sat the disconsolate remains of Valhalla. Their blades and helmets had been confiscated and piled near the central fires. Their shields were now being tossed onto the hillside to await the coming of the Vigiles, and their regimental banners – Raven, Storm, Hammer and Wolf – were being laid in the grass by hoplite Heavies who ensured their boots stamped over the colours.

The Vikings perched uncomfortably on the ground as the damp soaked into their breeches. All except two. Bjarke had howled and cursed and threatened endless blood on anyone who dared lay a hand on him, but now he stood in silence with his shoulders slumped. Next to him, hair pale in the weak light, Calder stared mutely as the Titans jostled her Raven banner. Heph's breath caught in his throat. He had so nearly killed her. He had almost allowed Boreas to gallop straight through her. Only at the last moment had he recognised the woman he might have loved and forced the horse aside.

Cleitus too was staring at the defeated foe, chewing his lip and trying to get his head around the ramifications of the last sixty blood-soaked minutes. He turned back and now there was shrewdness in his pig eyes. Wordlessly, he strode to where Valhalla's Triple Horn of Odin banner remained planted in the earth. With an audible grunt, he heaved it out and carried it back to the cavalry pair.

'Well,' he sneered. 'It's time we got you reacquainted with your comrades. I suspect they will be dying to meet our new King Killer.'

Calder watched the arrival of the helicopters with unseeing eyes.

Sweat dried to a crust. Hair matted across her scalp. Highland chill discovering the gaps in her chainmail. Hands flecked with blood – though not her own – and pain rippling through her right arm, where a Titan's horse had slammed into her.

But none of that mattered. Collapsed around her were the remnants of her Raven litters, and around them the detritus of the Horde of Valhalla. Torn from the jaws of victory, thrown from the heat of war, they sprawled limp and confused on the hillside, stripped of their shields and weapons. Stripped too of their helmets. Never before had they allowed their faces to be bared in the presence of the foe.

Do I even know these people? Calder's eyes flicked from one to the next. Of course she did. There was Geir, kneading his shoulder where an arrow had punctured him during the Raids. There too was Estrid, blood congealing around a head wound. And young Sassa, who had crouched with her in a den of lions. Calder knew each and every one of the faces of Valhalla. She had shared the Tunnels and Halls with them. She had toasted them with mead and ale, traded sword-strokes in the Practice Rooms and run alongside them through the tight closes of Edinburgh. And always those faces had shone with the confidence of warriors.

And yet... now she barely recognised them. They were ghosts, this Horde. Just a bunch of shell-shocked figures, slouched on a hillside, wilted, rudderless and bewildered. Even Bjarke was quiet. He towered next to her and glared at the guards, but his bombast had leaked into the mud and now his silence was louder than the thunder of the choppers.

Calder blamed herself and she wondered if the others

did too. It seemed that her entire existence in the Pantheon had been building to that one moment when the horsemen pounded across the battlefield and she had been the final, flimsy line of defence before the King. As every head had turned and every camera trained on her, she had known she must bring down those knights. But they had been too fast. Shaking and cursing, she had loosed her arrows and she thought she had hit the lead rider, but he had kept coming and in seconds was upon her. In that moment, she had seen her death in the flying hooves of the stallion and the iron point of his lance, but her destiny had changed. He had swung around her, and the shoulder of his horse had hit her like a freight train, slamming her into the mud so hard that her world had blackened. By the time she saw the sky again, it was over. Her King was dead and she had failed at the critical moment when her Palatinate had needed her most.

Bjarke murmured a warning and she forced her eyes to focus. A group of Titans were approaching, the fat Companion Colonel at their head. He planted his feet on the centre ground and regarded them imperiously. In his hand he grasped their Triple Horn standard. Up the Field, more Vigiles were disembarking from helicopters. Under the orders of Atilius and the powers vested in them by the Pantheon, they would soon take charge of the prisoners, but no one could stop this Titan having his moment of glory.

'It is over!' he shouted above the noise. 'Valhalla is gone. Expunged from the Pantheon. Do you understand?'

Bjarke spat and figures rose around her, but most tolerated these words without response.

'No man or woman is to utter that name again.' He

peered around at them, his little eyes squinting from behind his helmet. 'You are mine now.'

He turned to one of Nicanor's Heavies and swung the Odin standard towards him. 'Burn this rag.'

The trooper looked aghast.

'You heard me,' Cleitus hissed with menace. 'Burn it.'

The man clasped the shaft, glanced uncertainly at Nicanor, and then strode away towards the central fires. Around her, Calder sensed the Horde rising. Cohesion at last. Anger kindled as their banner approached the heat. Bjarke rumbled again and this time it grew into a cry as they saw the Triple Horn lowered and the first flames lick across their Colours. A wave of noise broke from the captive lines as black smoke blossomed into the sky and the flag erupted in a ball of heat.

Valhalla swore its defiance and, although she knew it was the final dying shout of a once-proud Palatinate, Calder howled as well and shook her fists at the bastard Titans.

The Vigiles arrived and tried to gain control of the situation, but Cleitus wasn't finished. He swung on his heel, grabbed a Companion and pushed him forward.

'This,' he yelled over the cacophony. 'This is the hero of the day. The soldier who won the Field of the Twentieth Grand Battle and the man who has destroyed you all.'

Cleitus attempted to grab the Companion's helmet and tug it off, but the man swatted him away.

'Take it off again,' the Colonel snarled.

The figure stood dejectedly in front of the Horde and gradually the noise died.

'Show them, damn you,' snarled Cleitus.

The figure did not respond, but then finally he sagged

his shoulders and reached for his helm. And even as he did, Calder understood. The man's chin might be clean shaven and his body clad in bronze and scarlet, but she knew him nonetheless. The lean, muscled limbs. The way he faced them with silent authority. She had danced with that Titan on the Palatine Hill in Rome, and he had once said he loved her.

Her hand fluttered to her mouth. *Oh god, no. Not you. Please, not you.*

Cleitus had expected the Vikings to erupt. He had wanted to feed on their despair. But, instead, as the Companion removed his helmet and the captives stared upon the face of a man who had shared their Halls, a man who had won them their Assets in the Nineteenth Season, who had stood with their finest Wolves and who had raced across the blood beach of the last Grand Battle into the arms of their foe, there was only a stunned silence.

'That bastard,' Bjarke whispered eventually and even though these were the last defiant words of Valhalla, Calder barely acknowledged them because the Companion was staring at her with eyes of sullen devastation. She wrenched her attention away from him and he slammed his helmet back over his face and stalked off.

A Vigilis officer shouldered past Cleitus and began a flurry of orders. The defeated Palatinate was now under his authority. They would be fed and watered and then removed from the Field. They were not prisoners, but any deviation from his commands would be punished with the utmost severity. His units took over from the circle of Titan Heavies and began to herd the Horde into columns in readiness for the trek out of the valley.

Dully, Calder looked around at the sombre faces of her Palatinate and then her hand came out to touch Bjarke.

'What is it?' he growled, and waited for her roving eyes to come to him.

'Where's Skarde?'

II

Sheeted in blood, his face still cratered with bruising from Bjarke's rooftop beating, Skarde was a vision of hell when the horsemen swept onto the Field. He had been glorying in the carnage as he cut his way through the last Titan defences to attack the Sacred Band, but gradually he sensed the violence lose its momentum as friend and foe stared across the valley. When he turned and saw the little cavalry unit wheel away from the slaughter and charge upfield, one overriding conviction came to him. *Run. Run from that valley and don't stop, because those riders are like nothing the Horde has ever faced and they bring with them the fall of Valhalla. The fall of Odin.* Ever since he had stepped from the darkness of Erebus, he had recognised that his salvation was only as durable as Odin's power. Without that protection, his enemies would crowd back and jostle for his demise.

In the moments before the klaxon, when every camera was focused on the other end of the Field and every warrior frozen in dismay, he had lowered his sword and inched through the gawking lines. No one had waylaid him, even though he passed so close to Agape he could have reached out and touched her. Then the spell was broken, and the Titans had howled their delight as the klaxon sounded to end Conflict Hour. He had dropped his sword and loped up the slope behind the Macedon Colours until he discovered a fold in the land and tumbled into cover.

The confusion would die in minutes and order return. Soon they would count the living and the dead and his absence would be discovered. He dumped his helmet, unbuckled his scabbard, heaved his chainmail over his head and slipped a thin seax knife down his boot. A drone whirred overhead, and he toyed with donning his helmet again, but speed was everything. Better to run unencumbered. He waited until he was certain the sky was clear of unwanted eyes, then broke from cover and threw himself down the opposite slope.

For thirty hard minutes he floundered through Knoydart's unforgiving terrain. Spindly heather caught at his ankles. Rocks skulked in the grasses, ready to trip him. Every dip led him into soft, sinking peat. At the sound of each helicopter, he threw himself into knots of thorny gorse. His ankles screamed and his lungs were molten. He stumbled to a stream and drank, then sat back on his haunches and eyed the landscape. To the south was an expanse of water. A loch perhaps or a sea inlet. That would be his first goal. Get to its shore and then attempt to take his bearings.

He followed the boggy banks of the stream, slipping and cursing. A pair of deer bounded away and then half the hillside disintegrated as the rest of the herd galloped upslope.

After another mile's grind, he spied a track bridging the stream and slowed to approach with caution. It was wide and well made, most likely an estate artery for stalking parties, and its unexpected appearance rejuvenated him. He gazed in both directions and guessed east would take him deep into the interior, so he turned the other way and began a steady lope along the track, grateful for the drier ground. He had not gone far when he noticed movement in the distance and threw himself to his knees. There it was again. A droplet of silver above the horizon, moving fast. Another drone? What the hell was one doing out here? Surely they couldn't be searching for him already.

The speck followed the curves of the track and then a mountain biker shot around a corner, wearing a silver cycling helmet, bright top, shorts and backpack – and Skarde knew instinctively that this man had nothing to do with the Pantheon.

He remained on his knees until he could hear the tyres on the stones and was sure the man was alone. Then he rose and blocked his way. The rider saw him and braked sharply. Skarde put on the best smile he could muster beneath his dirty white beard.

'Afternoon, my friend. A fine day to be out.'

'Aye,' the rider said warily and unclipped one foot from a pedal to balance.

'Where you headed?'

'Just a loop out to Camusrory. And you?'

Skarde turned on the spot and pretended to peer around him. 'I don't rightly know. I'm a stranger to these parts. Where do I get to if I keep following this track back the way you've come?'

The rider looked to be in his forties, with a belt of fat beneath his cycling vest, but he was no fool. He examined Skarde with suspicion, spying the blood on his cheeks and hands, taking in his sodden clothing and strange boots, as well as the lack of any rucksack or outdoor equipment.

'Inverie,' he replied carefully and began edging his front wheel round without taking his gaze from Skarde. 'I left my car there where the road ends.'

Skarde noticed the movement and stepped casually towards him. 'How long?'

'How long?' the rider repeated.

'How long to this Inverie?'

'Four hours, I guess, on foot.'

Skarde took another half-step closer and nodded towards the bike. 'I'll bet less than two on that.'

The man stared at this wild apparition before him, the blood, the grime, the dangerous eyes, and then something unsaid passed between them and words no longer mattered. He jerked his handlebars round and pushed frantically on the pedals. The bike responded. It was a good model, light and fast, and it should have saved his life.

But Skarde was faster.

The rider was just rising in his saddle when he was hit by the full force of the Viking and thrown onto the track. Stink and sweat enveloped him and he had time only to raise his head and blurt a surprised curse before a knife was rammed into his throat. The impact was so unexpected that he felt no pain, just the warmth of his lifeblood soaking down his front. He garbled something, then the knife came again, deeper this time, hard up through his mouth. His mind clouded and the last sounds he heard were the feral grunts of his killer.

Skarde kept his seax embedded until he felt the body relax, then scanned round for any sign of movement. Satisfied, he rose and began to drag the corpse off the track, but the rider's damn shoes were still attached to the bike.

Skarde kicked hard at each ankle, until the pedal unclipped, then tossed the body into the heather. There he stripped it, removed his own soiled clothing and changed into the biking gear.

He searched the man's backpack and discovered a sandwich, water, map and car keys, but no phone. He washed his knife in the stream and stowed it in the pack. He arranged his own clothing as best he could over the sallow corpse to conceal it from drones, then forced his feet into the narrow biking shoes and returned to the track to right the bike. It had been a lifetime since he had cycled, but he perched on the saddle, pointed the front wheel towards Inverie and made one final examination of the murder scene.

Over the next two hours, Skarde trundled along the track and found the man's car where the tarmac began just outside the tiny hamlet. As night descended, he stowed the bike in thick gorse, devoured the sandwich, then started up the ignition – and continued his long flight from Knoydart.

Kustaa's world imploded.

He had spent the afternoon alone in Valhalla, watching the feeds of the Battle. The Tunnels were empty and the Gates locked, and he had been enjoying the privilege of having the place to himself. He found cheese and grapes in the kitchens, opened an expensive Malbec and settled back in his Thane's quarters to watch the spectacle.

When he saw the horsemen enter the fray and tear up the Field, his mouth had hung slack. As Sveinn had fallen, Kustaa jumped upright and stared frozen at the screen, murmuring *no, no*, because he understood the consequences of that deathblow. For half his life he had toiled in the forgotten service sectors of the Pantheon, always lusting for a position that warranted his skills. Then, a year ago, that opportunity had come calling. The Horde of Valhalla had sought a new Thane to replace Radspakr. Kustaa had been interrogated by Atilius' personnel squads, taken apart in interviews and his CV dissected, until finally word had come that Lord Odin had selected him.

So when the Titans killed Sveinn in that distant valley, Kustaa burst from his office and paced into the Great Hall, one hand tearing at his wavy hair, because he knew the ramifications. The fall of the Palatinate. The ending of Valhalla. *His* Valhalla.

Ten minutes later came the first call and it was Aurora in the Operational Support Unit, shrieking incoherently. *Blood*, she was saying. *Blood everywhere.*

He assumed she was reacting to Sveinn's death and ordered her to calm down.

'That brat!' she spat between gasps.

'What are you talking about?'

'The kid... the kid from the Schola. The one *you* sent.'

'What of him?' Kustaa was angry. He didn't need her problems at a time like this.

'He's killed Odin. Stabbed him.'

Kustaa froze a second time.

'There's blood everywhere,' she choked.

'Calm down. Where are you?'

'In Odin's office above the OSU. He was up here with the kid, watching the Battle. Then security came bursting in saying the brat had run out of the building and disappeared. In all the commotion, he must have got past us without anyone noticing. So I took the lift up to check on Lord Odin. And... and...'

'And what? Tell me!'

'And he's in his chair and there's a knife in his throat. One from the kitchen, I think. And there's blood everywhere... and he's dead.'

'Does anyone else know?'

'No.' She started crying. 'Just me.'

'Don't let anyone into that lift, you understand? I'll be there in a few minutes.'

When he arrived, he ordered everyone to stay put, then took the lift to Odin's office and examined the scene, his hands trembling at the sight of the corpse slumped in its chair. Eventually, he went back down again and told everyone to go home. Then, reluctantly, he called the central Pantheon teams and said he needed to speak to Atilius about an urgent matter.

The Praetor was at his headquarters in Rome. He listened in silence, then told Kustaa to bar anyone from entering the OSU until his Edinburgh Vigiles were on site. He would be in the city as quickly as his flight could bring him the fifteen-hundred miles.

The Titans remained on the Field for several hours, cleaning weapons, tending wounds, paying respects to their dead, watching the Vigiles and *libitinarii* sort through the Horde's discarded clutter, then feasting and drinking around the sprouting fires.

Heph, Dio, Zephyr, Lenore and Spyro saw Pallas into one of the choppers to be taken to the Pantheon recovery wards and formed an informal guard of honour as Maia's body was wrapped in her cloak and carried to waiting Land Rovers.

Dio would not rest until the horses were checked for any strains or wounds, watered, washed and fed from the bags of oats he had remembered to bring from their camp. When he was finally satisfied, the team sought sustenance, but there were too many hoplites – high on victory and wine – wanting to prod the horses and cheer their success. So the unit had chicken and wine brought to where they perched beside their mounts and ate ravenously, watched by at least a hundred inquisitive faces and by the drones above. Always the drones.

As they were finishing, Agape approached.

'Diogenes,' she said, without wasting words on congratulations. 'When you have eaten, you and the team will oversee the return of the horses to the ferry and then to your camp. You will be met there by your bus and the horse transports. Sort what you need, see the beasts safely on their way, then get yourselves some sleep on the bus. You have earned it.'

Dio nodded and Agape turned to Heph.

'Walk with me.'

He swallowed his chicken and followed the Captain of the Band as she stalked away from the group. When they were out of earshot, she turned on him.

'You were late to the Field. There are rumours of drone footage showing you sitting on your lionskins while we mounted a desperate defence of our King and Colours.'

Heph looked her in the eye. 'I made the tactical decisions necessary at the time.'

There was a tense silence and he waited for her tirade, but instead she blew her cheeks out and shook her head in disbelief. 'My god. Both Kings gone. Never would I have believed it. Mark my words, there will be turmoil to come.'

'I assume that was factored in when Zeus decided to train a secret cavalry.'

'Perhaps, but no one could have foreseen this. Already orders have come that I must accompany the other officers on a flight back to Edinburgh. We are required there in a hurry. You will travel on the coaches with the rest of troops.'

'I will not. My place is with my team. I will see the horses safely returned to our camp and prepare them for their journey.'

Agape glanced briefly at the drones above. 'Heph, I don't think you understand the situation. You just became the most infamous soldier in the Pantheon. Not only here in Scotland but all around the world. Every Caelestis, every Palatinate, all the Curiate, every flash-Harry with a bucket-load of cash wagered on this Battle, now knows of Hephaestion. They will be gawking at that cavalry charge. Replaying it. Arguing about it. Thinking through the ramifications. And there will be some out there – many, perhaps – who will not be pleased by what you've done. We've made powerful enemies this day.

'So you won't walk back to the ferry with your six horses and four troops because I can't vouch for your safety when there's all these damn cameras still buzzing around. You will stick with the main body of the Palatinate, embark on the buses to the city outskirts, then take one of the waiting cabs to your home. And there you will stay until you hear otherwise. Do you understand?'

Heph bit his lip indignantly and refused to answer.

'You'll see the horses again soon enough, I can guarantee that. They have just become our most valuable assets and Zeus will ensure they are loved and pampered and protected like never before. But you need to keep your head down until this whole situation gets sorted and order is restored.'

Heph heaved a sigh, stared into the distance, then finally nodded his acceptance. 'Okay.'

'Stick with my Band and Parmenion's peltasts. Don't draw attention to yourself. Once you're back in the city, shut yourself away in your quarters and I'll contact you as soon as I can.'

And with that, she left him and boarded a Wildcat chopper with the other officers. Heph explained the situation to Dio, who got the team roused and ready to depart before the light faded.

'Go carefully, Heph,' he said, holding the reins of Xanthos. 'You're a celebrity now.'

III

Atilius arrived in the Valhalla Tunnels at eight in the evening, along with a dozen of his personal Guard of Vigiles from Italy. These fanned out to secure the Gates, while a specialist team departed immediately for the murder scene. The Praetor was in no mood for pleasantries. He led Kustaa up to the Council Room and slammed the door.

'A Caelestis of the Pantheon murdered!' he shouted. 'Here, in Edinburgh!'

'My lord, I—'

'Who is this boy? What was a student from the Schola even doing in your OSU?'

'He was working on a personal project for my Lord Odin, looking into a man called Tyler Maitland and his sister.'

This stoppered Atilius' wrath.

'Tyler Maitland,' he said more slowly.

'Lord Odin needed the boy's IT skills to research Maitland's background and find his sister.'

'And you knew about this?'

'Only what I've told you, lord. I've no idea who this Maitland is, nor why Lord Odin was so interested in him, and I know nothing of what the boy found.'

'Who else knows?'

'Just my Head of the OSU, Aurora.'

Atilius ground his jaw and thought. 'You'll not leave Valhalla,' he said eventually. 'Get downstairs and wait, while my teams oversee matters. We will need access to your systems. Give them any help they require.'

'Yes, lord.'

'The Vikings will be bused back from the Field and should arrive in the early hours. You and I will be here to welcome them and explain their new circumstances. Now, get out.'

The Valhalla Horde's departure from Knoydart was much as it had been planned long before the shock outcome of the Battle. They hiked the same route back through the moorland to the lone ribbon of tarmac, where the same buses awaited them. They changed out of their war gear and shared steaming buckets of water to wash away what they could of the slaughter. Wounds were tended and bound. Then they donned black hoodies and trousers, and devoured flatbreads, cheese, soup and a thick lamb stew from giant pans. Finally, as dusk settled, they clambered onto the buses and sank into sleep.

But the differences were more subtle. Instead of marching out in their usual litters, the procession was divided into groups of twenty, each separated by half a dozen armed Vigiles. When they removed their mail, it was stowed in crates and taken away, and Calder had the distinct impression it was the last they would see of that Viking war apparel. Six hours later, as the first lights of Edinburgh shone through the dark, they found no fleet of cars waiting on the outskirts of the city to smuggle them back to their homes. Instead, the coaches continued into the heart of the capital and parked up in a line at the top of the Royal Mile.

Glancing uneasily at each other, the Horde descended and allowed Vigiles to herd them down Milne's Court to the North West Gate of Valhalla. They filed past the empty Gatekeeper stations and along the Tunnel to the darkened Reception Areas and Armouries, then down steps into the Western Hall. No fires burned in the hearths and no delicious scents floated from the kitchens. Instead, they were directed on past the classrooms and the silent Practice Rooms, before congregating at last in Sveinn's Throne Room. Dead Sveinn. The irony was lost on no one.

A Vigilis captain climbed onto the dais in front of the longship prows and held up a hand for quiet. In the long pause that followed, Calder looked at the faces around her. Some were sullen, others creased with anger. But most were simply exhausted, broken by the freight of battle and drained by the totality of their defeat. She realised with a jolt how many carried wounds and just how few of them now stood in the Hall. Nigh on a hundred and ninety Vikings had marched into Knoydart, but she doubted there were many more than a hundred and fifty around her now. Asmund was dead. Bjarke had told her on the hike out. Stabbed by one of Parmenion's peltasts. Jorunn too. Brave Jorunn. She had made it from her hospital bed after taking an arrow at Waverley, only to take another during the struggle on the northern flanks of the Field.

Calder knew the Hammers had suffered against Nicanor's mighty sarissas, though she could see Ingvar leaning against one of the stone columns nursing a punctured shoulder, and Ulf had ghosted past her in the dusk as she tried to swallow hot lamb stew beside the coaches. The Wolves looked light too, but at least Ake and Stigr still stood. The same could not be said for the many wounded carried from the Field by *libitinarii*. Most should live, but they would unlikely see much beyond the Pantheon wards for many weeks.

So here waited the tatters of the Horde.

The door to the Council Chamber opened at the top of the stairs and from it emerged Atilius, Lord Praetor of the Pantheon, clad for once in modern trousers and a shirt, as though he had been given no time to don his customary robes. Behind him came Kustaa, Thane of Valhalla, also without his robes, hair combed and wavy, but his face dumbfounded.

Atilius took the steps slowly, nodded to the Vigilis captain and walked to the centre of the dais, where he eyed the waiting warriors.

'Welcome back. I trust you have fed and slept as best you can and that your wounds have been tended. These are not the circumstances under which any of us expected to meet. I am sorry you have lost your King. He was a good man. True to the Pantheon. Dedicated to his Palatinate. And there are many beyond these walls who will miss him as much as you.'

They were well chosen words, but no one had the energy to respond, and the silence lay heavy.

'The Rules, however, are the Rules. King Sveinn the Red was killed on the Field of the Grand Battle during the Twentieth Season by a sword in the hand of a Titan foe. As such, the King's Palatinate – the Horde of Valhalla – is now under the authority of the Titan Palatinate and will henceforward cease to exist. All that was Valhalla's – the

Schola, the Operational Support Units, the Highland castle and estate, the Palatinate records and funds, as well as these very Tunnels, now belong to the Titans.'

He waited to gauge the reaction. The gathered warriors glanced at each other, but none would speak.

'And this means you too,' the Praetor said slowly. 'This is not the end of your Pantheon journey. Be under no illusion, you are all still oathbound. You each remain a front-line fighter in the Pantheon, tasked with mastering martial skills and contesting the forthcoming Seasons under the orders of your immediate superiors. Your pay will continue as normal and your accommodation will remain unchanged. You are, however, now members of the Titan Palatinate and the Titan chain of command will decide how to deploy you in the Twenty-First Season.

'I assume I make myself abundantly clear. If any one of you fails to show up when decreed by the Titan command, or fails to obey an order, or thinks you can quietly disappear... you had better think again. The full force of the Pantheon's disciplinary regulations will be brought to bear. No one leaves the Pantheon until their oath has been fulfilled.'

Atilius stared around the Hall. 'Are there any questions?'

None were forthcoming.

'In that case, when I dismiss you, you will leave these Tunnels quietly and in good order, stopping to pick up nothing. Those of you who think they require further medical care should make themselves known to the Vigiles. The rest of you will return to your homes. You may continue your lives as usual until you are contacted by your new chain of command. I have only four mandates: you will speak of these events to no one; you will refrain from meeting with anyone who is present here tonight; you will not depart the city; and under no circumstances will you return to these Tunnels until explicitly ordered to do so by a Titan officer. I believe these requirements leave no room for confusion.'

Again he paused to allow his words to settle. He glanced at Kustaa, then swept his gaze back to the faces below.

'You are dismissed. Use only the Milne's Court Gate through which you entered.'

The Hall began to stir and there was a slow, wordless exodus up the steps.

Then, came an afterthought from Atilius: 'All except Bjarke and Calder.'

He did not use their titles. No *Jarl*. No *Housecarl*. And it was lost on no one as they departed.

Finally the movement died and only Calder and Bjarke were left.

'Come,' said Atilius, beckoning them towards the stairs. 'You are the last of Valhalla's Council.'

'There should be one other,' Calder said bluntly. 'Housecarl Skarde of Wolf Regiment, unless he has been carried to the morgues unseen.'

'We have been aware of his absence since the rollcall. He will be found and dealt with accordingly.' He waved for them to follow him up the steps. 'You too, Kustaa.'

The Council Room was just as Calder remembered it. The beautiful oiled map of Edinburgh still stood proudly in the centre of the room and the hearth had been stoked and lit. On a side table was a bottle of sherry, from which Atilius had been partaking. He poured himself another glass and sunk into the armchair beside the fire.

'Do excuse me. It was – as you can imagine – rather a

rushed flight from Rome. You may return to your own quarters shortly. In the meantime, I have one final task for you – which I will explain when everyone is present.'

He lapsed into silence and seemed to lose interest in them. Bjarke and Calder hovered on the other side of the map table. Kustaa, still ghost-pale and nervous, skittered over to Sveinn's corner desk and began to sort paperwork.

From the Hall came voices and a loud laugh.

'Ah,' said Atilius. 'About time.'

All heads turned to the door and in walked a heavyset bald man with shoulders almost as wide as Bjarke's and arms covered in freshly stitched cuts. His eyes roamed the room without comment, before settling on the occupants. Next came a slighter man with groomed blond hair and handsome features, though these too bore cuts and bruising. He smiled painfully and nodded to them. Calder looked askance at Bjarke. Did he have any idea who these newcomers were?

The laugh came again and then a third man entered and realisation flooded through the two Vikings. They might not have seen this man's scruffy red hair before, but they would know those squinting pig eyes anywhere, as well as the pallid, fleshy jowls and the pear-shaped physique. This was the bastard who had addressed them on the Field. Cleitus. Fat Cleitus.

Bjarke let out a low gasp and Calder felt heat prickling across her cheeks. How dare these Titans stride into the Council Room of Sveinn! The fat man barely acknowledged their existence. Instead he smirked. 'These rat tunnels are even more primitive than I imagined. No better than sewers. Twenty years they've been stuck down here.'

'Forgive my colleague,' said the handsome man. 'He does not show the respect due at a time like this.'

Cleitus turned on him. 'Watch your words. I'm senior officer here.'

The other man ignored him and addressed himself to Calder. 'I am Parmenion, Captain of Peltasts. And this is Nicanor, Colonel of the Heavy Phalanx.'

'We've come,' said Cleitus acidly, 'to see our new property. For what it's worth.'

Calder could barely think and she turned again to Bjarke, but the big warrior's eyes were on the doorway and his jaw hung loose. Calder followed his gaze and froze.

A tall figure had appeared. She was, Calder thought, without exception, the most striking woman she had ever seen. A lean strength exuded from her. Her arms were muscled under a figure-hugging sports top. Her eyes were green and studied Calder with unblinking steel. But it was her hair that took the breath away. Midnight blue. Blue like the ocean. Like the cloaks of the Sacred Band.

My god, thought Calder. *How could anyone wreak such havoc on the battlefield and then look as faultless as this?*

Agape, the Titans' greatest warrior, had entered the Halls of Valhalla.

Atilius put down his glass.

'So, your final task,' he said, addressing Calder and Bjarke, 'is to escort our guests around the Valhalla Tunnels.'

'We're not bloody guests,' Cleitus interjected. 'We're the new owners.'

Atilius regarded him and then demurred. 'The Colonel is correct. These Titan officers are the new overlords of these tunnels. You will show them around, furnish them with any information they require, then depart for your homes and remain there until you hear otherwise. I trust that is clear.'

Parmenion stepped around the table and nodded again to Calder. 'Please, lead on.'

Her mind a mess, Calder acquiesced and sensed Bjarke following her.

'I can't do this,' he breathed as they descended.

'I know,' she whispered and turned to him at the bottom.

The Titans were filing down behind them, Parmenion in the lead, then Agape, while Cleitus was japing at the top with Nicanor.

'Go home,' she breathed to Bjarke. 'I can escort them.'

He nodded his thanks and reached out to take her hand. 'Hail, Thegn Calder of Raven Regiment.'

'Where's that bear going?' demanded Cleitus as Bjarke departed without a backward glance. 'I didn't dismiss him.'

'I think,' said Agape slowly, 'you'd be wiser to let that bear be.'

Cleitus blustered and prepared a retort, then saw the light in Agape's eyes and bottled it. 'Right,' he said, and waved at Calder. 'Lead on then, woman. Seems it's just you.'

She took them through each Tunnel; opened the Gates and let them peer onto the streets. She showed them the Armouries and the changing areas, the kitchens and the classrooms. Then she stood aside to let them into the Practice Rooms and Cleitus punched one of the hanging pells in delight. Nicanor took a wooden sword and assessed the balance of a blade that was so much longer than their Titan shortswords. Parmenion found the archery area and ran his hands lovingly along the bows.

Calder felt Agape standing behind her and turned.

'What is your name?' asked the captain.

'Calder.'

'And what does it mean?'

'Dark waters.'

The Titan considered this. 'What is your status?'

'I am— I *was* Thegn of Raven Company, a position I inherited when Housecarl Freyja fell at Waverley during the Raids.'

Agape dipped her lashes. 'A sore loss. Housecarl Freyja was a great warrior. A true foe.'

'She was my inspiration,' Calder admitted softly.

The Captain of the Sacred Band did not respond, but, while the men played with weaponry, her gaze remained on Calder.

Finally, when they had seen all they wanted, Cleitus dismissed Calder and she walked alone through the North West Tunnel, back to the Gate onto Milne's Court and slipped out into the early light of a new morning.

The last Viking to leave Valhalla.

IV

After a seven-hour soporific journey in a coach full of unwashed bodies, Tyler Maitland found himself driven into the arms of Edinburgh by a silent taxi driver and dropped outside his apartment block in the West End.

He had just made it up to his penthouse, and was pouring himself generous slugs of whisky, when the buzzer sounded.

'Yes?' he said into the intercom.

'Callum Brodie?' came a man's voice, using the new identity Tyler had been given when he deserted the Valhalla Horde.

'Who wants to know?' Tyler asked guardedly.

'Check your phone.'

His phone? What the hell was the guy on about? Tyler had not been back to the penthouse for weeks. He had dedicated the past month to training at the farmhouse near the Ochils and the last time he had seen his phone was when he tossed it into a box on the front seat of the coach that took his cavalry to battle.

The man on the intercom had nothing more to add, so Tyler padded grumpily around his apartment. Lo and behold, on his bed sat his sports bag full of the clothing he had taken to the farm and in one of the pockets he discovered his wallet, watch and phone. He powered it up and a video message from an unknown number appeared on WhatsApp. He tapped it and Hera's face appeared.

'Pack what you need for a few days and go with my driver when he calls at your apartment. He can be trusted.'

Tyler deleted the message and swore. Couldn't they leave him alone even for one night?

'We good?' asked the man when Tyler pressed the intercom again.

'Yeah. I'll be down in five.'

Everything he needed was in the sports bag. He slung it over his shoulder, gulped the whisky and took a final look around the place.

'Where we going?' he asked as he exited the building and saw the man waiting beside a smart BMW, then he threw up his hand. 'Wait. Forget I asked. I'm sure it's a surprise.'

The man opened the back door. 'Not too far.'

The car took Tyler back over the Forth and he cursed quietly because it was less than an hour ago that the first cab had taken him in the exact opposite direction. They returned to Fife, but soon left the motorway and wound through dark lanes and sleeping villages. Eventually the car turned off and made its way uphill along a deeply rutted track. Tyler swivelled in his seat and could see lights extending into the distance as they climbed. Unease flickered up his spine. Had he been too quick to trust the message and permit this stranger to take him into the middle of nowhere? Agape had said to lie low; to keep his head down.

At last, the lights of a small house appeared and the car pulled across a cattle grid and parked outside.

'Where are we?' Tyler demanded belligerently and when the driver did not respond, he was about to reach around the seat and grab the man by the neck, but one of the rear doors flew open and cold night air, spiced with perfume, rushed in to greet him.

'Hello Hephaestion.'

He blinked and stared out. Hera, wife of Zeus, stood alone in the darkness, the lights from the house playing on her earrings.

'Hail, the conquering hero,' she said, smiling as Tyler grabbed his bag and extricated himself.

'What the hell? Why am I here?'

'All in good time.' She touched his chest with slim painted fingers and bent to the driver's window. 'That will be all. Return to the village and await instructions.'

Once the engine had dwindled along the track, Tyler realised he could hear sheep bleating in the dark. A speedy-looking Porsche was parked in the shadows, but Hera placed a hand on his elbow and guided him into the house.

It was an old cottage with a tight entrance vestibule and low ceilings, but when she took him into the main living space, he saw it was exquisitely furnished in dark oak, with gold-framed watercolours and antique crockery on the mantelpiece.

'What is this place?'

'A little gem in my husband's portfolio, although I think he forgets he owns it. I use it occasionally as a safehouse.'

'A safehouse?'

'In our line of business, it's always good to have somewhere unnoticed by the inquisitive eye.' She was dressed in designer jeans and a luxurious Arran sweater, her hair tied back and make-up lightly applied. 'Take your bag upstairs and make yourself comfortable.'

When Tyler returned, she was in the kitchen and she waved for him to sit at the big farmhouse table. 'I've Greek coffee on the stove and sweet bourekia pastries warming.'

'Thanks. I kinda thought it was dinner.'

'It's an hour before dawn.'

She served the pastries, then sat with a coffee and watched him eat. 'How *are* you?' she asked eventually.

'Exhausted. I've not slept for twenty-four hours, trekked god knows how many miles, sweated buckets... Oh, and I killed two people – one of them a King.'

She nodded slowly. 'Indeed you did.'

He finished a pastry and reached for his coffee. 'The last time we met was also over breakfast – in the Balmoral, seven months ago. And I said if you want to get out of the constant cycle of sparring with the Horde, you need to change the game.'

'And you've certainly proven that point.'

Tyler put down his cup and grew serious. 'Am I in trouble?'

'Not with Zeus. He's ecstatic. Loving every moment. As we speak, he's most likely calling the other Caelestes to crow about your success.'

'Huh, I'd love to be a fly on the wall when he speaks to Odin.'

'Odin's dead.'

Tyler froze and stared at her. 'How?'

'That's not your concern. But you need to start grasping the scale of the ramifications of your deeds.'

Tyler was quiet for several long seconds. 'Is that why I'm here?' he asked eventually.

'You've lit a fire, Heph, and it's raging out there. Until we know how to fight it, you need to stay low.'

He picked at a pastry, but his appetite had gone.

'So what happens now?'

'That's the question everyone's asking. Jupiter's called an emergency gathering of the Caelestia when the big issues will be thrashed out. I imagine it's going to be heated. In the meantime, we can progress with some of the known quantities. The Horde now belongs to us. That means everything – troops, equipment, property, administration, tech, training. Our Palatinate will double in size and there's a huge amount to be sorted and agreed fast. Then there's the question of a new Titan King.'

She paused and peered at him. 'It's not gone unnoticed that the drone footage shows your unit in no great hurry to go to the aid of Alexander.'

'Did you expect me to send them onto the Field the instant we arrived? Seven riders against two hundred Vikings already knee-deep in slaughter? I had to wait until the Horde was committed beyond the point of no return.'

Hera looked sceptical. 'And by so doing, you just happened to rob us of a weak, paranoid, coke-fuelled junkie of a King. You played a dangerous game, Captain. One false move and it could have been us who ended the day with no Palatinate.'

Tyler shrugged irritably and slugged his coffee. Hera decided to let the point rest. She retrieved the coffee pot from the stove and poured him more.

'It should be Agape,' he said. 'She should be the next Alexander. She's our best warrior by a country mile.'

Hera smiled thinly and sat again. 'Zeus has wanted Agape for his Queen for years. There is little doubt she would be the greatest Alexander of them all. But Agape does not want that honour.'

'Why ever not?'

'The role of a King – or Queen, though the Pantheon to its discredit is yet to have one of those – is to stay alive at all costs. To remain cosseted in the strongholds during the Raids and Blood Season. To stand behind the banners during the Battle. That's not Agape's style. She commands the Sacred Band, our most elite unit and quite possibly the most skilled company in the entire Pantheon, and she lives to lead them into the fray. She is a soldier, not a monarch and Zeus has come up against that irrefutable fact more than once.'

'Well, it can't be that pompous prick Cleitus. I didn't do all this to give him the crown.'

Hera bristled and Tyler knew he'd overstepped the mark. There was a strained silence and then she said simply, 'Sometimes even Caelestes must bow to the power of politics.'

He didn't know what that meant, but kept his mouth clamped, and eventually she began again in a breezier tone.

'This house is in the Lomond Regional Park in central Fife. It is roughly equidistant between the capital and your cavalry stables, so you should be able to move between both with relative ease. My driver's name is Stanek. He is lodging in one of the towns on the periphery of the Park, and I will give you his number. He will take you to your unit and to the Titan strongholds when needed. You are to avoid dallying or going anywhere else, especially in the city. You are the King Killer and I intend to keep you alive.'

'Are my team accommodated at the farm?'

'Diogenes is. The others are being given a few days' leave to recuperate, but they will return next week. There is much to be done. We must expand the Companion Cavalry, trawl for new volunteers from our lines, as well as those of Valhalla. I believe we will also inherit the Blood Credits that Valhalla earned during this year's Seasons, so we will have an expanded budget to equip and train your new recruits.'

'And just what are we training for? Who will be our next opponent?'

'That's what everyone is asking, from the Caelestia down. Do you understand the structure of the Pantheon?'

'Of course.'

She pointed to a drawer beside the Aga. 'There's paper and pens in there. Show me.'

Tyler retrieved the items and scribbled out the simple pyramid structure which Agape had drawn for him on the plane to Ulaanbaatar.

Legion

Huns   v   Sultanate

Kheshig   v   Warring States   Horde   v   Titans

Hera leaned forward and tapped his diagram with a long nail.

'This structure has remained unchanged for the Pantheon's

twenty Seasons. In the very early years, everyone started with equal resources, but the Legion rapidly dominated and accrued funds through military success and shrewd gambling. There were a couple of Seasons during which the Huns and the Kheshig changed places. The Kheshig had become significantly larger than the Warring States and was permitted to challenge the Huns – the smaller of the two Palatinates in the tier above. They fought a single Battle to determine who would face the Sultanate in the following Season. If this had happened on our side of the table – if we had simply become so much larger than the Horde – we could have challenged the weaker Palatinate above and potentially changed places.

'But we didn't. Instead, you killed Sveinn and now there's going to be only one enlarged Titan Palatinate with no opponent. We have unbalanced the pyramid and no one really knows what to do.

'The Huns and Sultanate have yet to contest their Grand Battle for the Twentieth Season. It's possible the loser will be required to face us in a fight for a place in the second tier.' She sat back and studied him. 'Even when we have subsumed Valhalla, our Titan lines will number less than three hundred and fifty. Do you know the size of these other Palatinates?'

'I know they've got a hell of a lot more.'

'Attila's Huns boast close to six hundred warriors and all on horseback. Barbaric and ill-disciplined they may be, but their mounted skills are even more feared than Genghis' jaguns, and when Bleda leads her Black Cloaks into the slaughter, there are few who can stand against her.

'The Sultanate is larger still. Seven hundred and twenty strong, organised around Mehmet's personal Janissary regiments. They could swallow our Phalanx.'

She lapsed into silence and let her words sink in.

'I guess then,' said Tyler eventually, 'I've some work to do with my five remaining horse troops.'

'You do indeed.' She smiled at him. 'But first, Hephaestion, you take a few days to rest. You deserve it. I've had this place well stocked. When daylight comes, you'll see it's beautiful outside. Enjoy the peace. Eat, drink, relax. You deserve it.'

She rose and prepared to leave.

'Zeus will want to see you soon. In the meantime, ponder what you've done. You've achieved something no one else in this Game has ever managed. You are our King Killer. And for a time at least, you are the most famous soldier in the Pantheon.'

V

Oliver's breath snagged in his throat and his heart juddered. Twenty yards from his hiding place, a fox trotted across the grass, spotted him and froze. He had never before seen one in the flesh and, in the cold soundless gloom of pre-dawn, from where he lay curled beneath a laurel bush, the predator looked as strong as a wolf. How utterly helpless he would be if the beast chose to launch itself at him. He imagined razor teeth sinking into his flesh as easily as his knife had punctured Odin's throat. With a terrified start, he remembered his shirt front was covered in the man's blood. Surely its stench would bring the creature rushing to the feeding frenzy. But, instead, his sudden movement alarmed it and it scampered away with its tail low.

He eased himself into a crouch and stared around at the dense shrubs, wondering what else might lurk in their depths. Sometime in the early hours, he had climbed a gate into Drummond Street Gardens, hopeful that the fenced perimeter would be a deterrent to the druggies and the drunks. He must have slept – though only the gods know how his frazzled mind could have closed down – and now his coat was muddied and his hair full of leaves and grit.

It had been four in the afternoon exactly – the last moment

of a Grand Battle playing out somewhere far to the north – when he had rushed headlong from Quartermile into a city bathed in soft spring sun. He had run with no thought, no plan, his limbs fuelled by terror alone. They would be on him in moments. The sirens, the helicopters, the shouts to '*Halt!*'. He had killed one of the most powerful men in the land and there would be no mercy. They would beat him, haul him to the deepest dungeon and brutalise a confession. He would die friendless and forgotten. The boy who had murdered a god.

So he ran. Through the streets, across junctions. Cars braked and pedestrians parted and he was convinced each and every one of them knew about the blood-soaked shirt beneath his coat. *There's the perpetrator*, they would yell. *Somebody stop him!* Their fingers would point. *That way, officer. Catch him. Never let him see the light of day again.*

But the sirens had not followed and the pursuers did not come and somehow he had found himself in Grassmarket, starting up the long staircase of Castle Wynd. The incline stalled him and his breath came in great burning gulps. People milled up and down and stared at this strange youth, so he tucked himself against the railings and peered around, trying to make sense of his new world. Evening was closing in, the sun low across the rooftops and golden on the walls of the castle above. Buses rumbled and voices twittered. Frustrated drivers honked horns. But there were no sirens and no commotions. Nothing to stir the otherwise normal waters of city life.

He had mastered his breathing and stalked more steadily up the steps to Castlehill at the top of the Mile where camera-toting tourists ignored him. He wanted to go to the police and tell them everything about the murder of his parents, but that would only lead them inevitably to the corpse of an aging man in Quartermile with a knife in his brain. He squinted along the Mile. The Valhalla Gates were down there. Could he thump on one of those until someone offered him sanctuary? He snorted angrily. What bloody idiot talk. He had just murdered their Caelestis. They would hoist him high and peel his skin.

Tyler. Tyler would understand. But he was on a battlefield somewhere in the lost northlands, dealing with the aftermath of slaughter.

So what should he do? He leaned on the parapet of the Esplanade, staring over the city. There were a million people out there just doing their thing and it dawned on him that none of them could he count as a friend.

He had loitered on the Esplanade for an age. Evening turned to dusk and the tourists departed. Crows argued in the trees on the northern slopes. Lights came on in the castle and the entrance closed to visitors. The casual warmth of a spring afternoon tiptoed away and the first tendrils of cold kissed him. He pulled up the hood on his coat and thrust his hands deep into his pockets, where his fingers found the USB stick he had taken from Odin's office.

Robotically, he began to walk onto the Mile, then left down the steep incline of Ramsay Lane with the bright shop fronts of Princes Street below. He let his feet take him and slowly a plan of sorts emerged. He would head to Learmonth and wait for Tyler's return. His brain was too tired to see all the holes in the idea, so he lowered his head and walked.

It was dark by the time he had reached the Water of Leith

and crossed at India Place, but the night brought renewed uncertainty. As every step took him closer to Learmonth, it was not Tyler who filled his mind, but his parents and the warm safety of his old home. This slowed him to a stop, because he knew he could not bear to look upon that place. Not tonight. Cold logic told him there would be nothing for him there but heartbreak. His home would have new owners, different curtains, new lights shining from the windows. And for the sake of his sanity, he must leave it well alone.

Night had closed around him and he had walked, aimlessly and without purpose, for miles. Great circles, everywhere and anywhere. The streets quietened and became rougher. Hunger gnawed at him. He tried asking for a hotdog at a street van near the galleries on the Mound, but when he could not pay, the man swore blue murder and threw what he had prepared in the bin. Later, Oliver was drawn by the deep scent of a McDonald's on Andrew Street just before it closed. They were happy enough to hand him a wrapped hamburger, until he could not hand them back a fistful of coins and then a uniformed security guard clapped him on the shoulder and walked him firmly to the exit.

And that was how – frozen, dirty, bloodied, exhausted and terrified – Oliver had found himself at the gates to Drummond Gardens. He had pulled himself over them and then crawled under the laurel bush.

Now he sat and cried as dawn coalesced around him. He didn't know why the tears came. Perhaps it was the shock of the fox or the sheer hopelessness of his predicament. But really they were for his mother. Over the last months, in the dark dormitories of the Schola, his silent tears had always been for his mother.

Somewhere beyond the railings a dog barked, and Oliver wiped his salty cheeks and forced himself to focus. It was a new day. The Battle was over and perhaps the Palatinates would be returning. Tyler had given him his phone number during their email exchange, but Oliver was damned if he could remember it. Maybe he could find a café and somehow get online. He stood gingerly, unzipped the coat and examined his shirtfront, caked in dried blood. It stank of death and miserably he concealed it again, stepped out from the shrubbery, thrust his hands in his coat pockets and walked back to the gate.

The fingers of his righthand touched the USB stick, but the fingers in his other pocket also brushed something. A long-forgotten scrap of paper, crushed into one corner. He extricated it and stopped dead.

A number was written on it. Not Tyler's. No, it had been a moment Oliver had long forgotten. A gift. An offer. *Ring me if you ever need to talk.*

Hope pulsed through him. Maybe, just maybe, Oliver did have a friend.

Kustaa sat at a desk which had once belonged to Radspakr, in the same Fife coastal property his predecessor had called home. A gift from Odin to his new Thane when Radspakr had departed the Pantheon so unexpectedly, and one Kustaa had sworn he would never give up. But now he had no eyes for the scene beyond the bay window as the first tendrils of sunrise slunk over the horizon, reddening the water and painting the distant ships in soft pastels.

Instead he focused his tired eyes on the screen in front of him. In the time after he had expelled everyone from the OSU, before he had called Atilius, before he had returned to Valhalla, he had scouted around the desks, searching for anything that might be of value in the testing days to come.

And he had found Tyler Maitland's laptop. The one Odin had passed to him many months before. The one he had given to Aurora with barely a thought. The one Oliver had worked on during his forays to the office. Kustaa had secreted it from the building, taken it to his car and hidden it in the boot.

Now he rubbed the sleep from his eyes and stared at the array of files on the screen. If he valued his position, if he wished for any chance to stay in the Pantheon, if he hoped simply to get through these next days with his life intact, he must discover why Odin and Oliver had prized this laptop. It was his only chance.

Oliver stalked along George Street, hands in pockets and eyes firmly on the early morning commuters. He had been selecting the friendliest faces, but so far that strategy had been hopeless.

'Excuse me, can I use your phone?'

Three attempts now and three rejections. A surly *no* from the first one, a lame *sorry, I'm late* from the second, and a wordless loop around him from the third. He had tried to clean himself up and hide his bloodied shirt under his coat, but he knew he must look sleepless, pale, desperate and unapproachable.

'Are you okay?'

The question came just as he had dropped his eyes to the pavement in defeat. She was in her early twenties, dressed in a cheap black trouser suit and plimsolls, with red specs and a stud in her nose. And, miracle, she had stopped and was looking at him in concern.

'I... yes... no. Can I use your phone?'

'Well...'

'It's an emergency.'

'Okay, I guess...' She pulled it from her shoulder bag, input the passcode and held it out to him.

He fumbled with the paper scrap in his pocket and tapped in the number written on it, then tried to smile his thanks as he waited for the line to connect. Five, six, seven rings and he fidgeted uncomfortably under her gaze. A voice he knew came on and told him to leave a message. He opened his mouth to speak, then creased his face in exasperation and clammed up.

'Problem?' the woman asked.

Oliver heaved a sigh and cut the call. He simply couldn't risk leaving a recording. 'No one picking up,' he said, handing the phone back to her.

'That's too bad.'

'Thanks anyway.'

She put the phone back in her bag and Oliver took faltering steps onwards, his head hanging disconsolately.

'Hey,' she said unexpectedly and he swung back to her. 'You said it was a really important call, right?'

'Yeah, really.'

'Well, I'm getting a coffee before my shift. You can walk with me if you want and keep trying the number.'

Oliver tried not to look too grateful. 'Yes, yes please.'

They continued along the street together as he tried the number repeatedly. When they reached the coffee shop, he followed her in and the scent was nirvana. She must have decided a lad in his state was likely penniless as well as phoneless, because she simply paid for two macchiatos, then looked him up and down and added a pastry to the order.

They stood near the door while he tore ravenously into the pastry and used greasy fingers to hit redial. Each time the same voice told him to leave a message and he put the phone down and awkwardly returned to his coffee.

Inevitably, time ran out and she began to shift and look at her watch. 'I've got to be going. The staff will have a phone. Maybe you can use theirs.'

Oliver nodded morosely. 'Yeah, sure. I'll try that.'

She shouldered her bag, then gave him a long look and shrugged. 'Just one more try, hey? You never know.'

One ring, two. And then a single word, hassled, irritable. 'Yes?'

Oliver was shocked, and for a heartbeat words failed him. 'Er... is that Mr Greaves?'

'Yes, who's this?'

He glanced at the woman and turned his body slightly away. 'It's Oliver.'

There was silence and then he heard a hand clamp over the receiver and muffled voices at the other end. Then Eli's voice came back. 'Oliver, where are you?'

'In the city.'

'Everyone's looking for you. It's crazy here. Vigiles everywhere. Rounding up the classes, taking rollcalls. The Schola's being tipped upside down.'

'You said when you gave me this number that if I ever needed someone to speak to, I could call.'

'And I'm glad you have. Where are you?'

Oliver picked his words. 'Can I trust you?'

'What?'

'Can I *trust* you?'

'Of course. That's my job. To consider the mental health of Valhalla's Schola pupils and be trusted by those that need to share.'

'Who's with you?'

'No one. I got rid of them. Believe me, it's damn hard to find a private moment with everything that's going on. You're supposed to be here. They're taking a rollcall of everyone.'

'If I tell you where I am, you seriously mustn't tell anyone. Will you promise?'

'Okay. But that woman, Aurora, is on site and seems incredibly keen to find you.'

Oliver's heart thundered in his throat. 'What's she doing there?'

'She turned up this morning and briefed all the staff that she needed to find you urgently. She's going to be pissed when the searches come up with nothing. Why didn't you show up at the OSU yesterday? You can't just go AWOL.'

'AWOL? Is that all she said?'

'Pretty much. Why? Is there something else I should know?'

Oliver held his tongue while he focused. Just absent

without leave. That's all Eli knew. He could sense the woman behind him looking at her watch again. 'Can you get to the city?'

'Not until it's settled down here. It'll be this evening, then a ninety-minute drive.'

'Seven o'clock then? By the Melville Monument in St Andrew's Square.'

'I'll try.'

'Alone. Don't bring anyone. Don't tell anyone. Promise me.'

'I promise,' Eli sighed. 'I'll get there when I can.'

VI

The year was only in its fourth month, yet the sun in its faultless blue heavens lavished summer warmth on the island of Capri.

Marcella Ballantyne would normally be on her yacht enjoying the more exotic climes of the Maldives or the Andaman Sea, but she had been attending to business in Berlin, then savouring an extended weekend of gallery openings in Paris. So now she reclined beneath the shade of her lemon tree orchard on the middle terrace, appreciating the clear spring air and waiting impatiently for Atilius to call. Beneath her, the lawns of her twelve-bedroom villa swept away between borders and cypress trees to an infinity pool at a cliff edge, and beyond that the azure waters of the Bay of Naples were studded with yachts and broken only by the three towering rocks of the Faraglioni.

She always referred to the place as *hers*, but in truth it was *theirs*. The estate had been snapped up by Julian in happier times, when he still found pleasure in delighting her with such gifts. During recent years, however, he had absented himself. Business meetings or the military demands of the Pantheon kept him in a constant cycle of movement between Rome, London, Tokyo and North America.

In much earlier days, she had maintained a jealous eye on his diary engagements. The man possessed a roving eye and, at six foot tall, blond and slim with a few billion in the bank, when he wanted attention, it was easy enough to find. It had proved nigh on impossible to block his flirtations, but marriage to him had brought wealth and privilege which she was damned if she would ever share with any jumped-up strumpet who thought she might be more to him than a one-night stand. So Marcella had guarded her husband closely.

There had been another reason to covet her relationship. Marcella first met a top-hatted Julian in 1989 at Royal Ascot and they had fallen for each other so swiftly that they had escaped to his suite and not emerged for three days. Despite his hectic schedule, they had revelled in a dozen more liaisons in the coming month, before she had felt confident enough to introduce him to her four-year-old son. Julian had been shocked and there followed fraught weeks when she had feared she might lose this golden opportunity, but she had mustered every feminine wile in her armoury and kept him coming back for more. The danger receded and when he impetuously put a ring on her finger that Christmas, she had resolved that no power on earth would ever take this newfound wealth, this new entitlement, these fresh luxuries away from her son.

A message popped up on her phone. Atilius was online and waiting. Well, let him wait. She poured herself a glass of sparkling elderflower cordial from an earthen jug and smiled as she wondered where Julian might be at that moment. She didn't even know what continent he was on. These days it no longer mattered. Thirty-two years of marriage and an almighty exchange of power had evaporated her jealousy. Julian could do what he liked, see whom he wanted. His affections were unimportant.

Despite being a man used to judging risk, he had nonetheless been too preoccupied playing with his soldiers to recognise the danger. She had come to him with a proposal and he had thought it benign enough. Inspirational, even. It would allow him to release all the administrative burdens which he found so tiring and permit him to focus solely on the military matters which he adored. So he had agreed to her plan and, nine years ago, he had bestowed on her the ultimate power in the Pantheon.

But he had failed to consider the ramifications.

Marcella tapped her phone and the Praetor's face appeared.

'Atilius,' she said curtly.

'My Lord High Jupiter.' Atilius inclined his head. The woman he saw on his screen was thin to the point of bony. Her skin was delicately lined and walnut, her hair in a fashionable pixie cut, dyed ebony to hide the grey, and her eyes mahogany and as sharp as her cheekbones.

'What news? Have you found the boy?'

'Not yet, ma'am.'

Jupiter gritted her jaw. 'Why not? I want him exposed. I want him beaten. I want him hung high for the world to see.'

'That might be unwise, ma'am.'

'Unwise! How *dare* you! A Caelestis – a god – has been murdered. One of our number. One of the Seven. That cannot go unpunished.'

'I merely think we should not be broadcasting this unfortunate incident far and wide.'

'Odin's demise is already rumoured everywhere. The rest of the Seven are up in arms.'

'Rumours are rumours, ma'am, and can be scotched. Facts, however, are more resistant. If we are seen to punish the culprit too publicly, we give credence to the stories surrounding the circumstances of Odin's death. Besides…'

'Besides, what? Spit it out.'

'Odin had just lost his Palatinate. Do you imagine he would have accepted that quietly?'

Jupiter weighed this and Atilius pressed ahead. 'I suspect our dear Raymond would have been damned if he was going to forsake his position without a struggle. Eventually, of course, we would have destroyed him – but not without an almighty fight. Our lord Odin was not a man of mild disposition.'

Jupiter peered out at the blue waters. 'So you're suggesting the boy did us a favour,' she said peevishly.

'A corpse is considerably easier than a kicking, swearing, fuming Raymond J Pearlman. I doubt we could have relied on him to return to his trading without being tempted to blurt to the world the story of his twenty years in the Pantheon. He would have held too much of a grudge. He would have been too desperate for attention. I suspect, one day, we might ourselves have needed to wield a knife.'

'I would have had no qualms.'

'I am sure not, ma'am, but this way is proving so much simpler. I will ensure Odin's Pantheon debts are all settled and all references to his Caelestes role destroyed. Then his personal matters can be turned over to his own bankers and lawyers. If there are palms that must be greased in return for silence, I will grease them. And that's an end to it.'

Jupiter nodded slowly, then pointed at the screen. 'But I still want the boy found. He is a witness, so I want him dealt with. But you may do it quietly.'

Atilius inclined his head again. 'As you wish, ma'am.'

Jupiter slipped a thin unfiltered cigarette from a gold case and lit it. 'So where is my *darling* husband?'

'Caesar is preparing to depart New York. He should be arriving at Ciampino Pastine in nine hours and will travel from there to his field camp. Valhalla's fall has come as a huge shock and he wishes to discuss options with his Legates.'

'Does he, now.'

'He will likely return to Capri in a couple of days.'

Jupiter blew smoke into the branches of the lemon trees overhead, drummed her fingers on the table and refrained from commenting.

'And what of this King Killer? Do we know who he is?' she asked eventually.

Atilius picked his words carefully. 'He is an officer in the Titan Palatinate, ma'am, who performed his duty.'

Jupiter smiled coldly. 'In other words, I'm to mind my business, am I, Praetor?'

'As you know, I am not at liberty to divulge the details of any Pantheon trooper in any Pantheon Palatinate. I have been entrusted with that obligation for twenty years. Break the sanctity of this contract and the Pantheon crumbles. My teams must remain independent from the authority of any Caelestis or King.'

'Even from the Lord High Jupiter?' she said slyly.

'Yes, ma'am. Even from you.'

Jupiter accepted this and there was a pause. She could see Atilius looking at something else on his screen and she sensed a moment of doubt, the faintest glimmer of unease in his eyes. 'Well, what is it?'

'I… I do have a picture of him, ma'am.'

'You offer me a picture, but no name.'

'It's doing the rounds anyway. He was captured bareheaded on drone footage after the Battle. I wouldn't want it to come as a surprise to you if the other Caelestes highlight it.'

'Send it.'

An image popped into the chat column and she enlarged it.

'A handsome enough fellow,' she said, after a few seconds' examination.

Atilius had been watching her intently. 'A face which is likely to be spread around the Pantheon, ma'am – and one, I fear, which may find its way into the public domain. I will do what I can to suffocate any media interest.'

'You'd better. He's a fool for allowing his image to be captured at a time like this. Get the picture offline, Praetor.'

'Indeed, ma'am. I will do what I can.'

Jupiter's attention had been drawn to someone making their way up the lawns from the infinity pool. 'That'll be all. Give my husband an appropriate welcome back to Rome and in god's name ensure you warn me before he turns up here.'

Atilius bowed and ended the call.

Marcella drew on her cigarette and watched her son approach. He was tall, muscular and athletic in his trunks. A thirty-four-year-old Adonis. Strange that he was blond.

So like Julian, yet not his son. She barely recalled the young wheaten-haired baseball player from the amateur leagues whose child she had borne.

'Who was that?' asked Fabian, towelling water from his ears.

'Just the Praetor.'

Fabian pulled a weary face. 'He found the boy yet?'

'He deems it unnecessary.'

'Well, just say the word and I'll send my Guard. We'll have what we need from the old fool quickly enough.'

Fabian poured himself a glass of cordial from the jug and Marcella changed the subject. 'Your father's on his way back.'

Fabian scowled, but resisted comment.

'So I suggest you get over to the Legion. I want you there to see what he has to say about Valhalla's fate.'

Fabian nodded. 'I'll fly after I've eaten.' Then his attention was drawn to his mother's phone. 'Who's that?'

She had left the King Killer's image on the screen. 'That, it seems, is a man with a growing reputation.'

Fabian leaned closer. 'I know him.'

'What?'

'I mean, I've met him. On Palatine Hill, at the Summoning last September. I had him beaten.'

'What was his crime?'

'Being an insubordinate little shit. He needed a lesson on how to act in the presence of his superiors.'

'Hmm. He just killed a King, so I suspect he didn't learn your lesson.'

'That little prick is the King Killer everyone's talking about?'

'Indeed he is.'

Fabian stared at the face. He remembered the beautiful woman on Palatine Hill, sheathed in floor-length silver, the one he – Augustus – had chosen to seduce. Then this Titan had asked her to dance and she had accepted and held him so close as they wheeled across the grass. Fabian's scowl darkened. 'Let me find him and have him punished.'

'Why? Because his fame is eclipsing yours?'

'Because he's a ball-ache and little people like that can't be permitted to rise above their station.'

Jupiter pondered the image, tapping the edge of her phone with gold-painted fingernails.

'No,' she said after long moments. 'Not for now. He's not worth the bother.'

VII

Oliver had chosen St Andrew's Square because its wide expanse provided him with sightlines. He wanted a meeting place where he could see who was approaching.

It was five minutes to seven and a pale April sun had already sunk below the taller buildings surrounding the square, the last rays stretching along George Street, sparkling off the shop frontages.

He stepped cautiously into the square and peered about. Shadows reached across the lawns from a smattering of trees and a few people sat on benches along the circular inner walkway. In the centre, Melville Monument stood alone, a single seagull perched on the viscount's head high above.

Oliver's eyes drank it all in, but nothing seemed out of the ordinary. No car waiting beyond the perimeter. No figures loitering beneath the trees. Steeling himself, he walked onto the lawns and headed towards the monument.

The hours since his conversation with Elliott Greaves had been interminable. The woman who had loaned him use of her phone had been kind enough to press a fiver into his palm when she departed and he had splurged it on a burger, double fries and a Coke. Now he was famished again, as well as cold to his core and beyond exhaustion. The smell of his bloodied shirt had long since fused with the sweat on him to create a deep musk that was altogether more feral.

He reached the monument and decided to stand in the shadow of the eastern side, so that those approaching would be dazzled by the dying sun. He thrust his hands in his pockets and shivered as the cold worked its way through him.

Will he come? He had wondered many times whether he had been a fool to contact Greaves. The man was, after all, an employee of the Valhalla Palatinate. His career and his money derived from the health and the wealth of Odin's Palatinate, and Oliver had just used a kitchen knife to cut off that source of funds.

He edged to the corner of the monument and checked people coming from the west. A man was angling across the lawns. A blonde girl with large sunglasses walked the other way. A couple traipsed past, weighed down with shopping bags. He looked again at the man, but it wasn't Elliott. The figure bent and retrieved a ball from the grass, then threw it for a terrier and disappeared under the trees.

Oliver turned back east, but no one in this direction showed him any interest either and none approached across the grass. *Come on.* Perhaps Greaves had been delayed. He had sounded harassed on the phone and Oliver could only begin to imagine what might be happening at the Schola as news of Odin's demise filtered down the ranks.

'Are we clear?'

Oliver whipped around at the sound of a voice so close. The blonde girl with the sunglasses had slipped around the corner of the monument and was standing only a couple of strides away. She wasn't looking at him and for a moment he thought her question must be for someone else. Then recognition sparked.

'Meghan?' he whispered, bewildered.

'Aye.'

'What are you doing here? Where's Greaves?'

'He's waiting in his car. He figured I'd draw less attention.'

'I told him to come alone.'

Meghan threw him a glare from behind her shades. 'If you've a problem, I'll happily be on my way.'

Oliver reached out in panic and gripped her elbow. 'No, of course not. I'm sorry. I'm just surprised to see you.'

'Follow me, then.'

She swivelled back around the column and began striding towards the traffic lights at the end of George Street.

'Everyone's been looking for you,' she said as Oliver walked next to her. 'Some woman I've never seen turned up at the Schola early this morning and has been demanding you're found. It's chaos. There are Vigiles everywhere. We've had no classes, no combat. Instead, everyone was rounded up in the Arena and we've had endless rollcalls and headcounts. The teachers look scared and clueless, even Frog and the other Hastiliarii, and no one seems to know what's going on. But some of the Final Year are saying King Sveinn was killed at the Grand Battle. Is that true?'

'I believe it might be.'

Meghan had barely said more than a few words to him before that day, but now she was anxious – full of questions and fearful of the answers.

'Killed with a sword,' she continued as they reached the junction and she checked for traffic, then led him onto

George Street. 'I know what that means. The end of Valhalla. The coming of the Titans.'

'So why are you here?' Oliver asked again, breathless to keep pace with her.

'They kept us in the Arena all afternoon while they tried to work out what was going on, but by five they knew we needed food, so they permitted us to leave for dinner in year groups. Once we were up top, I saw Greavsie heading fast for the car park and I managed to slip from my group and follow him.'

'Did you realise he was coming for me?'

'No. Although maybe I had some gut instinct. But that wasn't why I followed him.'

'Why then?'

'Because I'm not stupid. If Sveinn really has been killed with a sword, then the Schola is finished. The Titans may select the best of the Final Year, but they have their own Schola and don't need the rest of us. We'll be dumped back on the streets and everything I've done will have been for nothing. All that study, all that training. I remember only too well where I came from before the Pantheon found me and I swear I'll die before I let anyone drag me back there. So I figured Greavsie was my one chance. He's been the only person at the Schola who really gave a shit anyway. So I followed him and I pleaded with him. And he stood beside his car looking as scared and confused as any man I've ever seen, trying to tell me to go back to my class, but knowing full well that there was nothing left for me with them. I tell you, I cried and I made a scene and I held on to his car door until finally he waved me inside and told me to get down in the footwell while he took us through the gates.

'That was two hours ago. And now I'm here, picking you up. I've no idea why the hell everyone's looking for you, but I'm figuring this is a damn sight better than waiting in that Arena for the Titans to arrive.'

She broke her stride abruptly and veered over to a car parked along the roadside.

'Quickly,' she said, yanking the rear door open and indicating with her thumb.

Oliver threw himself inside and she slammed the door and jumped in the front passenger seat. The driver turned and Oliver found himself looking at the haggard, anxious face of Elliott Greaves.

'Oliver,' he said, jaw slack. 'They've been tearing the place apart looking for you. Why did you desert the OSU?'

Oliver took a breath to steady himself. 'Odin's dead.'

'Aurora briefed the teachers in great confidence. Said we were to tell no one on pain of death. So how do you know this news?'

In truth, Oliver had not planned what he would say when he met Greaves. But sometime during that brisk walk with Meghan, listening to her words, picturing the turmoil at the Schola and her desperation to escape, he had realised he too must entrust his safekeeping to this man. He had no other choice.

Slowly, he unbuttoned his coat and Meghan gasped at the blood stain.

'I killed him.'

Lana Cameron forced herself up from her bed. Since leaving the Valhalla Tunnels to their new Titan overlords, she had trudged solemnly back to her new flat overlooking the green space of Edinburgh's Meadows, forced a bowl of porridge down her throat, then collapsed on the bed and spent the day staring at the ceiling, drifting in and out of sleep, replaying images of the Battle. Time and again, the Titan cavalry charged at her, and Tyler, helmetless, sitting firm in the saddle with eyes boring into her, lowered his blade for the kill. Visions of her Ravens came to her too, spread out on the grass, bruised and broken; the light of defeat in Bjarke's eyes and the tall figure of Agape stepping wordlessly into Sveinn's Council Chamber.

She pulled back the blinds to find night already creeping over the Meadows and the lights of the University quarter twinkling bright beyond. A day wasted. She sighed, yet her limbs were still bone tired. She leaned on the sill and placed her nose against the cool glass. For the first time since the start of the Twentieth Year, she had no plans and no instructions. The Blood Season was over and, for now, she was surplus to Pantheon requirements.

With a jolt, she realised she could no longer go to the Practice Rooms to work on her bladecraft, nor sit with a coffee beside the Throne Room's roaring fire. Valhalla's Gates were closed to her. Sveinn was dead; Punnr and Brante as good as lost; Geir, Estrid, Sassa and Sten uncontactable. She was entirely alone and she was expected to sit tight and wait until the enemy informed her she was needed. But how long would that be? Days? Weeks? Perhaps this was the end of the Pantheon until the autumn heralded the start of the Twenty-First Year. Seven long months away.

Gradually, she began to grasp the fuller ramifications of

the fall of Valhalla. She thought of Odin, most likely raging somewhere at the loss of his Palatinate. Her mind wandered to the hospital wards where she had spent so many weeks in recovery and she pictured Nurse Monique. Would she lose her job now the Horde was gone? Would they cast her aside, kick her out of her flat in Marchmont and ship her back to Trinidad? So much upheaval, so much loss. All because of a man for whom she had once cared.

She found her phone hidden in her linen drawer, where she had left it before departing for the Battle. She powered it up and logged in to her online bank account. A new sum had just been paid in from the usual Pantheon paymasters. It was an eye-watering figure. A bonus for walking out of Knoydart alive. So the words of Atilius had been true. She might be a survivor of a Palatinate that no longer existed, but, like it or not, she remained a paid-up Oathsworn warrior of the Pantheon.

She laughed emptily because once upon a time a younger Lana Cameron would have been gratified to see such a sum in her bank. She would have headed out to spend it, booked herself a table at one of the pricier restaurants in town or gone dancing at the swankiest hotels below the Mile. But that was the young Lana. Nowadays, money meant nothing. The more she accrued, the less she felt entertained. It was Weregild. Blood Funds. And it came at too painful a price.

She dropped her phone on the bed and padded through to the open-plan living area to put the kettle on, then spotted an envelope beneath her door. Retrieving it, she saw there was nothing written on the outside. Intrigued, she tore it open and two keys fell onto the carpet. There was a note too, with a printed header stating *From the office of the Thane*, and a single handwritten line: *By order of the King*.

Lana picked up the keys and turned them over in her palm. The edges of her lips curled in a sad smile.

She brewed her tea, then phoned for a taxi, packed up a bag and dropped down the stairs to the front of her building, where the cab took her south along Lothian Road and into the backstreets below Blackford Hill. As she had done last summer, she stopped the driver in Hermitage Gardens, shouldered her bag and walked past hedge-lined front gardens to a back gate along a dark alley, which she opened with the larger key. She felt her way through an archway of shrubs and across a lawn, then dropped down to the rear of an expansive Edwardian house, its ground floor reconfigured in glass.

Using the second key, she entered and closed the door behind her. She paused to listen to the heavy silence of the place and breathe in the air which still held the scent of Renuka Malhotra.

Sveinn had kept his promise. As one of his last acts, he had ordered Kustaa to bestow Freyja's property on Calder, the new Housecarl of Raven Company. Lana had no idea if she would be permitted to keep it now Valhalla had fallen, for there would be new Titan conquerors with avaricious eyes for such a place.

But quietly, as she switched on the lights and once again took in the eclectic colours, the Indian fabrics, the rugs, the candelabra and the lamps of many hues, she swore she would fight every last bastard who tried to lay a claim.

Because this was the house where she had found sanctuary from Skarde, where she had been reborn as a true warrior of Valhalla.

Now it was *her* home. And she was damned if she would give it up.

VIII

Kustaa was clicking through the laptop's files for the umpteenth time when his front door's buzzer sounded. Shocked, he sat motionless in the pool of light from his desk lamp and stared out at the evening sea. He never had visitors. That was the whole point of this property. Nestled against the waters of the Forth, in a tiny village with neighbours who didn't pry, his privacy was assured. No one cared what he did. And no one ever called.

The buzzer went again and a cold suspicion crept upon him. Atilius. The Praetor had allowed Kustaa to go home, but perhaps he had changed his mind. The warriors of Valhalla were still Oathsworn, but the Titans already had their own Keeper of the Books and their own administration units. So Kustaa was expendable. A Thane with no Palatinate. Perhaps Atilius had given orders to commandeer the house.

The buzzer went again, this time held for long, angry seconds. Kustaa forced himself to his feet and padded quietly to the hallway to check the camera footage. It wasn't the Vigiles. Instead, a feral, livid face stared back at him. Shakily he depressed the intercom, but said nothing.

'Open the fucking door,' hissed the man. 'I know you're in there, you fool.'

With an intake of breath, Kustaa complied and he was knocked back as the door was flung open and Skarde burst in. He grabbed Kustaa by the throat and shoved him against the wall, a wicked thin knife caressing the Thane's jugular.

'Are you alone?'

'Yes.'

Skarde banged Kustaa's head back against the wall. 'Are you sure?'

'Yes, of course. It's just me.'

'Where's your phone?'

'In the lounge, on my desk.'

Skarde's eyes bored into him and then he relented and released his grip. He swivelled and checked outside, before closing the door and bolting it.

'Well,' he said. 'Aren't you going to invite me in?'

'Yes…' Kustaa replied shakily, fingering his throat. 'Come through.'

Skarde followed him into the lounge and scouted around before finally slipping the knife into his jacket. He was wearing a strange get-up of corduroy trousers, a chequered shirt, scuffed black shoes and a cheap coat, none of which fitted him and all of which looked grubby and creased, as though he had attacked random strangers and stolen their clothes. Even as Kustaa thought this, he wondered if it might just be true.

'I need a drink,' Skarde said.

'I'm sorry?'

'A beer, damn you!'

When Kustaa returned, Skarde had removed his coat and was just placing the Thane's phone on a table close to him. 'In case you get tempted to call someone,' he said, accepting the glass. 'And what's this?' He turned to the open laptop.

Kustaa swore to himself. Why hadn't he put it out of sight before he answered the door? 'Just some work.'

'Work? Didn't you see the Battle? You don't have a Palatinate anymore. You're just as out-of-work as I am.'

Thankfully, Skarde lost interest in the laptop and went to perch on the arm of the sofa.

'May I ask,' Kustaa said cautiously, 'how you know where I live?'

The Viking settled his gaze on him. 'Because Odin once brought me here to meet Radspakr and I guessed the place must have passed to you after Radspakr's death.'

'His death?' Kustaa jolted. 'I thought he retired.'

'Did you now?' Disdain flickered across the Wolf's features. 'I strangled him right here on this carpet.' He pointed to the centre of the room. 'Just about there.'

Kustaa gaped like a fish. 'You... you strangled him?'

Skarde drained half his beer and dragged a sleeve across his lips. 'So don't get any clever ideas.'

Kustaa hovered by the desk, unable to think. 'What... do you want?'

'I need to speak to Odin. He's the only one who can help me. After that bloody fiasco on the Field, I figured the Tunnels would be crawling with Titans and all hell will have broken loose in the city. So this was the only place I could think of. I assume you have Odin's number. Call him up. He owes me.'

Kustaa opened his mouth, but nothing came out.

'What're you looking like that for?' Skarde demanded. 'You stupid or something?'

'Odin's dead.'

Skarde gawked at him, his violent demeanour momentarily shaken. 'You'd better be talking gibberish.'

'I'm afraid I'm not. He's been killed.'

Skarde launched himself off the sofa arm and smashed a forearm into Kustaa's neck, dropping his beer and taking the Thane once more back against a wall. 'By the Pantheon? Because he lost his Palatinate?'

'Not the Pantheon,' Kustaa choked. 'A boy. A boy from the Schola killed him.'

The Prisoner's eyes bored into him. Ice-blue, yet fired with fury. 'A boy! What bollocks is this?'

'Odin had him working on something in his office at the OSU.'

Slowly Skarde released his grip and stepped back, rubbing his beard and shaking his head. 'Christ. I needed Odin. I *needed* Odin. He's the one who got me out of that prison and the only one who can keep me out now Valhalla's fallen.' He stared at the floor for long seconds, then raised his eyes to inspect the Thane for any hint of deceit. 'A boy, you say. Was he called Oliver?'

Kustaa was stunned. 'How do you know about Oliver?'

'Odin talked about him right here, just before he had me strangle the last Thane. So what was this Oliver doing in the OSU?'

'He was looking for someone. Someone Odin badly wanted to locate.'

Skarde impaled him with his gaze. 'Let me guess, this someone was Tyler Maitland?'

Kustaa's spine prickled. *How does this man, this killer, this thing, know all this?*

'We lost the bastard on the blood beach last year,' Skarde elaborated. 'Gave himself up to the Sacred Band and no one's seen anything of him since. I assumed the Titans got rid of him, but Odin was convinced he was still alive and so he got me doing some interrogating of my own.'

Kustaa's mind fluttered through visions of Skarde's interrogation techniques; of his leer as he leaned over Radspakr's corpse in this very room. What if the same fate awaited him? How could he get himself out of this predicament?

Flustered and deeply fearful, he gambled on his next words. 'Maitland is very much alive and this—' he pointed towards the desk '—is his laptop.'

Skarde stared at the computer. 'You've got Maitland's laptop?'

'I took it from the murder scene. The boy had been interrogating it to track Maitland's movements.'

Skarde approached and ran his hand over the rim. 'How do you know the bastard's alive?'

'I was scrolling through some of the documents and came across an old scan of his driving licence.'

'So?'

'So, it's the same face as the one on all the drone footage from the Field.'

Skarde peered at him. 'What are you talking about?'

'The fool was stupid enough to remove his helmet in front of the Valhalla prisoners.'

'And?'

'And Tyler Maitland is the King Killer.'

Hera was already seated when Zeus arrived at the buzzing Greek taverna on Shore Street in Leith and was shown to her table. They could have chosen the privacy of any of the fine dining establishments in the capital, but sometimes the ebullient atmosphere of this place was more attractive. It reminded them of the open-air seafood restaurants along Peyia's shoreline, which they had frequented in younger days.

'Hail the victor,' she said, raising her flute of champagne after he kissed her.

Zeus had watched the Battle from his offices in New York and this was the first time the couple had seen each other since the momentous events. He had rung her as his plane was touching down and had proposed a celebration over meze.

'How are you feeling?' she asked as he took his seat and the waiter poured him champagne.

'Elated, of course. Your cavalry was magnificent.'

'Mine?'

'It was your idea, my dear. What a result! Only you could have dreamed seven horsemen would have that impact. Twenty years of rivalry and we have finally emerged as victors.'

'Have the others called to congratulate you?'

'Most. They are full of admiration for a fight well won.'

'But?'

Zeus grew serious. 'But, they are deeply disturbed – as am I – by the manner of Raymond's death.'

They quietened as a waiter brought starter dishes of bread, humous, capers and a selection of pickles. Zeus drank his champagne rather too eagerly and helped himself to another, and Hera waited for him to resume.

'The Caelestia have seen the pictures. Stabbed in the throat, sitting at his desk, like a common murder victim, blood everywhere. How can this be? He's one of the Seven. A Caelestes. A god. *We* don't get stabbed. That's simply not how all this works.'

'I agree. Such a regrettable addendum to a fine victory.'

Zeus leaned forward. 'I've spent the last twenty years paying upwards of two hundred warriors to train in the use of blades. Blades like that kitchen knife in Odin's neck. What if one of them gets an idea and decides to pay us a visit?'

'It was a tragedy, my love. But an isolated one.'

'Nevertheless, a precedent has been set. A Caelestis has been killed and my five fellow lords are far from happy about it.'

Hera sighed and waited for her husband to calm down. He tore off a hunk of bread and jabbed at the humous.

'We both know Odin was mixed up in dark affairs,' she said eventually. 'He twisted the Pantheon Rules, cheated the odds, and it all caught up with him. He brought his death upon himself. It does not change how the rest of you run your Palatinates, nor the respect with which you are held by your Titan troops.'

Zeus chewed on his bread and his eyes grew lost. 'You know what saddens me the most? That he died my enemy. I always thought we had years ahead of us to make it up again. Do you remember how it used to be?'

'Of course.'

'I counted him as a good friend. Or as good a friend as it was possible to have in the double-dealing world of high finance. We'd worked on a few buyouts by then and made a lot. And then – when was it, '97 or '98? – he came to my London office with Julian Ballantyne.'

'I remember. I was in Athens – at that house in Vouliagmeni, trying to avoid your mother. You called me to say you'd met with them, and Julian had described a new project he was developing. *A game*, you said he called it. *A bit of fun.*'

'Ha! Some game.'

'It all sounded madness to me.'

'But that was the thing about Julian. He could persuade anyone to do anything. He won me over and I became the Caelestis of their Greek Palatinate. So, I have Raymond to thank for that and for everything that has happened since.'

Hera smiled reflectively. 'Those early days really were fun. All that brainstorming and planning how the game would work. To be honest, I thought the whole thing would last a few months and then you'd all forget about it. Remember how young Atilius was when he was first recruited?'

'Atilius made all the difference. An inspired hire. Once he was on board, it all started to come together. All our grandiose ideas finally took shape. He forced us to forge the Rules, to agree the financial arrangements, to conceive how it could be self-funding. And I began dreaming of how glorious it would be to recreate the might of Alexander the Great.'

'And the rest is history,' Hera added with a grin.

'Indeed.'

'My love, I've not said this to you often, but you know the Pantheon is a force for good, don't you? Many have died for it. Much blood has been spilled. But I believe you created something that has brought so many benefits. The children in the Scholae who are given new chances in life. The wealth that is shared out amongst all levels of Pantheon employees from the Kings to the backroom teams. The way this game you helped design has inspired so many people, even those not directly involved. The world is a more exciting place with the Palatinates in it.'

Zeus nodded and blew her a kiss, but then grew serious again and she waited for him to give voice to his thoughts.

'We should never have moved the Palatinate to Edinburgh.'

'Oh, not this again.'

'But it's true. The proximity with Valhalla fuelled the rivalry between us and I'm convinced it was why Raymond got so entrenched in messy dealings. He became desperate to beat us and he undermined the Rules too much.'

'Have you forgotten why we moved? Your business was firmly rooted in London and you spent all your time hopping over to New York. Athens was an absolute financial backwater. Twenty years ago the internet was in its infancy and none of us realised how online working would soon reshape the dynamics of the financial world. Back then, location mattered – and Athens was the worst place for your business.'

'That, and you couldn't stand my family,' Zeus interjected acidly.

'That too.'

There was an irritable silence, mercifully alleviated by the waiters bringing the main course. Dishes arrived of octopus, squid, whitebait, mullet, sausage, halloumi and stuffed vine leaves.

'And I know your other reasons,' said Zeus, shrugging away his anger and offering each dish to his wife first. 'Your friend needed your protection…'

Hera looked at him sharply.

'I've always known,' he said softly.

She ate and they were silent for a time.

'My point,' said Zeus eventually, 'is not that Athens was ever appropriate. We tried it for the first five years and the gods know it was tough. But we should have relocated to London. It was the obvious choice. One of the great cities of the world.'

'Have you forgotten that it was Odin who *invited* us to locate in Edinburgh?'

'He certainly offered it as a choice.'

'He did more than that. He pushed us to consider it. Back then, he was in love with the city. The Horde had settled in the Tunnels and he was busy extending them and creating a unique underground stronghold. He loved the Old Town. He used to rhapsodise about the atmosphere, the architecture, the whole *blackness* of the place. He had investigated the rooftops and thought they'd be perfect for another force. He used to keep saying that Edinburgh was built for two Palatinates.'

Zeus smiled despite himself. '*Get your goddamn asses up here*. That was a line he kept repeating.'

'And he was right. For fifteen years, the rivalry between Titan and Horde has been the most intense in all the Pantheon. The Raiding Seasons alone have become works of art, admired by the other Palatinates. The very fact that we have existed cheek by jowl, our blades almost kissing, has made everything so intoxicating.'

'An intoxication,' murmured Zeus, chewing on squid, 'which eventually got to Raymond. Got to *both* of us. Win at all costs. Look at you and me – so desperate to create a cavalry. And for what reward? To destroy Odin. And in the end, he died because of it. Stabbed in his office like a common criminal.'

Hera bit back a retort and they concentrated on their food. Around them, the taverna was filled with warmth and good cheer. It was someone's birthday and the staff brought in plates of pistachio kadaifi with sparklers stuck in each. Above the laughter, the place reverberated to the universal notes of 'Happy Birthday' and Zeus joined in with the obligatory applause.

While the staff cleared their table and Hera ordered desserts, Zeus decided to change the subject.

'Cleitus has been ringing me interminably.'

'Of course he has. His campaign to become the next Alexander is in full swing. Have you spoken with Agape?'

'Not yet.'

'Will you?'

'I am duty-bound to ask her and she will give me the same answer.'

'She would make a brilliant Queen, but we must accept that she is already a brilliant warrior and that is all she desires.'

'I have been thinking about Hephaestion,' offered Zeus, looking to his wife for counsel.

'I wondered if you might.'

'He was magnificent on the Field. Every trooper loves him. They are ready for his leadership.'

Hera let her husband wait for her thoughts. It was a critical moment. Heph was the King Killer and his reputation was sky-high across the Pantheon. Dangerous eyes were drawn to him. Perhaps in the coming months, as a new Season unfurled, his celebrity might fade and those eyes would turn to other matters. But to elevate him to King, to give him that honour after only two years in the Pantheon, would focus every eye on him all over again and keep them fixed.

'It's too soon,' she said simply. 'He crossed the blood isle battlefield to join us only twelve months ago.'

Zeus nodded his understanding and reached for the sticky baklavas which were arriving. His wife had spoken.

'Then it must be Cleitus.'

IX

Skarde let the hot water pummel his face and wash away the last grime and sweat and horror from the Battle. Alone in Kustaa's bathroom, beyond prying eyes, his shoulders slumped and he exhaled a long breath as the fatigue of his fight and his flight overtook him. Downstairs, Kustaa was preparing supper. They were an unlikely dining pair, but the Thane had little choice. As far as Skarde could see, this was about the safest and most comfortable place he could hide while the Pantheon grappled with its future.

He turned the water off, dried himself on the nearest towel and then padded through to the Thane's bedroom to rummage through his wardrobes until he found something better to wear than the assortment of clothing he had bludgeoned several victims into relinquishing on his journey out of the Highlands.

Kustaa had prepared a thick-slabbed rarebit for his unwanted guest and he hovered by the kitchen door as the man settled himself on a sofa and bit greedily into the food.

Only when Skarde had wiped the last strands of stringy cheese from his beard, did he focus his attention back on the Thane. 'What have you found on the laptop?'

'Just random documents, scans of old photos, emails, bills, the usual stuff. Nothing important.'

'So what the hell did Odin think was on there?'

'Perhaps nothing. But he wanted it checked by the boy anyway. I've spent most of today going through it in detail and, frankly, I think we're going to be disappointed.'

Skarde banged his plate down on a side table and stared venomously at the other man. '*Disappointed* isn't an option. *Disappointed* doesn't get us out of this situation. Seems to me we haven't got a shitload of other ideas. You just lost your Palatinate, Thane. No, wait, not *Thane*. Not even *Kustaa* now. You're a nobody with no place in the Pantheon. They'll come for your house soon, pal. Then your accounts. And then what? Your life? You think they'd be happy having the ex-Thane of a fallen Palatinate – the one with a murdered Caelestis – growing old with so much sensitive information in his thick head?'

Kustaa's face tightened at this, but he held his tongue.

'To be honest,' Skarde continued, 'I don't give a crap what happens to you. But, as for me, I just absconded from the Field and I'll die before anyone drags me back to that hellhole prison.'

Wordlessly, Kustaa picked up the discarded plate and took it through to the kitchen, where he ran it under the tap and stood in mute shock, dread sinking to the bedrock of his stomach. It had never occurred to him that the Pantheon might now consider him a liability, that they might want him silenced for good. He loathed the man in the next room, but when plights were desperate, sometimes you had to make a pact with the devil.

Steeling himself, he returned. 'Why don't you take a look at the documents yourself?'

Skarde glared at him, but then nodded. He pulled up a chair next to Kustaa and they clicked through every item on the hard drive and Skarde squinted at each, wrinkling up his nose in concentration as he willed something of value to reveal itself. They went through Tyler's emails and saw the exchange when Oliver first sent him a message from the OSU.

'They were actually communicating,' sneered Skarde.

'I don't know how. Our systems were all locked down and we had admin control of this laptop the whole time.'

'Well the boy got round those obstacles easily enough. He was having a laugh at your expense.'

While Skarde clicked on, Kustaa took a cautious sideways glance at him. The man smelt of violence. A fleshy, earthy, salty scent. The essence of a killer. As Skarde ran his fingers over the trackpad, his elbow was touching Kustaa's arm. The Thane's heart thudded. The revelation of Radspakr's murder right here in this room had shocked him to the core. Would that be his own fate, once Skarde had tired of his search? Would he too feel those fingers around his throat, pressing at his windpipe?

'What's this?'

Kustaa's attention refocused. Skarde had opened an old black and white image.

'Just Maitland when he was young. I guess he's probably fifteen.'

Skarde picked at a scab on his lip and studied the photo. 'Who are the two women?'

'I've no idea. The one in the middle's in an academic gown, so maybe it's a graduation. A college friend perhaps?'

'Or a sister?'

Kustaa leaned towards the picture. 'You think that's Morgan?'

'Don't see why not. They look similar. The sort of faces you want to punch.'

Kustaa flicked his eyes between the figures. 'I don't see what good it does us. No one knows where she is.'

Skarde was silent and Kustaa turned to see a thin smile toying on his lips.

'What?'

'Look who's in the crowd. Our poor, dearly departed Housecarl of Wolf Regiment.'

Kustaa peered at the faces until he spotted what Skarde had seen. 'Is that Halvar?'

'Halvar the Rock. All dressed in a nicey-nicey suit and staring at that girl like she was the last woman on earth.'

'Are the rumours true that they were in a relationship?'

'Viking and Titan, screwing like rats when they thought no one was looking.'

Kustaa sat back and puffed out his cheeks. 'So this is a picture showing the three people Odin was desperate to silence.'

'Aye,' Skarde murmured, transfixed by the image. 'The Titan traitor, Olena; her Viking lover; and the new King Killer.'

'Whose face is already in wide circulation,' added Kustaa. 'But only *we* know his real identity. And guess who was probably the last person to open this very same picture?'

'The boy who stuck a blade into Odin's brain.'

The two men looked at each other and Kustaa tried to get his head around this discovery.

'I think,' he said eventually, 'we may just have found ourselves a bargaining chip.'

After Oliver's bombshell that he had killed Odin, the journey was deathly quiet. Eli was lost in his thoughts as he drove. Next to him, Meghan sat taut as a bowstring. For his part, Oliver slumped in the back, with his eyes half-closed and his body spent.

Eli took them south, away from the lights of the city and into the borderlands. His mind wandered back to the days during the previous autumn when Oliver had been returned to the Schola from his posting in Valhalla's OSU in a state of furious agony. Eli had been called urgently from his home in the middle of the night. The boy was screaming and fighting anyone who came near. The Praefecti eventually got drugs into him and dragged him to the sickbay, where he had been lying heavily sedated and pale as a corpse when Eli arrived.

Nobody had seemed to know why he was so angry or why he had been shouting *murder* and screaming for his mother, but as Eli sat beside his bedside and squeezed the sleeping boy's hand, Oliver had mumbled about his mum, his face screwed up in pain.

Piper Mallard, the Head, had originally briefed Eli that Oliver was a special case; an Initiate to the Schola who had grown up in a normal loving family. Eli had pressed her to say more, but she could only warn him to keep a careful eye on the lad and deploy his training in mental health and psychology wisely. But as Oliver lay drugged and bereft, it became increasingly difficult to keep a handle on confidentiality. Piper briefed Eli again. For reasons way above their paygrade, the Pantheon had wanted to Initiate Oliver and this had necessitated the demise of his parents. Eli was utterly shaken by the news. He had spent years counselling many of the forgotten and destitute youngsters, the *lost children*, orphaned, missing, broken, who were regularly 'rescued' by the Pantheon and brought into the Schola system. But never would he have believed the Pantheon might kill a family to kidnap a child. It seemed, Piper said, that Oliver had somehow discovered this information in the OSU.

As the days passed, they reduced the drugs and Oliver became more conscious. Eli sat beside him and talked and tried to offer him reassurance and kindness. He knew it was way too little too late, but it was all he could provide.

Oliver had been moved back to the dorms and his physical strength returned. He became quiet and docile, accepting most instructions from the Praefecti without a word, but Eli could see the dark light in his eyes. The lad had smouldered with an anger that he could only just constrain. He had gone back to the OSU and continued with his duties, but Eli made a point of finding him each evening on his return to the Schola and although Oliver had nothing to say, his message had been plain enough: someday, somehow, he would find those responsible for the deaths of his parents and then hell itself would not hold enough fury.

Eli turned the car into the outskirts of Jedburgh, a market town on the border with England. So, it seemed, Oliver had found the man responsible and taken his revenge, and the blood of a Caelestis now stained his shirt.

'Where are we?' asked Meghan.

'Probably better for you not to know. Somewhere safe, away from the Schola.'

On a quiet residential street, Eli pulled the Mini onto a tree-lined gravel drive and parked up in front of a quaint semi. They stepped out and the dark greeted them. It seemed a million miles from Edinburgh's bustle.

'Is this where you live?' Meghan asked.

'For now,' Eli replied, and led them to the door. 'Please, come in.'

He had hardly been expecting visitors and the place spoke of a relaxed untidiness. Shoes discarded. A jumper thrown over the sofa. Sunday's newspapers spread across the coffee table, surrounding an unwashed mug.

Meghan stared uncertainly about her. The Pantheon had taken her from the clutches of a drug dealer and a pimp, and the Schola was all she had known since then, so she could not conceive of a room that held no threat. Oliver barely glanced around. He stood limply by the door and used his remaining strength to stay upright.

'Get yourself upstairs for a shower,' Eli said, scrutinising him. 'I'll look out some clothes for you. They'll be way too big, but I'll try to get some better fitting ones from the Schola tomorrow. And give me what you're wearing. We need to get rid of all of it.'

While Oliver washed, Eli showed Meghan to a small box-room bedroom downstairs. 'I'm afraid this is all I can offer you. I'll give Oliver the spare upstairs.'

Meghan was wide-eyed at the soft duvet and cushioned

headboard. When Eli had gone to the kitchen to make supper, she ran her fingers over the cotton and sat cautiously on the end of the bed.

Oliver came downstairs in a baggy tracksuit and handed Eli all the clothes he had been wearing in the city. Eli promptly stuffed them into a refuse sack and added Oliver's shoes as well. Then he sat them down to spaghetti bolognaise and from somewhere Oliver found the strength to eat.

'I'll be gone early tomorrow,' Eli said, as they cleared the things. 'Sleep in, get your energy back. Don't, whatever you do, leave the house or go out the front. You can use the back garden if you need to, but don't let the neighbours see you.'

And, with that, they separated to their respective bedrooms and sought the solace of sleep.

Skarde spent the rest of that evening in surly silence, drinking whisky and giving the Thane strange looks.

Damn the man, thought Kustaa. *Is he just going to slouch there, sinking whisky?* He didn't want Skarde getting drunk. He was frightened enough of him when he was sober. Kustaa made himself a cocoa and edged in and out of the lounge, but Skarde just stayed slumped in thought, his eyes shifting up to stare at the Thane – eyes which, to Kustaa, seemed to be weighing the benefits of keeping the Thane breathing.

When Kustaa finally dared head upstairs, he found himself cursing the lack of a lock on his bedroom door and he lay wide-eyed for an age, staring at the glimmer of light from the landing. At some point, he heard the tread of his unwanted guest on the stairs and a creak of floorboards outside his door. There was a terrifying silence and Kustaa held the duvet to his chin as though it would protect him like a coat of mail. Finally another creak and then the merciful sound of the door of the guest bedroom closing.

X

Sixty miles east of Rome, beyond the tourist hotspots and hiking trails around Lake Turano, deep in the beech forests on the far side of Mount Navegna, twelve acres of land had been cleared of trees, and the timber used to build a wide rectangular stockade. Around this, concealed in the woodland, was another fence, this one fifteen feet of high-tensile wire, with two thousand volts running through it to give the unwary trespasser a nasty surprise. Cameras were set every thirty paces and fed images back to a control room sitting squat in the forest, manned by personnel of the government's Arma dei Carabinieri.

From the air, keen eyes might spot a single road that twisted through the woods for eight miles, studded with checkpoints. When the trees relented, it straightened and passed under the main southern gate of the stockade. Beyond this, the same aerial eyes would see rows of colonnaded barrack blocks crowding either side, until the road reached a central crossing point where ornate villas had been constructed around a parade square. Beyond these, nearer the northern edge of the stockade, stood more utilitarian buildings. These housed mess halls, armouries, training rooms, baths, stables and a field hospital –

everything necessary to accommodate the needs of almost twelve-hundred Pantheon troops, divided into two cohorts of six centuries each.

For this was the field camp of Caesar's Legion, the greatest of the Palatinates.

And on that sparkling April morning, with the heavens a cobalt blue above the province of Lazio, a silver Maserati SUV carried Julian Ballantyne on the last leg of his journey. His private plane from New York had landed at eight-forty, to be met on the tarmac by his usual driver, who then whisked him through Rome's suburban tendrils on the ninety-minute ride to the Field of Mars, the name bestowed on the Legion's camp in honour of the original Field outside the walls of Ancient Rome, where countless military parades and triumphs had once played out.

The car took Ballantyne under the Praetorian Gate and past the rows of barracks, to the central square, where a single figure in a knee-length scarlet tunic and hobnailed caliga sandals awaited. The man stepped forward and opened the rear door.

'My lord Caesar.'

'Primus.'

The man was clean shaven like all in the Legion, with closely cropped grey hair and pale, smoky eyes. He was approaching his sixties, but still as lean and sinewy as a wolf. Cornelius was his name, but everyone referred to him by his honorific title. Primus Pilus. First Spear. Not an officer, but the Legion's senior Centurion and the most respected soldier in the Palatinate.

'How are the troops?' demanded Caesar as he strode towards his villa and First Spear fell into step beside him.

'Flavius has the First at basilica in the drill halls. Cassia sent the Second on quick-step marches to the east. Full equipment and a thirty-miler. She'll have broken them by dusk. The Praetorians are at the Palace.'

'Is the situation in Scotland common knowledge?'

'Yes, my lord. Sveinn's death was the talk of the camp last night.'

Caesar stopped by the arched entrance to his villa and turned on First Spear. 'And?'

'They laugh, my lord.'

'Laugh?'

'A Titan cavalry of seven! They respect the tactics, they applaud the secrecy and they acknowledge the deed, but the scenario is, nonetheless, comical.'

Caesar hummed sceptically in the back of his throat and then continued through the shaded villa entrance and into a private courtyard, where a fountain sparkled in the sun and coffee and fruit had been laid on a marble table.

'Is that all they talk about?'

First Spear tapped his Centurion's vine stick against his thigh. 'There are other mutterings. Odin is dead, they say. He could not stand the dishonour and killed himself just seconds after the Titan buried his sword in Sveinn.'

'Hardly the sort of news I want my Legionaries dissecting. Do we have a problem?'

'The moment Odin lost his Palatinate, he became a nobody.' First Spear shrugged. 'No one cares.'

Caesar accepted this in silence and then waved for his Primus to depart. 'Have the officers assembled in the Principia in thirty minutes.'

He poured himself a viscus coffee from the stovetop pot

and selected a handful of grapes. He could have partaken of a much heftier breakfast on his plane, but these days he ate little. He prided himself on his trim, soldierly figure, but, in truth, at sixty-nine years of age, his body wanted less anyway.

He sipped his coffee and stared unseeing at the bright waters of the fountain, his mind lost on the images he had seen of the death of Sveinn and the young King Killer as he reined his horse and returned to kneel beside the fallen King. There had been more footage when the King Killer had removed his helmet in front of the defeated Horde. It was a handsome face, filled with the exuberance of youth, and he was perhaps unaware of the shockwaves his actions had unleashed. Caesar's Legionaries might laugh at the events in Knoydart, but the King himself felt a frisson of excitement as he munched on his grapes. Something unprecedented had occurred on that Field, which would take this Game he had created into uncharted territory. For twenty years the Seasons had rolled by without a hitch and now, suddenly, this dramatic shift. The repercussions were only just beginning to reveal themselves, but Caesar already felt the tingles of anticipation churning in his gut whenever a new challenge faced him. Things were changing; he could sense it. Events were in play that could not be stopped. New beginnings. And that young face of the King Killer was at the heart of it all. The future of the Pantheon.

Alone in the courtyard, hidden from prying eyes, Caesar Imperator smiled.

Once he had eaten his fill of the fruit, he retired to his private quarters to rid himself of his travel clothes, shower and pull on a crisp white tunic trimmed with the broad purple stripe of Rome's equestrian class, along with gold-painted caliga sandals. Then he strode out into the sunlight of the main square once more and headed the short distance to the Principia, the field camp HQ.

He could have gathered his officers in the more palatial surroundings of the Legion's ceremonial headquarters in the Domus Aurea on Rome's Caelian Hill. The ruined complex had once been Nero's Golden Palace, and Caesar had spent a decade and a fortune excavating, restoring and developing it to reflect the opulence of Ancient Rome's most infamous emperor. Marble courtyards were recreated, surrounded by statues of the gods and filled with the scents of jasmine and bougainvillea, and the tinkle of fountains. A spa complex boasted open-air pools, steam rooms, a frigidarium, tepidarium and a hot caldarium. At the centre of the site stood a new amphitheatre for the Legion's formal ceremonies, as well as a gorgeous triclinium dining hall. Further out was a grass parade ground expansive enough to hold the Legion's twelve-hundred troops, and around this was more contemporary office space for Atilius' administrative teams to keep the Pantheon running.

Caesar was justly proud of his Domus Aurea, colloquially referred to simply as the Palace, but today was about military matters and so he had called upon his officers to meet in the martial simplicity of the Legion's field camp.

They were seated at the campaign table in the central sacellum chamber when he arrived – all bar one – and he could have guessed who the absentee would be. Beyond them, resting in state, was the Eagle standard of Jupiter, with the smaller standards of the First and Second Cohorts on either side. Incense burned in bronze cups and sunlight filtered meagrely through three small windows, creating a hazy, shadowed atmosphere which might have felt no different two thousand years earlier. The three officers rose and bowed their heads to Caesar. In one corner of the chamber, First Spear loitered.

'Where is he?' growled Caesar as he took his seat at the head of the table.

'On his way from your residence on Capri,' answered Cassia, Legate of the Second Cohort, her tone sharp and laced with irritation. She was a woman of heft – large-boned and strong beneath her white tunic. Her hair was cut short and platinum grey, flecked with strands of midnight. Her throat and arms were fleshy, yet even the most casual observer would sense the warrior fitness that exuded from her. She was in her thirteenth year in the Pantheon and had risen to command the six Centuries of the Second – almost five hundred troops, comprising scouts, archers, pioneers, one hundred basic *munifex* Legionaries recruited in recent years from the Legion Schola, three hundred more experienced *immunes* Legionaries, fifty senior *principales*, ten *optios* and five Centurions.

Caesar bottled a curse, but they could all see the indignation scrawled across his face.

Next to Cassia, Flavius, Legate of the First Cohort, shook his head imperceptibly and lowered hooded eyes on Valerius, Consul of the Legion, Praefect of the Camp and Keeper of the Books, who sat opposite. The three of them were used to these theatrics. The absentee was Augustus and although he might be a fine soldier who led his Praetorian Guard with dash and aplomb, he was also the son of Jupiter, and that made him arrogant, entitled, lazy and endlessly insubordinate to his stepfather. In time, so Augustus was convinced, the Pantheon would be his, and the day when old Caesar stood aside could not come too soon for him.

'Then we will begin,' Caesar said and indicated for Valerius to pour him a cup of watered wine from an amphora on the table. 'As you will all know, these are uncharted times. Two days ago, King Sveinn the Red was killed by a Titan blade on the Field of Battle in a place called Knoydart in west Scotland. As the Rules dictate, his Valhalla Palatinate is forfeit and will be subsumed into the Titan lines. The Horde's Edinburgh Tunnels now belong to Alexander, as do the Viking Schola, training bases and funds. Odin's time in the Pantheon is at an end and the seven-strong Caelestia has become six.

'Most critically of all, the demise of Valhalla has unbalanced the Pantheon's structure. Alexander's force will now double in size, but he faces no immediate foe next Season. So he awaits direction. The Caelestia will meet in an emergency counsel next week to agree a way forward, but before they do, I wish to hear the advice of my officers.'

This was not an unusual request. Caesar often liked to consult them about strategy before the Caelestia could get their hands on it. He was, after all, the founder of the Pantheon, the man who had first dreamed it up, who had first given birth to the idea of this worldwide Game. So, in the eyes of his Legion officers, he had every right to consider Pantheon strategy. In the early years, he had taken his seat amongst the Caelestes, attempting to be a god as well as a general. Once upon a time the other Caelestes had been his friends, his colleagues, his peers, but the situation had become awkward and unsustainable. Caesar could not sit upon the Council of the Gods, as well as lead his Legion in the field. He must choose. So he had given his place on the Caelestia to his wife and focused his attention on the Legion.

And for this, his officers respected him deeply. He was, first and foremost, a soldier and a general. It was his passion for the ancient warrior codes that had driven him to create the Pantheon and he gave the best of himself when leading the might of his Cohorts into battle.

Naturally, however, he could not entirely forfeit Pantheon strategy. Why should he? When critical Pantheon-wide issues arose, he would invariably bring his officers together to consider views, then use his remaining influence to whisper advice to Jupiter and the other Caelestes to ensure decisions were swayed his way. Usually, it worked.

'Valerius,' Caesar said, tasting his wine. 'Perhaps you will brief us.'

'My lord.'

Valerius was a small balding man, with an ever-widening paunch and a taste for high cuisine, fine wines and even finer young men. But, like the others, he still kept himself fit and believed in the hard disciplines of the Legion, while overseeing the business of the Palatinate with shrewd brilliance.

'Six days ago, the Sultanate and the Huns completed their Blood Season amongst the alleys and squares of old town Istanbul. By the end of the final Blood Night, the scores stood at eighty-six Blood Credits to the Huns and a hundred and fourteen to the Sultanate. In nine days, they are due to take to the field for their Grand Battle on the grasslands of Hungary's Hortobágy Reserve. Mehmet will boast seven hundred and twenty-four troops, of which two hundred and seventy are his household Janissary regiments. The Huns, for their part, will bring five hundred and ninety-two horse warriors, of which almost half comprise Bleda's Black Cloaks.'

'And Alexander?'

'Numbers are not yet confirmed. Obviously, the Titans and the Horde have already contested their Grand Battle and now the victorious Titan Palatinate will number approximately three hundred and fifty.'

'Of which seven are mounted,' interjected Flavius with sarcasm.

'They will attempt to enlarge that number,' replied Valerius, 'but they won't have much time.'

'Hmm, indeed they won't,' Caesar said. 'So, Legates, Consul, give me your thoughts.'

There was a long silence and then Cassia was about to offer her opinion, when there was a bustle at the door and Augustus strode into the chamber, dressed in jeans and a blue shirt.

'You're late,' barked Caesar. 'And you're dressed improperly.'

'Hello to you too, my lord. Would you have me go and change, and then be later still?'

Caesar seethed, but he set his face in a scowl and jerked a finger at a chair. 'Sit down and let us continue.'

Augustus' blond hair shone even in the muted light and his skin was bronzed from hours beside the pool on Capri. He smiled and helped himself to wine without glancing at the others.

'I understand your Praetorians are at the Palace,' said Caesar.

'They are. The accommodation is so much more preferable than these barracks.'

Caesar did not reply, but his lips pursed sourly. With an effort, he turned to Cassia. 'I believe you were about to offer an opinion, Legate.'

'Yes, my lord. Valerius had just briefed us on the current state of play with the Sultanate, the Huns and the Titans,' she summed up for the benefit of Augustus. 'The Sultanate and Huns are due to meet for their Grand Battle in nine days. Despite the changed circumstances in the tier below them, I suggest that they are permitted to continue with these plans and to face each other on the Field. As usual, the winner will then challenge us to a further battle later in the month, but I think it appropriate that the loser also prepares for a second battle, this time with the Titans. The victor of this clash will then be confirmed in Tier Two.'

'And what of the loser?' prompted Flavius. 'They are left in Tier Three with no opposing Palatinate?'

Cassia shrugged. 'Perhaps they join the Kheshig and the Warring States in a combined Tier Three next year.'

Augustus snorted and Caesar turned coldly to him. 'You have a better idea?'

Augustus looked his stepfather in the eye. 'There is a King Killer out there. A simple *captain* who led his seven-strong unit onto the Field at the very end of a Battle his Palatinate was losing and then got lucky. A man who, with one swordstroke, has become an overnight sensation. And now Alexander dreams of things beyond his reach. I say it is the duty of the Legion – and the Legion alone – to reinforce the status quo.'

'You would have me lead my Cohorts against Alexander?'

'It is the only action that matters. We are the masters. We must step into the fray, destroy this King Killer and send the Titans packing. Order will once again prevail and the other Palatinates will be reminded of their natural place.'

'We would outnumber them four to one.'

Augustus shrugged. 'Then hold back the First and Second and let my Praetorians alone cut Alexander's lines to pieces.'

Caesar felt Cassia and Flavius stiffen at this affront and he held up a finger of caution. Augustus grinned and swigged his wine and there was a stony silence.

'What say you, Flavius?' Caesar asked eventually.

The Legate of the First Cohort was a towering man, even when all six and a half feet of him was seated. He too was in his sixties and had been on the journey with Caesar from the start, rising through the ranks of Legionaries and Centurions to become one of the most senior commanders in the Pantheon.

'Putting our Imperial Legate's last preposterous comment aside, the nub of what he said may have merit.'

Augustus snorted again. 'Merely the nub, dear Flavius?'

'It might indeed be appropriate for us to take to the Field against the Titans and set an example at this critical juncture. Better than waiting in the background for others to determine events.'

Caesar was silent as he pondered, stroking a finger along the rim of his wine cup. 'I hear you, but I doubt the Caelestia will agree. Ördög and Kyzaghan will not countenance keeping their Palatinates in the wings to allow us to take centre stage. They will demand their right to wage battle and the others will agree. None of them wish to see us parade our superiority on the Field yet again.'

Flavius demurred to Caesar's judgement.

'Valerius,' Caesar continued. 'You have not spoken.'

The Consul rested his hands on his paunch and let the others anticipate his thoughts. 'My lord, much of the talk so far has been about the other Palatinates and the Caelestia. For my part, I have been considering the Curiate.'

Caesar nodded knowingly. 'I thought you might.'

'From what I hear from Atilius, they number over a thousand now and their close associates amount to five times that. Their passion, their support and – most vitally – their boundless enthusiasm for wagering their money is what has kept our little sport running over all these Seasons. And we must remember that a sport is precisely what the Pantheon really is. We would amount to nothing without the commitment of our fans.'

The soldiers around the table rarely liked to be reminded that their precious military machines were essentially just playthings in a very large game, but they knew the truth in Valerius' words.

'Our precious Curiate,' the Consul continued, 'has rarely – perhaps never – been so engaged as they are right now. What occurred in Knoydart was the equivalent of a goal in extra time or a touchdown against all the odds. A King is dead. A Palatinate has fallen. A new, unlikely hero has emerged. The shock has sent the Curiate into raptures and they can't get enough of it. They are primed for the next move we make, ready to wager untold fortunes on what the Pantheon does now and we must not squander this opportunity.'

'So, in your opinion, what should that be?'

'They love the Titans, my lord. Maybe by next year, the

fervour will have passed, but just at the moment, Alexander and his King Killer are the headline acts. The Curiate don't want to watch Mehmet's Sultanate and Attila's Huns have their Grand Battle like any other Season, as though nothing of huge import has just occurred. But nor do they want to see the might of your Legion take to the Field and overpower the Titans with sheer numbers.'

'Then what?'

'A three-way fight, my lord. Keep your Legion in reserve for now and let the other three Palatinates meet on one Field and see what transpires.'

'But we know what will transpire,' interrupted Cassia. 'The Sultanate and Huns together are a combined force as large as ourselves. They will simply wipe the Titans from the Field.'

Valerius eyed her with a glint of mischief. 'Who says they'll want to play it that way?'

For a moment, no one answered.

'You mean...' pondered Flavius, '...that they might ally themselves with Alexander?'

'I mean, Legate, that on a Field of three, any number of alliances, double-dealings, changes of heart, are possible. Mehmet and Attila have spent most of the last two decades throwing their soldiers at each other. I think one, or even both of them, will see the presence of the Titans as a golden opportunity to change that impasse.'

Caesar inclined his head in admiration.

'So we just sit the whole thing out?' demanded Augustus tartly.

'For once,' mused Caesar, 'perhaps we have to accept we are not the main attraction.'

'And the Curiate,' added Valerius, 'will quickly realise the myriad possible outcomes in a three-way struggle and it will loosen their moneybags faster than ever. What a show it could be.'

The Legion's officers thought about this and then watched Caesar to glean his opinion.

'I will consider the options overnight,' he said after a few moments, 'and then advise Jupiter accordingly. She will persuade the Caelestia on our behalf.'

'Will she?' Augustus asked, smooth as silk.

He left the question hanging and Caesar glared at him, but did not rise to the bait.

'In the meantime, I wish to review the Legion on full parade this evening at seven. We may not yet be called to Battle, but I will nevertheless inspect the immaculate precision of my Centuries. Cassia, when will the Second return from their march?'

'By five, my lord. I will have them ready.'

Caesar nodded. 'And, Augustus, you will bring the Praetorians from the Palace.'

His stepson chewed his lip frostily and did not reply.

'Did you mishear?' Caesar enquired acidly.

'No, my lord,' came the surly response. 'I will have them here.'

XI

The Valhalla Schola rarely had visitors.

There were never parents' evenings or local community events. Government inspectors did not call. New teaching staff were rare and sporting encounters with other schools unheard of. So when Eli pulled into the car park beside the wisteria-clad main building and found it full of vehicles he had never seen before, he knew the day was going to be very different.

He had left Oliver and Meghan sleeping and had stood in his driveway for several minutes debating whether he was being stupid leaving them alone. What if they decided to take flight as soon as he had gone? In the end, he reasoned that they had nowhere else to go and they knew it.

He stepped cautiously from his Mini and peered around. With all the turmoil, most of the teaching staff would have chosen – or been required – to stay on site the previous night and he hoped his absence had not been noticed. Grabbing his leather satchel, he made his way past the old building and onto the quadrangle. The classrooms around the perimeter were empty, but it was still only eight-fifteen and he supposed the students would be breakfasting in

Hall. He dropped down the steps to the staffroom and a stale fug of old coffee and burnt toast made his nostrils flare as he entered. Slumped in armchairs were four of the teaching staff, pale, worn and morose.

'We thought you'd done a runner, Elliott,' said one of them snidely.

'I'm sorry,' he stammered. 'An unavoidable commitment.'

The man snorted. 'That's rich.'

'Meaning?'

'Meaning, the way things are going, I doubt any of us will be getting out of this place for a while.'

Eli dumped his satchel by his desk and approached the group. 'What's been happening? Who's are all the new cars?'

'Titans,' said an arithmetic teacher for Year Two. 'They've sent a delegation from their own Schola, which arrived in the early hours and disappeared into the Main Building with Piper.'

Eli perched on the arm of a chair and tried to compute this new information.

'What are they doing here?'

'What do you think? They've come to assess the students.'

'And us,' added the first man with a hollow laugh.

The arithmetic teacher ignored him. 'Piper brought them out of the Main Building an hour ago – and you've got to give her credit. She'll have been fighting for all of us in there, for our futures – for every student and every member of staff and all that we have here – and she still came out looking as smart and professional as I've ever seen her.'

'So where are the Titans now?'

'They've split into groups. Some are down in the Arena with Frog and the Hastiliarii, assessing the combat skills of the Final Year students. Others are preparing to watch Year Three on the Assault Runs in the woods. There's more of them with the Estates team, inspecting the buildings.'

'So, what of you? Are you just killing time?'

'We're waiting to be interviewed.'

Eli understood. 'To see if we're worth keeping.'

'Pretty much. The smart money's on the Titans keeping this Schola running in some reduced capacity.'

'But they won't need all of us.'

The woman nodded. 'I'd expect the Initiates and Year Two to be dumped back into social care and most of us staff are going to be walking out of here with a redundancy cheque.'

'And just to rub it in,' said the other male teacher, who looked barely older than the students themselves, 'they're all masked.'

Eli leaned his head forward in shock. 'Surely not.'

'They don't want us seeing their faces until it's determined which of us is staying and which leaving.'

Eli whistled softly and was about to ask more, when the door from the rose garden opened behind him and a startled voice called his name. It was Cristina, his mental health colleague, and she stared at him from the doorway, so he rose and followed her outside.

'Where have you been?' she asked as soon as they were beyond earshot.

'I'm sorry. I was needed elsewhere.'

'Christ, Eli. I've been working all night. Do you realise

how stressful this whole situation is for the kids? The Vigiles are still marching around helmeted and now the Titans have arrived masked. The usual timetable has been turned upside down. And if any student gets emotional, they've been offloading them on to me. I've five in the garden now and another eight in sickbay.' She looked him up and down. 'Your absence at such a critical time has been noted.'

Eli held out his hands in submission. 'What can I do?'

'Go check on the ones in the garden, while I get myself some breakfast. They need some good old-fashioned reassurance and then we must get them back to their Year groups. Much better for them that they're not left out of proceedings at such a critical time.'

'Sure, I'll take over.'

'I'll grab some food and then go check on the ones in sickbay.' Cristina made to return to the staffroom, but she turned back with a final piece of information. 'They've still not found Oliver.'

Eli spent the rest of the morning with the students. Most were simply scared by all the change, the demons of their past lives resurfacing, so he gave them quiet words of advice. Sometimes he sat with them in silence. A few he even hugged. Each time he walked one back to their Year group, it seemed another was being brought to him.

After lunch, Cristina took over and he was called for interview with a masked Titan, who sat behind the teacher's desk in one of the empty classrooms and did not introduce herself. She pilloried him with questions about his background, his training, his duties and his temperament, and he guessed from the substance of her inquiries that she must be in a similar field. Perhaps she came from a Titan mental health unit. He knew he was in a fight to keep his job and he gave the best of himself to her, but his mind kept drifting to the two students hidden in his Jedburgh house, and a nagging voice in his head insisted on asking why he was bothering with the interview. His actions last night had already dictated that he would never again be safe in the employment of the Pantheon.

She released him after an hour with no concluding remarks and, having checked that Cristina was okay, he drifted down to the Arena, where Year Three were now being put through their combat drills while Year Four had been removed to the woodland assault courses. Vigiles and Titans stood in masked groups, watching the students and muttering amongst themselves. Spade and Thumbs led each exercise, bawling out commands with as much enthusiasm as they could muster, while throwing poisonous glances at the observers. Frog watched from the sidelines and Eli walked quietly over to him.

'How's it going?' he asked.

'How'd you think?' the Hastiliarius growled. 'The youngsters aren't stupid. They know this is it. Pass the test or they're out of here. Bastards have stamped numbers on all their arms, see? That way, they can just stand there behind their masks and assess all the kids, then mark their number down in their notes. One column for in and one for out. Simple as that.'

He spat into the sand.

'Will many get through?' Eli asked.

'Most of Year Four. The Titans need the extra numbers

and our final year students are skilled enough to switch to Titan ways of war. Year Three, I'm more dubious. Some will be selected maybe, but they won't want the bother of training up the weaker ones. It's Year Two and the Initiates that worry me most. They're being brought in later, but the Titans are only going to take those who show real promise. Bad times, Greavsie. Bad times.'

'What about you and the other Hastiliarii?'

Frog watched Spade and Thumbs for several moments. 'We're old Viking dogs who can't learn new tricks. I've never held a hoplon or fought with a shortsword or hefted a sarissa. Our time's up.'

'I'm sorry,' Eli said quietly. 'We've had our disagreements, but I've always respected how you developed the kids.'

Frog laughed. 'Yeah, yeah. It's all a bit late now to say how much we loved each other.' He held out a hand and they exchanged a firm, perfunctory shake. 'Fare you well, Greavsie, wherever the road takes you.'

Eli wandered away from the combat trials and took the lift back up to ground level. He decided to head to the sickbay to check on the intake, when he heard the click of heels behind him and a woman with a blonde bob that defied her age approached.

'Elliott Greaves?' she asked. Her lips were as red as her bloodshot eyes and her mascara did nothing to conceal the stress and exhaustion scrawled across her face. 'I'm Aurora, head of the Operational Support Unit.'

'I know. I was at your briefing yesterday.'

'And I think we spoke a couple of times on the phone last autumn.'

'I remember. When Oliver had a breakdown after being posted to your unit.'

'Yes, our elusive Oliver.'

'I had my work cut out for me to cool his anger and help him back to strength.'

'I'm not sure your efforts were effective.'

The two of them assessed each other awkwardly and for a moment neither knew how to continue.

'Is your OSU as full of Titans as this place is?' Eli asked.

She nodded and rapped her hands against her thighs, and he could see the manic fear coursing through her. 'You realise it's all over, don't you? All gone. They'll take everything from us.'

'So what are you doing here?'

'Still looking for Oliver. I hoped to find him before the Titans arrived. Now they're here, the trail's going cold.'

Eli knitted his brows. 'On whose authority are you looking for him?'

'On whose authority?' she repeated sharply.

Eli squared up to her. 'I'm sorry. Maybe I'm missing something. Our Palatinate has fallen. You're no more the head of the OSU now than I'm the head of mental health. We're all just waiting for the Titans to decide what to do with us. So, on whose authority are you looking for Oliver?'

'On Kustaa's. Thane of Valhalla. His name still carries weight.'

Eli gave her a long look. 'No, it doesn't. Go home, Aurora. Your presence here is unnecessary.'

He turned on his heel and continued on his way to the staffroom.

'Wait,' she called and trotted after him. Now she came close, and her tone was conciliatory and purring with promise. Her eyes flitted around nervously, as she whispered up to him. 'We must find the boy. He's so important. Have him and we have a bargaining chip.'

'A bargaining chip?'

'Don't you want to keep your job? You could be a marvellous counsellor for the youth of the Titan Palatinate. If we have Oliver, we can negotiate for new jobs.'

She glued her bloodshot eyes to him, fingernails touching his lapel. 'You knew him well. You helped him last time. Can't you think where he might be hiding?'

Eli carefully prised her fingers from him. 'I'm sorry, Aurora. I don't know where he is and I wouldn't tell you even if I did. Whatever you think you want him for, it's over. I suggest you go home.'

Eli stepped away and departed again.

'You were in a hell of a hurry to leave last night,' she called after him, venom in her voice now.

That stalled him. 'What do you mean?'

'I watched you on the security feeds. You marched away like you were late meeting someone. Like someone really needed you, from the expression on your face. Why such a hurry, Mr Greaves, when all your colleagues stayed at their posts? Where were you going?'

'Home. Where do you think? To get some rest before another difficult day.'

'I hope for your sake you're telling the truth.'

Eli waved her away and turned his back on her again. 'You're in no position to issue threats.'

As he reached the staffroom, her voice carried to him, frightened and angry. 'The Titans are battening down the hatches. None of us is going anywhere until they're done. So I hope there's no one special waiting for you at home.'

XII

Tyler Maitland crouched on the rough grass and munched on his second bowl of cereal.

It was three days since Hera had taken her leave of him and since then he had seen no other human soul except distant farmers whistling for their dogs and the occasional toy-like tractor in the valley. The views were stunning. Fields sloped from where he perched and ran smoothly to the shore of a reservoir, cradled by the volcanic cones of West and East Lomond summits. A high pressure had slunk across central Scotland and there was early summer warmth in the air, drying the grass and tempting him from the shadows of his cottage. Mid-April meant lambing season in Fife and from everywhere came the bleats of mother ewes as their youngsters danced and tumbled and cavorted with abandon.

He had never experienced the solitude of such a rural idyll and he supposed he should be grateful for the chance to recuperate, but his brain had perversely refused to embrace the peace and instead wound itself into knots of anguish.

He mourned Sveinn. Over and over again, he replayed the jolt as his sword broke through the King's chainmail and he glimpsed the wide, astonished moons of Sveinn's eyes.

He saw the blood creeping from the King's lips as he cradled his head, and heard the rattle of the last oxygen in his lungs. Memories tiptoed further back to a torchlit night when he had first laid eyes on the sovereign of Valhalla at the Oathtaking ceremony for the Nineteenth Season. Sveinn had been regal then in silver mail, his long tresses catching the light from the flames. His voice had been deep and soft, the tone of a man accustomed to commanding with ease. Tyler had been awestruck.

Never, never, would he have believed it would be a blade in his own hand that ended the life of this King.

He recalled Sveinn telling him about his son in California and he hoped there might be a family funeral. But instinctively he knew that the Pantheon disposed of its corpses – even its regal corpses – in a manner far less public.

Tyler grieved too for Maia. The quiet attention she had given to every task. The way her face could explode with mirth. Her motherly composure towards Pallas and her artful teasing of Zephyr, so subtle that the man had never noticed. The evenings shared over the washing-up, small talk and soap suds. The habit Maia had of placing her forehead on the muzzle of her mount and whispering secret words. Tyler wished he knew what those words had been and why the ritual had been important to her.

He craved the routine of the stables. Hera assumed she had been doing him a favour by granting him these days alone, but the time could have been spent so much better with his cavalry. He missed the horses. The sweet scent of their hay. The soft rumbling of their breath. The warmth of their flanks. And he missed Dio bringing a reassuring discipline to every hour.

And finally, there was Lana.

She tugged at him and he knew not how he should react. He had forgotten the feeling of her body as she had danced with him on Palatine Hill, but her words still came to him strong and clear: *We're foe now. What we were has no meaning.*

But that was before he had spied her blonde ponytail in the last line of defence on the Field and swerved Boreas around her; before she had sat amongst the defeated warriors of Valhalla and watched him with haunted eyes.

Now they were no longer foe. He had killed her King and they would be reunited under the one banner of the Titans. Could she forgive him? Could they perhaps find again what they had once thought they held? He had no answers. He only knew for sure that every day, every hour, as he idled his time away in those hills, Lana Cameron kept creeping into his heart.

It was raining gently in Jedburgh when Oliver came downstairs, just a pitter-patter on the patio beyond the kitchen's French doors.

Elliott had not returned the previous day and the two teenagers had spent a second sombre evening lost in their woes. When he had left that morning, he had raised no possibility of not seeing them later, so events at the Schola must be changing fast.

Oliver filled the kettle, then went to see if Meghan was up. The front room was deserted and so too was her box room. He returned to the kitchen and pressed his face against the French doors and there she was. Despite the wet, she was sitting on a tree stump at the far end of Elliott's unloved lawn, wearing one of his raincoats with the hood pulled up and cradling a mug of coffee. She seemed to be looking into the trees beyond, perhaps listening to the crows or simply lost in her thoughts.

The kettle came to the boil and he brewed himself tea. The first night in the house, he had slept like the dead as the sheer weight of exhaustion had overtaken him, but the second had been a much more intermittent affair and, as he spooned out the teabag and threw it in the bin, his movements were slow and heavy. Any relief at being found by Elliot had been replaced with a deep, implacable emptiness.

Whichever way he had spun it during his waking moments under the blankets, he could see no way forward. Life had hit a brick wall. He might have detested his months in the OSU, but every day there had been structure and purpose. Between his nights in the Schola dorms, his long commutes to the OSU and then his hours at his desk, he had been kept rigorously timetabled, and beneath it all there was the conviction – growing like a tumour – that someday, somehow, he would avenge the murder of his parents.

And now he had done so.

And his parents were still dead. And his heart was still broken.

Nothing, he realised, was going to bring them back or mend his wounds, least of all plunging a blade into an old man's throat. If he was honest, he was shocked by his own actions. As he replayed the images of Odin's appalled eyes and the liquid sounds of his gasps, it was as if it was someone else striking the blow. Not Oliver Muir, the boy who used to be so passive. Where had such energy and hatred come from? Where had it gone?

He stirred his tea and looked out at Meghan. And what now? He had been so obsessed with vengeance that he had never thought about what lay beyond. The authorities thought he had drowned in the Forth and the Palatinates wanted him for the murder of a god. He had no family, no home, no Pantheon, no purpose. Even when Mr Greaves did come back, Oliver could think of no next move.

His whole reality was just this house, this kitchen, this mug of tea – and the girl at the end of the garden.

He eased open the doors and stepped onto the patio. If she heard him, she made no response. The rain pattered on his head, but in a strange way it was refreshing, a sign that life kept going. He walked onto the grass with his eyes focused on the back of her hood. This girl – this woman – was the one element which didn't fit with his emptiness. She wasn't supposed to be here. His battered mind could just about understand the reasons for his actions in the OSU, the logic of why he had reached out to Elliott Greaves and how life had brought him to this house. But she was a surprise, a piece that didn't fit. She simply shouldn't be here.

Yet, here she was, sitting silently on her stump while the rain cooled her coffee, and he found himself overwhelmingly grateful.

'A penny for your thoughts.'

She took an age dragging her gaze from the woodland. 'I don't think you want them.'

'Try me.'

She sighed deeply. 'I'm angry, Oliver. Bloody damn steaming livid at the unfairness of it all. I was one of the triers in the Initiates. You know that. You might have been off on your jaunts to the OSU, but I was keeping my head down and working hard at everything they threw at me. I studied in class; I learnt what they told me to. I bested the assault courses and mastered the martial training in the Arena. Put a wooden sword in my hand and I could beat Gregor every time. And you know why? Because the Pantheon was the best thing that ever happened to me.'

'I'm sorry,' Oliver said softly.

'Sorry? What the hell have you got to be sorry for? It's that bastard who put a sword in King Sveinn who should be apologising. I bet he never thought about the consequences for the rest of us.'

'You should not have fled the Schola.'

'Of course I should. The whole place was in its death throes. Any fool could see that. I'm an Initiate, no use to anyone now. If I'd stayed, they'd probably already be dumping me back in the foster system. I won't allow that. Coercing Greavsie into taking me was the best thing I could have done.' She frowned at him. 'Although I wasn't expecting you to turn up and tell us you'd murdered Odin.'

Oliver smiled weakly. 'Yeah, that's rather limited our options.'

'Do you think something's happened to Greaves? Perhaps they saw him help me and now he's been detained.'

'I suspect he's just got caught up in everything that's going on at the Schola and he'll be back when he can.'

'But what if he's not? What if we never see him again? What the hell are we supposed to do? Do you have a plan? Because I sure don't.'

Oliver raised a hand in an attempt to placate her, but he

could think of nothing valuable to say and she threw the remains of her coffee on the grass irritably.

'I'm sorry, I just need some space at the moment.' She rose and handed him her empty mug. 'I'm going for a walk.'

'Greavsie said we shouldn't.'

'Screw Greavsie.'

She stalked off round the side of the house and he imagined her striding down the drive and starting along the road to town, her head down against the strengthening rain. He sat silently for a few moments, staring into the trees as she had been doing and berating himself for not having the right words for her. Then he tipped his tea on the lawn and headed towards the kitchen to get dry.

But Meghan was not on her way to town. She came back around the corner of the house and hovered on the edge of the lawn with an odd expression on her face.

'What?' he said, changing direction and the first shivers of alarm running up his spine.

'We have a visitor,' she replied mechanically and her eyes were wide.

He strode to her with his heart thumping because he could see the fear of god in her and knew implicitly that something dangerous waited around the corner.

'Hello, Oliver.'

He stopped dead and his lungs spasmed once.

Aurora stood before them, her make-up messed, her hair dishevelled and her expression drained. Behind her, one of the security guards from the OSU waited beside a car in the driveway. 'I've spent a long time looking for you,' she said.

'Where's Mr Greaves?'

'Mr Greaves won't be troubling us.'

Oliver's eyes drifted down her body and he saw what had frozen Meghan. Aurora held her arms loosely at her side, but there was no mistaking the snub-nosed barrel of a pistol in one hand.

'Is that real?' he asked.

'Do you think Valhalla only has spears and arrows?' She raised it slightly towards them. 'Odin's very own. He always kept one in his desk. Perhaps there would be some kind of justice if his bullet entered his killer's throat.'

For a heartbeat, he thought to run; to push Meghan with him and flee for the trees.

'Don't,' Aurora said sharply, as if reading his mind, and brought the weapon to bear. 'Don't think I wouldn't use this.'

The moment passed and Oliver raised his hands. 'Did Greaves tell you where to find us?'

'He didn't need to. He's too stupid for subterfuge. You and he were thick as thieves when you had your breakdown last year and so I suspected he might know something about your whereabouts. His actions gave him away and then it was simply a matter of finding his address on our databases before the Titans took them over.'

Meghan found her voice. 'Wh-what do you want?'

'What do I want?' Aurora's reply was righteous and sparked with indignation. 'Justice. That's what I want. Your friend here murdered a god and destroyed my Palatinate. Do you know how many years it took me to fight my way to the headship of the OSU? Fifteen. Fifteen years of devotion and service to Odin. And then the old man gets himself killed and my whole career falls apart.'

She waved the gun at them again and Oliver took an involuntary step backwards.

'Well, I'm not walking away so easily,' she hissed. 'If Valhalla has fallen and the Titans have no need of me, then I have to be more creative. So I thought to myself, there's one prize still out there worth having. Everyone's talking about the King Killer – but what would happen if I found the God Killer? There must be people of power who will reward me richly if I bring them the boy who murdered a Caelestis.'

Meghan shook her head. 'You don't have to do this.'

'Oh yes, I do.'

'Please, Aurora,' Oliver said softly. 'Let's find a different way.'

'You should have thought of one before you stabbed Lord Odin on my watch.'

Keeping the gun levelled at them, she reached into her pocket and retrieved a phone. One-handed, she punched in a number, while her eyes never left Oliver's.

A voice came on at the other end.

'It's me,' she replied. 'I have the boy.'

There was a silence and then the voice came back with instructions. She confirmed and cut the line, then focused once more on Oliver.

'Get in,' she said, waving the gun towards the car.

'Where are you taking me?'

'Shut up and get in.'

Oliver looked to Meghan and she nodded. Keeping his hands raised, he stepped slowly towards the vehicle and the security guard opened the rear door. With another glance at Meghan for reassurance, Oliver got in and the door was slammed.

Aurora switched the gun back to Meghan.

'What are you going to do?' the girl asked quietly, her hands still raised.

Uncertainty danced across Aurora's face and she did not respond. She had her prize now. The presence of this girl was a problem she didn't need. It would be so easy to squeeze the trigger, but a shot in these quiet suburbs would bring the neighbours running.

For long seconds she stared at Meghan, while the guard started the engine and turned the car in the drive.

At last, she came to a decision. With a final flourish of the weapon, she hauled open the other rear door and got in beside her captive.

Meghan let out a ragged breath and lowered her arms. The last she saw of Oliver was his face turned back to her as the car pulled out of the drive and headed north.

PART TWO

OVERLORDS

XIII

As dusk arrived and darkness reclaimed the views, Tyler heard the low murmur of a car engine in the valley and strode outside to see headlights approaching. It was the same BMW that had brought him to the Lomonds and the window eased down to reveal Stanek's face.

'Orders have come to take you to the city,' he said.

'The city? Not to my cavalry stables?'

Stanek shook his head.

'Oh well. Should I pack a bag?'

'You need nothing.'

Tyler stepped back into the lobby to retrieve a coat, then slammed the door of the cottage while Stanek turned the car. Neither man was in the mood for conversation, so Tyler sat silently on the backseat as he was taken once again through the darkened Fife towns, across the Forth and back into the heart of the capital.

It was only nine-thirty when Stanek pulled up halfway down the Royal Mile near Gray's Close and the pavements still bustled with tourists and residents alike.

'You're expected in Ephesus,' said Stanek. 'Go around the back of the hostel and take the steps up to the floors above.'

Tyler alighted and slunk down the close to the rear of

the backpackers' hostel and discovered rusting metal steps which had probably once been a fire escape. He peered around and waited until he was sure he was unobserved, then loped up the flight of stairs and rang a bell. A camera trained on him and after a few moments he heard the click of a lock. He pushed his way through to an old, musty-smelling corridor with peeling magnolia walls and a loathsome pink carpet, at the end of which was a spiral staircase climbing to an oak doorway. This time there was no bell, so he knocked smartly. A lock clicked again and the door was opened by a silver-haired man in black civilian clothes.

'Ah, Hephaestion, welcome.'

The man stepped back and Heph found himself entering an entirely different environment of brightly lit stone and marble, with doors off to each side and the scent of aloe hanging in the air. Almost a year before, he and Dio had passed through this reception on their way to the office of Simmius after they had won their death fight against Alexander's champions, but he had never before entered Ephesus by the old staircase.

'My name is Ellis, one of the entrance-keepers. I believe you know Ephesus, but in case you don't have your bearings, showers and pool are second on the right. Changing rooms beyond. Armouries third on the left and the Gardens on the fifth floor can be accessed from the stairs at the far end. The War Room is the final door on the right. You are to be in there for ten.'

'Gotcha.'

'Your attire is already prepared for you.'

Heph followed Ellis' directions through to the showers, where the smell of aloe grew even more intense. Beyond, he discovered again the pool where he and Dio had feasted after their victory, lit softly from below to reveal the serpent-head of Medusa crafted into the tiling. The water looked inviting, but he was on a tight schedule, so he skirted the perimeter and entered the changing areas. The rooms were deserted, except for a single open locker, in which hung a scarlet tunic, soft leather ankle boots with closed toes, a thick belt and a fine wool cloak for warmth.

Silently, he changed and belted the tunic tight at the waist, then stepped to a full-length mirror to check his image. It felt good to be back in Pantheon clothing, a sign that his wait was over. He ran a hand through his short, tousled hair and then over his clean-shaven chin. He missed his long tresses and goatee beard. He had started growing them as soon as he escaped school, as a two-fingered salute to that old life of structure and conformity, but there was no disputing the new haircut now gave him a genuine military bearing. Before him in the mirror, an officer from ancient Alexander's imperious, conquering armies stared back.

'Hephaestion,' a voice boomed over his shoulder. Nicanor came striding into the room and began stripping off his jacket, plaid shirt and jeans. 'You joining us?'

'I am expected in the War Room shortly.'

Nicanor – down to his underpants – opened a locker and retrieved a similar red tunic, boots and cloak. He was a huge man with a toned, muscled physique which could only be the product of hours in a gym. His athlete's legs, crooked nose and shaven head reminded Heph of a typical second rower in a rugby scrum, and he remembered seeing him in the heart of the tumult at the Battle, bellowing orders as he strove in vain to keep his Phalanx Heavies in formation.

Nicanor laced his ankle boots and then straightened and regarded Heph. 'That was a hell of a stunt you pulled.'

Heph shrugged. 'A *stunt* which only succeeded after months of hard training.'

'You and your little squad were quite the secret. It's almost a year since I first clapped eyes on you. Back then, your hands were bound and you were pleading for your life in front of Alexander. I saw you one more time, when you and your friend fought for your lives in the circle and earned your places in this Palatinate and then you disappeared. Gone, forgotten, thrown from the Pantheon, so I was informed. Months passed and the whole of the Twentieth Season played out. Then, just days ago, you swoop out of nowhere on the back of a horse and kill the King of Valhalla.'

There was a tense pause and Heph steeled himself for the inevitable insult, but instead Nicanor smiled and held out a giant paw. 'It's a bit late to say welcome, but welcome anyway. In my opinion we needed someone to stir things up and, boy, that's just what you and your horse troops have done.'

Heph accepted the man's hand and saw the twinkle in his eyes and, in that moment, decided that he might like Nicanor.

The big Titan led him out of the changing area and ushered him down the stone corridor into a large room of white marble tiles. Dominating the centre of the floor was a vast mosaic depicting central Edinburgh in a myriad of different colours. Heph gasped at the beauty of it and let his eyes linger on the Old Town streets he knew so well and the principal buildings of the Royal Mile. On the rooftops, the four Titan strongholds were shown in red and at different key points along the surrounding closes, while the Valhalla Gates were meticulously plotted in green.

Set around the mosaic were seven cedarwood chairs with mother-of-pearl Stars of Macedon inlaid on their backrests. Behind these was a table laid with pots of coffee and water jugs, and beside this stood Parmenion and Agape, both also dressed in tunics and cloaks.

'Well, well,' said Parmenion. 'The King Killer. I wondered if we might be seeing you this evening.'

Heph realised Simmius was standing in a corner consulting a screen, but he did not look up or acknowledge their arrival.

'Caffeine?' asked Agape and when Heph nodded, she poured him a cup of thick black Greek coffee.

He was just indulging in the powerful taste when there was an exclamation from the doorway. 'Who the hell invited him?' Cleitus glared at Heph.

'I did,' answered Simmius, still without looking up.

Cleitus reddened. 'This is the Titan Council of Commanders and I demand to know why that *boy* is present.'

Simmius put down his screen and graced Cleitus with his attention. 'My lord, Hephaestion is Captain of the Companion Cavalry and, like it or not, that earns him a place on our Council.'

'But he's captain of six troops! No, wait, one of them got themselves impaled so make that only *five* troops. How can he possibly be counted amongst our senior officers?'

'Because the Companion Cavalry is now a formally recognised regiment in its own right, which Zeus has personally nurtured and which, I would propose, has already more than proved its worth. It will sit beyond the jurisdiction of the Heavy and Light Brigades and will have its own line of command.'

'Then to whom does it report?' blustered Cleitus.

Simmius regarded him coolly for a moment, then inclined his head. 'Directly to the new Alexander, my lord.'

Cleitus quietened and considered this. Then he scrutinised the other occupants in the room and nodded slowly. A small, enigmatic smile twitched on his lips and he began to walk across the mosaic towards the chairs. Instead of heading for his usual position on the far left, all eyes followed him as he set a course to the central seat.

Parmenion's face tightened. 'Are we to understand that Zeus has already made his choice?'

Cleitus' smile broadened as he turned to them, though his eyes remained hard and reptilian. 'Oh yes, Zeus has decided.'

With languid nonchalance, he eased his bulk into the chair and folded his hands magnanimously across his belly. 'Black Cleitus is no more.'

'Behold, your new King,' Simmius intoned without expression. 'Alexander of Macedon – High King of the Titans, Commander of Companions, Protector of Pella, Persepolis, Ephesus and Thebes, Lord of the Sky-Gods.'

There was a stunned silence.

Cleitus had always been the most likely candidate to succeed the last Alexander, but none of them had expected Zeus to make the selection with such alacrity. Parmenion's eyes drifted to Agape, and Heph knew he was thinking just what he himself had put into words after the Battle. *It should have been her. Agape is the only rightful leader of this Palatinate.*

The awkward hush was broken by further movement at the door and a seventh figure entered the room. Heph had never seen this man without his helmet, but he could not mistake his tight, raw-boned features and malicious gaze.

'Ah, Menes,' said Simmius. 'Welcome to your first Council.'

'Somebody had better explain,' rumbled Nicanor.

The new Alexander glared at him. 'As your sovereign, I do not expect to *explain* decisions to my officers. However, on this occasion, I will elaborate. Zeus called me two days ago to bestow on me the powers of the King of Macedon. As one of my first acts, I have promoted Captain Menes of the Companion Bodyguard to my old position – Colonel of Light Infantry. He is now line commander of the Companions and also of Captains Parmenion and Agape, and thus a new member of this Council. I trust this is sufficient explanation.'

Parmenion and Agape exchanged glances and Heph could see the anger flushing their faces. With the ascent of Cleitus, they would rightfully have expected one of them to take over as Colonel of the Lights, a position which still allowed them to command their own units in the field. Menes was a more junior Captain and this decision was a flagrant disregard of their experience and seniority.

'My lords,' Menes responded quietly, giving each of them a curt nod. 'I am honoured by this opportunity and look forward to steering the Lights to many fine victories in the Seasons ahead.'

'Well said,' agreed Alexander, clapping one hand on a

knee. Then, with elaborate slowness, he extended the same podgy hand towards the centre of the mosaic and held it there. 'And now, before we continue with business, you will each swear your Oath of Fealty.'

Once again the room was silent and for painful moments no one moved. Eventually, Agape put her cup back on the table and walked onto the mosaic. Stopping in front of Alexander, she dropped to one knee, took his hand, leaned forward and placed a kiss on his knuckles. Keeping her lips so close that they brushed his skin, she spoke solemnly.

'I swear to obey the authority of my King – Alexander of Macedon – and submit to his commands. I will honour his Lion Standard and defend his life with my own. Let the gods be my witness.'

Alexander's flaccid features creased into a leer at the sight of this beautiful, powerful woman bent before him with her face lowered between his knees and for a heartbeat his desire was clear for all to see. Then he controlled himself, straightened his expression and allowed her to rise. Agape stepped away and took a seat in one of the chairs.

In turn, the other officers also knelt, kissed his hand and recited the words, until only Heph was standing.

'Well, boy. Give me your Oath.' Alexander stared at him malevolently, daring him to refuse.

Heph approached and forced himself down onto one knee. He focused on the hand and saw how it wobbled. Freckles dusted the fingers and the nails were stubby and bitten, with grime beneath. As he brought his face close, he caught a distinct tang of old garlic. He yearned to grab the hand and yank the bastard from his throne, but instead he forced himself to touch his lips to the middle finger and then recite the words he had heard the others speak.

'I swear to obey the authority of my King – Alexander of Macedon – and submit to his commands. I will honour his Lion Standard and defend his life with my own. Let the gods be my witness.'

Alexander removed his hand and pulled Heph's chin up until their eyes met. 'And that's that. Your Oath is binding. You're mine now, boy.'

Heph bit his tongue, rose and took the final seat on the outer edge of the group, while Alexander looked around him in triumph. Only a few short nights ago, he had thought the Titan Palatinate so weak that he had bargained with Odin for a coveted senior post in a newly victorious Valhalla. Yet, from the jaws of defeat had sprung a surprise so complete as the winds of change had come howling on the backs of seven riders. Now, here, in this War Room, all his dreams had fallen into place. Suddenly, *he* was Alexander, master of all he surveyed.

'Simmius, you may update my Council of Commanders.'

The Lord Adjutant inclined his head towards his new King and swiped the screen in his hand. 'My lord, I think we can say these are unprecedented times. Our Titan Palatinate is experiencing an almighty upheaval and there is so much still to be decided by Zeus and the Caelestia. However, I can brief you on the latest information at my disposal.'

'Do it.'

'We have not yet received formal confirmation of casualty numbers from the *libitinarii*. I can, however, tell you that our losses our grave. There is no doubting that we were on the losing side of the Battle until its very last moments. Informal numbers – comprising the dead and hospitalised wounded – from the two Raids at the zoo and Waverley Station, the four Blood Nights and the Grand Battle, are as follows:

Lion of Macedon x 1 = 50 Credits
Colonel x none
Captain x none
Platoon Lead or Dekarchos x 6 = 18 Credits
Companions or Band (elite) x 15 = 30 Credits
Cavalry x 1 = 10 Credits
Phalanx or Peltast x 34 = 34 Credits
Total Losses (provisional) x 57
Remaining Titan numbers: 78

Nicanor whistled softly. They had all fought in that final blood frenzy around the Lion of Macedon banner, but the numbers were still worse than they had feared. Fifty-seven friends and comrades were down, some facing agonising weeks in the Pantheon wards, most already in early graves.

'And our erstwhile foe?' asked Parmenion.

'The Horde of Valhalla enjoyed much of the offensive action during the Battle and, thus, their casualty rate was lighter. Informal numbers from the Raids, the Blood Nights and the Battle are:

High King x 1
Jarl x none
Housecarl x 1 = 8 Credits

Hersir or Thegn x 3 = 12 Credits
Wolf or Raven (elite) x 11 = 22 Credits
Drengr x 27 = 27 Credits
Total Losses (provisional) x 43
Remaining Valhalla numbers: 161

This time Nicanor laughed ruefully. 'A hundred and sixty-one shields remaining. That's double our numbers. They would have murdered us in the Twenty-First Season if we hadn't killed Sveinn.'

'But we did,' spat Alexander angrily. 'High King times one. Didn't you hear Simmius? Those hundred and sixty-one shields are *mine* now. Every last one of the bastards. How many does that make, Adjutant?'

'Two hundred and thirty-nine, my lord.'

'Two hundred and thirty-nine. The largest the Titan Palatinate has been for almost a decade. We are a force to be reckoned with once again.'

The other officers glanced at one another uneasily. It was hardly a total to inspire fear in the other Palatinates.

'My lord,' continued Simmius, 'I do have some unexpectedly good news to impart. Atilius has confirmed that not only can we spend the sixty-nine Blood Credits we earned during the Twentieth, the Caelestia has agreed that the losing Palatinate's efforts should not go unrecognised. We are, therefore, entitled to spend the Blood Credits Valhalla would have earned this year, including the fifty Credits for the sad loss of the last Alexander.'

'So how much is that?' Nicanor asked.

'Valhalla's Blood Credits are one hundred and forty-two.

Added to our Credits of sixty-nine, that gives us a total of two hundred and eleven Blood Credits to spend.'

There was a momentary silence and then every face split with a grin and Alexander smacked the arm of his seat in triumph.

'Two hundred and eleven,' he crowed. 'What a victory. What a conquest. We are transformed!'

'And may I suggest that we spend them fast, my lord,' added Simmius. 'The death of King Sveinn has thrown up a huge number of questions about what happens next for our Palatinate and the Caelestia have many key decisions to make. However, I suspect we will not have the leisure of the Interregnum to prepare for our next challenges. Events may happen quicker than we expect.'

'Agreed,' exclaimed Alexander. 'Spend the damn Credits. I want troops in my lines. Take every student from our Schola who can wield a sword effectively. Look too to the Valhalla Schola before it closes down. Recruit their final year students and any other individual who we deem worthy of a place in our Companies. Fill my phalanx. Burgeon my hoplite lines. Select a few of the best to be Dekarchos, but reserve most of the funds for one-Credit troops. That way we can grow our mass most effectively. Imagine it, my officers – another two hundred sword-arms! A Palatinate of over four hundred Titan soldiers.'

Nicanor, Parmenion and Menes cheered, but Agape and Heph exchanged silent glances.

'My lord,' Agape interjected. 'I hope you will spend on more than one-Credit hoplites.'

'Of course, Captain,' Alexander replied magnanimously.

'You may scour our current troops to select the best to join your Band. It is only fair that your Company reaps the rewards as well.'

'My lord, I was not speaking of my Sacred Band. I was thinking more of our new Companion Cavalry.'

'What? Those horse soldiers? At ten Credits a pop? Not likely. I'm not wasting this golden opportunity on four-legged beasts. Zeus tried that last Season and we very nearly lost the Battle.'

'But we didn't lose it,' Heph blurted. 'Because Zeus' seven horse troops won the Battle for you.'

Alexander forced his bulk upright. 'How dare you speak to your King in that tone, Captain. You have been in this Palatinate for barely a year and on this Council for barely an hour, so you will not have opinions above your station!'

Heph could not stop himself. He too sprang to his feet and faced Alexander across the mosaic map. He was about to shout back words of defiance, but Agape was waving him silent behind the King's back and he bottled his anger.

Alexander, however, was scarlet. 'What? You dare to challenge me? Your sovereign? Sit down, you little prick, before I have you removed!'

Heph steeled himself, glanced at Agape and then forced himself back into his chair. The King remained upright, breathing heavily and fuming. Everyone waited until his fury cooled, then he eyed each of them and finally seated himself again.

'My lord,' Parmenion ventured cautiously. 'Captain Agape has a point. Our cavalry was so effective in Knoydart because it arrived as a surprise on the Field. That surprise, however, has gone. Everyone in the Pantheon, from the Warring States to the Legion, now knows about our Companion Cavalry and they will be expecting them in any future action. Seven is a pitifully small number if they are to have any chance of further success.'

Alexander was still glowering and breathing heavily, his jowls sagging onto his chest. For long moments he stared at the map and refused to respond. Finally, he snapped, 'I will give you four.'

'Four, my lord?' Simmius queried.

'Four damn horses. *If* you can find the riders amongst our lines.'

'So that's forty Credits,' confirmed Simmius.

'It is,' seethed Alexander and his eyes turned to Heph. 'A huge cost, so you'd better make it worthwhile.'

Simmius checked his screen. 'Hephaestion, you still have the budget for seven horsemen despite the loss of one rider and one horse at the Battle. So you now have authority to purchase five fresh stallions and to recruit five riders from our current lines, bringing your Cavalry to eleven.'

'*My* Cavalry,' growled Alexander, his eyes still on Heph.

'Of course, my lord,' said Simmius with just a sliver of irritation in his tone. 'That goes without saying.'

'And what of the Vikings?' Menes asked evenly.

'The Adjutant is correct,' Alexander replied. 'We must move swiftly in case events come faster than we expect. Get them in. Get them back to their Tunnels and train them relentlessly in their new weaponry. They are Titans now. I want them proficient in the use of a shortsword, a sarissa, a javelin. I want them practised in the art of defence with a hoplon shield. I want a hundred and sixty hoplite troops ready to expand our lines at a moment's notice.'

'It will take me time to change the records,' warned Simmius.

'Damn your records. You can sort all that later. Don't waste precious days allocating Titan names to those bastards – that can all come later. They can keep their heathen names for now. Just get them looking like Greek warriors and herd them into the Bladecraft Rooms.'

'How will we incorporate them into our Companies?' queried Parmenion.

Alexander chewed his lips. 'We won't,' he concluded eventually. 'Not yet. Those that show promise over time can be promoted to our units, but for now they're all inexperienced, useless Titan troops and I won't have them contaminating our true lines. They will comprise an auxiliary regiment; our greenest and least skilled hoplites, who can be deployed in action where and when we deem fit.'

'Who commands?' Menes asked.

Alexander considered this. 'You do,' he decided. 'I trust you can select your best Dekarchos to be your second-in-command for the Companions, so you can devote your energies to training this new auxiliary regiment?'

Menes nodded. 'I can.'

'Train them hard, Captain.'

'You have my word on that.'

'What of the Viking officers?' asked Parmenion.

'No damn officers! They are defeated foe and I will not honour their old hierarchies. They will all become the lowest of our hoplites, the greenest of our troops. If they prove themselves in the future – well, damn them – I will reconsider then.'

Heph could not stay silent. 'No officers!' he exclaimed.

'That's what I said, Captain. Do you suffer from hearing problems?'

'But... but...' Heph was so shocked that he could barely get his words out.

'What our colleague is trying to say,' interceded Agape, 'is that the Horde was filled with warriors of great distinction. Jarl Bjarke. The Wolf litters. The Berserkers. They are mighty warriors who have proven themselves time and again on the Field, as we well know to our cost. To demote them to basic hoplites would be a criminal waste.'

'They are defeated foe,' Alexander snarled. 'They have forfeited any seniority they might once have boasted. They are also untrained in our ways of combat and in the use of our weapons. So I will not permit them the honour of bringing their past seniority into our lines.'

'But their *pride*!' Heph gasped. 'They are the Horde of Valhalla. You cannot reduce them all to your most junior troops. It will break them.'

'It's *supposed* to break them, you idiot. There's a hundred and sixty of the bastards. As Nicanor said earlier, that is twice our own number. I will not risk giving them a sniff of authority or command. They will be junior hoplites, each and every one, without exception. And I will use them in future action as I see fit. Do I make myself clear?'

Heph dropped his eyes and stared at the map. 'This is wrong,' he said softly.

But the King's mind was set. 'Simmius, find me a name

for this auxiliary regiment and get hold of the Schola to identify the best trainers we have. Bring them here and get them working on these new troops. I want them fighting like Titans within weeks.'

Agape watched Heph writhe with his private angst, then turned to Alexander with another question. 'Where do we base them?'

'In their god-forsaken Tunnels, I suppose. I'm not having them enjoy the luxuries of our strongholds. Besides, we will have many more newly recruited Titans from the Schola, so Ephesus, Persepolis, Thebes and Pella will soon be bursting.' He twisted to look at Simmius. 'How is the conversion of the Tunnels proceeding?'

'It's underway, my lord. We will have them looking and feeling like Titan ground as soon as we can.'

'Find a new name too. Valhalla is a name which no longer exists in this city.'

'Yes, my lord.'

'I have a suggestion,' said Menes smoothly.

'Speak.'

'Why not call it Alexandria, lord?'

There was silence. The commanders looked around at each other and waited for someone else to speak. Alexander rubbed his chins thoughtfully.

'The greatest city of the Hellenistic age,' continued Menes. 'Founded by Alexander the Great himself. What more apt way to mark your kingship, lord? Through our complete victory on the Field, you have the opportunity to found a new stronghold, just as Alexander himself once did.'

The King began to grin. 'I like it. *Alexandria*. The newest of our strongholds. Titan ground beneath the Mile. Simmius, it is agreed. Proffer this name to Zeus and if he consents, send out news to the rest of the Pantheon. Today, I have founded the second Alexandria.'

XIV

It was dark when the car pulled into a Fife coastal village and eased through the gates of a big house above the shore.

Oliver had spent the journey hunched against the rear passenger door, his cheek pressed to the window and his knees folded up to keep himself as removed as humanly possible from the woman next to him. He dozed fitfully, but every time he glanced her way, she seemed alert and watchful, her attention rarely faltering and her gun still gripped with purpose. She had shown up at the house without her usual heels and business suit, and instead wore sensible shoes and hiking trousers. The remnants of her heavy perfume overpowered the cramped space and made him wish he could hold his breath forever. Her blow-dry was unkempt and her make-up fading, exaggerating the deep lines scrawled across her face and lending her a menace which her ma'amship in all her office finery had never possessed. Sometimes, in the OSU with Jed and the other Tech team members, he had played along with their jokes at her expense, but he wasn't laughing now.

'Out,' she said brusquely, the first word she had uttered since they had left Jedburgh.

The central locking was released and Oliver stepped into a salt-scented night. His movement triggered a light and then the door of the house opened and a figure emerged. He had tried to imagine to whom Aurora had placed a call and who might be waiting to receive them. Pantheon authorities, perhaps? A Vigilis commander or Atilius himself? Maybe one of the new Titan overlords, or some twitching, heartless jailor who would chain him and cast him deep into a Pantheon cell. He had even wondered if this was the start of a final journey to the horrors of Erebus.

So the sight of Kustaa's wavy hair and plump form was something that sparked hope. Here was a man Oliver did not fear, an insipid man, an inadequate Thane. Someone with whom Oliver might be able to negotiate.

Aurora was clambering out of the other side of the car and it was the first time her gun was not levelled at him. For a desperate moment, Oliver thought of making a run for it. Kustaa was in no shape to give chase and the woman would have to be one hell of a crack shot to hit him in the dark. *Burst into action, right now! Get through the gates and race down the road!*

But his limbs never twitched and the idea wilted on his brain, because at that moment a third person came from the house. Oliver could make out little more than a figure silhouetted against the inner lighting, but it was enough to appreciate the strength of the man, his hands held ready by his side, the hyena gait of his legs, and Oliver knew instantly that if he ran, this man would catch him and break him.

'Who's this?' Aurora demanded in alarm and waved her weapon at all of them.

'Introductions can be made once we've settled our guest,' replied Kustaa.

'You never told me there would be anyone else here.'

'My dear, Aurora, I suggest you come inside before someone gets hurt and I will explain everything.'

She battened her lips, but only half lowered the weapon.

Kustaa focused on Oliver. 'I'm sorry to drag you here under such circumstances, but I'm sure you realise what an uproar you've created. There are a lot of people who wish to speak with you, some of a lower moral character than others. So we feel your safety is best guaranteed by hosting you here, away from prying eyes and out of harm's way. I'm sure you understand.'

He signalled for the driver to depart and they waited until the gates had closed. Then he led Oliver towards the house and the other man stepped grudgingly aside. Up close, his features were blade-thin, his face bruised and lacerated. His hair and beard were the colour of a corpse, like week-old snow or putrid milk, and his eyes crawled over Oliver, penetrating and shrewd, a hair's breadth from violence, assessing and taking the measure of him.

Oliver understood implicitly that this man would kill him with no more contrition than stepping on a snail and the knowledge drained him of any resistance.

Without objection, he allowed Kustaa to escort him into the house.

Heph felt physically sick as the Council ended and he could finally escape. He avoided the changing areas and took himself instead up a floor to the Ephesus garden, where he paced along the walkways beneath olive and fig trees, clematis and jasmine. The night had turned sour and rain pattered on the glass roof, but he barely noticed.

His head was consumed with memories of his old friends from Valhalla, how glorious they had once looked in their Viking apparel, the fervour in their eyes as they drank to the Norse gods, the straightness of their backs when they pinned their Bloodmarks to their mail, and their pride in the Wolf, Raven, Storm and Hammer banners. He too had felt that pride and known implicitly that none of them stood firm in the shieldwalls for the benefit of the Pantheon or for Odin's sport or for the lure of money; they braced themselves beside their brethren simply because the Horde meant everything to them.

Yet now – because of his own actions – that Horde was lost. The banners had been burned, the Tunnels renamed, the regiments disbanded and their Viking finery discarded. Never again would they heave on their mail or shoulder their limewood shields, and none of them would ever die with a longsword in their hand. Not for a moment had he thought this would be the inexorable result of his actions on the Field.

They would loathe him.

They would hate the Titans. They would abhor Alexander.

And, most of all, they would despise themselves.

Heph groaned aloud and pushed angrily through the arms of giant ferns that reached across the walkway.

'Hephaestion,' came a voice from the other side of the border.

He had no idea how long Agape had tracked him, nor how much she had seen of his furious, tearful face, but he was past caring. He rounded on her and strode across the carefully cultivated earth.

'He's mad. That fat bastard's so far up himself, he's lost touch with any critical faculty he might once have possessed. Or maybe he's just always been a thick-headed moron.'

'Have a care, Captain. Like it or not, he's your King now.'

'But a man like that shouldn't be. He has no right to style himself "Alexander". The real Alexander, the Lord of Asia, would never have treated his respected enemies with such disdain. The opposite, in fact. He embraced their cultures. He clothed himself in Persian robes. He married an Afghan bride. He took part in their local customs wherever he went. He encouraged his soldiers to marry Persian women. And he learned from the best of his foes and adopted their battlefield tactics – the cavalry of Darius, the war elephants of Porus. This was how he conquered the greatest of empires and forged the cultures of east and west into one. By respecting his enemies. By permitting them to keep their pride and their spirit, so long as they fought for him.'

'That's wishful thinking and never going to happen in the Pantheon, Heph. The Horde of Valhalla is beaten and that's the end of it.'

Heph stepped close to her and almost reached out to grip her arm. 'You don't believe that. I know you don't. These are uncharted waters for the Pantheon. A Palatinate has never been dissolved before, so there are no precedents. We could have united the Vikings under Alexander, if we had used our heads – and if we had selected the *right* sovereign.'

Agape examined him grimly. 'Seditious talk, soldier.'

'Oh come on, we all know the throne is yours by right. You are the Titans' greatest officer. Favoured by Zeus. You need only have accepted and the throne would have been yours.'

'I am a warrior, Heph. A swordmaiden. A Captain of the most accomplished unit in the entire Pantheon. Why would I ever give that up to hide behind the shields of other soldiers?'

'You could have been a warrior queen. You could have led from the front. The Lord of Asia did. That's what made him so adored and so respected by his enemies. He rode at the head of his lines and took himself to the heart of the most bitter fighting.'

'But that's not how the Pantheon works, and you know it.'

'I hear tales that Caesar leads his Legion. He gave up his place on the Caelestia to be at the head of his Centuries.'

'Caesar has the strongest force of arms in the Pantheon at his disposal. He is protected by more than a thousand Legionaries.'

Heph took a juddering sigh and forced himself to hold his tongue. He stepped away and gazed over the greenery to the Titan throne sitting lonely and empty in the wide expanse of marble at the centre of the garden. 'You can dice it whichever way you want,' he said quietly, 'but you know this isn't fair.'

'Since when was the Pantheon ever fair? We may dislike our King's decisions, we may consider them short-sighted, perhaps even foolhardy, but we are officers in the Titan Palatinate and we follow the orders we are given.'

Heph shrugged in surrender and kept his silence until the heat in his chest had cooled. Then, without meeting her eyes, he asked simply, 'Can I see Valhalla?'

'I think you mean Alexandria.' She examined him. 'Yes, you can, but only if you are going to act as a Titan Captain.'

He nodded. 'I will. You have my word.'

'Then you must change back into streetwear and head to the old South Gate down Blair Street. It's the only one currently in use.'

And so he did.

He strode through the rain to Blair Street and, just like the old days, slipped down the iron steps to a lowly, graffiti-riddled door and faced the camera which was filming him from a shadowed corner. When the door clicked, he eased it back on its hinges. Inside, the Gatekeeper room was manned by new personnel, men who looked at him without recognition and who only permitted him to proceed after checking their database records.

He walked silently through his old haunts, keeping his promise to Agape and never allowing his surging emotions to show. Everywhere he went, Pantheon contractors busied themselves transforming the place into a new Alexandria. The walls of the Tunnels had already been stripped of the beautiful sheet silver which had depicted scenes of fjords and longships and victorious Viking armies. In the Throne Room, the dais was empty and Sveinn's mighty dragon-headed prows we stacked in a corner ready for removal. The tapestries were gone; the Regimental banners taken down. In the Western Hall, the giant Triple Horn of Odin engraved into the sandstone floor had been pried up one flagstone at a time and now an ugly rubble hole waited for the new overlords of Alexandria to refashion it. The great hearths remained as they were, as did the drinking benches in the corners of the Hall. But they were empty and silent, and try as he might, Heph could not even recall the Norse hymns that had once been sung from them over ale and mead and mutton stews.

When he was done, when he had filled his eyes with the loss of it all, he took himself out South Gate and stood in the night, feeling the city breathe around him, his tears mixing with the rain. Finally, empty and broken, he called Stanek and sat in silence as he was taken back to the hills and the sheep and the solitude.

XV

Jarl Bjarke was not the submissive type.

But Jarl Bjarke was no longer a Jarl and after a week confined to his Leith apartment, pacing the rooms, eating junk, drinking too much and constantly examining what he could have done differently to change the course of the Battle, he was a man depleted when his phone finally rang with new orders.

Meekly, he accepted the instruction to head to South Gate on Blair Street, even though it was still daylight and the caller gave him no indication of their identity and spoke of a place called Alexandria. When he arrived, wearing blue jeans, T-shirt and leather jacket, the street was filled with pedestrians going about their business in the blustery iron-grey conditions of a spring afternoon.

It was rare for him to enter the Tunnels during daytime hours and it was unheard of to do so in the company of at least ten other former members of the Horde. They had all arrived at the designated time of three o'clock and trooped down the steps in a disconsolate line. Civilians cast their eyes over them from the pavement, but could never guess what reasons these men had to be going through the tiny graffiti-smeared door below and they gave them no further thought.

Once inside and through the secondary secure doors, the group was made to queue quietly like schoolboys, as a handful of officious administrators checked their details on the computers in the Gatekeeper quarters. Four more ex-Horde members arrived, burgeoning the number to fifteen, but that was all, and Bjarke noticed they were all from different regiments and of varying seniority. No pattern. No reflection of the old structure of Valhalla's lines. No other officers.

And no women.

When they were checked in, an austere, whippet-thin man wearing a black polo-neck told them to follow him and led them down the Tunnel towards the Reception Areas. Bjarke found himself seventh in line and it didn't even occur to him that once he would have flattened anyone who dared walk ahead of him.

The Tunnel looked different and it took him several moments to realise the walls were bare. The Norse panoramas, wrought in silver, were gone. There were gasps and murmurs around him as the others noticed. The sight should have stirred him to fury, should have made him want to smash the thin man's brains against the stone, but all it did was turn his stomach with foreboding.

When they reached the entrance to the Reception Area, the man stopped them and told the first five to proceed through to the showers.

'Clean yourselves,' he said in a disdainful tone. 'Wash your hair, then take a towel and go through to the changing rooms.'

Once again, Bjarke waited in the queue, listening to the sounds of the showers and keeping his eyes from the others. Then he was called through with the next five. He stripped and placed his clothing on a bench beside the lockers and took himself into the warmth of the water. He soaped and rinsed his long blond hair and massaged conditioner into the braids of his beard, then walked back to the lockers and wrapped a white towel around him. The administrator glanced disapprovingly at his tattoos, especially the serpent that writhed around the back of his neck.

Once the five had fixed towels, they padded barefoot after the man as he led them towards the main changing rooms. Bjarke noticed three other black-clad figures fall into step behind them and these had short blades on their hips. Unease prickled up his spine and his old warrior instinct flickered. He glanced back at them and drank in the alertness of their postures. They knew something he didn't and they were preparing for a struggle.

So what was ahead? Why had they been called here and told to wash?

Bjarke clenched his fists and stepped into the changing room. Set in the centre, between the rows of lockers and benches, were three chairs.

And with gasps of horror, the five Vikings realised what awaited them.

A chill had risen from the earth, but the stars still burned above and the air was filled with garden scents. Lanterns hung from the lemon trees on the terrace. The borders below were aglow with expertly concealed lighting and the blue haze of the pool shimmered in the dark as though suspended above the ocean itself. Beyond this, the bay twinkled with its own stars, the lamps of a hundred yachts, and from somewhere out on the water, a lone voice crooned local folk songs.

Jupiter pulled a shawl around her shoulders and drew on a thin unfiltered cigarette as she waited for her husband. Caesar had arrived late that afternoon and thankfully taken himself off to his quarters in the east wing without seeking her out. They had agreed via text to meet at nine on the terrace for an al fresco dinner and she had completed her online engagements with her diary secretary, her personal shopper and her house manager of the Palace in Rome before bathing, dressing and ordering prosecco and aperitivo dishes alone on the terrace.

Fabian – as usual when his stepfather was home – had remained on the mainland, most likely primping himself for a tour of the capital's best clubs with a swarm of acolytes in tow. He had always been a moderate drinker, but of late he had developed a pill habit, which electrified his natural conceit and made Caesar fret that his stepson's tongue would loosen too much in the wrong company. What could tall, blond, muscled, wealthy Fabian possibly be tempted to whisper in a girl's ear that would dazzle her even more? *Darling, I'm the Imperial Legate of the Praetorian Guard.*

Caesar joined her on the stroke of nine. They greeted each other with awkward pecks on each cheek and she poured him a glass of prosecco. The house staff emerged with antipasti dishes and the couple sat picking at them and looking out at the lights. As usual, they limited themselves to superficial niceties until the time was right to speak of more important things. She asked him about New York and he asked her about Berlin. She told him of the gallery openings she had attended in Paris and he went into tedious detail about some stock options that were proving challenging.

Eventually, the staff returned with a risotto of local catches from the bay and then steak and a side dish of chicory salad. Neither of the Ballantynes were fans of dessert, so once Caesar had finished picking at his steak, they had coffee and glasses of grappa brought, then waited until the staff had cleared the plates and left them in peace.

Jupiter lit another cigarette and examined the profile of her husband across the table, lost in his thoughts. He looked tired and leaner than ever. In quiet moments like this, she still felt for him. She could remember the younger man and the passions they had once shared. The heat from the relationship might have cooled, but her respect for him had never faltered. Only *her* Julian could have built a finance empire of such prodigious proportions, then grown sick of it and spent his last two decades devoting his ardour to the creation of a worldwide game. Only he could have abandoned the boardrooms and the super-rich social engagements to dream instead of leading a Legion. She might not love him anymore, nor even perhaps tolerate him, but she had to admire his vision and tenacity.

She decided the time was right to break into his reverie. 'I trust your days at the camp were well spent?'

Almost regretfully, he eased himself from his thoughts and turned to her. 'I had the Cohorts paraded and watched them drill. Cassia and Flavius are keeping them in good condition.'

'Primed for the Battle to come.'

Caesar resented needing to respond. He knew she was probing the limits of his powers as a mere King. 'Perhaps,' he answered eventually.

Jupiter kept her tone light. 'Only perhaps? The eventual victor between Kyzaghan's Sultanate and Ördög's Huns is scheduled to meet my Legion in the final Battle of the Pantheon Season, as has happened without fail for the last fifteen years. Are you suggesting there is any doubt?'

'*Our* Legion,' he said quietly.

She considered this, drawing deeply on the cigarette and exhaling twin plumes of smoke from her nostrils. 'Our Legion,' she conceded at last.

Caesar swallowed his grappa irritably and poured another. 'Let's not play games tonight, Marcella. It's been a long trip, I'm tired and there are important things we must speak of. The death of Sveinn has thrown many questions into the air.'

'You think I'm not aware of that? You think I don't know why you ended your meetings early in New York, why you've spent five days cosseted with your commanders and why I'm graced with your presence tonight?'

'Are you suggesting events don't warrant my attention?'

'I'm reminding you that Kings look to the running of their Palatinates and leave Pantheon strategy to those of higher rank.'

He could not help himself. 'I am *Caesar*!' he exploded.

'Indeed you are.'

She let him cool and there was silence. The singer was still crooning somewhere in the distance and there was a brief shout and the smash of a plate from the kitchens.

'I've already been in touch with all my fellow gods,' she said, choosing to step back from confrontation. 'There is a great deal of angst about events. They are horrified that Odin – *Raymond* – could have been so easily murdered and angry that the culprit is still at large. It is a travesty, Julian. A slur on the whole Pantheon. What could be more sacrosanct than the safety and untouchability of the Caelestes? Do you think *I* could be at risk? Could there be eyes out there in the night right now dreaming of the notoriety to be earned from killing Lord High Jupiter?' Her jaw tightened as her train of thought developed. 'What if the killer was hired? What if someone out there is paying for the deaths of the Caelestes? One of the Curiate perhaps. Someone who's lost a fortune to the Pantheon and bears a grudge.' She glanced around at the gardens. 'Perhaps I am unsafe here.'

Caesar leaned towards his wife. Her momentary fragility was strangely compelling. 'My dear, I'll have the guard doubled, but you've no reason to worry. Raymond's loss saddens me deeply. It was a gross lapse in security and a tragedy so unexpected that we must look deeply into the circumstances to ensure it can never happen again. But it was a one-off. Of that I am certain. Raymond was playing fast and loose with the Rules. He thought he had his actions well hidden, but any fool could see them. And he made enemies. Last week one of them came calling. But there is no threat to the other Caelestes, least of all you.'

She accepted his reassurance, but her expression remained rigid.

Caesar picked his next words prudently. 'But, if truth be told, it is *Sveinn's* demise which has more ramifications.'

'There is anger about that too amongst the other gods. Malutin and Reis are incensed. They think Petrou broke the spirit of the Rules by hiding his new Titan Cavalry and by pretending he had not spent his Credits. Tuesday's meeting is going to be fun.'

'Malutin and Reis are naturally going to think that, because they feel threatened. Their Hun and Sultanate Palatinates have spent more than a decade happily sitting in Tier Two, facing each other and vying for the right to challenge our Legion at the end of each Season. Now, out of the blue, Petrou has thrown all this in the air. He has destroyed the Valhalla Palatinate, he has subsumed their warriors, and he now has every intention of shaking up Malutin's and Reis' cosy little state of affairs in Tier Two. So before you step into that room with the Caelestia next week, we need a plan.'

Normally, Jupiter would have bitten back at these words. With a man like Julian Ballantyne for a husband, she had always known she must keep him leashed; must maintain some kind of power over him that would guarantee her marriage and guarantee the privileged future of her son. That power had come when he offered her his place on the Caelestia and she had vigorously held it over him ever since.

But this time, she did not challenge what he said. Perhaps it was the shock of Pearlman's murder or maybe the reluctant concession that the troubled waters running beneath the Caelestia were too deep and she needed his help to navigate a course.

'Do you have some suggestions?' she asked in a more conciliatory tone.

He leaned towards her, his eyes intense in the lantern light and his grappa forgotten. 'I do.'

She stubbed out her cigarette. 'I am cold. Come, bring your drink. I have the fires lit in the loggia. I will consider the merit of your thoughts there.'

XVI

Lana was holding a Matsyasana yoga stretch in the peaceful front room of Renuka's beautiful house beneath Blackford Hill, when her phone pinged.

Over the last ten days of waiting, she had fallen automatically into the three-fold structure that Renuka had practised. The mornings were the Awakening, an envelope of time when she tried to be at peace with her thoughts. She ground coffee and heated bagels and sat by the giant glass doors to watch birds on the feeders. She let her mind rove over the events of the last few weeks and months, analysing the Battle, contemplating Sveinn's death, worrying for her Ravens and pondering the man called Hephaestion who had danced with her on Palatine Hill, spurred his warhorse towards her across the Field, stared disconsolately at her from the ranks of the victorious Titans, and once, long ago, kissed her unreservedly and told her he was falling for her.

Try as she might, nothing made sense and peace did not come easily. So, in the afternoons, she took herself to the front room and devoted herself to the Finding, easing herself into various Yogic asana postures and focusing on breathing exercises. A tiny voice in her head often asked what the hell was the point, but she insisted the activities provided structure and let the days pass quicker.

Renuka's weapons had been removed by the Pantheon when she died, but Lana still descended to the basement each evening, cranked up the music and worked herself on the gym equipment until her muscles screamed and her body was slick with sweat.

The message that tenth afternoon took the usual form. A few terse words from an unknown WhatsApp account which self-deleted after reading. She was required to report at the East Gate on Market Street at midnight. This was followed, however, by a new addendum: *Non-compliance will result in the severest punishment.*

Right, she thought. So that's how the bastards want to play it.

She was damned if she was going to disrupt her routine on their account, so she still spent the evening working out in the basement, then showered and ate a hearty supper. She booked a taxi for eleven-thirty and left the house with her muscles singing from the exercise, her hair washed and tied back, and her mind set. The best of her. Ready for whatever the Titans were about to throw her way.

She entered the East Gate through the Market Street vaults just before midnight and discovered the Tunnels alive with bustle. She found Estrid and Sassa in the changing rooms and hugged them and tried to smile as they stripped and pulled on the scarlet tunics awaiting everyone. Then Geir came through from the men's area and she was about to embrace him too when she realised he looked different. His expression was so bleak that it took her several moments to realise what had changed. His beard had gone.

'You shaved it off,' she murmured, coming close to him.

'They did,' he spat quietly. 'We're fucking Titans now, aren't we? Baby-chinned Sky-Gods.'

His face was spotted with nicks and red-raw rashes, as though his skin protested the change as much as he did.

Calder led them into the Tunnel and saw that the other men were similarly shaved. Worse still, their long warrior hair had also been chopped. Geir had always been cursed with minimal growth on top, but most of the other Viking men had prided themselves on their tresses. Now they were all hacked back into ragged, clumsy schoolboy cuts and it was as if their fighting spirits had fallen to the barber blades as well. They kept their eyes averted, barely wishing to acknowledge the women, feeling gauche and embarrassed under their gaze.

The press of the numbers shuffling past the Eastern Armouries and down towards the Throne Room suggested to Calder that the entire Horde had been summoned. They came from each Tunnel, drawn inexorably to the wide space of Sveinn's Throne Room, pressed shoulder to shoulder. As she approached, she could hear the hum of lowered voices, the murmur of comrades meeting again, but none of the boisterous din which would once have signalled the gathering of the Horde.

She pushed through the crowd and they deferred to her because she had been Housecarl of Ravens and it was natural to let the officers congregate at the centre. Yet now there were no insignia of rank, no outward evidence of seniority. They were just a crowd of rudderless individuals, all dressed in identical scarlet tunics and closed-toe sandals.

When Calder reached the open floor at the centre of the

gathering, she realised the dais was unlit and sheathed in shadow. She looked instead across the Hall to where burlier figures waited in the habitual place of the Hammers. She met the haunted gaze of a big, muscled blond man and for a heartbeat she failed to recognise him. Then she gasped and could not stop her hand coming up to her mouth.

Bjarke saw her reaction and his features tightened. His chin and cheeks were pale as summer cream after so many years hidden from the sun, but also blotched with painful red spots, like the complexion of a teenager. His short hair stuck up as though he had only just risen from bed. He looked, somehow, twenty years younger, yet irredeemably older, his shoulders slack and his back drooping. Calder forced her attention away and spied Ingvar next to him. Huge, glorious Ingvar, broad as a bus, now similarly diminished. And there too were Stigr and Ulf, but now they were sheep, not wolves.

Above them, the door to the Council Chamber opened and the murmuring in the Hall spluttered and died. Onto the darkened dais trooped ten Titans, armoured in bronze and bearing blades, but for the first time without their helmets, and from the Chamber above came a single man, similarly attired. He was lean as a hyena beneath his armour, the tendons on his thighs like vipers above his greaves as he descended. His breastplate gleamed, his right hand rested on the pommel of his shortsword and his tight, hollow face studied the crowd with vulpine interest.

He walked onto the dais and came to the edge, legs apart. He watched them for long seconds, taking them in, letting the moment extend. Silence. Every face turned up to him.

'I am Menes, Colonel of the Brigade of Light Infantry in

the Titan Palatinate, Commander of Companions, Officer in Charge of Peltasts, Scouts, Archers and the Sacred Band.'

They might not have recognised the face, nor cared for the titles, but they knew the name well enough. He had risen through the Companion ranks after Timanthes had fallen in the cellar. A hard bastard, by all accounts. A foe who killed Vikings with pleasure.

And now he stood in Sveinn's old Hall, without helmet and without fear.

'Welcome,' he laughed and exposed a ragged set of teeth, 'to New Alexandria and the Hall of Zeus!'

With theatrical pomp, the lights above the dais came on and the crowd gasped. Gone was Sveinn's throne. Gone too his mighty Viking prows. In their place, hung from the ceiling, was a giant Star of Macedon and the wall behind was covered by a vast golden lion on a scarlet background.

'You stand at the heart of the fifth Titan stronghold,' Menes exclaimed. 'New Alexandria. And it will be your home as you train in our inaugural auxiliary regiment.'

The insult of the Titan symbols strung high in Sveinn's Throne Room at last lit a spark and a venomous hum rose as the Vikings rediscovered their spirit. Every one of them knew friends who had died fighting against those symbols. They had all seen colleagues hacked and stabbed and trampled while those banners flew above the heads of their adversaries, and it was too much now to watch them flaunted in their own halls. The hum became shouts and the Horde shifted and pulsated. Ingvar was at the front, the humiliation of his shorn hair forgotten, swearing at Menes and reaching for him. They would mount the dais, grab the man, tear him limb from limb.

Menes drew his shortsword and yelled for reinforcements. The ten Titans bared their blades and weaved into line either side of him. At the same instant, more Titans came from the Training Rooms. These were not armoured, but they carried sharpened iron nonetheless and they fanned out along the wings of the crowd. The Horde outnumbered their new masters ten to one, but they were crammed together and their tunics provided no protection from the short stabbing skills the Titans were moments from employing. Resistance would be a bloodbath and all knew it.

Ingvar felt a restraining hand on his shoulder and he spun to look down at the slight figure of Calder.

'This is not the time, Hammer. But I promise you, there will be another. Desist and step back.'

Ingvar glared at her with violence throbbing through his veins, but he recognised her authority and saw the steel in her eyes. With difficulty, he contained his temper and leaned close to her. 'Another time, Housecarl. We will stand together another time.'

'You have my word.'

Menes had grabbed one of the foremost warriors clambering onto the dais and was holding his sword to the man's throat. 'Back, you dogs! Another movement and I will order the killing to begin.'

He stared at them with unalloyed hatred, tinged with fear, but resisted the temptation to slice the man's jugular. One wrong move like that and it could have sparked the whole place into uproar again. He shoved the man off the dais.

'Get them in order,' he yelled to the line of armoured

Companions next to him and they dropped from the dais and marshalled the Vikings back into the centre of the Hall.

Gradually the Horde cooled and the moment of danger passed. Menes wiped his sword arm across his mouth and glared viciously down at them. 'Do that again,' he said, pointing his blade at Ingvar, 'and it won't be just your hair I cut off.'

He sheathed his weapon and took a moment to master himself, then pointed to the unarmoured Titans who had emerged from the Training Rooms during the flashpoint. 'These men and women are going to be the centre of your world for the next few weeks. Some come from our battlelines, many from our Schola, where each year they teach and shape our new intakes. They will run your lives. Their word is command. You will listen to everything they say and you will obey. They have only one task: to turn each of you heathens into a soldier worthy to stand beneath the Lion of Macedon banner.

'So you will train every hour given you. You will listen to them, watch them, learn from them. You are, of course, not trusted with real iron, but you will handle Titan sparring weapons of wood – the shortsword, the hoplite's dory spear, the javelin and maybe even the sarissa. You will each carry a replica hoplon shield until your arm screams and it has become one with your body. You will forget your Viking shieldwalls and your untamed heathen antics on the battlefield. Instead, you will learn the art of the Titan battleline. How to absorb the impact of your foe on your hoplon, then the coordinated push, the step forward and the stab. Absorb, press, thrust, retract – the way of the hoplite; the skills which carried Alexander's armies across the globe.

'Fail to listen, fail to learn, fail to make the grade – and you will be punished with the utmost severity. Remember, you cannot leave the Pantheon just because your poor King died and your pathetic Horde was destroyed. You are Titans now. You are the most junior of our intakes and you will train until you fall. Or face the consequences.'

He paused to eye them. The fire had gone from the assembly and most of the Vikings looked at the ground or stared off into the distance; hearing his words, but refusing to meet his glare. Calder caught Bjarke's glance and something passed between them. A silent avowal between Valhalla officers that this wasn't over yet.

'You will be divided into groups of thirty,' continued Menes, oblivious. 'Then allocated numbers for your unit. Your training masters will tell you when each unit is required here in Alexandria.

'For those of you who succeed, it has been decided by Alexander and his Council of Commanders that you will constitute a new regiment of basic hoplite heavy infantry. You will be known as Hellenes, soldiers of the Hellenic regiment – named after the Hellenic League in ancient times, which was a confederation of Greek states created by Alexander's father and used as a tool to unify all Greek forces under the Macedon banner. The name is apt, I think, as we shape you into a new body of arms beneath the Titan flags.

'Obey your training officers. Master your new weapons. Aspire to be Titan hoplites and one day – perhaps sooner than we all realise – you may be permitted to stand in our lines on the Field of Battle and face whichever new foe our lords decree.'

Oliver's internment in Fife inspired a murderous tension in the household.

Kustaa played the role of host, offering him food and drink as though he were a valued guest, but Oliver ignored everything placed in front of him. Aurora watched him like a hawk and refused to call him anything except *the God Killer*. In her opinion, they should be beating him for information, not feeding him. As for the other man, he held his tongue, though his poisonous glances at Aurora suggested he would happily choke her first.

Eventually, they bundled him upstairs and locked him in a bedroom so they could mutter and argue below. They must have decided they could do nothing more with him until morning because Oliver heard someone come upstairs and test the lock, and after that a long silence descended. He heaved hopefully at the window, but it refused to budge, so he slumped on the bed. The night lengthened and he must have slept.

The next day, Kustaa escorted him downstairs and offered him breakfast. Oliver desperately wanted to ignore the food, but the man with the bruises was not present, Kustaa was gentler in his approach and the toast smelt too divine. So he filled himself and accepted hot tea, while Aurora hovered by the kitchen door and examined him with frightened eyes.

When he was done, Kustaa quizzed him about his motives for murdering Odin, but Oliver responded only with non-committal grunts and the Thane could press him no further. Aurora slammed Tyler's laptop in front of him and demanded to know what he had been looking for and what he had discovered. He made a pretence of clicking through a few screens and pointing out some bits and bobs, but they both knew he was giving them nothing of value. Soon, the other man appeared and lurked somewhere in Oliver's periphery. His silence was as malevolent as his face and his scrutiny pressed around Oliver like the coils of a constrictor.

Kustaa took him back upstairs and locked him in the bedroom again while debate sparked in the room below. It seemed to Oliver that Aurora and Kustaa were fearful of a situation they had conspired to create, but they were even more terrified about how to resolve it.

At the end of the first day, all three of them came for him and forced him through the kitchen and then down a flight of steps to an underground utility. Alongside boot racks, drying machines and a sink, they had arranged a fold-out bed, a TV, a table and chairs, a small sofa and a pile of magazines. Oliver recognised a prison when he saw one. With a shrieking heart, he struggled in their grip and kicked and spat. Kustaa tumbled in the melee and Oliver thought he might break free, but then the open palm of the scarred man smashed into the side of his skull so hard that he was thrown back against the table and his legs folded under him.

As his mind blackened, the last thing he heard was a growled obscenity.

XVII

The Gods of the Pantheon flew into Rome one by one in their private jets.

Mikhail Malutin landed first. No longer the mighty Russian bear who, a quarter of a century before, had spent Hallowe'en at Julian Ballantyne's Hampshire residence and watched his first weaponised blood duel in his host's basement auditorium. Now he was a man struggling with diabetes and rampant cholesterol levels, his jowls slack, his moustache unkempt and his muscles weak from a sedentary lifestyle, but he still ate and drank like a prince. His bellow could still quell armies. And he revelled more than ever in the notoriety of his alter ego: feared Ördög, Caelestis of the Pantheon's bad-boy Palatinate.

He had been at the Hun field camp in Hortobágy, observing the sweeping spectacle of his black-bannered cavalry as it prepared to meet the Sultanate for their annual Battle, when news of Sveinn's death and Odin's murder came through. He had demanded an emergency meeting with Attila and his officers to hear their response, and when the proposal arrived from Jupiter to gather the Caelestia in Rome, he had choppered back to Prague and boarded his plane.

Jacob Steinberg came next. An Israeli by birth, an American by citizenship, he had not originally wanted the Kheshig Palatinate when Julian visited his Manhattan offices twenty-three years ago and made the suggestion. But the more Steinberg looked into it, the more he had warmed to the idea. Genghis Khan was indisputably the world's greatest ever conqueror, with an empire that dwarfed those of Rome and Macedon and Persia. The ancient shamanist religion of the Mongols also worked its magic on Steinberg. There was something so wild and passionate about the gods of the grasslands and the trees and the waters. And then there was Tengri, Lord of the Heavenly Blue Skies, a name so synonymous with the endless horizons of the Mongolian plains that when Steinberg finally embraced his new Palatinate and touched down near the Khan Khenti, it swept him away.

Perhaps it was because it was all so utterly different from his usual self. Plump, pasty, myopic and balding since his twenties, Steinberg had always looked exactly like what he was: a financial whizz, a mathematical geek, who spent his days stuffed behind computer screens, running his figures, weighing his odds. Even the limitless wealth he mined, so appreciated by his wife, had always been an irrelevant by-product to him. For Steinberg it had always been about the maths. So Julian's Pantheon had offered him something intrinsically appealing: the opportunity to run an army's budgets and to play with finance at the highest levels with the Curiate's gambles, but also the secret delight of being the Lord of the Heavenly Blue Skies.

Next to land on Rome's puddled tarmac was Zhang Huateng, the last of the original five who had gathered in

Julian's Hampshire basement all those years ago. He was sixty-seven now, yet he had barely aged. Slim, spruce and chic, everything about him – his posture, his clothing and his speech – was elegant. Hailing from a humble background in rural Jiangsu and now based mostly in Shanghai, his stellar career had made him something of a darling with the Chinese government, who viewed him as a perfect example of Sino economic growth and soft power. While he had never told anyone of his secret Pantheon life, there were many in his homeland who suspected – or wanted to believe – that he was Xian, the ancient god of birth, and Lord of the Warring States Palatinate.

Like most of the Caelestes, Huateng spent half his life in the air and he arrived in Rome now sipping a soda, alert, briefed and ready to do business.

The fourth arrival was the first of the pair of Caelestes who had not been present at the Hampshire gathering in 1997. Hakan Reis had been born into wealth in the suburbs of Ankara, the second son of a Turkish industry magnate. He had studied finance at Yale and the Judge Institute in Cambridge, then met the other Eagles in Chicago. A playboy in his youth, he had quickly become a lively regular at Julian and Marcella's parties, and he had embraced the concept of the Pantheon on the very day Julian had first broached it with him. He was intensely proud of his Turkish ancestry and the martial might of Turkey's history and he had seized upon the idea of a Sultanate Palatinate, sweeping Julian up with his fervent enthusiasm. He had wanted to be Saladin, but Julian had reminded him that Saladin was a warrior, not a god, and so they had agreed on Kyzaghan, who, long before the coming of Islam, had been the Turkish deity of war.

Now, over two decades later, Reis was an obese, heavy-lidded, wheezing figure, whose playboy lifestyle had broken his body and his three marriages. But his passion for the Sultanate burned as hot as ever, though now it invariably manifested itself as jealousy and suspicion of his fellow Caelestes, and an abiding hatred of Malutin, the god of the Huns and his great rival in Tier Two.

Finally, last to land, as the rainclouds over Rome gave way to late afternoon sun, came Zeus. Nikolas Petrou had been born in Nicosia and married his childhood sweetheart. He had befriended Raymond J Pearlman amongst the cut-and-thrust of the financial scene in Eighties Manhattan and they had stayed close as their fortunes had soared. Petrou's quiet intelligence was much admired amongst the key figures of the world's trading centres, though few would have guessed this mild-mannered, silver haired, happily married family man was also one of the Pantheon's great gods. It had taken some time for him to warm to the idea when Pearlman had first introduced him to Ballantyne and it had required days of consideration and discussion with his wife before Petrou was seduced by the wonders of reimagining the magnificence of Alexander the Great.

He had remained seduced ever since. It was an integral part of his Greek-Cypriot ancestry and he loved his role as Zeus. Normally his calm acumen was admired by his fellow Caelestes, yet this god was not beyond making surprise moves which could throw the Pantheon into a tailspin. In Year Five, he had suddenly upped his whole Palatinate and moved it from Nicosia to Edinburgh. The other Caelestes had choked on their fine wines and protested, but Odin had welcomed the arrival of the Titan Palatinate in his city and the furore had died.

Now, once again, Zeus was at the heart of turmoil. He had played a secret hand that had resulted in a dead King, a murdered Caelestis, a fallen Palatinate, an unbalanced Pantheon structure, and a whole heap of angry gods.

Skarde sat in a leather reading chair, a bottle of whisky close to hand, waiting for Kustaa to speak. The Thane had placed himself on the sofa opposite and from his frenetic fussing and fidgeting over the last hour, he was obviously agitating himself into making a proposal to the Wolf.

Aurora had stepped outside for yet another smoke and Skarde toyed again with the idea of following her out, breaking her neck and throwing her over the cliff. The woman was a liability and extraneous to needs, but he kept reminding himself that Kustaa alone could not be trusted with the boy's captivity. The lad was too damn sharp. He would find a way to befuddle the Thane and make a break for freedom. Aurora might be a complete pain in the arse, but she would happily shoot the boy dead if he so much as made a lunge for the front door. So, at least for the time being, Skarde would let her live.

Kustaa finally found his voice. 'I have an idea.'

Skarde settled his attention on him, but refused to speak.

'On my phone,' the Thane continued, 'I have the numbers for my fellow Quartermasters in the other Palatinates.

We communicate from time to time about administrative issues.'

'You mean Simmius and the like?'

'Simmius, yes. Belgutei from Genghis' jaguns. Valerius of the Legion. All of them.'

Skarde stirred himself and reached behind the sofa to grab the coat he had worn when he first arrived. From a pocket, he retrieved Kustaa's confiscated phone. 'What's your passcode?'

Kustaa told him and Skarde tapped it in.

'These Quartermasters, show them to me.'

Kustaa came over and indicated the six names and their respective Palatinates as Skarde scrolled through the contact list. When they were done, the Viking harrumphed and switched the phone off.

'What of it?'

'Like me, each Quartermaster not only serves his respective King, but also supports the offices of the Palatinate Caelestis. They each have the ear of a god.'

Skarde nodded thoughtfully, but held his tongue, so Kustaa waded in further.

'We know the identity of the King Killer and now we also have the God Killer. Can you imagine the precedent set if the Caelestia let the murder of one of their number go unpunished? They will reward us generously for what we can give them.'

'So we contact one of these Quartermasters?'

'I suggest Valerius of the Legion. We go right to the top. And we demand a call with Jupiter herself.'

Skarde turned the phone over and over in his hand, his brows clenched in a deep frown.

'Not a call,' he said at length. 'This has to be done in person.'

'We can hardly drag Oliver to Rome,' Kustaa protested.

'I didn't suggest that.'

Aurora could be heard coming back through the front door.

Kustaa kept his eyes on the Wolf. 'If you're proposing what I think you're proposing...' he said quietly. 'Don't you dare dream of double-crossing me.'

Skarde laughed derisively. 'Are you threatening me?'

'I mean it,' said Kustaa, pointing a finger at him. 'I've come too far for some bastard like you to cheat me.'

'Have a care, Thane.'

'I've given you a roof, provided you with the King Killer's identity and brought you Oliver, so you owe me.'

Aurora came into the room and instantly felt the tension. 'What's going on?'

'I mean it,' said Kustaa coldly without taking his eyes from the Wolf.

Skarde returned his stare, then relented with a snide guffaw and waved a hand at Aurora. 'Nothing for you to worry yourself about.'

The next morning, Skarde did not appear and Kustaa became increasingly jittery.

'Have you seen that bastard this morning?' he demanded of Aurora, who shook her head.

He went outside to throw away the whisky bottle that Skarde had been cradling and found the driveway empty. He hurried back inside and searched for the keys to his Mercedes AMG. Nothing. He levered himself behind the sofa and found Skarde's filthy coat, but the pockets were empty. No knife. No phone. Then he rummaged through his desk and swore. No laptop.

'Call my phone,' he said, striding back into the kitchen where Aurora was preparing a meagre breakfast for their prisoner.

Together they listened to the rings until it clicked into the answering service.

Kustaa swore again and climbed the stairs to listen at Skarde's bedroom. Not a sound. He knocked impatiently. No answer. Another knock, louder, and then he swung open the door. The bed linen was thrown back and the curtains drawn.

Skarde was gone.

XVIII

It was customary for meetings of the Caelestia to be meticulously slotted into crammed schedules and for the gods to take it in turns to select a venue. There was much sharp rivalry about who could find the best location and who could provide the most extravagant entertainment. One year, Malutin bought an entire island near the Seychelles solely for the purpose of hosting the meeting. He oversaw construction of luxury chalets on pontoons which reached out from the golden sands onto crystal clear waters. Another year, not to be outdone, Hakan Reis took them all into the sands of Arabia, to a city of Bedouin tents, complete with a private jacuzzi for each of them and steam rooms where the skies never rained. When it was Steinberg's turn, he invited them to a resort high in the Andes and flew in most of Rio's adult entertainment industry

But this time, it was Rome. It was always Rome when there was trouble. This time diaries must fit around the Pantheon. This time there would be no entertainments. It was business, plain and simple.

After their rushed flights, they had each spent the night in the best apartments of the Legion's Domus Aurea complex. Some would be more jetlagged than others, but they were all well accustomed to an international lifestyle and they each made their way across the marble courtyards and around the Palace's fountains in good time for Jupiter's scheduled start.

They gathered in the awesome basilica at the centre of the complex, with its colonnaded exterior, cross-vaulted ceiling and giant marble supports. Caesar had raised it from the ruins of the site when he first planned the construction of his new Palace, and it had been designed with such an eye for detail that it looked as if it had been magically transported from the glorious age of the Roman empire.

The Caelestia greeted each other over coffee, making small talk in smart-casual attire like delegates attending a finance conference. At a given signal, however, the waiting staff retired, phones were switched off, doors were closed and guarded, and real names abandoned. This was Pantheon time now and each of the five men remaining in the vast room ruled a Palatinate, so they would use only their celestial titles.

When they were seated around a large circular table at the centre of the basilica, Jupiter entered. They heard her heels on the marble floor and turned to watch her walk to her place in front of a giant frieze of the Roman gods. She wore a black trouser suit, set off with diamonds hanging from her ears and a simple brooch depicting the Imperial Eagle. She did not smile. Her jaw was set firm and her eyes betrayed no emotion.

She knew that, to them, she was an outsider. When Ballantyne – founder and architect of the Pantheon – had dramatically forfeited his position as Lord High Jupiter and declared he would instead lead his Legion in the field as

Caesar, they had been shocked, but they had also admired his decision to be what he wanted. It was his damn Game after all. Let him stand with his Eagles and feel the throb and thunder of real battle.

But they had never expected Marcella to be his replacement. They had known her for many years as Julian's wife. A formidable operator in her own right, a party organiser of extraordinary flair and a sufferer of no fools. But Lord High Jupiter, most senior of the Pantheon gods? That was a step they had found hard to countenance.

In truth, she had done a tremendous job. The Pantheon was stronger than ever, the Legion supreme, he rivalry of the Palatinates as intense as it had ever been and the professionalism of the support units unsurpassed. Technology was ensuring the Vigiles' camera feeds were more and more extensive and the increasing use of drones meant the Battles could be watched in super hi-res around the world. Law enforcement and media were bought and muffled. The fan bases were more vociferous than ever. And, most important of all, money was rolling in as rich punters clamoured to join the Curiate.

Jupiter had justified her position, but on a personal level, she had kept herself removed from the other Caelestes. They disliked how she had sidelined her husband and ensured his voice was rarely heard amongst his old Caelestia brethren. They knew her increasingly fractious marriage influenced her politics in the Pantheon. And they unanimously resented how she had groomed and installed her son into one of the most senior roles in the Legion. They all had children – some more legitimate than others – but none of them had ever brought them into the Pantheon. It was simply not the way. Some around the table in the Domus Aurea suspected Jupiter impatiently awaited the day when Caesar dwindled and Augustus could take his place.

One other individual entered the basilica and sat quietly at a table separate from the others. Atilius, Praetor of the Pantheon, would record proceedings and speak if he was directed.

'Welcome,' said Jupiter, in a far from welcoming tone. 'Thank you for getting here at such short notice, but I think we all agree a meeting in person was necessary. A Palatinate has fallen and one of our own has been murdered.'

It was lost on no one that a seventh seat had been placed around the table and left empty – a simple, emphatic gesture that Odin was gone.

'Has the killer been found?' Kyzaghan demanded without preamble.

'His arrest is inevitable; it is only a matter of time.'

'How much time do you need? It's Edinburgh, barely a village by the standards of most cities.'

'I can assure you we have our security teams at full stretch to apprehend the culprit and it will not be long.'

'What do you have to add?' said Ördög, pointing a finger at Zeus. 'It's your damn city too.'

Zeus opened his palms in supplication. 'I'm hardly best placed to know the circumstances of Odin's death when it took place in his Valhalla offices.'

'But it's your antics on the Battle Field that led to his death, of that we must be certain. You played fast and loose with the Rules.'

There was a murmur of agreement.

Zeus objected. 'I earned my Blood Funds in the Nineteenth

and I spent them fairly and within our agreed guidelines at the start of the Twentieth. I simply chose not to reveal *how* I spent them. There is nothing in the Rules to suggest I have acted inappropriately.'

Tengri spoke up, his accountant's mind focused on the details. 'You introduced a new force towards the end of the Battle Hour and from a direction that was not your agreed end of the Field. That's like a twelfth man in a soccer match running onto the pitch from the sidelines and scoring a goal because the opposition's defence did not see him.'

'Again, there is nothing in the Rules that explicitly states an entire Palatinate must be openly at one end of the Field at the start of Battle Hour.'

Tengri harrumphed and Kyzaghan swore quietly beneath his wheezing.

Xian had remained silent, but now he angled his slight figure towards the giant Ördög on his left. 'I question your assertion that Odin died because of our colleague's creative interpretation of the Rules.'

Ördög raised his arms and growled in exasperation. 'What are you saying, man? Do you think it's a coincidence that Odin was knifed minutes after his King was killed on the Field?'

'I'm saying, my friend, that there is no logical reason for his murder to be directly linked to the death of King Sveinn. In the moment of his King's demise, Odin lost his Palatinate, his status in the Pantheon and his reputation. There was no need to kill him. So we cannot discount that the timing was indeed coincidence.'

Ördög heaved a sigh, but bottled a response.

Kyzaghan shifted his bulk to stare first at Atilius in one

corner and then at Jupiter. 'Find who did this,' he rasped, his voice dripping with venom. He pointed a stubby finger at Jupiter. 'Beat a confession out of him or her and then string them up.'

'I can assure you,' Jupiter responded, 'the culprit will feel the full force of Pantheon reprisals.'

'Don't bandy words at me. Death! That is the only reprisal for the murder of a Caelestis. We will accept nothing less.'

'Indeed,' said Jupiter solemnly.

'And make sure you film it, Praetor. I want to *see* this execution.'

'My lord,' Atilius inclined his head.

There was a pregnant silence, then Jupiter sat forward and marshalled their attention. 'And now to matters more strategic.'

'Indeed,' muttered Xian.

'We have a Palatinate without a foe. A hole in the third tier of our pyramidal structure.'

Ördög glared at Zeus. 'Don't you dare even *think* you can prepare a Challenge to Tier Two. Your little games with the Rules give you no right.'

'I most certainly do have the right,' exclaimed Zeus, affronted.

'This is Tier Three business,' Kyzaghan agreed with Ördög, their rivalry briefly put to one side. 'Let them sort it out and don't bother the more powerful Palatinates.'

Zeus frowned. 'With Valhalla incorporated into my lines, along with the extra Blood Funds I have earned this Year, I will soon be able to field four hundred troops.'

'And seven cavalry.' Ördög smiled and Kyzaghan guffawed.

'Eleven, actually.'

The basilica echoed to the bellowed laughter of the Tier Two Caelestes.

'This is unhelpful,' Jupiter interrupted sharply. 'I have not summoned you here to make light of the situation.'

'No one has *summoned* anyone,' Tengri answered, with warning in his tone.

There was a tense pause.

'I have a Battle to prepare for,' Kyzaghan wheezed, 'against this man Ördög here. We fight for the right to face your Legion in a few weeks, Jupiter, so I don't care what the others decide to do in Tier Three.'

'Let them fight it out,' Ördög growled. 'Loser gets bumped from the Pantheon.'

This time it was Tengri's turn to be affronted and for a moment the basilica's calm was broken with shouts. As the heat of the words died, Xian spoke up.

'I must remind everyone that the Rules are specific about the situation we find ourselves in. A King has been killed by a foe with a sword in their hand. That results in the fall of the losing Palatinate and its incorporation into the winning Palatinate. The Rules then state that this enlarged Palatinate may Challenge the Palatinates in the Tier above. There is no ambiguity about this.'

'But it's preposterous,' Kyzaghan retorted. 'Zeus and his Titans are no match for us.'

'But it's the Rules,' Xian said with quiet steel.

Ördög swore and threw out a hand at Zeus. 'All right, make your Challenge, Zeus. It will be a bloodbath.'

'But which of you does he Challenge?' Tengri asked and this stalled the debate.

'Ördög's Palatinate is the smaller,' said Kyzaghan. 'It must be his Huns who face Zeus.'

'Like hell!' Ördög rose from his seat and the full hateful intensity of their rivalry came storming back. 'I own six hundred of the finest mounted troops in the Pantheon, each at a cost of ten Blood Credits. That dwarfs your budget.'

'Yet you have failed to rack up a single convincing victory in eleven Seasons!'

'I have swarmed over your Janissaries in every Battle we have waged.'

'Your Black Cloaks are dirty, ill-disciplined bandits who have no right to call themselves an army!'

Ördög thumped the table. Kyzaghan struggled to his feet and squared up to him, while Xian sat stone-faced between them.

'Gentlemen,' said Jupiter and her rigid tone cut through the noise. 'I have a proposal.'

Eyes turned to her.

'Well, spill it,' said Ördög angrily.

'Sit down,' she replied, and with such authority that after a few moments, the men complied.

'I assume this is a proposal that Caesar has also considered?' asked Tengri archly.

Jupiter worked her jaw. 'He has been briefly consulted.'

'We are all ears,' said Xian.

'A three-way Battle,' Jupiter announced briskly. 'The Sultanate, the Huns and the Titans.'

The hall was silent. The Caelestes glanced at each other.

'A three-way Battle,' Kyzaghan parroted. 'In just one hour?'

'No time limit,' Jupiter said sharply, as though it were a mere morsel she cast into the conversation.

Again, there was a long pause as each man grappled with this.

'No limit?' Ördög questioned quietly, suspicious that there was some trick afoot.

'You fight until one King is killed with a sword. The end of another Palatinate. Then we reshape the five remaining Palatinates into a simpler structure. We do away with the pyramid. Going forward it can be two in the bottom tier, two in the middle tier, and the Legion at the top. Problem solved.'

It was Zeus' turn to be perplexed. 'But... but... three of us on one Field?'

'What's the matter?' laughed Kyzaghan coldly. 'Worried we'll destroy you?'

'If I were you,' interceded Xian softly, 'I'd be more worried about who forms an alliance with whom. Friends come and go on a battlefield.'

This stoppered Kyzaghan's goading and he and Ördög glanced at each other with renewed suspicion.

Xian focused on Jupiter. 'The destruction of another Palatinate. Are you sure this is wise? We would be reduced from seven to five in just one Season. Could the Pantheon come through it intact?'

'Of course it could,' Jupiter replied dismissively. 'Nothing is set in stone. We will adapt.'

'And what of the Curiate? Could they bear the loss of another Palatinate?'

'They will adore the drama of it all.' Jupiter signalled to the Praetor. 'Atilius, speak.'

The Praetor rose from his place at the separate table. 'My lords, wagers from the Curiate are off the Richter scale since the fall of Sveinn. Others clamour to join. Interest has never been at such levels. Our friends and supporters are mesmerised by what may happen next and the news of a three-way fight with the certain death of a second King will send them into raptures. Fortunes are there to be made. We will be awash with blood wagers.'

The Caelestia digested this. Tengri scribbled some notes on a pad. Xian ran fingers over his chin. Ördög and Kyzaghan still glared at each other, weighing up the risks and opportunities.

And Zeus sat dumbstruck, his heart thumping.

'If one King falls,' Tengri said eventually, looking up from his pad. 'How will the defeated Palatinate be divided between the others?'

Jupiter had already prepped the answer to this question with Caesar. 'If the two victorious Palatinates share an equal part in the victory, the troops and funds of the fallen foe will be divided up between them. If one Palatinate plays a much more significant role in the downfall of the losing force, that Palatinate will receive all the troops and funds.'

There was logic in this and the Caelestes accepted it without comment.

'And what of us here today?' Ördög asked carefully.

'What of you?'

'One of us will lose their Palatinate and their place around this table.'

'Of course. One of you will depart the Pantheon. You will lose your troops, your Blood Funds and your rights. But, if you leave with dignity and silence, you will not end on the point of a knife as Odin did.'

The gods bridled at her words, but they held their tongues

and so she gave them time to consider. The hush was broken only by Kyzaghan's wheezing. Eyes shifted around the table. Minds calculated risk; imagined scenarios. Some already thought of alliances and double-dealing. Promises that could be made, then broken. Opportunity. Glory. Treachery.

'So where will this Battle be?' Kyzaghan rumbled.

'We already have a location,' answered Ördög with contempt. 'Your Sultanate is due to meet my Palatinate on the Hungarian steppe, so I say we stick to that plan and invite Zeus to the party.'

'That gives you home advantage.'

'As you had it last year.'

'But this time the stakes are much higher.'

'Gentlemen,' Xian interrupted, holding his palms up for calm. 'I suggest you continue this debate later, but if logistics are already well underway for a confrontation in Hungary, then this should remain the preferred plan. Atilius, do you have anything to add?'

'My agreement, lord. I have transport, accommodation, security and camera units already preparing in situ, so keeping to this location would be the least complex scenario.'

The others accepted this proposal in silence, although Ördög and Kyzaghan continued to exchange glares. Before anyone could frame further questions, Jupiter spoke. 'So I think we have a firm proposal before us and I suggest we vote.' She turned to her left. 'Tengri.'

Tengri pushed his glasses up his nose, consulted his pad, then rocked his head. 'I am not convinced that the death of another King is an attractive objective, but I agree the wagers of the Curiate alone will more than make up for this. So you have my support. I say aye.'

'Kyzaghan.'

The Lord of the Sultanate looked blackly around the table. 'Aye, dammit. I will still be standing at the end of it and we won't need the extended time. We will roll over Alexander and his Titans in less than an hour.'

'Xian.'

The Warring States Caelestis looked small between his two neighbouring colleagues, but his word was always held in high regard. 'There are risks. Nothing goes to plan on a battlefield and we cannot predict the ramifications of such a fight. It may not be as clean-cut as you suggest, my lord Jupiter, nor as rapid as Lord Kyzaghan thinks. Events will bite us in some way, mark my words, and we may come to regret the conclusions of this meeting.' He held their attention. 'But… this is not my fight. My Palatinate will wait in Tier Three beside the Kheshig and observe the outcome. So, aye. May the gods not toy with us.'

Jupiter turned her eyes to Ördög. 'And you?'

Ördög glowered around the table. 'My Huns have never shrunk from a challenge. *I* have never shrunk from a challenge. My Black Cloaks will destroy whoever dares take to the Field against them. They will bathe in the blood of their foe.'

'So you agree?'

'Of course I agree. Aye.'

Finally, she looked at Zeus. 'It is the actions of your Titan troops that have brought us to this table today. You have defeated Valhalla. Are you now prepared to make your

Challenge for Tier Two and face the blades of the Sultanate and the Huns on one Field?'

Zeus' calm, handsome features betrayed no emotion, but his insides roiled. He had never expected a dramatic proposal such as this and he wished he had time to consult Hera. But Jupiter was correct; the entire situation was down to his own scheming, the creation of his little Companion Cavalry and the man called Hephaestion who had plunged a sword into Sveinn and become the Pantheon's exalted King Killer.

He could not step back from the brink now.

'Aye,' he said quietly.

Jupiter smiled grimly. 'Then we have our decision. At the first feasible opportunity, the Hun, Sultanate and Titan Palatinates will meet on the Hortobágy Plain in Hungary and none will withdraw until one King has fallen to a sword blade. Atilius, consult your teams and furnish us with the earliest date by which you can have preparations ready. We will then feed out details through our usual channels, giving our many valued supporters time to assess odds and place bets. Thank you for your time, gentlemen. If there is no further business, I will close the meeting.'

It was done. The Caelestia had spoken.

XIX

Tyler's heart sang as Stanek drove him through the Ochil Hills, down the deep slash of Gleneagles and into the gentle countryside of Perth and Kinross.

The little cottage in the Lomonds had served its purpose. It had provided peace so he could think and refuge from the storm blowing through the Pantheon, but now his time there was over and beside him on the seat sat a kitbag into which he had packed his belongings. At last he was returning to his Cavalry and a smile twitched at the corners of his lips. It had been only two weeks since the Battle, but it felt like an eternity and now he had friendships to rekindle, horses to love and recruits to train.

Dio was waiting in the yard when the BMW came up the track, and the moment it halted he strode forward and threw open the rear door.

'My Captain,' he grinned, standing smartly to attention in his mucking-out overalls. Then the two men embraced and he whispered into Tyler's ear, 'It's damn good to have you back, Heph.'

'Damn good to be back. I've been kicking my heels.'

They stepped apart and Dio grabbed Heph's kitbag,

as though about to escort an important guest to his accommodation.

'I've only been getting snippets of news out here,' he said, 'but I think we might have stirred up a hornet's nest.'

'You could say that.'

'So, Cleitus is King. We got messages on our phones announcing his accession, all proper-like, with every last one of his damn titles.'

'I hope one of them was "twat".'

'You and him not hitting it off?'

They had been approaching the door to the farmhouse, but Heph pulled away and went to perch on the gate into the fields, where he lit a cigarette and squinted at the hills.

'He's destroying the Horde – and doing it with malicious glee. Valhalla's been renamed Alexandria and every Viking image has been torn down. I hear rumours he's had all the men's beards and hair shorn and he's turning every Viking into a low-rank hoplite and forcing them into a new auxiliary infantry regiment called the Hellenes.'

A shadow passed across Dio's face and he dumped the bag and leaned on the gate next to his Captain. 'That is a grave slur on the memory of Valhalla and everyone who ever fought beneath the banner of Odin.'

'It's not just a slur, it's thick-headed and brainless.'

Dio examined his friend and chose his words with care. 'Isn't it exactly what we expected to happen once we killed Sveinn? Valhalla must become Titan, just as we had to bend a knee and become Titans after our surrender. We were shaved of our beards and told we must learn new customs, grip new blades and fight with new skills.'

'Of course Valhalla must become Titan, but we could

have been so much more ingenious. Cleitus could have sworn them to the Lion banner, then granted them the right to fight as Vikings. We would have led a hundred and fifty experienced blades into battle, with their units, their hierarchy and their pride intact. Instead, we've got a single bloated, unwieldy regiment of foot, with few honed battle tactics and zero morale.'

Heph was becoming riled and Dio decided to close the subject down. Instead, he shrugged and asked gently, 'So, would you rather say hi to the people first or the beasts?'

Heph smiled despite himself, hopped off the gate and stamped out his cigarette. 'The beasts.'

'Boreas!' he cried in delight when they entered the stables and his stallion came to the front of his stall and nickered in welcome. Heph climbed in beside him and ran his fingers lovingly through his mane and along his coat. 'He's in fine form.'

'Of course he is,' said Dio, perching on a haybale. 'You think I'd have it any other way?'

Heph placed his head against his steed's neck and felt the warmth and the gentle rumble of his breath. The stable was scented with hay and dung and animal musk, and its peace was broken only by the shifting of hooves and the occasional tossing of a mane. For long moments, he did not move and was content just to drink it in.

Then he lifted his face. 'You know, this is my happy place.'

'Mine too, fella. Everyone in this heartless world needs a happy place.'

Heph spent another twenty minutes greeting the rest of the horses and Dio's mighty stallion, Xanthos, gave him a soft headbutt. Then he came to the stalls at the end of the block and found them filled with five new beasts – two chestnuts and three greys munching on nets of hay.

Dio came to lean on the stalls next to him. 'Same fine stock. Arabian. All stallions again. Great leg strength and bone structure, and pretty good dispositions. Whoever finds these for us knows their stuff.'

'So we are to be eleven.'

'I know it sounds so few,' said Dio, contemplating the horses, 'but there's a hundred and ten Blood Credits in these stalls. Zeus is doing what he can for us.'

Heph broke his own gaze and turned to his friend. 'And what of the riders?'

Dio grinned. 'They're in the house, awaiting the arrival of their Captain.'

'Then let's meet them.'

They headed out of the stable and strode back across the damp grass.

'Things have changed,' Dio said as they walked. 'You remember how sceptical Zephyr and Spyro and Lenore were when they first arrived?'

'Too well. We were just some mad experiment back then that no one wanted to be part of.'

'It's different now. We're the heroes of Macedon. Every last Titan witnessed our arrival at Knoydart and cheered our charge across the valley, and now we've been inundated with volunteers to join.'

'Any of them good?'

'I discounted those with no riding experience, then had the rest brought here. Even some of those were pretty abysmal and I kicked them straight back to the city. But I've picked six for you. Like us last year, they've no experience of riding without saddle or stirrups, but this time there's one essential new ingredient.'

'Which is?'

'They're *keen*, Heph. They *want* to be under your command; to claim a place in your Companion Cavalry.'

Heph laughed. 'Well I hope I don't disappoint.'

The farmhouse smelt of coffee and toast when they entered and the kitchen was crammed with nine bodies breaking their fasts.

'Attention!' Spyro cried when he spotted Heph at the door and the bustle died.

Spyro stepped into the middle of the room and brought a fist smartly up to his heart. 'Welcome back, my lord.'

Heph examined the proud Titan, a former elite soldier in Agape's Sacred Band, and saw the sincerity in his eyes. He stepped forward and took Spyro in a hug. 'It's good to see you.'

For a moment, Spyro was shocked, then he relaxed and hugged Heph in return. He was grinning broadly when they parted and others came forward. Zephyr gripped Heph's hand and then there was Lenore, her eyes dancing, her lips an enigmatic crescent.

'We've missed you,' she said softly, just for him, and took him in a light embrace.

Heph wished the room would light up with Pallas' smile, but the lad's arm was still in a cast and he would lie in a Pantheon ward until next Season. So Heph looked instead at the six new faces circled around the table. Two men and four women, all wide-eyed and transfixed by his presence.

Spyro took the initiative. 'Introductions are in order.' He

beckoned them forward one at a time and Heph shook their hands.

He knew the men already. Thales and Philemon. They were both from Parmenion's peltasts and he had met them at the *Agonium Martiale*.

'You helped me on with my scale armour,' he said to Thales, remembering the streaks of silver along the sides of the man's hair.

'I think I did,' Thales replied. 'About the only time you wore the peltast rig.'

The women he might have seen in the Titan lines, but he could not place. Melitta and Phoibe came from Nicanor's Heavy Brigade, sarissa bearers, the former very tall, the latter thick-set and strong. Elinor and Roxana were Companions, blade-sharp troops once under the command of Menes.

'Alexander's Bactrian wife,' Heph said to Roxana and she frowned in puzzlement, but let the comment pass.

He studied each of them as they waited on his words. Tension creased their faces, but they looked fit and ready for the challenges to come.

'Thank you for volunteering,' he said. 'You come from fine units and I am grateful that you deem a place in my Cavalry worthy of your commitment. Dio tells me you are all strong riders and I believe you have already been introduced to our friends in the stables.'

He paused to consider. 'I can't promise it's going to be easy in this unit, nor can I tell you what awaits. Last year, we were Zeus' secret little unit, without much pressure of expectation, but with a carefully timetabled schedule to be ready in time for the Grand Battle. Now we are famed throughout the Pantheon and watched by every eye, but our schedule is shrouded in mystery. We may have months to prepare or we may have weeks. No one is privy to the plans of the Pantheon gods. Most challenging of all, we don't even know the identity of our foe. Will we face foot soldiers or cavalry? Shieldwalls or mounted charges? Your guess is as good as mine.

'So all we can do is focus on being the best we can. Work hard. Wake every morning with the will to learn. Listen to Diogenes. Follow the examples of Lenore, Spyro and Zephyr. Love your horses. Put their welfare and comfort first at all times. You will fall. You will hurt. Riding without saddle and stirrups, while mastering the skill to attack and defend, is a steep challenge.

'I can't say what we will achieve. I can't tell you what will be demanded of us. I can only promise that if you give me your sweat, your willpower and your hearts, I will champion you and we will have fun and we will be one family.'

They cheered at this and thumped their hands on the tabletop and Heph hoped they would release him from their gaze.

'I think that deserves a coffee, sir?' Spyro suggested.

Heph nodded gratefully. 'I think it does.'

They fed him toast too and while they were busy, Dio laughed in his ear. 'Where'd you learn to speak like that? Have you been practising in front of a mirror?'

When they were ready, Heph led them out into the morning sunshine and across to the stables, and watched as Dio slipped into training mode and walked between each of them with words of advice as they prepared their horses. For the time being, they would ride with saddles and full tack, but soon they must slip into the ancient ways of their Macedonian forebears.

Heph waited with Boreas beside the stable door, the merest smile of pride on his lips, as his little Cavalry mounted up and took to the field.

Valerius, Consul of the Legion, was being chauffeured home from his Palatinate when his private phone rang. He had spent six days at Caesar's field camp in the forests beyond Mount Navegna and he was considering how he would spend the weekend at his city home in the Scala quarter of Rome.

He was tired after the rigorous demands of the camp. Caesar had been in one of his more manic moods and, as usual, his instructions had fallen into the Consul's lap to action. Now Caesar had departed for Capri and the camp was settling into weekend training, so Valerius felt at liberty to steal forty-eight hours amongst the distractions of the metropolis. He would most likely partake of a quiet lunch at his favourite restaurant, then arrange one of his more flamboyant parties for that evening.

He consulted his phone irritably. Very few souls had access to this number, but the caller was one of his fellow Quartermasters, the new Thane of Valhalla. He had known Radspakr well since the early years and been shocked by his sudden disappearance. 'Retired' was the official parlance, but Valerius wasn't so green as to believe that. Radspakr had been removed permanently; almost certainly killed. Valerius kept his nose out of Valhalla business, but he was deeply curious to learn what the Thane had done to deserve his demise.

He racked his brain to think of the name of the new Thane. Kustaa, that was it. Some fellow from the back-offices, got a lucky break. Or maybe not so lucky, now that the whole Valhalla Palatinate had fallen during the man's first year in post.

And then Odin had been murdered. A Caelestis killed by an unseen hand. Something was very rotten at the heart of Valhalla and now this Kustaa – a fellow with whom Valerius might have exchanged a forgettable word during one of the Quartermaster meetings – was calling him.

'Yes?' he said, putting the phone to his ear.

'Is this Valerius, Quartermaster of the Legion?' came a strained voice.

'If you have this number, I assume you know whom you are calling. And am I speaking to Kustaa?'

There was a long, hesitant pause. 'No.'

Valerius straightened. 'Then you had better get off this line, very quickly.'

'Wait. I'm calling from Kustaa's phone. My name is Skarde. I am the Housecarl of Wolf Company in the Horde of Valhalla. I have very important information to impart.'

Valerius had not heard the name before, but his instincts stopped him from disconnecting. If this was indeed a housecarl from the former Valhalla Palatinate, then he would most certainly be a man in desperate plight. And desperate men invariably had loose tongues. 'Then tell me.'

There was another pause. 'My information is for Jupiter personally.'

Valerius barked a laugh down the phone. 'Ha! Is that so? Who do you think you are to propose a meeting with the

Lord High Jupiter? And why should you think I can help you? This call is over.'

'No, wait! Don't hang up. I swear she will *really* want to hear what I have to say.'

Valerius brooded. He needed to be cautious. Kustaa's phone could have been stolen by anyone – a scammer, a reporter, even someone from law enforcement. On the other hand, pretending to be the Housecarl of Wolf Company would be an audacious story if untrue. 'I need more than that.'

A muffled curse came down the phone. 'Okay. It's about the King Killer and the murder of Odin. I know who the King Killer is and I can give Jupiter the God Killer.'

Now the caller had Valerius' undivided attention, but still he was careful. 'You expect me to believe that?'

'I expect you to believe that Odin was killed in his office in Edinburgh by a single stab wound to the throat. Contact Atilius. I'm guessing you can get that verified.'

'And what do you desire in return?'

'I have my demands, which I will put to Jupiter in person.'

'You have demands, eh? I suspect Jupiter is unaccustomed to listening to demands.'

'Do we have a deal, for Christ's sake?' the man cursed.

'A deal?'

'Will you arrange an audience with Jupiter? She's your damn Caelestis.'

Valerius pondered this unexpected development, peering out at the suburbs of Rome. 'Where are you?'

'Scotland. Edinburgh.'

'I will organise a flight.'

'And no bloody funny business. Anyone tries anything and I'll destroy what I have.'

'My dear man, if I wished to employ any *funny business*, you'd be dead before I tuck into my dinner tonight. I've said there will be a flight and there will be. I will have the arrangements sent to your— To Kustaa's phone. Will we be having the pleasure of the Thane's company as well?'

'No. Just me.'

'Very well. Be on the flight. And when you land, we can decide if what you have is valuable enough to disturb Jupiter. *Buon viaggio*, Housecarl Skarde.'

XX

News of the Caelestia's decision spread like wildfire.

The Palatinates of Kyzaghan's Sultanate, Ördög's Huns and Zeus' Titans would come together on a Field of Battle on the Hortobágy steppe in Hungary on the twelfth of May, three weeks hence, to bring the Blood Season of the Twentieth Year to a dramatic close. It was shared on Pantheon messaging systems and proclaimed in the halls and camps of every Palatinate. Phones beeped across continents as the privileged and the wealthy were sent live links to the latest odds and invitations to Pantheon viewing channels.

Unofficial briefings also lit up the unofficial channels. Of the three Kings – Mehmed the Conqueror, Attila the Scourge of God and Alexander the Lion of Macedon – it was said that one must die that day. A Palatinate must fall. This was how the Pantheon would restructure after the actions of the King Killer.

Monetary speculation went into overdrive.

In Persepolis, Alexander had a private audience with Zeus. Those who witnessed the King emerge said he was white with shock. His anger fell on anyone who crossed his path as he stormed to his private chamber and locked himself away. If the rumours were true, if a sovereign must die, then Alexander knew well enough of the might of the Janissaries and the endless black cavalry lines of the Huns, and terror leaked from him. After the Battle in Knoydart, he had grabbed at the crown with lascivious glee, but perhaps he had also grabbed unwittingly at his own death warrant. A King for just a few weeks. The shortest reign in Pantheon history.

At his camp in Hortobágy, Attila gathered his commanders under the roof of his mighty log house and plotted tactics. He realised as clearly as his master, Ördög, that this was the opportunity to break the cycle of conflict with the Sultanate. Over the years, the two sides had come to know each other's strengths and weaknesses too well. They could guess manoeuvres before they occurred. They could respond to every enemy probe and every new formation. And, most of all, the Kings could read each other's minds like long-lost family. But this time, the presence of the Titans changed everything. There would be a new dynamic on the Field, new patterns and new unknowns. And where there were new unknowns, opportunities were never far behind.

So Attila – frugal, vulpine and dangerous – hunched around the great fire at the heart of his log house and listened, gimlet-eyed, to the thoughts of his commanders. There was Uptar, Horse Lord of the First Horn, which consisted of a hundred and fifty of Attila's most loyal warriors, who provided a swirling blanket of protection around their King. Then there was Ellac, Horse Lord of the Second Horn, once again a hundred and fifty strong – the fleet and fast archers, who could rain storms of iron onto an enemy and disappear in a heartbeat. Finally, there was Bleda, a commander so wild and intimidating that even

Attila wondered if he could control her. The light from the flames flickered over her gaunt face, glittered on her blood-red fingernails and illuminated the disconcerting sight of her front teeth where she had filed them to points. She led almost three-hundred Black Cloaks, the punch of his heavy cavalry, which could sweep across a Field and fall upon the foe like a wave.

Eight hundred miles south east, deep beneath the pavements of central Istanbul and feeding off the dark, dank tourist hotspot of Justinian's sixth-century colonnaded Basilica Cistern, other forgotten cisterns had been tunnelled and renovated over two decades to accommodate the quarters, armouries, bath houses and training facilities for Mehmed's Sultanate troops. Light and warm, these tunnels were the heart of Palatinate life, though ceremonial occasions demanded his troops occupy a wing of the opulent Topkapi Palace on its hill above Old Istanbul; and on the grasslands of central Anatolia across the Bosphorus, his seventy-strong Sipahi cavalry was stabled.

Mehmed was a soldiers' King. He had risen through the ranks over many years and preferred a blade in his hand to a crown on his head. Short in stature and slow to anger, he nonetheless wielded his ruby-encrusted *kilij* – a one-handed single-edged scimitar – with the reflexes of a man half his age. At night during the Pantheon Conflict Seasons, he habitually wore silver mail under plate armour, and stalked through the armouries, stroking his lavish moustache. In the wake of the momentous news about the Battle, he spent hours assessing the Yaya infantry brigades and his two hundred and seventy Household Janissaries, the fanatical heart of the Sultanate, while his Agha officers led individual skills sessions – one-to-one combat, formation manoeuvres and plans of attack.

In Edinburgh too, in similar armouries beneath the cobbles, the new Hellenic regiment of hoplite infantry was grudgingly put through its paces. Two hundred bronze breastplates had been forged, as well as knee-length greaves and basic, non-plumed helmets. They must learn to move and fight in this kit, and grow accustomed to the limited field of vision between their helm's cheek protectors. So they wore this armour as they practised in the Training Rooms of New Alexandria and the air hung heavy with the sweat and stink of them.

They fought in lines with wooden hoplons and shortswords, and their instructors shook their heads and exchanged disconsolate glances. These troops had honed their skills with Viking longswords and war axes. They were intimately acquainted with the reach and killing space of such weapons and knew the devastation of a swinging blade. But now they were told they must get in close and stab with short, fast thrusts. It was so alien. They would strike from too far and overreach. They would attempt a swing and be castigated from the sidelines. They would hunker into shieldwalls and get yelled at to maintain their hoplite formation.

But the greatest problem – the one no quantity of acerbic swearing by the instructors could alleviate – was that these Hellenes did not bring their hearts to the fight. They hated the symbols of Macedon that hung in their Halls. They derided their new King. What had he ever been to them except a distant figure hiding behind his lines at the opposing end of a battlefield? If he lost his life in the coming struggle, they would likely add their cheers to those of the other Palatinates.

Calder hated the circumstances as much as any of them, but she also noticed that more and more of them looked to her for guidance through these dark times. Sveinn was dead. So too Freyja and Asmund. Halvar was gone. And Bjarke, shorn of his beard and hair, was a ghost of himself. Between the sparring, he would glance at her with empty eyes that whispered silent words: *This is not our fight.*

Calder might wear the rig of a junior hoplite like everyone else, but they still believed in her as the Housecarl of Raven Company. Her former troops – Liv and Geir, Estrid and Sten – habitually sparred alongside her and followed her lead, but gradually, over the nights of repetitive training, the rest of the Horde began to gravitate towards her.

One evening, late into a session, a voice spoke into her ear, reedy and hesitant, 'What should we do?'

It was Ulf.

Memories flooded her of the man's arrogance during her first Armatura season, of him tracking her through the forests of the Sine Missione, of his face as he came to murder her atop Edinburgh Castle. Now he waited on her words. How the wheels of time toyed with them.

Her reputation had first grown when she had entered a lions' enclosure to seek an Asset. She might have failed to find it, but they had toasted her courage on the ale benches of the Western Hall. Then they had watched footage of her charging into the darkness of a tunnel at Waverley, a forlorn attempt to chase down a Titan Raiding party and the first Viking to stand over the body of the fallen Freyja. Finally, the Horde had witnessed her leading the last line of defence on the Field of Knoydart, the woman who fired an arrow onto the helm of the King Killer and who stood defiant against the onrush of his cavalry. They watched and they remembered.

Her response to Ulf – and her response to all of them each night, as she concentrated on her training with renewed vigour – was the same: *Keep practising. Learn to use these weapons.*

'We may not give a damn about a Titan King, but when the Janissaries and the Huns come for us, we must be ready. We do not fight for the Macedon flag. We fight for our honour and our lives.'

She was right and they all knew it. They followed her example and trained hard, and while they might listen to their instructors' hoarse shouts, it was to another leader that they looked. As the hours ticked by towards the great Battle, the Hellenes forged a fragile fighting spirit.

On the other side of the Forth, surrounded not by the salty tang of sweat, but by the cold earthy scents of Perthshire, Dio took the Companion Cavalry through their paces. The new recruits did not have the luxury of time and on the eleventh day, Dio pulled out lionskins and declared that they must ditch their saddles. The new cadre floundered and wobbled. They lost coordination and forgot their newly-learned principles of formation riding. Elinor fell hard and was out for two days with a bruised spine. Phoibe's horse went lame and could not be ridden for a further five.

In the worst moments, Heph would lose his composure and shout, 'For Christ's sake! Get it right! This is the Huns coming for us!'

And Dio would scowl at him, until his Captain raised a placatory hand and mouthed a silent apology.

One morning, as Zephyr led the recruits in a trot while carrying lances, Dio sat on the fence next to Heph and asked, 'In all honesty, what can eleven riders do against six hundred?'

'Live long enough to make a difference.'

'And how do you propose we do that?'

'Zeus once gave me some essential advice in a letter. They were words from Belgutei. Wait. And wait again. Hold to the single critical moment in the Battle. Do not be distracted by the many different struggles; focus only on the one that matters. When you find it, and you know the moment has come, hurl yourself at it with all the violence you possess.'

Dio raised an eyebrow. 'I'm not sure Bleda and her Black Cloaks are going to let us wait.'

'Then we must avoid her for as long as we can. When the moment arrives, we will know it.'

A couple of hours' drive south, in the quiet rural surroundings of the Borders, a young girl woke each morning in a house on the outskirts of Jedburgh and despaired that she was powerless to do anything except wait and hope. Eli had returned to find Meghan still in the garden, cold, soaked and distraught at the abduction of Oliver. She had yelled at him that they must go to the police, must find a way – *any* way – to rescue him.

It had taken Eli several days and all his professional skills to calm her. He had no knowledge of where Aurora lived or where she might have taken her hostage. Nor could he seek help at the Schola. On the very day Aurora had come for Oliver, the place had formally closed and he had been cast out.

One thing he knew for certain was that he could not submit to Meghan's pleas to go to the police. That was a hole way too deep to scurry down. So he brought her soup and cooked her meals and gave her space and peace and assurance.

'He'll be okay,' he would say when she was in the mood for listening. 'That woman won't hurt him. He's no good to anyone unless he's alive and kicking. He's a survivor and he'll come out of this in one piece.'

Eli had no job now and no inkling of his future. Technically, he didn't even have a place to live. The house was the Pantheon's and one day people would come to claim it. But, until then, he knew he had just one goal: to be there for this girl, whatever the coming weeks might bring; to help her overcome her turmoil and to set her on a path towards a brighter future.

And in a small village on the Fife coast, a stone's throw from Tyler's old cottage in the Lomonds, the man known as Kustaa – once Thane of Valhalla – stared out bay windows at the garden and the sea beyond.

He could see the blonde head of Aurora smoking on the lawn and he wished he could rid himself of her presence. She had been in his house for a week, pacing it like a caged animal, jumpy and brittle, and still ferociously determined to emerge from this mess with money and privilege and immunity.

Beneath the floorboards, in the utility area, they had made Oliver as comfortable as possible. He had light and heat, a bed, a chair and a television. He was permitted upstairs to wash and even to share meals with them, although these were such silent, hateful affairs that he rarely accepted the invitation.

It was three days since Skarde had disappeared with Kustaa's phone and laptop, and with them any access to the workings of the Pantheon. Kustaa could contact no one in his old Palatinate. He could get into no databases, no records of personnel, no Valhalla emails and no messaging systems. His old life was gone and the Pantheon was closed to him.

He distrusted Skarde with every fibre of his being. Nothing felt right about waiting in the house with their precious prisoner, while that man was at large. Instead of loitering in Fife like fools, they must take the initiative. If there was even a chance Skarde might betray them, he should do something to put the bastard on the backfoot.

An idea had come to him during the early hours while he lay in bed. It was a memory of a place. A secret place. A stronghold owned by Valhalla, but only ever known to Odin and his immediate entourage. Such was its secrecy that the new Titan administration would not have discovered its existence.

It remained a place unrecorded. Off the books. A place forgotten.

XXI

April rushed headlong into May. The days might be lengthening, but for the horse troops of Macedon the time before they would be called to arms was evaporating faster than the morning dew.

Dio was merciless in the punishing schedule for his new charges. As light blossomed in the eastern sky each morning, he paced the farmhouse, banging on doors and kicking bodies out of sleeping bags. Bleary-eyed, bruised and miserable, they stumbled across to the stables and mucked out, groomed and fed the horses. Only then did he permit them to return to their own comforts.

He allowed an hour for breakfast and Heph appreciated the ingenuity of Dio's regime. His friend understood that the company would work far better for the remainder of the day if they were granted this time to prepare. Bodies came alive during that hour, spirits warmed, caffeine kicked in and porridge anchored stomachs.

In the mornings they rode unencumbered by weapons, each day becoming more accustomed to the feel of their mounts without saddle or stirrups. They stopped at noon to give the horses a second feed and to gulp down toasted flatbreads with cheese and tea. The afternoons were for weapons-handling, riding with lances and blades. As skills improved, he replaced their hardhats with the plumed headgear of the Companion Cavalry. Grins broadened and backs straightened, but they quickly realised how much these bronze helms encumbered their vision. Seeing enough to angle their mounts towards a given point was one thing; spotting a target hanging from a rope was quite another.

'They'll get there,' Dio assured Heph one evening when they were the last to depart the stables, though his tone lacked conviction. 'I'll drill them harder than ever. Thank god we still have a week.'

But Dio was wrong.

The very next afternoon their session was interrupted by the churn of large vehicles and into view came four horse carriers.

'Oh please god, no,' muttered Dio.

Ordering the Company to stay put in the field, he accompanied Heph back to the farmhouse and waited while the carriers squeezed into the yard. From the lead vehicle emerged the same lank-haired, pot-bellied man who had transferred the horses to Knoydart in March. He lit a foul-smelling roll-up and squinted towards the stables.

'Orders were for double the number of vehicles this time. How many you got? No more than twelve?'

'Eleven,' said Heph.

'Okay, three in three and two in the other.'

Dio stepped forward. 'There must be some mistake. It's only the third of the month, so there's more than a week until the Battle. I need another few days here.'

The man snorted and smirked knowingly with his team as they descended from the carriers. 'Sorry pal, it ain't

Knoydart this time. I gotta get your fine fellas down to Newcastle for embarkation tomorrow. Once over the water, we've still got a twenty-hour drive. The horses will need to be out of the carriers twice on that journey, so we have to build in stays at proper stabling. And I'm guessing a serious horse fella like you is going to want them acclimatised to their new surroundings at the other end before you start riding them too heavy-like.' He offered a sympathetic shrug, as though he gave a damn about Dio's timetable. 'So we gotta take them today.'

Dio was wild-eyed. 'You're putting my horses on a boat?'

'It's not your typical passenger ferry, pal. Don't worry.'

Heph and Dio looked at each other. In all the rush to hone the new recruits into some semblance of an effective Cavalry, neither had considered the logistics of getting eleven horses to Hungary.

Dio strode round the back of the lead vehicle and yanked the doors open. The interior was as it had been for the trip to Knoydart. The space was divided into three separate stalls, each large enough for one horse. Beyond these was a storage area and then a separate section with bunks, a small kitchenette and a toilet.

'How long have we got?' asked Heph, coming to stand beside the man while Dio fretted inside.

'Ought to be on the road by five.'

Three hours. They would need to work fast.

Dio jumped from the carrier and jabbed a finger towards the man. 'You're not taking my beauties without me. Not all the way to bloody Budapest.'

The man began to protest, 'Look, pal—'

'Don't "pal" me! That wasn't a question; that was a statement.'

The man looked to Heph for support.

'I think he means it.' Heph shrugged.

The man swore quietly. 'I need two of the vehicles for my men. But you can have the other six bunks if you insist.'

Dio nodded. 'Okay. That's more like it.'

The man stamped on his cigarette. 'So, five o'clock departure, it is. You'd better get sorting what you need.'

'Feel free to use the farmhouse kitchen,' Heph said to the men, then grabbed Dio's arm and steered him back to the gate. 'So what's the plan?'

'I figure I'll take five of the newbies, if I have your permission. The more time they spend with their mounts, the better. And we may have a couple of days to run through some manoeuvres when we get there.'

'Fine. Take whoever you want.' Heph looked at the Company lined on their mounts, awaiting them. 'It's bad eh, my friend?'

'It certainly is. We're not ready.'

'We're going to have to be.'

Lenore, Spyro and Zephyr reacted professionally to the news and put the recruits to work stabling and grooming the horses, then packing straw, feed, water, coats, armour, weapons and all the rest of the paraphernalia needed by a horse unit. The shock of the sudden activity was scrawled over the faces of Phoibe, Thales and Elinor, so Dio kept them moving, letting them have no time to ponder what awaited. They were all experienced members of the Titan lines. They had faced the blades of Valhalla on more than one Field. But this was different. This time they would be leaving Scotland. This time they would be advancing into battle on horseback. And this time, they faced foe who were little more than phantoms of their imaginations and as limitless as the stars.

At last they were ready and the horses were coaxed into the carriers and fastened in their stalls. The creatures nickered, and flicked their tails, but they trusted their handlers. Dio had selected Phoibe, Roxana, Elinor, Melitta and Thales to accompany him and he sent them off to stow their belongings. When all was done and they were selecting their bunks in the carriers and belting themselves into the passenger seats, and the transport team were sealing up the backdoors and shouting instructions to each other, Heph stepped close and embraced Dio.

'See you in a few days.'

'Aye. Who knows what we'll be facing.'

Heph held on to his arm. 'Whatever it is, we'll face it together.'

Dio shook hands with the other three men and hugged Lenore, then waved once and hauled himself into the front of the lead carrier. The vehicles spluttered into life, took an age turning and processed down the drive.

Silence reasserted itself. The bustle was gone and the five remaining Companions loitered disconsolately.

'Come on,' said Spyro eventually. 'Those stables aren't going to clean themselves.'

The gloom was mustering by the time they had finished and Zephyr, Spyro and Philemon returned to the farmhouse to crack open wine and prepare food. Lenore and Heph shook out the final hay nets and reattached them to the walls in each stall.

'How are you feeling?' he asked quietly and she took so long answering that he thought she had not heard.

'Frightened,' she said simply.

'It feels unnervingly empty without our beloved beasts.'

'It certainly does.'

'Do you wish you'd never joined this Cavalry?'

'I sometimes wish you'd never plunged a sword into Sveinn's belly.'

He stopped fiddling with the final net and looked at her. The quiet hung as he waited for her to elaborate. She placed the last excess tack into a crate and sealed it, then turned to him.

'Like you, I've only been in the Pantheon for two Seasons, but I got to understand the Horde as my foe. They were a clever and dangerous enemy, but I studied their city haunts, I understood their methods and my fellow Titans were experienced in how to counter them. I guess I found the risks acceptable.' She brushed strands of straw from her tunic. 'Because that's what this is all about at the end of the day, isn't it? The equilibrium between the rewards we receive and the risks we're prepared to face. Once that balance is blown apart, the Pantheon stops functioning.'

Heph closed the stall door and leaned against it, but did not interrupt her.

'Now everything feels so utterly incomprehensible. I can't begin to imagine what faces us out there. I've never been to Hungary. The other Palatinates are little more than stories to me. And I've no idea how anyone even begins to fight a three-way Battle.'

Heph sighed in understanding. 'I hear you and I feel the same. I've spent sleepless hours on that farmhouse floor, but

I've tried to tell myself that it's the unknown which I fear the most. We can't picture the foe in our heads. We can't visualise the landscape or imagine how the Battle will play out. We can't even get our heads around the journey. But, like today, when the carriers turned up unexpectedly, when events happen, we adapt to them and they will be far less frightening than our imaginations have led us to believe. Hungary's not so exotic. The Field will look like any other Field – a green space with grass and trees, probably in the middle of nowhere. And when we see the other Palatinates for the first time, we'll have the rest of the Titan Companies around us. Remember, with Valhalla joining us and the new Blood Credits that were spent, we will number upwards of four hundred.'

Lenore looked as though she wanted to say more, but thought better of it. 'Come on. Let's get back before those boys have scoffed everything.'

They put out the lights and locked the door, but when they were halfway across the grass, she lingered in the dusk. 'I guess fear is a natural part of this game we play.'

'The Pantheon thrives on fear.'

'But this is different and you know it.' His response had irritated her. 'We're eleven riders, Heph. *Eleven*. Luck was on our side at Knoydart, but it won't be a second time.'

'You don't know that,' he said gravely. 'Anything can happen. The future is a mystery.'

'For god's sake, the future's always a mystery. By definition, the future is nothing more than our imaginations. But this particular future holds one undeniable truth and it's a truth that terrifies me.' Her tone was so bereft that it held him. 'We are now the most notorious unit in the Pantheon and you are the infamous King Killer. When those six hundred Huns sweep towards us, they won't care about the other Titan Companies; they'll have eyes only for the eleven of us. The Rules of this Battle dictate that a King must die, but there's also glory to be won when the Companion Cavalry is destroyed and the King Killer has fallen to their blades.'

XXII

Heph shared a disgruntled meal in the warmth of the farmhouse kitchen. He tried to maintain a relaxed exterior, but Lenore's words had upset him. When they had eaten their fill, he made a surreptitious call to Stanek and then helped clean the crockery while he awaited the arrival of his driver.

'I'm heading into the city,' he said when headlights shone through the windows.

They sensed his black mood and accepted the announcement without comment. Once he was enveloped in the darkness of the back of the car and the countryside of Perthshire was shooting invisibly past, he found his hands were balled into fists and his heart was pounding. Was Lenore right? Did he really have such a reputation? If so, then he was undoubtedly leading his ten Companion riders to their deaths.

He had no idea why he was going to Edinburgh or what he was planning to do. He simply needed the space. When they reached Princes Street, he asked Stanek to stop the car and alighted. 'I'm okay for the rest of the night. I'll call you tomorrow.'

He paced past the lights of the big stores. It was ten

twenty-five, but the pavements were still busy and traffic trundled along the street. He cut across Waverley Bridge and then began the climb up Cockburn into the Old Town. Rain started to spot onto his face and he grumbled as it became heavier. He was a Titan officer. He could have sought shelter in the rooftop gardens of Ephesus or the spa of Persepolis, but instead he was drawn to deeper haunts. He switched direction and jogged up the long steps of Warriston Close to the rusted metal door that had once been the North Gate of Valhalla. He stared through the rain at a camera in the wall and heard the buzz of acknowledgement.

The new Gatekeeper team had their databases sorted and this time there were no fumbled attempts to identify him.

'Welcome, Captain,' the lead man said and it was strange to see no beards or long hair.

'Who's in tonight?'

'The Colonel has companies one to three of the Hellenes in the Hall of Zeus.'

'The Colonel?'

'Menes, sir.'

Of course. Scum always floats to the top.

Heph headed along North Tunnel, oblivious to the new Macedonian tapestries bedecking the walls. He stripped in the changing rooms and pulled on a clean tunic from the lockers, then followed the sounds of human exertion and wood on bronze. As he approached the steps down to the main Hall, he stopped and beheld the sight before him. Over a hundred hoplites, helmeted and clad in bronze, were stretched out in parallel lines, stepping forward in unison and thrusting short wooden blades at the air in front of them. Then they repositioned and did it again. Bareheaded

Titans patrolled the edges of the Hall, pointing out mistakes, shouting advice and sometimes striding into the mass and physically forcing someone to rethink their movements. On the dais sat Menes with a flagon of wine, speaking with one of his senior Dekarchos.

Heph folded his arms, leaned against the wall at the top of the steps and pondered the display, trying to imagine these lines standing firm against the Janissaries and the Black Cloaks. He was so absorbed that he did not notice heads beginning to turn his way and murmurs swelling. Someone called and pointed at him and more Hellenic helmets twisted. Gradually it dawned on him that the angry eyes in the recesses of the bronze were those of his former Viking compatriots.

He cursed himself. He knew, of course, that the Horde had been forcibly transformed into the new Hellenic regiment. He had been present at the Council of Commanders when it had been decided. But his mind had been far away, locked on Lenore's words, and he had not considered the situation. The troops beneath him not only saw the King Killer idly observing their shame, they also saw the Wolf traitor, the man who had run from their lines on the blood beach and surrendered to Agape. The resentment swelled and the Titan instructors cajoled them from the edges and waded in with their clubs. On the dais, Menes stood and peered imperiously at the insubordination.

Before the instructors could react, a helmeted hoplite detached from the formation and snaked through the lines towards Heph. He recognised the slim, muscled figure, the curve of the hips and the rope of blonde hair over one armoured shoulder, and his breath caught.

She was on the steps before he could do more than straighten and unfold his arms.

'You fool!' she said furiously, but quiet enough that it was only for his ears. 'What stupidity brings you *here*?'

'Calder, please, I didn't mean any offence.'

'Offence? You think it's fitting that you should come and watch our disgrace? Well take a look!' She waved her wooden blade back at the crowd. 'Have a good long look. See what you've done to us.'

He stared into her eyes and held her gaze for a heartbeat. 'I apologise. I was stupid. Please forgive me.'

'Get that bloody woman back in line!' shouted Menes.

'Ignore the bastard,' Heph implored, even as burly Titans came for her. Then, a spontaneous, almost mad, idea. 'Midday tomorrow.'

'What?'

'Noon tomorrow. Outside the Galleries. Meet me.'

'You're crazy.'

'I beg you, meet me. *Please*.'

Arms came around her and began to drag her back into the lines. He wanted to launch himself at the men accosting her, but he knew it would be the spark that disintegrated any semblance of order. So he watched helplessly as she cursed and pushed them off her and shouldered her way back to her place in the formation without a backward glance.

'Is Agape in tonight?'

The Titan Gatekeeper consulted his screen. 'Says here she's in Pella.'

Heph nodded, pushed through the Alexandrian Gate

and continued up Warriston Steps to the Royal Mile. The rain had passed, but the pavements were slick now and the dwindling traffic splashed through puddles.

Pella was the most compact of the Titan strongholds. It had no Bladecraft Rooms or baths, no Council chambers or gardens. What it did contain on any given Conflict Night was the Sacred Band. As the most western stronghold – and therefore the highest on the slope of the Royal Mile – it was the best strategic location for the Band to sweep from the rooftops and descend fast in any direction they were required. The limited space also made the presence of other Titan companies impossible, and the Band valued this privacy.

Once past the cameras and the security doors, Heph presented himself at reception on the third floor above Brodie's Close, but his status as a Titan commander did not automatically allow him further. Instead, he was made to wait until Agape had been contacted and she appeared in person.

'Hephaestion. An unexpected visitor to my stronghold.'

She was wearing a scarlet tunic with black leggings and boots, and her hair had been freshly coloured blue and tied back into a knot.

'Yeah, well, most of my unit and my horses are already halfway to Budapest.'

Her eyebrows raised at this. 'So soon?'

'My sentiments exactly.'

She eyed his jeans and street clothes. 'Technically, I should get you to change before we go further, but it's only me here tonight, so I guess your appearance will have to do.'

She led him up tight stairs which passed changing rooms,

showers and lockers, then opened up into a wider loft space with scattered sofas and tables. Ladders reached for hatches in the ceiling.

'Our exit points,' she said. 'We can be out of those in a flash when the call comes.' She pointed vaguely at the other doors. 'Map room. Armouries. Massage cubicles. Mess hall and refreshments. Security and IT. And BOC.'

'BOC?'

She led him to the door and opened it. 'Band Operations Command. It's my space as senior officer. I don't welcome visitors, but I guess I'll have to make an exception.'

He followed her in and discovered a tiny room painted in deep aubergine, with two leather chairs, reading lamps and a mahogany desk. On a corner table was a bottle of Shiraz, a half-filled glass and a travel book about the ancient sites of Mesopotamia.

She saw his surprise. 'On Conflict Nights, this is where I prepare for blood. At quieter times, I find it a more cerebral space.'

She reached into a cabinet above the desk and produced a second glass. 'You wish to partake?'

'I guess. Today seems to be full of surprises.'

She poured him a glass, then settled back and watched him as he perched in the other chair.

'So what brings you to Pella?'

'I don't know. This afternoon I lost my Cavalry. By dinner, I was in such a foul mood, I had to be alone. In Valhalla— I mean, in Alexandria, I bumped slap bang into most of the Horde and nearly got lynched. So I pointed my feet west and they brought me here.'

'Well, here's to accidental visitors,' she said and they clinked glasses.

He tasted his wine and murmured approval. 'Actually, I do know why I'm here. I wanted to ask our greatest warrior how we prepare for a three-way Battle?'

Agape pursed her lips at this. 'A foolish term. There's no such thing as a three-way battle, because battle is always a thousand smaller ways. It's the moments when you are eye to eye with your foe and one of you must die. Battle turns on those intimate contests and it doesn't matter how many armies or Kings or banners are actually on the Field. Kill your foe; it's as simple as that. Whatever flag they honour, whichever King commands them. Then kill the next one who gets in your face. And the next. And maybe when they stop coming, you will look up and realise it's your army's banner that flies victorious.'

Heph scowled. 'I hope there's a more encompassing strategy than that. Zeus and Alexander better have their heads deep in planning, otherwise we're going to be up the bloody creek with no paddle when that klaxon kicks off.' He controlled himself and took a moment. 'Someone close to me told me that she's frightened. She painted my fame as a liability. Told me I have a massive target on my chest, and that means the troops around me will also be in the eye of the storm.'

'Your Companion Cavalry are indeed now famed throughout the Pantheon.'

'Just as your Sacred Band has been for years. So I'm asking you to tell me straight how I can look my unit in the face when the Huns and the Sultanate bring upwards of thirteen hundred troops onto the Field, and tell them I'm leading them into a fair fight.'

Agape made him wait. She topped up her glass and then considered him in the lamplight. 'Here's the truth of it. Kyzaghan and Ördög don't really care about taking the head of Alexander. If a King must fall, they don't want it to be him. We're small-fry to them. The insects on the muzzles of the big cats. Those two have been locked in rivalry for over a decade, always bruising each other, always taking flesh wounds, but never landing a knockout blow. So they see us as the opportunity they've been waiting for.

'Don't get me wrong, they'll tell Mehmed and Attila to attack us with fury, but they'll save their real heavyweight lines for the moment they see a chink of weakness open up in the ranks of the other one. That will be the critical moment of the whole Battle. And it will also be our critical moment.'

'How do you mean?'

'Our priority is to ensure we still have some semblance of a fighting force when that critical moment arrives, because what we do next may determine the outcome of the Battle. The foe will be locked in mortal combat. Their attentions will be averted from us. And in that moment, we have a chance to do something unexpected. To insert ourselves where they are weakest and land a blow they will remember forever.'

Heph's face was intense as she spoke, but then a new thought clouded his expression. 'Except we have a coward for a King. He'd rather we quake around his banner.'

Agape acknowledged this. 'Kings like him are bystanders on a battlefield.'

'Then why won't you make a Challenge, Agape? There's still time. Force him to fight. Zeus will support you, so too Nicanor and Parmenion. He will die on your blade and you will lead us onto the Field.'

'That is not my destiny.'

'He's a liability! A weakling and a fool. He's taken the might of Valhalla and degraded them to resentful Greek foot soldiers. He has to go.'

'Then you make the Challenge.'

Her words caught him and he gaped at her in silence, searching for the sarcasm.

'Me?'

'Your stock is high. You are the King Killer. Our troops look to you. If you beat Alexander, they will acclaim you King in his stead.'

'Are you serious?'

Her look was enigmatic. 'Maybe I am.'

He took a breath and shook his head. 'I can't. I've been a Titan for less than a year. It's not the way of the Pantheon.'

Agape laughed unexpectedly. 'My dear Hephaestion, I don't think there's one thing you've done since the Venarii parties recruited you that could be described as the way of the Pantheon.'

He tried to smile too, but her suggestion troubled him and when he eventually bade her farewell and stalked back to a West End apartment he had not occupied for over six months, his mind was awhirl and his mood blacker than ever.

XXIII

Marcella swam a lazy length of her cliff-edge pool and gazed at the yachts moored far below.

One of her attendants strode down the lawns and waited until she turned her head. 'He's here, ma'am.'

She did not respond and he left her in peace, while she swam another couple of lengths. Finally she stepped from the water, slipped on a robe and reached for her gin limoncello, but there was a fly in it. She scrunched her nose petulantly and flung both drink and glass over the cliff.

She made her way up the lawns, giving herself time to smoke a cigarette, then descended steps at the side of the villa to a series of whitewashed outbuildings. Two heavies stood by one of the doors.

'Well?'

'Nothing on him except a phone, ma'am, which he refuses to unlock until he's spoken with you.'

Marcella dropped her cigarette and stubbed it out. One of the heavies held the door open for her, while the other retrieved the discarded butt. Inside the bare stone room was another guard and a metal table with two chairs. In one of the chairs sat a bound and blindfolded man with striking white hair. Marcella seated herself opposite and appraised him.

The man had a tough physique beneath his T-shirt and arms that bore many scars and a few new bruises, but she could tell he was nervous. Her heavies had no doubt been less than warm in their welcome.

'You wanted to see me,' she said eventually.

'I'm not seeing much of anything at the moment,' he answered through gritted teeth.

'The blindfold stays on in my presence.'

The man considered this for several seconds, then accepted the condition. 'Is this Jupiter?'

'*Lord High* Jupiter. You may call me "ma'am". And to whom do I speak?'

'Skarde. Housecarl of Wolf Regiment, the Palatinate of the Horde of Valhalla.'

'There is no such Palatinate.'

'Aye ma'am. More's the pity.'

'You're a long way from Scotland.'

'I come bearing gifts.'

'Consul Valerius tells me you were quite insistent on that point. He says you called him using a private number that you had no business knowing and told him you had information about the God Killer. Information you steadfastly refused to divulge to him in person, even when he resorted to more physical means to loosen your tongue.'

'It is for you only, ma'am.'

'And what do you want in return for this information?'

The man's lips drew back in a snarl. 'My Palatinate is gone. My regiment too. I have no rank. No position. No role in your Pantheon. But when my King lived, I was a

Wolf, one of the hunter killers of Valhalla. I led litters. I savaged Titans. I was feared by all. Let me serve you ma'am. Give me a place in the Legion cohorts. I will fight for you. I will kill for you. Your word will be my command.'

'My word is every man's command.'

'You may task me with anything. Whether on the battlefield, in the city, during Conflict Hours or outside them, I will carry out your every wish with lethal efficiency.'

Marcella sat back and assessed him. They were strong words, spoken with a strenuous arrogance that was appealing. He didn't look a fool. It took balls to get an audience with her and she sensed he was not a man who wasted people's time. 'You have two minutes.'

'Do I have your word that you will give me a place in your Legion?'

'You have my word on nothing. I will assess this information of yours before I decide.'

Skarde gritted his teeth in anger and a low growl vibrated in his throat.

'Ninety seconds,' she said, unimpressed.

'Okay, okay. I know where the God Killer is hiding. I can take you to him.'

Marcella was not about to give him the satisfaction of knowing his revelation had intrigued her. 'What makes you think I need to know where he is hiding?'

'Because he killed a Caelestis,' Skarde blustered. 'One of your number. The Pantheon clamours to see him punished.'

'How *dare* you tell me what the Pantheon wants,' she snapped furiously and Skarde braced for more punches from her henchmen.

'I'm sorry, ma'am. I didn't mean to speak out of turn.'

'What evidence do you have that this person is the God Killer?'

'Evidence? We know it was him. He was with Odin when he died.'

'Did anyone see him strike?'

This wasn't going well. Skarde did not know how to respond.

'I thought as much,' Marcella said more levelly. 'Well, it seems you don't as yet have much of value to bargain with. You will provide us with the location of this so-called God Killer and I will send someone I trust to make their own judgement. You will remain in my care until I have received their feedback and only then will I decide what is to be done with you, Wolf.'

Skarde forced a change of tack. 'I have something else to offer – about the King Killer.'

'I'm not interested in the King Killer.'

'On my phone I have a photo of him.'

'I've already seen one.'

Marcella was bored of the conversation and made to rise.

'Not *this* picture, you haven't. You must look at it.'

Something in his desperation made her pause. She sighed and snapped her fingers. The guard pulled Skarde's phone from his pocket and gave it to her.

'What's the passcode?'

Skarde did not reply. He was dismayed that his news about Oliver had been met with such lack of enthusiasm, so now he needed to time his remaining revelations with extreme caution. He started with what he thought was a mere titbit. 'The King Killer's name is Tyler Maitland.'

Marcella sat stock still. Her pulse quickened. 'Maitland? How is that spelt?'

'M-a-i-t.'

There was silence. Marcella's mind drifted far from the room. Maitland? That name again. But it has to be a coincidence. How many Maitlands in Scotland?

'And how do you come by this name?'

'I was trusted with matters of a sensitive nature by Lord Odin. Tyler Maitland was one of these.'

Odin? What had that old bastard been scheming?

Marcella gathered herself. 'I asked you for the passcode.'

Behind his blindfold, he had noticed the new stridence in her voice. It confused him, but he dared to hope he might still pull something from this meeting.

'There's a picture on there,' he said, 'that not only shows Tyler Maitland, but also his treacherous sister and the Valhalla Housecarl she loved and with whom she conspired to bring about the fall of a Palatinate.'

'Just give me the damn code.'

He told her. 'You'll find the picture in Photos.'

Marcella pulled it up.

And that's when her world ignited.

Her hands shook. Her heart thundered. Blood roared in her ears. Somewhere above the noise, the man was saying more about Maitland's sister and star-crossed lovers and Odin's obsession, but she had ears for none of it. Her vision was filled only by the other woman in the picture. The other one.

Abruptly, she backed away, knocking the metal chair over. Without a word, she pushed the guard aside and marched into the sunlight.

'Hey!' she heard Skarde shout, before he was silenced by a muffled whack.

Marcella strode up the steps and onto the lawns, one hand still gripping the phone, her lips drawn back in a rictus of fury. Her heart thumped and her head pounded.

That bastard! That conniving arsehole!

Fabian was somewhere up on the verandas and she skewed right to avoid him, onto a path surrounded by planting. She forced herself to stop and to control her breathing as she stared over the greenery to the sea. Furiously she stabbed at the phone and pulled up the picture again. There was a bench and somehow her legs took her to it and she slumped down. Tears came now, salty and warm, running down her nose. She swiped at them angrily, because it had been years since anyone had made her cry.

She willed herself to calm down and took stuttering gulps of air. Slowly, the thumping in her head lulled and the hot emotion subsided, replaced once again with steel. She dried her tears with her palms and stood to stare at the horizon.

You... bastard! All these years, all this time, you've been lying to me and you thought you could get away with it.

She closed the app on the phone and marched back to the little stone room.

'Where is he?' she demanded as soon as she shoved open the door.

Skarde was hunched over the table, still bound and sightless. 'What?' he croaked.

'Where is this Tyler Maitland?

'With his bloody horses, I guess, but I don't know where. He's Titan now.'

'And how was Odin involved?'

'He said Maitland was a big prize, someone he was desperate to find. Him and his sister.'

'His sister?'

'She's in the photo too.'

Marcella pulled the image up on the phone again and forced herself to look at it once more.

Eventually, an implacable weight settled in her stomach and she said tonelessly, 'You will remain in detention here until I have considered this matter further.'

Skarde's protest was choked back by an arm around his neck.

Marcella strode from the room, taking with her his phone.

XXIV

'Hi.' The syllable was uttered so irresolutely that it barely came to Tyler over the noise of the traffic on Princes Street and the churn of voices on the esplanade outside the Royal Scottish Academy.

He had been sitting on a bench for ten minutes looking out across East Princes Street Gardens in all their spring glory. Beside him were two takeaway coffees and with every minute that passed, he had become more and more convinced they were destined for a bin.

He swivelled to the sound of her voice and squinted at her from under the brim of his hat. 'I didn't think you'd come.'

'Nor did I. I've walked past you twice already and both times nearly headed home.'

'Well, I'm glad it's third time lucky.' He rose and handed her one of the cups. 'Cappuccino, right?'

She took it with a half-smile.

'I thought we'd just walk,' he continued. 'Probably easier than a table somewhere.'

They began to amble listlessly onto Princes Street and east towards the Scott Monument. His head had been full of words to say to her, but quite suddenly it was empty and they walked in awkward silence, just two souls amongst the burgeoning crowds on a bright Saturday in the heart of the city. He was overwhelmed by her proximity. He thought he recognised her scent, but it might simply be his mind playing tricks. She was dressed in a grey woollen coat, with a navy skirt beneath and ankle boots. Her hair was loose and straightened and there were pearls in her ears. Memories flooded him.

To his surprise, it was she who broke their silence. She glanced over the road to Jenner's, the old department store, which was now being transformed into a hotel, and said simply, 'I miss that place.'

'Do you remember when we met in there for coffee?'

'We didn't *meet*; you followed me. I had no choice but to let you put your tray down next to me.'

'Back then, I didn't even know your name. You were just *Miss Pearl Earrings* to me.'

She lifted a finger to one lobe self-consciously. 'We were so worried we might be seen. We feared the Pantheon had eyes everywhere.'

'Now look at us. We couldn't give a damn.'

She grew pensive again and they walked on towards the junction with Waverley. 'Innocent times,' she said, almost to herself. 'Times when we thought the Pantheon was about how many weights we could lift when Halvar shouted at us.'

Instinctively, he shepherded her across the main junction away from the Old Town on its hill above. He wanted them to avoid the alleys and closes which held such complicated emotions. So they turned towards St Andrew's Square and walked into the embrace of New Town.

'Are you going to tell me why you wanted to meet like this?' she asked eventually.

'I needed to see you again.'

'You saw me last night. And before that, you saw me clearly enough when I fired an arrow onto your helmet and your horse damn near broke my spine.'

'I don't mean that. I mean I needed to see *Lana* again. Do you realise it's been more than a year since we were together simply as Lana and Tyler in your house by the Leith?'

'I'm not the same Lana now. Too much blood under that bridge.'

For the first time, he turned his head as they walked and looked at her properly. 'Yes, you are,' he said firmly.

She didn't like his comment and they progressed in silence past St Andrew's Square. Eventually, she asked, 'So is that the point of the hat? Turning back the clock to earlier times?'

'Maybe. I don't know. I just thought I'd be easier to spot in the crowd.'

'It doesn't look as good on you without the long hair.'

He bristled. 'Yeah, well, my new style wasn't a matter of choice.'

She halted him suddenly with a hand to his chest and scowled. 'Okay, let's stop this banter. It took a vast amount of willpower for me to turn up today and I didn't come for the small talk. I've already asked once why you wanted to meet and not got a decent answer, so I'll try one more time. Did you have something you needed to say to me?'

They were on the brink of the slope down to Drummond Place. Across the rooftops was an expansive view of the silver waters of the Forth and Fife beyond. The Lomond hills rose like pimples on the horizon. He focused on her and tried to come up with a response to her question. He knew he did have something to say to her, he just hadn't expected the moment to arrive so soon and now it had, it sounded all wrong in his head. He opened his mouth, closed it, then opened it again, as his tongue formed syllables before his brain could properly assess them.

'I wanted to tell you I still love you.'

Her scowl evaporated and she stared at him in mute shock.

Then she stepped away and looked at the view. 'You've said some stupid things in the time I've known you, Tyler Maitland, but that takes the prize.'

He didn't know what reaction he had hoped to elicit, but it wasn't that. He struggled to respond, but all that came out was, 'It's true.'

'True?' She rounded on him so angrily that people on the pavement opposite glanced over. 'This from the man who fled from our lines on the blood beach, off on some forlorn search for his sister and forgot all about me.'

'I *never* forgot about you.'

She jabbed a finger at him. 'You abandoned me. You left me to face events that were so much worse than anything your little adolescent brain could ever imagine.'

'But—'

'No! There's no "but" anything.'

She swung away and he thought she would leave, but she remained where she was, peering out at Fife. Neither spoke. Kids ran past. A lorry beeped loudly as it reversed into a narrow drive. A gull squawked from a streetlight above.

He saw her shoulders sag and her eyes close for a few seconds. Then she said in lower tones, 'Love... That's a heavy word, Tyler. Perhaps the heaviest of all.'

'That's why I don't use it lightly.'

'But I fear you do. In this game of blood, you see me as someone who offers security, someone to be at peace with. You think I'm more than the others because with me you can step outside the game. You can remove the weight of your armour and dispose of your captain's rank. You can unburden yourself of your secrets and you can just be your real self.'

'Is that so wrong? The things we do in the Pantheon don't define who we can be beyond it. I would have loved you without any damn Pantheon.'

Again, he felt her eyes roaming over him.

'Would you? I doubt it. Can you imagine us together without any Pantheon? What would we have done? Got married in a sweet little ceremony with flowers and a white dress? Bought a terraced house and worked nine to five to pay the mortgage? Had a couple of children, owned a dog? Spent our Sundays cooking roasts and dozing on the couch?'

His jaw tightened. 'There's no need to be facetious.'

'I think this is probably the best time to be facetious.' She enunciated her next words as though attempting to explain a complex problem to a child. 'Tyler, we're officers in the Pantheon. We're washed in blood. We're inured to violence. We've watched friends die. What the hell is love supposed to be in a world like that?'

'Perhaps it's the most important thing.'

His answer stoppered her and she turned back to the

view. He held his tongue because he could feel her struggling to vocalise whatever was going on inside her.

Finally, she tried a different tack. 'We might have shared many experiences, Tyler, but... we don't truly *know* each other. Doesn't that matter to you?'

'Of course it does.'

'You can't love someone if you don't know them.'

'We've stood together in shieldwalls, for god's sake! What more do we need to know? Most people go on a few dates and fall in love. You think they know each other?'

At this, she gave him a long, appraising look, but didn't respond.

'Lana, we've packed more into two years than other couples fit in to a lifetime. I love you because of everything you are and everything we've shared.'

He thought there might be pools in her eyes, but she had swivelled again so he could only see her profile and it could be the cool breeze coming from the Forth.

'Tyler, like it or not, we're Pantheon. We'll walk away from here to the biggest battle of our lives. I'll go back to Viking units whom you not only abandoned, but ultimately betrayed. You'll don your plumed helmet and scarlet cloak and ride as the King Killer into the heart of the enemy. And we'll laugh at this conversation.'

His stomach lurched. 'Will you really laugh?'

'No,' she responded guiltily, seeing she had hurt him. 'That was poorly phrased.'

'I'm not some smitten idiot. These aren't feelings I'm just blurting out a week after meeting you. I've considered these emotions for more than two years. I've played with them. I've dissected them. I've recognised there are huge challenges between us, bloody great voids of conflict! But, in the process I've also got to know you much better than you realise, both as Lana and as Calder. I've seen the real you in all its raw wonder. And I've come to understand that what I feel for you… is love.'

He had her attention. Her eyes were fixed on him, unblinking.

'I know we're Pantheon,' he continued, his face creasing as he struggled to express himself. 'I get that. But the Pantheon doesn't own all of me. One day, if I survive, I intend to leave. I will walk away and live my real life. But I know deep in my heart that I never want to walk away from you again.'

His words petered out.

She watched him for an eternity, then dropped her eyes and murmured, 'Oh Tyler, Tyler. The gods play with our hearts.'

She stared at the pavement and he could see the warring emotions on her face. He wanted to reach out, to take her hand and squeeze it, but he was glued to the spot.

Finally, she inhaled and mastered herself. 'I think I should go now. It's for the best.'

Nausea welled in him, but he had no more fight. He nodded numbly and sighed in surrender. 'As you wish.'

He kept his eyes on the horizon as she shifted hesitantly from his vision. Her heels tapped a few yards up the slope and then stopped, and for a heartbeat he thought she might throw herself back to him, but when her voice came, it was bleak and hollow.

'Freyja's dead.'

He turned and knew she was calibrating his response, but all he could think of to say was, 'I'm sorry. She was one of the best.'

It was not enough. If ever he had needed the gift of oratory, it was at that moment and she looked at him in disappointment.

'She was much more than that,' she said quietly. 'But perhaps it's for the best that she never saw Valhalla's subjugation.'

She made to depart again, when another question arrested her. 'Have you heard from Oliver?'

'Oliver? I had an email from him a few months ago asking what I was up to, but otherwise I've not heard from him for over a year. What makes you ask?'

She held her response. They were only days from battle on a foreign plain. They needed every ounce of focus and commitment. How could she tell Tyler of the deaths of Oliver's parents, of her suspicions that he had been forcibly subsumed into the Pantheon Schola system? It would blow Tyler's mind. He would raise hell trying to locate the lad at a time when his troops needed stable command more than ever.

'No reason,' she said. 'I just wondered.'

And with that, she left him.

'Mikhail, it's good of you to spare me the time.'

'Come now, Marcella, I think we can do away with the pleasantries. What can I do for you?'

Her emotions were under control. Her tears were gone, her shock locked away. Now her woman's heart was encased in cold, unforgiving iron.

All those years of deceit. All those thousands of conversations when she could have been trusted with the knowledge.

She felt like such a fool.

'I have a favour to ask of you.'

The line was poor. No doubt Malutin was deep in rural Hungary overseeing preparations with Attila.

'Have a care what you ask,' he growled. 'I'm days away from a showdown with Hakan's Sultanate and I'm not about to let politics get within a furlong of my Huns' battle plans.'

'Of course not. I would never dream of proposing anything of strategic disadvantage to you.'

Malutin harrumphed down the phone. 'I mean to take Mehmed down this time. Without the limit of a single Battle Hour, my Horns will tire him into submission.'

'I will be watching with bated breath.'

'So what do you want?'

'It's the Titans that interest me.'

'Those maggots. I've told Attila to play with them, give Zeus a bloody nose, but it's Mehmed I want, not Alexander.'

'Justly so. Alexander is insignificant in the grander scheme of things. But my favour does concern his troops.'

'Spit it out.' Malutin's voice was laced with suspicion.

'I want the head of the King Killer.'

Malutin barked with laughter. 'Has he become an irritant?'

'His profile is much too high for any single soldier in the Pantheon. The feeds of his cavalry charging at Sveinn are still being shared everywhere.'

'His cavalry? His damn cavalry is eleven horses! I have six hundred. We can destroy him with our first charge. Marcella, he's nothing. Why are you troubling yourself?'

'Trust me when I say he has set a precedent that must not be allowed to take root.'

'We've already agreed another King must die at Hortobágy. So there will be another King Killer, one of my trusted Huns who will have buried their blade deep in Mehmed's heart.'

'Then the Titan King Killer will not be missed.'

Malutin was silent for several seconds, mulling over her request and wondering what she wasn't telling him.

'What's in it for me?' he demanded eventually.

'What's always in it for people like us. Brief your syndicates. Massage the odds. Create the demand and set your bluffs. Wager on his death at a certain hour in the Battle, on a specific regiment of your Huns to claim his head. Select the weapon and the precise manner of his death. Do whatever you damn well want to guarantee a small fortune for yourself and your allies. Just make sure he's dead before the Battle is done. You said yourself your cavalry can kill him on demand.'

Malutin took his time answering. 'Money is money, but I have associates who would be only too grateful for advance intel on a guaranteed action. I will consider it.'

'I will be indebted to you.'

Malutin had been about to end the call, but he paused at this. 'Your debt, Marcella, is something to be valued.'

'So I will give it. You may ask me any favour if you do my bidding during this fight.'

She could sense him teetering on the brink. Finally, he relented.

'You will have his head.'

PART THREE

DISCOVERY

XXV

'If half a thousand cavalry pour over that horizon, we had better know what we're damn well doing,' growled Dio from his station just behind Heph, and softly enough for his Captain's ears only.

The Palatinate was formed up in battle order on the plain of Hortobágy, a hundred miles east of Budapest, and Heph thought he had never before seen light like it. An ocean of sky extended in all directions and afternoon sun bounced off helmets and breastplates, hoplons and sarissas, uninhibited by cloud or shade. He had ensured his unit drank a bellyful of water before departing camp, but the heat was not severe enough to threaten dehydration, nor the climate dry enough to induce thirst. Indeed, the grass was green and the streams they passed were full.

The light, however, glared down on them and forced their heads to bow and their eyes to scrunch. Even Boreas had lowered his neck despondently.

Although the land was featureless, the Vigiles unit that had led them from camp in an electric Jeep had halted them here in the shallowest of natural bowls. Ahead and to their left, the plain rose just enough to inhibit their views and conceal what might lie beyond. Heph guessed they were

261

facing north, but the sun was still too high to gauge with any confidence.

The klaxon would sound at three, the usual start time selected in order to accommodate the privileged Pantheon audiences in their multitude of time zones. Far to the east, it would already be evening in Tokyo and Shanghai, where the ultra-rich would be gathering for expensive dinners and private viewings. In New York they would be breakfasting on salmon and bagels and on America's west coast, the Curiate would be hauling themselves awake in the last hours of darkness to hit the caffeine and settle in front of their live feeds.

For the first time everyone had cleared their diaries beyond the usual hour, because on this occasion there would be no cessation of the conflict. No klaxon to signal an end to hostilities. The struggle might continue all afternoon. The sun might dip, the shadows extend, the light fade and still the troops might wage war. For the Caelestia had decreed that once blades were drawn, none should be sheathed until one of three Kings lay dead, his blood spilled by a sword in hand, his killer standing over him.

Heph touched his heels to Boreas' flanks and wheeled to peer down the Titan lines. His eleven riders were stationed on the left flank of the Palatinate, providing the flimsiest of screens for Nicanor's Phalanx. Beyond the forest of sarissas, Alexander had surrounded himself with his Companions, Menes to the fore. Next to them were Parmenion's peltasts, arranged loosely, javelins in hand. And when Heph squinted into the distance, one hand up to shield his eyes, he could just see the mass of the new Hellenic regiment on the far flank. Their lines weaved in unmilitary fashion and their hoplons were propped against their legs while they waited, but they looked a formidable enough number. He thought of Calder somewhere amongst them. How strange that she wore bronze today and stood once more under the same banner as him.

He could not see the Sacred Band. Perhaps they were hidden amongst the Companions or maybe they loitered in the small stand of trees that anchored the Titans' far flank.

On another day, Heph would have been impressed with the Palatinate's number. The assimilation of Valhalla instantly swelled the Titan headcount to two hundred and forty. Then the combined total of Blood Credits won by both Palatinates during the last Season had totalled over two hundred, allowing Alexander to harvest every pupil in the Titan Schola who could handle a blade, and even some from the erstwhile Valhalla Schola. Taking into account a forty Credit expenditure on the new horses and a series of two-Credit elite troop recruitments, the Palatinate still boasted nigh on four hundred blades. Nicanor's Phalanx had six additional rows of twelve, Parmenion's peltasts were almost fifty strong, and the rag-tag remnants of the Companions had been transformed into a hoplon-count of sixty.

It was a mighty force, but it dwindled in comparison with what awaited them. And every Titan knew it.

Alexander stood in the centre of his revitalised Palatinate and fear radiated from him. One King must die that day and the weight of this knowledge buckled him. He had been manic in camp, barking wild-eyed orders, but on the march out he had fallen silent and trudged solemnly after the Vigiles, displaying no more authority than the greenest Schola recruits in the back lines of the Phalanx. Two sturdy Companions carried the Lion and Star of Macedon banners. In previous Battles, when the Rules were understood and the enemy in sight, they would have driven them into the ground and protected their King with their lives. But today there was no sign of the foe. No movement for as far as the eye could see. So the banner bearers stood uncertainly, waiting for a command from their sovereign.

Alexander spotted Heph out of line and signalled furiously for him to return to his station. Heph ignored him long enough for most of the Palatinate to witness his insolence, then clucked and turned Boreas back.

Dio drew up next to him on Xanthos. 'I don't like it,' he whispered. 'If this is the Field, then where the hell is our opposition?'

For once the roar of helicopters was absent, but the sky was filled with the whir of drones zipping backwards and forwards to record every angle. Spread along the horizons were Vigiles camera teams, but this time they stood in the open backs of Jeeps.

Heph nodded towards them. 'Look at those guys. Static filming stations were used for the previous Battles, but now they're in vehicles.'

'Maybe this isn't the Field.'

'Or maybe this Field is a hell of a lot bigger than we assumed.'

In the commanders' briefing earlier, he had learned that the perimeter of the Field would be marked by lines of red flags and no Pantheon trooper should set foot outside it. Sure enough, beyond the copse of trees on the far brow of the natural bowl, flags broke the horizon like a physical fence line, but in all other directions, they were absent.

'Christ, this is good horse country,' Dio said, squinting at the unbroken grassland.

'Just what we didn't need.'

'My thoughts exactly. Where are the bogs and forests and mountains of Scotland when you need them? The sort of terrain that might break up six hundred bastard Huns. And, remind me, how many mounted troops can Mehmed boast?'

'Seventy – and they're called Sipahi. Easily differentiated from the Huns because they're big-horse heavy cavalry, wearing chainmail that hangs to their knees and helmets that rise to points. They'll carry small round shields, lances and curved scimitars. If they care for authenticity, they may even have feathers in their helms. Even their horses are armoured.'

'To be frank, Heph, I'm just planning to kill anyone who's not wearing Titan bronze.'

'You should know your enemy, my friend. It might save your life. I've been to your home. I've seen your library. I know you're as much a student of history as I am.'

In the days before the call to depart Edinburgh, Heph had shut himself off in his West End apartment and googled the hell out of the Sultanate and the Huns. He had watched every unauthorised film clip that had somehow slipped online; blurry, distant images of wild horsemen and squares of Sultanate infantry. He had peered at each charge, each melee, hitting the replay button time and again.

Then he had done a deeper dive into the known history of Mehmed's armies in the sixteenth century. He could find little on the Yaya infantry regiments, but the few illustrations he had discovered suggested they were lightly armoured with steel breastplates and carried spears and small, manoeuvrable shields. The Janissaries were the heavy infantry, bedecked like their cavalry kin in knee-length chainmail, iron wrist-guards and the same pointed helmets. The history books said they used to be Christian slaves, trained as captives and indoctrinated in the ways of the Sultan until they became Mehmed's most fervent soldiers. They had been feared throughout the Sultan's empire and now they were a force to be reckoned with in the Pantheon.

In camp during the preceding days, Heph had gathered his little cavalry and attempted to furnish them with his findings. He wanted them to be able to recognise the different units of their opponents and to understand their fighting strengths. They listened with rapt attention, but he was dubious that he had been a good enough teacher.

The organisation of the Huns, he admitted, was altogether more indecipherable. They all wore black robes, thick fur hats and boots and were minimally armoured. It was rumoured that the men amongst them despised facial hair and would scratch or burn their cheeks to hinder growth. Heph suspected this was just an online story, stirred up by the obsessives on the fan-sites who yearned for good old Pantheon villains, but it made him uneasy nonetheless.

Like his new cavalry, the Huns rode with no stirrups and only cloth saddles, but they had the benefit of years of training behind them, and their mounts were tough little steppe ponies, agile and well-balanced. Battle tactics constituted a howling, screaming, lightning-fast chaos, but trawls through more Pantheon fan-sites revealed that

Attila's Palatinate was divided into three sections, based loosely on the concept of two horns surrounding an enemy, before a heavy attack punched through the centre.

Uptar commanded the First Horn, which also formed Attila's personal guard – his most loyal troops. Ellac led the Second Horn, armed with curved composite bows. Heph remembered his visit to Mongolia to witness the skills of Genghis' mounted archers and he feared Ellac's Second Horn would be just as proficient. He imagined them swirling five hundred yards beyond reach, loosing lethal volleys of arrows, then galloping away while twisting and sending reverse parting flights into the Titan lines.

And then there was Bleda, a name that had only recently grown infamous amongst online fans after she allegedly accused her commander of misconduct and oversaw his long, hideous death, along with four of his loyalists, impaled on stakes driven into the soil of Hortobágy. Now she was captain of Attila's Black Cloaks, the most feared and wildest troops in the whole Pantheon. They would come with spears and curved blades, brandishing ropes to lasso hapless foe and drag them away. No one knew what happened to those unfortunate enough to be ensnared like this, but many of the Huns wore human skulls as their face masks.

It was little wonder that in classrooms, chatrooms, staffrooms and coffee houses across the world, the same phrase was repeated: *Win or die, but don't ever get captured by the Black Cloaks.*

A shout broke Heph from his thoughts.

The Heavies had spotted movement and arms began

to point. He followed their fingers and saw three riders approaching from the horizon at a slow trot.

'What have we here?' growled Dio and he glanced back at the Companion Cavalry arranged in column. Lenore and Spyro met his eyes. Zephyr glowered behind his helmet, but the newbies shifted nervously and strained to make out the approaching riders.

'Huns,' said Heph. 'The horses are too short and stocky to be anything else.' He squinted hard into the light. 'One of them's carrying the Crowned Eagle banner. My god, I think this could be Attila coming.'

'Finally. I was starting to think we'd have to start without them. So where's his wild army?'

Heph was silent, examining the empty grassland beyond. No rising dust. No sparkle of sun on blades. 'I don't think he's bringing his troops.'

'Then what the hell does he want?'

'Maybe it's a tradition in these parts. Some sort of Kingly pow-wow before it all kicks off.'

A commotion was breaking out down the line near the Titan flags as those around Alexander came to the same conclusion.

'I spy more company,' said Dio, dragging Heph's attention back to the horizon. Sure enough, another group of three riders had appeared to the east and approached at the same steady pace. 'Still think he's not bringing his troops?'

Heph raised his hand to shield his eyes from the glare. 'I already said you should know your enemy. Those are big beasts and they sure aren't carrying Huns.'

Shouts from along the line forced him to turn. Alexander was jabbing a thumb at him and hollering.

'You better see what his highness wants,' said Dio, but Heph was already encouraging Boreas to move.

He trotted along the front of the Phalanx, inclining his head to Nicanor as he passed.

'A horse!' shouted Alexander when Heph was in earshot.

'My lord?'

The King was crimson and sweating beneath his ornate armour. 'You think I'm going to trudge out there and address those bastards on foot? I am the Lion of Macedon. I am their equal.'

Heph shifted his weight and waved for Dio to join them.

'Lend him Xanthos,' he said quietly once Dio was beside him.

'You're kidding me.'

'Just for this. Nothing's going to happen.'

With an expression like thunder, Dio dropped from the broad back of Xanthos, placed his mouth against the beast's ear and whispered words of reassurance, then led him resentfully to the King.

'Have you ridden before, my lord?' asked Heph.

'Damn you! Just get me on the thing.'

Alexander flung an impatient arm over Xanthos' spine and grabbed at his mane.

'My lord!' Dio almost manhandled his King away from the horse and cupped his hands. 'Give me your left foot.'

Somehow, with much cursing and struggling and a helping pull from Menes on the other side, they got Alexander's bulk mounted and the King sat rigid, gripping the rein and gawping.

Heph eased Boreas forward and took hold of Xanthos' noseband. 'I'll lead you, my lord?'

Alexander nodded petulantly, then snapped, 'Agape, where are you?'

The Captain of the Sacred Band appeared from nowhere amongst the Companion lines.

'You come too. Show them you are on this Field.'

So the little party moved cautiously out from the lines. Heph kept a firm hand on Xanthos and walked Boreas at a slow pace.

Just this once, Alexander's dignity was Heph's priority. In front of the rival Kings and every watching Titan, he dared not risk his King falling on his fat arse.

Agape paced beside them, her expression hidden inside her helmet, but her blue cloak, blue plume and blue hair would remind the rival Kings that Alexander could call upon this most accomplished of warriors.

The three groups converged and stopped within earshot, a ring of land between them no wider than the centre circle on a football pitch. Nine figures on the expanse of Hortobágy Plain, watched by four hundred pairs of Titan eyes and every available drone.

It was Mehmed who spoke first. 'My lord,' he said with grace, and inclined his head to Attila. 'Once more our Palatinates join on a Field of Battle.'

Attila responded by leaning over and spitting copiously into the grass.

Mehmed ignored the gesture and turned his attention to Alexander. 'Welcome too, my lord.' He placed his hand against his mailed chest and dipped his head. 'We have waited many Seasons to meet you properly.'

Heph was impressed with the man. His tone was courteous, his bearing regal. As was customary, the upper half of his face was covered by a gilt-silver mask, but his eyes danced and his teeth dazzled beneath a luxuriant moustache. Precious stones hung from his silver mail and a single huge sapphire was embedded in the centre of his spiked helmet. He sat upon a giant chestnut stallion wearing its own coat of silver mail, and behind him one of his Sipahi commanders held the Golden Crescent banner aloft.

'Where are your troops?' Alexander demanded belligerently and, although Mehmed's expression faltered in surprise, he recovered and smiled again, though now with no warmth.

'They are here and keen to make your acquaintance.'

'You demand to know where his troops are?' Attila interrupted in angry, heavily accented English. 'Who are you to speak like that? You, who comes to my country uninvited and brings four hundred foot-soldiers in sandals.'

He leaned and spat again without removing his glare from Alexander. He was wearing head-to-toe black, save for a leather breastplate over a fur robe that looked voluminous on his thin shoulders. The plate was scratched and gouged, his boots caked in dust and his hair lank and greasy where it fell from his fur hat. Beneath him was a shaggy, unkept little pony with a mane so long that it covered one eye, but the creature looked muscled and fit. From Attila's saddle-cloth hung what Heph hoped were dried vermin, but he feared might be human scalps. An aroma rose from these shreds of flesh and from the horse and the man himself that was deep, musky and alarmingly unpleasant. Worst of all, the King's face was covered by the front half of a human skull, its lower jaw absent so his mouth and chin were visible. His sun-darkened flesh was scored with livid white scars and

Heph remembered the rumours about the Hun tradition of cutting and burning their faces to destroy their beards.

He remembered too all those childhood days when he and his mates would talk in thrilled voices about the Pantheon. Not just the Vikings and Titans of their home city, but also the wonders of the further flung Palatinates, those figures who were just fleeting visions, snippets of legend, and none more so than the terrifying tales of Attila, Scourge of God, the demon of the Pantheon. Now he sat astride his pony just yards from Heph and the air almost crackled with violence.

'Uninvited?' fumed Alexander. 'I don't need an invitation. I'm here because I've already killed a King and I will kill another before the day is out!'

They were good words, if they had not been spoken by a fat scarlet man quite obviously desperate to stop himself sliding from his horse.

Mehmed was motionless, watching Alexander. Attila raised a bony hand and pointed at the Titan. 'I will make you eat those words. I will stuff them down your throat even as you choke on your lifeblood beneath my boot.'

Alexander took a breath and prepared another barrage, but Mehmed interjected. 'My lords, I did not come to trade insults.'

There was silence and Heph became aware of the unwavering attention of another rider to his left. He flicked a rapid glance. It was a woman with long, dark hair and skin almost as pale as the skull covering her upper face, and he guessed instantly that this must be Bleda.

She saw his furtive peek and, to his surprise, in the presence of the Kings, she had the audacity to speak.

'Are you the King Killer?' she asked him in cold tones.

Alexander scowled, but waited for Heph to respond.

'I don't recognise that title,' said Heph, bringing his gaze to bear on the woman. 'I am Hephaestion, Captain of Companion Cavalry in the Palatinate of the Lion of Macedon.'

For once, Alexander murmured his approval and even Mehmed dipped his head respectfully, but Bleda sat unmoved, her eyes tracking every line of Heph's helmeted head.

Attila chuckled darkly. 'I think the commander of my Black Cloaks wants a new skull mask.'

At this, Bleda pulled back her lips in a rictus grin and Heph physically jolted at the sight of her teeth filed into predator fangs.

He forced his eyes away and tried to gather himself.

Bleda's grin faded, but as she removed her gaze, she met the unwavering eyes of Agape. If anything passed between them – a challenge, an insult, a message – it was too subtle for the men to notice.

'My lords,' said Mehmed with a sigh. 'I fear we are achieving little. I came here to meet you both, to look you in the eyes and to wish upon you a fair fight. One of us must die today. It is decreed. Just as this sun will fall over the land and bleed red as it sets, so one of us must also fall and bleed our life into the soil.'

'And what if it is you that dies, Mehmed?' snarled Attila. 'What if the Horns of Uptar and Ellac break through your Janissaries this time? Are you ready to meet your fate?'

Mehmed touched his mailed chest once more. 'I am a Pantheon King and I accept the Rules set by the Caelestia.'

Attila laughed at this, though he must know his master,

Ördög, would be watching the feeds with undivided attention. Indeed, the hum of the drones gathered above was almost too invasive. In a moment of clarity, Heph realised what an incredible scene this must be for the watching audience. Three Palatinates, three Kings gathered in a circle, speaking words, laying challenges, moments before the greatest Battle in the history of the Pantheon.

'We do not stop until one of us is dead,' said Mehmed for the benefit of the cameras.

'Until one of us is dead,' repeated Attila.

'Only with a blade in hand,' added Mehmed. 'If one of us is felled by a projectile, it does not count and the struggle must continue. Even nightfall cannot bring an end to it. Is that understood?'

Alexander nodded curtly and Attila once more relieved himself of a copious amount of saliva.

'Pray that one of you dies soon,' he growled. 'You will scream for your mothers if my Black Cloaks come for you in the dark.'

There was nothing else to be said. The hour was upon them. The circle broke. Attila, Bleda and the Hun banner-bearer thundered back across the grass in a series of whoops. Mehmed's retinue trotted to the horizon and disappeared.

Heph was so wrapped up in contemplating the woman who wanted to wear his skull that his thoughts were only broken when Alexander exploded that he was going too fast and the Lion of Macedon almost slipped sideways in a heap right in front of his own troops.

When the man's feet were finally back on earth and Xanthos had been returned to an indignant Dio, Agape came to Heph and offered her hand. 'It begins, Hephaestion.

What we do this day will live long in the annals of the Pantheon.'

He gripped her hand and nodded, his eyes drifting over her shoulder to the Hellenic Regiment and his mind filled with Calder. 'Watch over Valhalla,' he murmured to Agape. 'We need them on our side.'

She could have reprimanded him for the use of that name, but didn't.

Nicanor and Parmenion and even Menes came forward and shook hands too. Then the commanders returned to their units and the klaxon shrieked across the plain.

Conflict was upon them.

XXVI

Nothing happened. The blare of the klaxon faded, the drones whirred and the plain extended before them. Boreas shook his mane and stomped a hoof. Someone coughed.

'What the hell happens now?' murmured Dio.

A rumble of unease rose from the regiments. Alexander had retreated to his banners deep within the protective cordon of his Companions and was looking around, waiting for someone else to take the initiative.

'I guess it's up to us,' said Heph. 'Let's have a look.'

He twitched Boreas forward. Dio waved an arm and the rest of the Companion Cavalry followed. The little column eased up the gentle gradient to their left and trotted along the rim to a broad summit. The grassland swept away in soft undulations, decorated with occasional copses of woodland. A river slithered its way to the east, spanned by a couple of bridges and fringed with reedbeds. Larger hills jostled on the far horizon and perhaps there were houses and roads and normal modernity, but on the plain itself there was no human life.

'That's the western perimeter,' said Dio, pointing to a distant line of red flags running on the left until they disappeared in a fold of land. Of the far northern perimeter, there was no sign. 'Must be at least ten square miles.'

'Probably more.' Heph was gauging directions and thinking about the departure of the Kings. 'Mehmed went that way,' he mused, pointing northeast to the mountains, 'and Attila over there.' He indicated the distant dip where the western flags disappeared. 'If the Field is a rectangle and we're standing along the southern base, then I think the foe are gathered in the two far corners.'

'A long way,' commented Dio.

'Not on horseback.'

Heph was studying the terrain. The lower areas of grassland formed natural channels for rapid movement, while the little rises created optimal vantage points. A sporadic column of woodland copses ran from where the Hellenes were currently stationed, with the river half a mile beyond.

Spyro was squinting at the perimeter flags. 'There's a lot of room on the flanks. They could come up either side and encircle us if we don't keep our backs to the southern edge.'

'Agreed,' replied Heph. 'But we need to get out of that bowl. We can't see anything down there.' He swung round and jerked his javelin towards Roxana and Thales. 'Tell the King to bring the lines forward to the higher ground. Make sure the Hellenes stay locked against the trees.' The pair made to depart, then Heph had a further thought. 'Inform the King of the river and the two bridges. If we can get to the nearest one, it's just possible we can hold it and force the foe to funnel over. Might give an advantage.'

Roxana saluted with a raised javelin and they cantered down the slope. The Companion lines opened to let them through to Alexander. After a long pause, the King could be seen gesticulating and then gradually, like a beast slowly waking, the Titan lines spasmed, tightened and moved forward.

'Company,' warned Dio, snapping Heph's attention back to the skyline. A group of horsemen had appeared on a distant knoll near the north-western corner. 'Huns?'

'Most likely,' said Heph. 'It's the direction Attila took.'

'They'll be able to see our units advancing.'

'Indeed. And during the pow-wow, he and Mehmed will have been studying our formations. It wasn't by chance that they ensured the meeting took place so close to our position.'

'Stupid.' Dio shook his head.

'Too late to worry about it now.'

The Phalanx was moving ponderously and the rest of the Palatinate was strung out towards the trees. They came up the rise and could at last also see the wider horizons, but the advance had opened gaps between the regiments. Heph watched them with an uneasy frown. These Titans did not yet understand cavalry warfare. They saw no threat in the gaps.

'Here they come,' said Spyro tensely.

Heph turned back north and, sure enough, a new mass of horsemen were rounding the knoll on which sat the Hun scouts and were cantering fast into the open lands in front of the Titan advance.

For a moment the Companion Cavalry sat in awed silence. The approaching mass might only be a fraction of Attila's forces, but it was still a sight none of them had ever witnessed. A hundred and fifty mounted warriors, sheathed in black, glinting with iron and steel, a growing thunder of hooves, eating up the grassland, and the first wild cries.

'The Black Cloaks?' asked Dio breathlessly.

'More likely Ellac's Second Horn. Soften us up with arrows first.' Heph's eyes were back on Alexander. 'Christ, he's exposed down there. Menes has his troops too loose. We've got to get Alexander inside the Phalanx, then close it up with a proper Companion shield line. Follow me.'

'We're retreating?' Spyro shouted as Heph was turning Boreas.

'We'll be overrun if we stay here. We have to bide our time.'

'But—'

'Get moving. Our moment will come.'

They tore down the slope. Heph slowed as he approached Nicanor. 'Cavalry coming. Get into spear formation. We'll bring the King inside.'

He didn't wait to listen to Nicanor bellowing commands, but he knew sarissas would be levelling and the outer ranks dropping one step behind, while those inside moved outwards to create a hollowed spear with Nicanor himself at the point. Menes waved for his Companion lines to open enough to permit Heph's unit through to the King.

'My lord, cavalry moving fast towards us. We need to get you inside Nicanor's phalanx.'

'I'm staying here.'

'You're not safe here, my lord. There's a hundred and fifty horsemen about to hit this spot.'

That stopped Alexander's protests. His mouth opened and his jowls wobbled, then he saw the sense and allowed

Heph to lead him unceremoniously out of the back of the Companions and towards the open rear of the Phalanx.

For a desperate moment, everything was chaos. Heph twisted round and could see the horde of enemy riders accelerating towards them, an exultant cry on their lips as they spotted the disarray.

'Dio!' he yelled. 'Tell Menes to follow. Get his troops round the back of the Phalanx, in a shield line to defend the rear. Zephyr! Halt Nicanor. What the hell's he doing still marching forward. We need stationary defence.'

Zephyr shot off; Dio too.

Beyond the Companions, Heph could just see Parmenion's peltasts in a swirling panic, but it was too late to help. On the far flank the Hellenes had forsaken a shield line and were running for the trees.

'Christ,' hissed Heph and had to forcibly stop himself from grabbing Alexander's cloak and literally dragging him into the Phalanx.

At last he had the King between the twin arms of Nicanor's formation, which was finally halting and bracing sarissas. Menes, thankfully, understood the plan and had not questioned Dio's orders. The Companions came loping around to the rear of the Phalanx and began tightening into line.

'Get inside!' Heph yelled to his cavalry. 'All of you in.'

There was thunder in the earth and the shriek of war in the air.

'Get inside! Here they come!'

His unit was in. Zephyr too. Dio almost didn't make it, but forced Xanthos through the hoplites just as they were sealing shut the spear. The Hellenes were near the trees and

Parmenion was exhorting his peltasts to follow. Only the gods knew where Agape and her Band were.

Horsemen flowed around the Titans like an unstoppable river of lava and the sky was filled with deadly iron-tipped shafts.

'Shields!' screamed Heph, but his voice was drowned out.

Ellac was upon them.

The Hellenic regiment was commanded by a strong grey-haired female Dekarchos selected by Menes. She was a decent officer and the Hellenes had endured her orders in camp, but with the horse warriors of the Scourge of God pouring towards them, they listened only to one natural leader.

It was Calder who took the decision to break formation. The moment she saw the massed cavalry accelerating into a full charge, she knew the Hellenes could never stand their ground. She pushed through the forward ranks with her dory spear held high and the once proud warriors of the Horde strained to see her.

'Get back in position,' the Dekarchos shouted furiously, but Calder ignored her.

'Valhalla!' she yelled. 'Get into the trees.'

She began to run and the ranks broke with her and suddenly it was a race of life and death. The Huns spied vulnerable backs and redoubled their howls as they galloped to get within bow shot.

The Dekarchos cursed in shock as her regiment disintegrated, then started to run as well. The first arrow took her in the small of her back. The power of a composite bow discharged the missile at such velocity that it broke through her bronze cuirass as though it were tin and she fell dead to the ground, unmourned and unnoticed by her fleeing soldiers.

Stigr and Ake were in the lead and almost into the woods. Arrows rained down, thunking into the ground, bouncing off helmets, burying into bronze and linen, flesh and bone. Calder's heart pounded in her mouth; her lungs burned white hot. *Don't stumble. Don't go down.*

Around her, friends and comrades were flailing as shafts hit, but she could not distinguish individuals in their strange new armour and there was no time to stop and help. The trees beckoned. Something hit her hoplon so hard that it spun her, and for an instant she was gawping at a wall of skull-faced riders no more than thirty metres behind, every arm extended with a curved bow, ponies snorting and grimacing with the effort. Somehow she kept on her feet, righted herself and ran again.

The trees came to her. Just a small copse, barely any protection, but something physical to break the wave of cavalry. The Hellenes tore into the wood and flattened themselves against trunks. Arrows whammed in an incessant storm, but the Huns knew better than to keep coming.

'Shields up, spears!' Calder shouted.

Hoplons were wedged against trees and spears created a bristling wall between each trunk.

Seemingly without a word of command, the horsemen wheeled like a terrifying flock of starlings and galloped along the edge of the wood, still loosing arrows with deadly accuracy. Any chink of exposed flesh was targeted. Around Calder, troops were hit in necks, arms, legs, even in the small gap between their cheek protectors. But the killing was weakening. The Huns dared not come into the trees. Their line would have to break around the trunks and infantry could reach up and tear them from their mounts.

Calder pressed herself against the aromatic trunk of an elm and stared around. Bjarke was there, peering back and nodding respect at the clarity of her command. Many were down, but her foresight had saved most from annihilation.

She realised their pursuers were just an offshoot of Ellac's Second Horn and the majority were galloping in a giant, surging circle around the Phalanx. For long moments she simply watched the carnage. After the terror of the chase, her mind was numbed. She could think of nothing more than staying beside her tree and holding on to it for dear life. Then she thought she spotted the distant plumes of the Companion Cavalry in the heart of the storm and a vision rose in her. Of Tyler. Of her friend.

The Hun pack that had been chasing the Hellenes numbered about sixty and were now themselves spreading into a sinuous line and bending around the far end of the copse in an attempt to surround their prey and maintain a constant rain of death.

Shouts arose near Calder and her mind came back. She realised Parmenion's fifty peltasts were still exposed on the plain. Somehow, miraculously, the Huns had missed them and now they too were running for the trees. The Hellenes began to cheer. For the past twenty seasons, these Titans might have been their foe, but they were a damn sight more worthy of their allegiance than the wild devils on their steppe ponies.

Calder yelled her encouragement, for this was a small

hope amongst the carnage. The Huns were turning their mounts and spotting the new prey, but they were at the other end of the woodland and they took precious moments changing direction and gathering speed. The peltasts ran for their lives. Arrows curved through the sky and began hammering into bronze. Titans fell, some dead weights, others flailing and crawling. The Huns came galloping back past the sheltering Hellenes, but their attention was fixed on the troopers in the open.

On angry impulse, Calder leapt from behind her tree and ran out of the woodland. She bounded five paces and thrust her spear into a black-clad Hun, whose torso was exposed as he raised his bow for another shot at the peltasts. Cheers blossomed behind her and more Hellenes raced out and stabbed at the passing riders. If the Huns had held swords, they could have cut their attackers down, but their blades were sheathed in their belts and their bows were useless in such close quarters.

In moments, the riders were past, but the Hellenes had brought down six and, more importantly, it had stalled the charging horses enough to allow most of the peltasts to reach the trees.

'Back,' hollered Calder, even as one of the Hellenes stepped too far into the passing storm and was trampled under hooves.

The rest realised their advantage had dissipated and they hurled themselves back to the safety of the elms.

The Huns were furious that their prey had escaped. Some slowed their ponies beside wounded peltasts and tried to grab them and drag them away.

'Bastards,' spluttered Bjarke, and Calder had to restrain him from charging into the open again.

But most of the Huns had been shaken by the Hellenes' sudden attack and they took their ponies far enough from the trees to continue an arrow-storm beyond the reach of Hellenic dories.

A Titan with ornate silver fish-scales came crawling to Calder and nodded his thanks.

'We are in your debt,' said Parmenion.

'Don't thank us,' spat Bjarke. 'You're just the lesser of two evils.'

'Nevertheless,' said Parmenion evenly. 'I do thank you.'

Bjarke growled and returned his attention to the swirling mass around the Phalanx. 'If those bastards keep up this rate of fire, your Titans are doomed.'

'The Huns are light cavalry. Lethal against disorganised infantry, but they won't break through Nicanor's sarissas.'

'And surely they'll run out of arrows soon,' said Ingvar hopefully from a nearby trunk.

Bjarke shook his head. 'If so, Attila can replace them with his First Horn and Black Cloaks, while they replenish.'

A new voice spoke up, nasal and frightened. It was Ulf, helmet lost, crouching behind his hoplon a few yards away. 'And where's Mehmed?'

'His infantry will take longer to get here,' said Parmenion dismissively.

'But his cavalry won't.'

'He'll keep his cavalry as close protection for his infantry.'

'That's not what I've seen,' Ulf countered, but drifted into quiet.

'Go on,' encouraged Ingvar. 'Tell us what you know.'

'I've watched footage of previous Battles and read commentaries. Mehmed stays within the walls of his infantry, but he sends his Sipahi horsemen wide, keeps them on the flanks out of sight, so that Attila can't throw everything he's got at the infantry because he has to keep some of his horsemen back to counter the Sipahi.'

'So what's you point?' demanded Parmenion.

'My point is that Mehmed's cavalry is heavy armoured horse. If they come up the flank this time, they can smash through your precious Phalanx and kill your King. And then it'll all be over.'

No one spoke. Parmenion examined Ulf, then turned back to the struggle, then finally shifted his gaze to Calder. 'Raven,' he said quietly, as though he had already accepted her authority in his Palatinate. 'Housecarl.'

This drew looks from all those within earshot.

'What do we do?'

Calder did not reply. All this time, she had been hunched with her back against the elm, looking in the opposite direction towards the river and the reedbeds, which ran lazily north.

'Housecarl?'

They waited on her words.

Finally, she spoke.

'We go on the offensive.'

XXVII

S omehow the Phalanx was holding.
But the endless rain of arrows looping over Nicanor's troops meant the presumed safe ground inside the walls of sarissas was the worst place to be.

Heph crouched on Boreas with his shield raised overhead, but he could provide no protection for his horse other than countless prayers, which he sent spiralling up to the heavens. Every missile that landed nearby made Heph's heart hammer at the thought that the next one could pierce Boreas. He had wondered about dismounting and lying the horse down, but that would make the target even larger. He tried to hold his hoplon over Boreas' head, but it was a long stretch and removed any protection from his own body. All he could do was stand his stallion still and hope they could come through this together unscathed.

The rest of the Companion Cavalry had reached a similar conclusion. They had pulled apart to avoid presenting a mass of horseflesh for the Huns to target, but all just stayed atop their mounts, heads down, shoulders slumped and hoplons held above them.

Alexander was crouching in the midst of his closest

Companion Bodyguards and banner-bearers, their hoplons forming a bronze shell over the King.

He glared at Heph. 'What are you doing, you heathen coward? Get out there and *fight* those bastards! That's what you're here for.'

'We can't fight cavalry of that number,' Heph snapped. 'We'd be annihilated and you'd be in even deeper shit.'

'Well do something! Don't just sit there – get me out of this mess!'

Even as the King protested, Heph heard a grunt of pain. Zephyr had been hit. A shaft had thumped into his bronze cuirass and sunk its iron head into his ribs just below his collarbone. A delicate ring of scarlet squeezed out around the arrow and ran down his armour in a single, artful line.

'Zephyr!' shouted Spyro.

'I'm okay,' the older man waved back, but his shield-arm dropped.

There was a shriek of animal pain. A shaft was embedded in Roxana's stallion and the animal bucked in terror and slammed her to the ground. She rolled from its pounding hooves, heaved herself upright and tried to grab the projectile, but there was no way she could get a proper grip when her mount was wheeling and shaking. Its rump thumped her as it spun and she fell again with a sharp cry, then it cantered along the inside of the Phalanx perimeter, snorting and stamping, until it finally shouldered through the lines and broke for the open plain.

Heph guided Boreas alongside the fallen rider and leaned down to help her up.

'I'm okay.' She was winded and shaken, but otherwise uninjured.

'We're taking a beating,' Dio yelled from across the space. 'We've got to do something.'

Heph looked around. The King was still cursing at him, but it was a distraction he didn't need and he let it wash over him. Menes had the Companions tight along the rear of the Phalanx, closing up the bottom of the spear formation. Nicanor stood tall at the very point and roared at his troops to hold their position. The long sarissas were unbloodied because Ellac's troops were content to do their killing from a distance. Heph suspected that even if Attila sent his Black Cloaks or First Horn with blades bared, they would not break through Nicanor's Heavies.

He tapped his heels and urged Boreas closer to where Nicanor stood, then dismounted and pushed his way between the Heavies.

'Hephaestion!' exclaimed the big Colonel when Heph's hand on his shoulder turned him.

'We're sitting ducks. Can you move without breaking formation?'

'Aye, as long as Menes can keep his boys and girls clamped across our arses, or we'll have the bastards pouring in from behind. What's your plan?'

'Get us to the trees.'

Nicanor glanced over to the small woodland where Parmenion was holding out. 'Not big enough to get us all under there.'

'Just the King's retinue and my Cavalry. Can your Heavies stay out and weather this storm?'

'If this is all Attila's got, then aye.'

'Over to you then, Colonel.'

'Make sure Menes knows the plan.'

'I will.'

'You stay,' Calder said to Parmenion, who crouched next to her. 'Keep them occupied.'

The contingent of Huns who had been giving them their undivided attention since the Hellenes had reached the safety of the trees, were strung out in a long line, galloping back and forth along the edge of the wood and firing deadly shafts between the trunks.

'They'll realise soon enough,' warned Parmenion.

'Just give us a few minutes.'

'That I will. Good hunting.' He watched her slink back through the trees to where her Hellenes knelt on the other edge of the wood. It was quieter there, all except a handful of drones and a unit of Vigiles filming from the back of a truck. The river was fifty yards away across open ground, its banks and shrubs and reeds beckoning.

Parmenion's forty peltasts locked shields against every trunk to block their enemy's view and to give an impression of greater numbers. As the horsemen swept past once more, he led his troops from cover and they flung their javelins. Horses reared. Riders fell. Cohesion was lost. Some steered their mounts away from the trees. Others tried to rein the pace of their ponies and reach for their blades. Parmenion drew his own sword and stabbed the nearest rider in the thigh. The woman was trying to fire her bow point blank at him, but he grabbed it and hauled her down, then stabbed her twice through her leather breastplate.

'Retreat!' he yelled above the bedlam.

They could not hope to give the Huns a proper fight. In

moments, the enemy would re-organise and be on them, then they would cut the Titans to shreds.

But the peltasts had done enough. They had distracted the foe and now they ran once more for cover.

The moment Parmenion attacked, a hundred and forty Hellenes surged out of the trees on the other side and followed Calder down to the river. They pushed through the shrubs and dropped over the bank into reeds, then tightened around her and waited for orders.

The Huns gave cry when they saw the Titan Phalanx finally shake itself awake and begin to move towards the trees. They circled even more wildly, each warrior releasing an arrow, drawing another and firing again. Nicanor shouted orders and his Heavies endured; faces down, scalloped shields tied to their left shoulders, sarissas held firm and knees bent to find the best purchase on the ground beneath their boots. Step by step the Titans walked and the Huns could do little about it except scream louder and mass their horses around this armoured behemoth.

Heph felt a sharp sting as he held his shield aloft and was surprised to see blood running from his exposed bicep into the upturned sleeve of his tunic. An arrow must have sliced him so finely that he barely felt the impact.

'You okay?' checked Dio, trotting over and spying the wound.

Heph nodded.

'You have a plan?'

Heph was about to answer when his attention was caught by movement up on the same rise his cavalry had first used to spy out the land. Dio saw his expression and wheeled Xanthos around, then whistled grimly. 'I was beginning to wonder where the rest of them were.'

Lined along the rim of the bowl were almost three hundred new Huns. Each carried a spear and a leather shield, and they sat their horses and watched the scene from behind impassive skull masks.

'Uptar's First Horn or Bleda's Black Cloaks?' Dio asked.

'Got to be Bleda. Only she commands that number.'

Shouts had gone up from the Titan lines as they saw the new threat, but the Black Cloaks showed no sign of movement.

'What are the bastards waiting for?' growled Dio. 'Think they'll try to smash us?'

Heph shook his helmet slowly. 'They're not heavy enough to take our lines and they know it. Attila's probably holding them back until he knows where Mehmed's cavalry is. If he permits Bleda to engage and then the Sipahi turn up, the Huns are going to be in big trouble. And also...'

'And also what?'

'Nothing.'

'Don't keep it to yourself.'

Heph pursed his lips thoughtfully. 'Just a hunch. Something in the way Bleda spoke to me. I think she sees Alexander's head as the second prize. What she really wants... is us.'

Dio peered at him above his helm's cheek protectors. 'The Companion Cavalry? Why? We're eleven souls. Nothing to her.'

'We're the King Killer Cavalry and she knows it. What greater fame than to take down the man who killed a King?'

Dio studied the massed horse troops. 'Well, she can't get us in here.'

'So she'll wait.'

The Titan infantry was making good ground and Dio signalled to the rest of their little cavalry unit to keep moving. Even as they responded, Zephyr's grip suddenly loosened on his rein and he fell, heavy as a stone, the arrow still protruding from his shoulder and the blood still just a single rivulet painting the front of his cuirass.

Spyro thundered over and leapt from his horse. He knelt beside his fallen comrade and pulled off Zephyr's helmet, then bent his head close to the other man's face. After a few moments he looked to Heph and his jaw was slack with shock. 'He's dead.'

Dio swore and spurred Xanthos across to the pair, but the big horse's momentum jolted and a despairing scream broke from its jaws. An arrow was buried in the stallion's chest, so deep there was only a few inches of ash and feathers exposed. Xanthos went down, knees buckling, hind quarters giving way. Dio tried to jump free, but his right ankle jammed between the ground and the creature's ribs, and he was trapped.

'Xanthos!' he cried and stretched himself towards his mount's terrified eyes. 'Xanthos, my beauty.'

The horse rolled and beat his hooves in the air. The movement released Dio's ankle and he scrabbled clear, then crawled back to his precious mount and flung his arms around the beast's neck. He reached for the arrow, but Heph arrived and jumped from Boreas.

'No,' he shouted and grabbed Dio's wrist. 'Don't extract it.'

'Get away, you bastard.' Dio wrenched Heph's arm away in fury, but he didn't attempt to clasp the arrow again. Instead he wrapped himself around Xanthos' head and tried to calm him. 'There, my beauty. Stay still; we'll sort you.'

Dio's face stretched livid in grief.

Around them, the Phalanx was still walking and the perimeter of Heavies closed on them.

Heph gripped his friend's shoulder. 'We have to move.'

'Get lost, Heph. I'm not leaving him.'

A few yards away, Spyro was dragging Zephyr's corpse and Lenore had dismounted and was slapping at him. 'Leave him, you idiot. He's dead. You can't do anything.'

The boots of the Heavies approached.

'Diogenes!' Heph shouted. 'Get up!'

Dio ignored him and held the horse, stroking its mane and whispering reassurance. The beast was snorting and still beating the air with its hooves, but the movements were slackening.

Heph grabbed at his friend's shoulder. 'Get up. You stay and the Huns will kill you in sight of us all.'

Dio released Xanthos and sprang to his feet, ready to punch his Captain's head from his shoulders. 'I'm not leaving him.'

'Yes, you are, you fool,' Heph swore back, then swung his attention towards the other group. 'Spyro, get on your goddamn horse!'

Spyro glanced at him blackly, but Lenore used the moment to hit him hard on the shoulder.

'You heard the Captain.'

He focused on her, then looked over the helmets of the advancing Heavies at the waiting Huns. His shoulders slumped and he released Zephyr's wrists, nodded once to his fallen comrade, then followed Lenore to the horses.

Heph returned his attention to Dio, who was once more slumped next to his dying mount. The Phalanx perimeter was upon them and the Heavies opened up to step around horse and rider.

Heph drew his sword and leaped beside Dio.

'What are you doing?' Dio managed to demand between his gasps.

'Dying with you.'

The Heavies passed them and the land opened up and all that was in front of them were a hundred mounted Hun archers. They howled as they spied the huddled group and chivvied their horses towards them.

'Heph, you bastard,' said Dio, finally releasing Xanthos and rising to his feet. 'Get back.'

'Not without you. We die together.'

Dio's body juddered in grief as he cursed, then he drew his own blade. 'I can't abandon him,' he said plaintively to his Captain.

'You abandon him or we die. Your choice.'

Dio howled, then grabbed Heph and propelled him towards the retreating Phalanx. They left Xanthos still squirming in the dust and barged back through the Heavies.

'Take Zephyr's horse,' Heph ordered and Dio was beyond argument now.

They both mounted and Dio paused just long enough to see his beloved stallion surrounded by a jostling crowd of Huns. He caught a final glimpse of the regal head raised to the sky and then Xanthos was gone.

The little cavalry trotted across the ground inside the

Phalanx and could see that the front arm of Heavies was almost at the woods, but another mass of forty Huns was blocking the way and firing point blank into the Titan lines. The Phalanx stalled, hunkering back from the fusillade.

Then there was a blur of movement from the trees. Blue cloaks, blue plumes. The Sacred Band sprinted into the midst of the enemy and leapt at the backs of the riders. Ellac's archers were taken by total surprise as these bronze-clad warrior gods launched themselves onto their ponies, and blades cut at Hun throats, stabbed into Hun spines, chopped at Hun legs. The Heavies arrived and jabbed their sarissas at exposed pony flesh and everything descended into a seething, frenzied melee.

In moments, it was over. Those Huns who could still ride kicked their mounts into frantic escape and galloped for the distant grassland.

The way ahead was open for the Titans. The Sacred Band allowed the Phalanx to weave through them and then Nicanor halted his troops with a huge bellow just as they reached the first trees. The entire formation ground to a halt.

Heph steered Boreas towards the King.

'Out!' he shouted and urged the Bodyguard to propel Alexander through the opening line of Heavies and into the trees. The King complied without comment, his face sheened with sweat beneath his helmet.

'You too,' Heph signalled towards Menes and his sixty Companions, who had held the rear of the Phalanx with true grit. They needed no further encouragement to race for the trees.

Menes paused beside Boreas. 'What next?'

'No idea. Getting the King to the trees was the entirety of my plan.'

Menes grimaced, but nodded. 'Well, it worked, Captain.'

He jogged towards the wood, while Heph urged his own riders to do likewise.

Dio was sullen beneath his helmet, his jaw damp with tears. Spyro too was grim. Roxana was on foot, her horse running wildly across the plain with an arrow still embedded in its hind quarters. Heph saw tall Melitta had a wound above one knee. She had found an opportunity to remove the missile and bind the puncture, but her cloth was now stained crimson. She gave him a hard glance, daring him to comment, for once she had been a sarissa maiden and she was damned if she would submit to pain.

Nicanor busied himself closing his Phalanx into its usual wedge formation and lining them so that their sarissas protected the length of the treeline. The Huns could whoop and cry and swirl, but no amount of arrows was going to get them past his troops.

Lenore trotted to Heph. 'Well done,' she said quietly.

'Indeed,' he replied, his eyes on the distant rise where the Black Cloaks had not moved.

Amidst the mayhem, silently and calmly, Bleda watched and waited.

XXVIII

Calder had paused just long enough to glimpse the peltasts retreating, then led her troops on a stumbling jog upriver. It was tough going. Shingle banks tripped them. Deeper pools slowed them. Sometimes the reeds spread in such number that they almost swallowed the regiment and the gurgle of the river was accompanied by a hum of soft curses as hoplites tripped and sank and shoved their way through the thickets.

The drooping sun caught on their bronze armour, but Calder was thankful the Titan command had never thought them worthy to wear scarlet cloaks and plumes like the regular Companions.

Ulf was beside her and he kept looking beyond the far bank to the line of perimeter flags.

'You still think they'll come this way?' she asked.

'They'll use the edge of the Field to make ground and then cross at the bridges.'

'The bridges?'

'The first one's not far ahead.'

'How do you know?'

He shot her a glance as though she was a fool. 'I studied satellite images of Hortobágy Plain before we left Scotland.'

They ran on in silence, but Calder could not help wondering what a strange and complex animal this man Ulf was.

The river meandered around a bend and their way was impeded by a vast reed bed that extended from bank to bank. The first of the Hellenes began to chop at the greenery with their short blades and push their way in, but the going was slow and the rest of the ranks bunched behind.

'This is bloody pointless,' Bjarke snapped and waded for the far bank.

'Wait!' Ulf called in alarm, but it was too late. Bjarke climbed the bank and stepped onto the grass beyond.

'What do you see?' Calder called up.

'Not a damn thing.'

'Are you sure?'

'Grass and flags and that's all.'

She clambered up beside him and took stock of the surroundings. The sun was beginning to sink behind them, bathing the distant mountains in a warm glow. The perimeter flags ran towards the hills in a straight line, leaving a corridor of grassland about two hundred yards wide and empty as far as the eye could see.

'Okay,' she said cautiously. 'We'll get them out and advance along here until we pass the reeds.'

Ulf had joined them. 'There's the bridge,' he pointed.

The reeds extended for half a mile, but beyond them was white masonry.

Bjarke waved an arm and began cajoling the troops out of the river. They gathered behind Calder and she led them in a column along the bank, eyes strained for any sign of movement.

After several minutes, Bjarke came close to her. 'I think that fool Ulf is wrong. We're just pissing about on the edge of the Field while all the action's back over there.'

'You think we should return?'

'I think we're wasting our time here.'

Calder suspected he was right. 'We'll get to the bridge and then decide.'

She was about to say more when her attention was caught by three drones zipping towards them. They hovered above the Hellenes then two shot back the way they had come.

'If we're wasting our time,' she said, 'what are they doing out here?'

At the same instant, sunlight sparkled on metal in the far distance. She stopped in her tracks and Bjarke peered askance at her. 'What?'

'There. Look. Armour.'

Dust rose from the horizon and little by little a column of cavalry hove into view.

'It's them,' said Ulf. 'They're coming for the bridge.'

Where the Huns had been wild and untamed, there was an ordered magnificence to this advance. They came four abreast, barely a shred of flesh visible beneath silver mail, steel helmets garnished with feathers, long shields with the crescent of Mehmed, and lances held aloft. The horses too were heavily armoured, so that only their ears and legs showed.

The Sipahi spotted the Hellenes. Sharp orders were passed down the column and the first lances lowered.

'We must get back into the reeds,' squeaked Ulf.

'Wait,' said Calder firmly.

Bjarke peered at the mass of horsemen and then at her. 'I think the lad might be right.'

'Wait,' she said again and it was enough to silence him.

The Sipahi were passing the bridge. They had decided this quarry was more valuable. They would crush these Titans, then return to the crossing with their blades bloodied. They broke into a canter and began to eat up the ground.

'Spread out,' she called over her shoulder.

The troops shared uneasy looks, but even though they all now wore this loathsome bronze armour, she was still their Viking housecarl. They formed lines across the grass between the river and the flags, hoisted their hoplons, weighed their dories and hunched ready.

'Calder,' Bjarke warned. 'Are you sure about this?'

'Wait,' she repeated.

The ground began to shake. The air roared. The Sipahi eased into six abreast, chose their mark and took their horses up to a full gallop.

'On my signal,' shouted Calder above the maelstrom. 'Turn and run thirty paces along the bank, then – and only then – switch course. Are you ready?' She raised her spear aloft. 'Wait...' The horsemen let out a unified yell of triumph. The feathers on their helmets rippled. The points of their spears reached for their prey. 'Now!'

As one, every Hellene turned tail and raced along the grass. A hundred and forty troops, running for their lives and desperately counting to thirty. Bronze armour clanked. Helmets tipped over eyes. Breath burned through lungs.

'Twenty-two, twenty-three.'

The Sipahi must be upon them. They would be trampled. Skewered. Left for dust beneath the hooves of these giants.

'Thirty!' Calder yelled. 'Get into the reeds!'

They needed no prompting. As one, every hoplite veered

towards the river and leapt over the bank into the arms of the giant stems. They ploughed through them, cursing and shouting, tripping, splashing and falling.

And the Sipahi came too. The bloodlust was upon them. The wonder of the charge made their hearts pump and their faces split in manic grins. To see the backs of fleeing infantry was what every cavalry unit lived for. To run them down. Overtake them. Spear them. Hack them. The sheer beauty of the slaughter in those moments...

The cavalry launched itself into the reedbed. Still six abreast, they were a wall of steel and horseflesh, flattening everything in their path. Greenery snapped, hoplite armour bent, bones were pulverised beneath hooves. Their lances lunged and found the spines of their foe, then retracted and thrust again. The screams of dying Hellenes were choked into silence by the water. For precious moments the cavalry was relentless and the riders laughed in mad delight as everything fell before them.

They were seven ranks in by the time they began to lose momentum and the first of them realised the peril. The rocks and the reeds had forced them apart and they no longer rode knee to knee. The horses started to stumble and twist and lose cohesion on the difficult terrain. Instead of an unstoppable punch of steel, every trooper in the Sipahi realised they were about to face their own individual fight.

From the reeds came a hundred yelling, blood-frenzied infantry like nothing they had experienced before, stabbing with their dories and their shortswords, grabbing the cavalry's lances and hauling them from their saddles. The Sipahi tried to draw their scimitars, but they were dragged down and their long mail coats were useless in the river. Blades severed horse hamstrings to collapse the beasts and trap their riders. Helmets were thrown aside, fingers grabbed for their throats. Heads were splintered on rocks and faces held beneath the water. Everywhere there was cursing and grunting and the smell of blood and horseshit and fear.

The ranks still on dry land reined back hard and churned in confusion, trying to back up enough to escape, but infantry launched themselves from the river and broke into the tumult, ducking under the lances and hacking at horse and rider alike. The cavalry still had the advantage of height, but in such close quarters they could not make it tell. For every Hellene they impaled, another two grabbed at them and hauled them down.

Somewhere amidst the frenzy, Calder killed methodically. She left her dory in the flank of a horse, drew her sword and stabbed into a rider's thigh. Bjarke was on top of a fallen man, breaking his face on a stone. Ingvar shouldered into a horse with such force that the beast stumbled to its knees. Ake leapt on top of a white stallion, pulled the rider's head back and sliced her knife across the woman's throat.

Chaos, mud, water and terror.

At last, the remnants of Mehmed's vaunted Sipahi broke and fled north, galloping along the perimeter flags as fast as their mounts would carry them.

Back to their King.

Back to tell him that his cavalry was broken and that there were devils in the ranks of Macedon.

XXIX

The struggle on the plain had faltered into an uneasy stalemate.

The Titans hunkered in the trees, their hoplons wedged against trunks while arrows thudded into wood and grass, bronze and bone. But now the Huns fired more in hope than in expectation. With Nicanor's Heavies lined along the perimeter of the woods, Attila's Second Horn could not close on the foe and their arrows were mostly an irritant.

The Black Cloaks had not moved from their vantage point. They knew well enough that even their number could not sustain an effective attack into the trees, so their prey was safe for the time being. But one false move into the open and they would be upon the Macedon troops.

Heph's Companion Cavalry had tethered their horses together at the centre of the woods and he ordered his riders to use their hoplons to shield the creatures. He forced Melitta to sit and have her thigh attended, and he left Dio well alone as his friend slumped a few strides from the rest of them, his face creased and angry.

Alexander stood within a tight circle of his Bodyguard and sheathed his fear by barking demands at his officers to demonstrate some decisive action. He reserved his most acerbic venom for the absent Hellenes, whom he had concluded were Viking cowards who should never have received the privilege of wearing Titan armour. He was vitriolic after Parmenion briefed him that the Hellenic Regiment had run to the river with the intention of heading north to seek out Mehmed, but when he learned they were now led by one of their own number, he became convinced that the Valhalla bastards had fled to save their skins.

Agape came to stand beside Heph and he commented facetiously, 'When I asked you about a three-way Battle, you said we would have to kill and kill again and keep killing until it was over. We're a couple of hours into this, the sun is getting lower and, so far, I've done nothing but hide.'

'It's not yet a three-way Battle,' she replied with disdain.

And that was the issue on everyone's mind. While Nicanor supervised his Heavies, Parmenion, Menes, Agape and Heph gathered in a huddle and asked the same question: *where is Mehmed?*

The answer came, at last, from the north.

The first sign of a change was when another throng of horsemen appeared in the distance. Their turbulent movements could only mean these were Uptar's First Horn come to play. It was Agape who spotted the smaller mounted group tracking the First Horn, which stopped on a gentle rise half a mile from the waiting Titans. The sight of the crowned eagle banner told them this was Attila himself who watched the action and issued commands.

Heph counted the little group and could make out no more than eight riders. One King, so close and so sparsely protected. Heph's mind toyed with distances and odds, and wondered how fast his nine remaining Companions could cover the ground at full gallop.

'Don't even think about it,' said Agape quietly. 'Bleda would tear you apart before you were halfway.'

Their attentions were dragged back to the horizon. Behind the mob of Huns, something was coming. The late sun flashed on iron and steel, and fired the colours of many flags. It was moving slowly – slowly like Nicanor's Phalanx – as it took one ponderous step at a time and let the horsemen swarm around it.

'Infantry,' said Menes.

'Well disciplined,' added Parmenion, 'if the Huns aren't bothering them.'

'And using the same tactics as us,' said Agape. 'Mehmed will be deep inside that square and the Huns can't do a thing about it.'

Heph began to see how the Sultanate and Hun Palatinates had spent so many years fighting each other to little effect. Attila was too quick and Mehmed too well protected. Stalemates all round.

Yard by yard, the infantry approached. Uptar's horsemen attempted wild sorties, but were incapable of breaking through the wall of pikes. A large contingent of Ellac's archers rushed away from the Titan woodland to assist, assessing angles and raining arrows down on Mehmed's banners, but the Sultanate King wore steel from head to toe and swatted the missiles away with disdain. The Battle was in balance. Only one force could make a difference – Mehmed's heavy Sipahi cavalry – but of them, there was no sign.

Drones floated above the struggle, keeping higher

than usual to avoid a sky full of deadly projectiles. The Vigiles filmed what they could from careering Jeeps, their cameras and the eyes of the watching Curiate all focused on the Sultanate and their galloping foe.

And that was when Heph decided it was once more time to change the game.

He left the huddle of officers and walked out of the treeline to the waiting Heavies before pushing through their lines to their colonel.

'You again,' said Nicanor as he watched the approaching Sultanate.

'Yeah, me again. That lot over there, you realise, have been going through the same motions for at least the past six Seasons. Mehmed can never catch Attila, and Attila can never get inside Mehmed's square.'

'And your point is?'

'They've never before shared the Field with a Titan Phalanx.'

Nicanor examined him. 'You think we should change the odds?'

'Imagine what would happen if you marched over there and broke Mehmed's lines.'

'We'd be inside in minutes, but we'd need back-up or they'd wheel in on our flanks.'

'They wouldn't have time, because as soon as you break a hole, the Huns will follow you in like a swarm of furious bees.'

'That could get pretty hot.'

'You won't be the recipient of their stings. There's a King in that square. Break the perimeter and let Attila's mob do the rest.'

Nicanor grasped the plan and nodded slowly, a smile beginning to crack his jawline. 'Kill the King.'

'One dead King and this is all over. Nicanor's the hero and the rest of us don't even need to leave these trees.'

'Have you run the plan past Alexander?'

Heph raised his eyebrows beneath his helmet. 'You think I need to?'

Nicanor hesitated, then snorted. 'Bollocks to him.'

Heph grinned and gripped the other man's shoulder. 'Go do what you do best, Colonel.'

He let Nicanor bring his troops to attention and pass orders down the lines. The front rank of twelve levelled their giant sarissas and the second rank brought theirs down over the shoulders of those in front. The other fifteen ranks closed up, with sarissas vertical, while those on the flanks also levelled their weapons and angled them out.

Alexander had seen the movement and broke from his Bodyguard as Heph returned to the trees.

'What in the name of the gods is happening?' the fat King bellowed.

'Nicanor has business with that square,' Heph answered flatly.

Alexander coloured in indignation. 'Just who the hell does he think he is to take any action without my command?'

'Well, you'd better go and stop him then.'

Heph walked back to his cavalry and met a glare from Agape. 'What have you done?'

'You told me in Pella that our role in this fight would be to wait until we saw a chance to do something unexpected. Well, I saw that chance.'

Every eye watched as the Titan Phalanx heaved a great sigh and paced away from the trees.

Ellac's archers whooped in excitement and tore after the Heavies to circle them and shoot arrows high into the air, so that they dropped onto the close-packed bronze helmets.

Heph turned his gaze to the Black Cloaks on their ridge. Riders were charging up and down the line, unit officers quite obviously attempting to interpret just what the hell was happening. Then a huge body of cavalry, perhaps half Bleda's command, broke from the line and surged down onto the plain. A moan broke from Titan lips beneath the trees as they imagined the impact of such a force breaking upon the flanks of the Phalanx and, for a few aghast heartbeats, Heph feared he had miscalculated.

But Bleda understood what was at play. She had not sent her Black Cloaks to charge the Phalanx. Instead, they swept past it and joined the First Horn in a great circle around Mehmed's square.

Kill the King.

Heph had wagered that Bleda would grasp the situation. Never before had the Huns benefited from an unstoppable armoured column like the Heavies. She knew what would happen when they made contact with Mehmed's infantry and she wanted her Black Cloaks ready to strike.

But she had not sent all her force. Half of them still sat and watched the Titan woodland. And Heph swore quietly, because he knew for whom they waited.

The Sultanate square had halted. They had seen the approaching danger and planted their feet firmly, ready for impact. Ellac still harassed the Phalanx, sending flight after flight of arrows to bounce off helmet and strike flesh. Gaps appeared as Heavies fell and those behind stumbled over the bodies, but Nicanor kept the pace relentless, bellowing commands and focusing on nothing but the infantry ahead. Closer now. Closer.

And then something that none of the watchers under the trees had expected.

A new body of infantry appeared from a dip in the western slopes adjacent to the Sultanate square. Six abreast in column, tightly packed, and armoured in steel from head to toe. A host of Huns were already harassing them, but it made no difference to the pace of these new arrivals. They came fast, with spears and shields and banners, marching onto the plain and angling towards the side of Nicanor's Phalanx.

'Janissaries,' stated Parmenion in alarm.

'You fool, Heph,' scolded Agape. 'You damn impetuous fool.'

Heph tried to make sense of it. 'I thought they were in the square.'

'You thought wrong. The square must only be the Yaya troops.'

'But I thought they were just light infantry.'

Parmenion glared at him. 'Light, yes, but also with years of experience in how to keep Huns at bay.'

Heph stared open-mouthed and began to understand the ramifications of what he had set in motion. The advance of the Janissaries was too fast, the angles too tight. Nicanor had no hope of turning to meet this new threat. He could only maintain his attack on the square, but his left flank would take the full brunt of the Janissaries' advance and there was not one chance in hell that it could hold. The Phalanx lines would break in half and then every Heavy would be at the mercy of Janissary and Hun alike. It would be a bloodbath. A massacre.

Agape was already marshalling her Band, determined not to abandon Nicanor to his fate.

'You can't go out there,' Heph protested. 'Bleda's still got a hundred and fifty Black Cloaks waiting for you to do just that.'

'You should have thought about that before you started meddling.'

Her blue cloaks came around her and Menes began barking orders to his Companions. Alexander stood dumbfounded, barely comprehending what was happening.

Heph cursed venomously, wedged his helmet back on and strode for his cavalry. If Agape and Menes were insistent on dying, then he must ride as well. He flung orders to his unit and they rose and began mounting. He could see the fear in their eyes, but no one hesitated.

'Looks like the shit's hit the fan,' Dio growled as Heph seated himself on Boreas.

'And it's all my fault.'

Agape had already brought her Band to the edge of the trees and now began to run into the open without so much as a glance back. Heph snatched a look over to his left and saw the first Black Cloaks begin to trot down the rise.

'Bloody hell. Here they come.'

He raised his hand and prepared to signal the advance.

'Wait,' said Spyro.

Heph swung round and was about to berate him, but

the blond Cavalryman was staring towards the Janissary column.

'They're not going for the Heavies.'

Heph looked back and his breath caught. Out on the grassland, Agape had seen it too and she braked hard and brought her Band to a halt.

'What the hell?' said Dio.

The Janissary column was swinging past the Phalanx. Two mighty infantry units eyeing each other and passing almost shoulder to shoulder without attacking. The Heavies continued their progress towards the Yaya square with no break in momentum and the Janissaries marched south. The Huns milled around everyone in utter confusion and Attila could be seen gesticulating madly from his hillock.

'What's happening?' demanded Alexander.

Agape already knew. She had turned her Band and was running for the trees again. Bleda realised too. The Black Cloaks wheeled around in a vast mass and galloped back up the slope to their own vantage point.

And finally the penny dropped for Heph too.

'Why aren't they hitting Nicanor?' Menes shouted from the head of his Companions.

'Because,' Heph retorted, 'they're coming for us.'

XXX

A flurry of activity broke beneath the trees as the Titans prepared themselves for the onslaught, but they all knew they were in trouble.

Taking into account dead and wounded, Menes had roughly fifty Companions around Alexander, Parmenion marshalled forty peltasts, Agape led a Sacred Band of twenty-five and Heph could count on nine Companion Cavalry. A shade over a hundred and twenty blades to protect the Lion King of Macedon from two hundred and seventy heavily-armoured Janissary infantry, Mehmed's most zealous soldiers.

Whomever commanded that regiment had taken a momentous and potentially Battle-changing decision. Instead of cleaving Nicanor's Phalanx in two, he or she had weighed the odds and decided that Mehmed could take his chances amongst his Yaya infantry, while the Janissaries went for Alexander's head. It would all come down to a race. Which of those Kings could be killed first?

'Stop them!' Alexander bellowed towards Heph, his face livid beneath his ornate helmet. 'This is all your fault, you cretin. So get out there and stop that column!'

'If he tells me one more time to do something suicidal, I swear I'm—'

'Then ignore him,' said Dio brusquely. 'Can we do anything to make up for this mess?'

'Not in these trees. We'd be better dismounted.'

'What about attacking the rear of the column?' suggested Lenore.

Dio nodded. 'That's a valid proposal. We could at least take some of them from behind and sow confusion.'

Heph was unconvinced. 'Not until they are much, much closer, because we'll draw too much attention.'

'You afraid of Bleda?' Dio countered.

Heph looked beseechingly at his friend. 'You know I am,' he answered quietly and Dio swallowed his frustration and held up a hand in apology.

Menes organised his Companions into two rows of thirty and tried to draw them tight enough to link hoplons and meet their assailants in the traditional line of battle, but the trees forced gaps and made them bunch and weave around each trunk. Parmenion stood his peltasts behind, braced to fling their javelins and then draw blades.

Agape jogged over to Heph. 'If they remain in column, they'll punch through us, but they'll be vulnerable on the flanks. Take one side and I'll take the other. Do what you can.'

Heph nodded his agreement, still stung that she had called him a fool. She returned to the other end of the Companion line and prepared for a flank attack. He drew his cavalry together and trotted forward between the trees, ready to close on the column.

That was all the time they had. The Janissaries were singing a marching song, marking each step with a solemn note. Their pace had not faltered. Their spears came down, their shields aligned in rows of six and they stormed into the woods.

The first trunks forced them to part and weave around the immovable objects, but it was not enough to undermine their momentum. The Companions roared in defiance, took a step forward and the lines met.

Order broke down. Nothing mattered but the snarling desperate fight for survival. Janissary spears smashed into hoplons. Shortswords reached beneath shafts and stabbed for groins and thighs. Peltast javelins flew twenty yards and clattered into mail and steel. The Sacred Band came at a rush from the side, tearing into Janissary torsos, punching with shields and stabbing with blades before the Sultanate troops could respond. Heph kicked his heels and took Boreas between the trees at a canter. The horse knew the danger ahead and whinnied with the adrenaline rush. He stamped his hooves high and allowed his full heft to hit the flank of the enemy column.

The Janissaries caved in under the weight of the horses. The entire column broke in two and Heph's unit pierced the midst of the Sultanate's infantry, punching with their spears until they snapped, then unsheathing swords and stabbing down. The stink of blood and fear rose like a tide and for frenzied moments Heph was conscious of nothing except the desire to kill. His lance took a man in the throat. His next lunge pierced the chainmail on the back of a female trooper, but left the point stuck in her. He grabbed his sword and scythed down at a moustached jaw grimacing beneath a tall, masked helmet, just as the man grabbed his leg and attempted to throw him from Boreas.

Then sense returned and Heph realised his troop had almost broken the column in half, but were now surrounded by enemy. There were bodies beneath them, being trampled into sludge, but also causing the stallions to stumble and falter. Spears and swords were turned on the creatures and began to thrust at their flanks.

Heph yelled at his cavalry to get out, but already it was too late. Phoibe's horse went down beneath her and she disappeared amongst the deadly steel. Elinor was grabbed from her mount and hauled down, where she was stabbed and stabbed again. Silver-haired Thales, who had once helped Heph on with his peltast fish-scales, just had time to look at his captain before a spear was thrust beneath his cuirass and he fell backwards over the rump of his horse. Philemon was fighting like a man possessed and his horse was screaming as it was punctured. Melitta kicked at an assailant with her wounded leg. Heph saw Lenore attacked from all sides and realised she was moments from being dragged down into the blood tide. He urged Boreas forward, stabbing relentlessly at everything below him, came next to Lenore's mount and grabbed the bridle. She wrenched herself free of the grasping hands and he pulled her stallion with him as Boreas exited the fight on the other side of the column.

'You okay?' he demanded and she nodded, though her cuirass was bright with blood and her thigh was lacerated.

Dio broke through to them too, but Spyro was deep in the struggle, sword slashing as hands reached for him.

Heph was about to charge back to him, when a shout from Lenore spun him round. The Janissary column might have been broken, but their lead ranks had crushed through the Companions and were deep in the woods. Then Heph saw what had made Lenore shout.

Alexander. Stupid Alexander, that worthless fool. He had fled from his attackers, run with his Bodyguard right out of the trees and onto the open plain.

Heph shook with rage. His heart yearned to go to Spyro's aid, but his head told him it was the King who mattered.

A smattering of Companions were running after their King, Menes leading them, but Agape and Parmenion were too deep in the slaughter to realise. Only horses could get to him fast enough. Only cavalry could stop the fool and herd him back to the trees.

Spluttering with every expletive he had ever known, Heph wrenched on his rein and took Boreas around the churning bodies. Lenore was at this shoulder and Dio a yard behind. They galloped past the Companions and peltasts, as the Titan lines folded under the sheer weight of the Janissary momentum, and Heph realised this was the end. They could not hold.

Then a new roar came to him from the other side of the woodland. A roar he knew well. From the corner of his eye, he saw bronze-clad warriors charging from the river and hurling their heathen cries at the Sultanate infantry. At their fore came a woman with blonde hair falling from her helmet and blood glazed across her breastplate and Heph gasped at the sight of his friend. The Hellenes had not fled. The Hellenes had not ignored the plight of their Titan conquerors. They rushed into the trees and fell upon the Janissaries, as Vigiles camera teams raced behind them in a desperate bid to film Viking and Companions standing shoulder to shoulder against a common foe.

Heph's heart surged at the sight, but he had no time to appreciate it. His fool of a King was still running across the grassland, a ragged comet tail of Companions in his wake. Heph steered Boreas through the final trees and then let him have his head as they broke free. Together, the three riders hurtled across the grass, cloaks billowing behind them, plumes catching the reddening rays of the setting sun.

They were glorious to behold and they were a sight not lost on Bleda. With a guttural command through her filed fangs and a nudge of her pony, she brought her Black Cloaks to attention and signalled the advance.

Attila too had seen the Titan King break from cover. He was beside himself with joy. Madly, he waved at Ellac below him and pointed her back towards the woods. As she gathered her forces and set her course for the Titan banner, Attila could not contain his excitement. The Titan Phalanx had broken through the Yaya square and Uptar's First Horn was tearing inside to find Mehmed. The Janissary column had flushed Alexander from his hiding place and now nothing could stop Bleda from cutting him to shreds. Attila laughed at the sheer delight of it all and kicked his little pony into a gallop down the hillock towards the Titans. He wanted to see Alexander fall. He wanted to witness it personally.

Heph overtook his wheezing idiot King and wheeled Boreas around in front of the tiny group.

'Get back!' he yelled, yanking his horse to a halt. 'The Hellenes have come. We can still hold the woodland!'

But it was too late and he knew it.

The King was gasping for breath and his wild eyes

focused momentarily on Heph before being dragged away to a vision beyond. Menes too was halting and staring in terror at what was approaching. Dio and Lenore slowed their mounts next to Heph and peered open-mouthed behind him.

With a deep breath, Heph turned Boreas and looked upon the coming of Death.

Bleda led them. Almost two hundred black-cloaked, skull-masked devils, screaming their war cries, kneeing their snorting ponies and brandishing their blades above their heads, flowing across the grass in a vast black wave.

'This is it, my friend,' said Dio. 'It's been an honour to be led by you.'

Heph's heart juddered with emotion at these words and his eyes watered. 'Thank you,' was all he could manage in reply. 'Thank you for everything.'

'So are we just going to sit here?' Dio demanded with a mad grin. 'Or are we going to leave this Game in glory?'

Lenore raised her sword. A wild, blooded maiden of war. 'The Companion Cavalry of Macedon.'

'The Companion Cavalry of Macedon,' Heph and Dio repeated.

Then the three riders urged their brave horses forward.

The drone cameras caught everything. Across the world, every member of the Curiate gasped and choked on their food.

In his private lodgings outside Edinburgh, Zeus stared numbly at the destruction of his Palatinate.

In Istanbul, Hakan Reis – Kyzaghan, lord of the Sultanate – watched transfixed, a sheen of cold sweat seeping into every orifice as he realised how close his own Palatinate could be to falling. Mehmed was minutes from death, but this foolish Titan King would die first.

In a mansion not far from Hortobágy, Mikhail Malutin – Ördög, Caelestis of the Huns – pounded the table with his giant fist and roared in triumph. Alexander would die, but so too might Mehmed before the klaxon sounded. The glory was his.

On a terrace beneath lime trees, Marcella Ballantyne let her cigarette burn down between her fingers as she watched her laptop screen, entranced. She stared at the three Titan riders charging towards the mass of Huns and her eyes were glued to the lead figure. The King Killer. The bastard upstart who had no place in her Pantheon. Now was the moment. Tyler Maitland was about to die and that was all that mattered.

And then Death changed her mind.

XXXI

Bleda was at the front of her raging Black Cloaks, eating up the ground towards their prey. The air was filled with the cries of her warriors, but she herself held her tongue. She had seen the three Titans spur their tall stallions towards her and she marvelled at their actions. Such mad fools, such heroic idiots, yet *such* honour.

Her eyes were riveted on the lead rider. The Captain of Companion Cavalry. The King Killer, who thundered towards the very heart of her massed attack. He must be a man who understood that no one was remembered for when or where they left this world, only for the manner in which they departed.

Pride surged through her. Pride for this glorious horseman in front of her and for the man she had hoped he would become.

Drawing a deep breath, she let rip a piercing shriek and raised her blade in a gesture that demanded the attention of her commanders. Then she wrenched her rein and drove her startled steppe pony away from the oncoming foe. Shouts and signals tore through the packed Black Cloaks as they followed her lead and the entire massed cavalry wheeled to the north.

'What the—!' Heph jerked back on Boreas' rein in shock.

The Black Cloaks had come so close that the ground trembled and their stink assailed him. The nearest riders glared at him and shouted obscenities, but they followed their commander and flew past without so much as a swing of their blades.

On they stormed, Bleda in the lead.

On towards the one group that now stood in their way.

Ellac realised the changed dynamic before anyone else.

She had never liked Bleda. Never trusted her since her sudden appearance in her Palatinate. The woman, Ellac had thought, was a tempestuous, capricious, unreliable new presence, who had embraced Hun culture by slicing at her own skin, filing her teeth and impaling her commander under false pretences.

So Ellac knew implicitly what was about to happen.

She threw her bow aside, dragged her blade into the growing dusk and yelled at her Second Horn to do likewise. They massed behind her and charged towards their fellow Huns.

If Attila ever understood what was coming for him, he never had a chance to react.

One moment he had been grinning from ear to ear and believing he might conceivably be the only King left standing at the end of this fight. The next, his most senior commander was leading her Black Cloaks straight at him.

He blinked and swallowed and opened his mouth to remonstrate, and then she was upon him.

Bleda buried her sword so deep inside her King that its point broke his spine and came out the other side. She released it and flowed past with a single screech on her lips.

Behind her, her Black Cloaks swarmed in confusion, utterly incapable of understanding whether they should be following their commander or worrying about their King. Bleda herself had acted on impulse and now that the blood craze was clearing, she had no idea what to do next, so she kept riding because there was no going back. Nothing to stop for. It was over and she knew it.

Bladeless, she galloped straight towards the oncoming ranks of the Second Horn and the fury of Ellac. It all happened so fast that she would never know whether it was Ellac's sword that took her down or that of one of her followers. The Second Horn flowed around her and steel caught her through the ribs, shattering bone and piercing organs. She lost grip of her rein and cartwheeled over the rump of her pony and everything went dark.

Heph spurred Boreas towards the confusion.

The Hellenes were sprinting across the grass in full war-cry, desperate to fall on the milling Huns, and Heph was taken by the battle-lust too. All the pent-up fear, all the holding back and waiting for the right moment, came flowing out of him and he galloped.

Wait, Zeus had once said. *Wait for the decisive moment.*

Well, this was the damn decisive moment.

Dio and Lenore followed and the Companions charged into the backs of the Black Cloaks, just as the Hellenes too reached the jostling mass.

The Black Cloaks were disorientated. Dusk was upon them and the gloom only made everything even more confused. Their King was down. The Second Horn was attacking them. Ellac had bloodied Bleda and knocked her from her horse. Hundreds of baying Titans were rushing them. The Black Cloaks yelled in anger and swung their blades at Hun and Hellene alike. Everyone was hacking and grunting. Blood washed the soil with the same crimson coat as the western sky. Horses reared and screamed. Bodies fell.

Heph stampeded into the midst of it all, lunging with his sword and bludgeoning with his shield. Boreas was a giant amongst the steppe ponies and the stallion ploughed through them, biting and kicking and clearing a path. Behind him, Dio and Lenore cleaved.

Heph didn't know what impulse drove him. Something about the woman with the filed fangs. Something about the way she had regarded him before the Battle and then taken one long stare at him just before she steered her entire cavalry away and rode to kill her King. He hacked his way through the seething mass, knocking Huns from their mounts, shouldering ponies aside, letting Boreas take him forward.

Finally, he spied her lying almost forgotten amongst the churning horses.

She was alive, just, and as her masked head struggled to rise from the ground, he jumped from Boreas and ran to her. Without thought for the blades and hooves around him, he flung himself down beside her and put his hand under her neck. Her eyes stared wildly at him from behind her skull-mask. Her lips were dragged back in pain and there was blood oozing between her terrifying teeth. Her skin was as pale as alabaster and her raven hair hung lank over her shoulders.

She was trying to say something. She grasped at him and he brought his ear closer.

'Brother,' she hissed.

'Yes,' he said. 'Yes, we have been brothers-in-arms today and I thank you.'

She gurgled in angry frustration and creased her face into concentration to find her voice again.

'Brother.'

'Yes, yes. Blood brothers. You have done great things, Bleda.'

She shook her head in exasperation and her blood-red fingers closed on his cloak, dragging him even closer, so that her breath was on him.

'I did this for you, brother. Always for you.'

And that was when Heph understood.

His lungs froze. His ears rang. The violence subsided into emptiness. All he saw was the woman before him. The woman who had shared his life, brought him up, loved him.

Sister.

Morgan.

XXXII

Morgan Maitland died of her wounds on the Field of Hortobágy Plain, in the arms of her brother. He had removed her skull mask and flung his helmet aside and they had shared a few treasured seconds of silent communion, seconds during which the years dissolved to nothing. Once more they were just children, sleeping in the same bedroom in Leith, playing on Portobello beach, grinning over hot chocolates, running lawlessly around the Craigmillar estate, crying and arguing, laughing and teasing, loving; sweet memories before their mother died, before the Pantheon arrived in their lives, before the violence subsumed them both.

When Morgan's pupils finally glazed and stilled, he had clutched her to him and pinned her so tightly as he shed tears onto her cheek, not noticing the stink of her hair or the abomination of her mouth, just remembering the girl she had once been. Somewhere the klaxon sounded. Emotions poured from him, raw and confused. He had found her. After all the years of searching and praying, he had found his sister when and where he had least expected.

And then he had lost her again.

It was Diogenes who came for him.

'Heph,' he said, gripping his Captain's shoulder. 'Heph, you must step away.'

Heph was beyond words. He held his sister tighter and shuddered as shock and despair leaked from him.

'Heph, you have to step back.'

He wanted to thrash Diogenes. How dare the man intrude on this moment. How dare he invade the time Heph had with his loved one. He wanted to spin and beat him into silence.

But instead, strength drained from his limbs and he had no resistance as he felt himself pulled gently from his sister. His body parted from hers, his fingers trailed across her face and lost contact and then his friend was turning him and placing a guiding arm over his shoulders.

Diogenes walked his Captain back through the mass of Hun horsemen and not one of them raised a hand against them. The klaxon had signalled the end of the conflict and they watched the party in silent bemusement. Their King was dead, killed by their own commander, and she, in turn, had fallen to Ellac's blades.

And the only person who wept for Bleda was this Titan officer.

Blood cooled on iron. Lenore gathered Boreas and Dio's new mount and the steppe ponies touched muzzles with the thoroughbreds. Then the Huns parted and permitted the little party to walk onto open grassland.

Several hundred yards away, Alexander was spitting orders at the Hellenes to herd them into a marching column. He was unhurt, his armour bright and bloodless. At the other end of the valley, a horseman in silver plate scanned the scene. The Phalanx had broken Mehmed's square and

Uptar's First Horn had surged to within cutting distance of the Sultanate King, but the klaxon had announced the death of a different sovereign. So Mehmed sat his stallion and stared across the grass towards the little group of Titans.

Marcella stared, too, from her Ops Room beneath the villa in Capri.

She had shouted at her team to get out and now stood alone, surrounded by screens, watching the feeds from Hortobágy again and again, clicking to different drones, zooming in, panning out and slowing the images down.

She punched in a secure number on her mobile. 'Did you trick me?' she demanded in cold fury.

'Trick you?' roared Mikhail Malutin. 'I've lost my Palatinate, you bitch! *Focus on the King Killer*, you said. *Bring me his head*, you said. Well, damn you, you won't get rid of me that easily.'

She cut the call and went back to studying the images. Why had it happened? Why would a Hun commander kill her own King? She watched again as the King Killer held his foe in his arms and wept as she died. She zoomed in on their faces. They were speaking, but the cameras could not pick up the words.

And then, as she scrutinised their expressions and their touches, realisation dawned on her. She strode to a small safe, spun the locking mechanism and retrieved Skarde's phone. Once more she inspected the photo on it, then gazed again at the feeds. And she understood.

She marched from the Ops Room and climbed spiral stairs to her villa's grand marble entrance vestibule.

'Bring me my son,' she said in her most imperial voice to the security personnel on the door. 'And afterwards I will see the Viking again. Have him prepared.'

'What is it?' asked Fabian irritably when he found her on the upper veranda. He still had a phone clamped to his ear and obviously thought the person on the end of the line warranted his attention more than his mother.

Marcella ran a finger across her throat. 'Get rid of the hussy, whichever one it is.'

He saw the fire in her eyes and guessed he should do as she bid. 'I'll call you back.' He cut the line and pocketed the phone. 'Well?'

'Did you even watch the Battle?' she asked incredulously.

Fabian shrugged. 'Until I got a better offer for my attention.'

Marcella took a moment to control her irritation by selecting a thin cigarette from a gold case and lighting up. 'Where's your father?'

'Don't call him that.' Fabian scowled. 'Where do you think? At the camp with his Legates, where he always is when there's Pantheon on TV. He expected me to be there too, but I deferred.'

'I bet you did.'

'So what do you want?'

She would not explain the truth to him because his rage would be too much.

'Who is your most trusted Praetorian?'

This focused him. 'Domna.'

'Is she good?'

'Why do you ask?'

Marcella drew on her cigarette and regarded her son. 'I need her to go to Scotland.'

Skarde was waiting in the outbuilding complex, barefoot and bare-chested. Once again, he was blindfolded and bound to his chair.

'I want Tyler Maitland dead,' she said without preamble as she took the seat opposite.

'He seems to have that effect on everyone,' Skarde muttered, and kept his head bowed.

'Can you do it?' she asked, examining the man. She could still recognise his strength and arrogance, but he seemed to have wilted since their last conversation and she wondered if her assistants were a little too zealous in their attentions.

'I take it he survived the Battle.'

'Just answer my question.'

Skarde took an age responding. Sensibly, he understood that what he said here would determine his future. At last, he raised his head and there was a hint of an ironic smile. 'Probably not.'

'Why?' she demanded, surprised by his reply.

'Because the Titans hide him away. I don't know what he told them when he surrendered on the beach last year, but they seem to value him enough to wrap him up in cotton wool between Battles and keep him from prying eyes.'

She digested this and unexpectedly felt her rage beginning to bubble again. She had kept it in check since leaving the Ops Room, but now it was threatening to boil over.

'Wait,' she snapped to the henchmen behind Skarde as she rose and stalked back out into the sunlight.

She stood on the lawn amongst borders of azalea and jasmine and raised her face to the blue heavens. Why could nobody ever be relied upon to get something done? Why did she always have to sort it herself?

She forced deep breaths to control her frustration.

She remembered the expression on Atilius' face on the video call when he had first sent her the image of the King Killer. Did he know what this man meant to her? The Praetor was so punctilious in his management of the Pantheon systems, so rigorous in his criteria; she doubted Tyler Maitland could ever have been recruited and have risen through the ranks without the unseen hand of Atilius easing his path.

And what of the other Caelestes? Were they in on the secret too?

She trembled with rage. It was all a plot to weaken her. Well, she would meet this challenge head on and destroy it without the aid of anyone else. She was Jupiter, Lord High Caelestis of the Legion and she would have her vengeance.

She stormed back to the compound.

'Who knows?' she demanded.

'What?'

'Who else knows about Tyler Maitland and his sister?'

Skarde was silent.

'Tell me or you'll die wearing that blindfold.'

He struggled to think. He knew he had only one chance to play this right.

'Ten seconds,' she warned.

'Four,' he replied.

'What?'

'There are four who know.'

'Give me their names.'

Skarde shook his head and laughed hollowly. 'No.'

He heard the henchmen take a step forward and for a second Marcella was tempted to let them crack his skull, but then she froze them with a finger. 'You refuse to tell me their names?' she clarified.

'If I do, you'll have no more use for me.'

His head was held high now, his chest thrust out, daring her. She considered him for long seconds and wrestled with her options.

'You realise I could have you tortured until you are screaming their names over and over again, pleading to tell me everything if only I will make the pain stop?'

'My tolerance for pain will surprise you.'

She could not deny his cocky indifference was strangely appealing. No one ever spoke to her like that and certainly not when they were blindfolded, beaten and half-naked.

'You walk a thin line, Viking. I don't think you know just how precarious it is. But... but perhaps there are better uses for you than the rack. If I send you to Scotland, will you kill them for me?'

'How will you reward me?'

She had to swallow her first indignant response and said more calmly, 'You will have a place in my Legion.'

'When we last met, you would not give me your word on that.'

'Then you have it now. You will return to Scotland with one of my hand-picked Praetorians and you will locate these four individuals and you will kill them. When my Praetorian has confirmed their deaths and when I have proof that they are the *only* people who know about Tyler

Maitland's search, then – and only then – will I welcome you into my Legion. Do we have an agreement?'

'And what about Maitland himself?'

'If the Titans wrap him up in cotton wool between Battles, then we must bring him out to Battle once again.'

Skarde pondered this strange turn of events. He had travelled to Capri in the belief that the God Killer's internment in Fife was his winning card, only to find Jupiter was much more interested in the King Killer. Now, all he had to do to turn his fortunes was to go back to the house in Fife and murder the captive and his two captors. That accounted for three out of four. The final one would take a little more work to locate, but he would relish every moment of the killing.

'Yes, we have an agreement.'

'And god help you, Viking, if you try to play me. No place on earth will harbour you. I will find you. I will beat you. And then I will give you the slowest, most painful death of any man in history.'

XXXIII

For the second time in barely a month, Heph found himself the centre of attention in the aftermath of a Pantheon Battle.

As darkness descended, almost two thousand warriors milled in confusion. All the aggression and violence had dissolved when the klaxon sounded and now they simply stared at one another, murmured to friends, tended their wounds, drank greedily from streams, checked on those less fortunate, or collapsed where they stood. The coming of night only added to the bewilderment.

Many had been too deep in the mess of Battle to know why the klaxon had called an end. Now they stood shoulder to shoulder beside their enemy and wondered which King had died. Others had seen the Huns clash with each other and they whispered of treachery. Some had even glimpsed the little Titan cavalry in the centre of the turmoil and rumours fluttered across the Field of a bronze-clad knight who had smote a sovereign and taken his crown. Just a few had been close enough to see the King Killer properly and now, even in the failing light, they floated around him in awed silence. Janissaries wandered from the trees and removed their helms to see him better. Huns slumped on their ponies and tried to comprehend what had happened.

As for the Titans, they kept a reverential distance from Heph, somehow comprehending – yet not quite understanding – that events on this Field had again changed everything and that this man, this survivor from Valhalla, was once more at the beating heart of it all.

Flames flickered as the first mess fires were kindled. Helicopters thundered in to discharge torch-wielding Vigiles and *libitinarii*. The camera teams in their 4x4s parked up and flooded the plain with their headlights. Field canteens were erected and hot food prepared. A specialist team dropped from a smaller chopper and hurried to the site of Attila's corpse to confirm the manner of his death and to ascertain the precise chain of events that had led to a Hun sword being buried in his chest.

Heph slouched on the grass and let it all wash over him. Dio and Lenore disappeared to find the rest of the Companion Cavalry. The last they had seen of their fellow riders they had been deep in the murder of the Janissary advance and the pair feared what they might find in the woodland. Boreas nickered next to Heph and hoofed the grass, perhaps wondering at the stillness of his master. Alexander's voice rose and fell above the hum of the armies, pompous and triumphant, though few shared his enthusiasm. A clanking came from the north as Nicanor mustered his Phalanx and brought them slowly back across the plain.

Menes appeared in Heph's vision and dipped his head in respect. 'Damn bravest thing I ever saw.'

Of Calder, there was no sign.

At last, Agape found him and hoisted him up. 'Take your horse and walk with me.'

'My unit,' he mumbled.

'They are awaiting you. It's time for you to leave. Right now.'

Despite the darkness, he found himself propelled away from the crowds, back into the dip where the Titans had first drawn up their lines, then through the flags on the southern perimeter. Lights from several vehicles could be seen ahead as well as the shadows of humans and beasts.

Dio strode out to meet the pair. 'Not good,' he said grimly.

'Tell me,' Heph replied.

'Phoibe, Thales, Elinor and Zephyr are dead. Roxana's missing.'

'Spyro?'

'He lives. He's with the medics. Melitta too.'

'So who's here?'

'Just Philemon, Lenore and the two of us.'

'Christ. And the horses?'

'Boreas and the two that carried us into the Huns.'

'And that's it?'

'The Janissaries have spent years fighting Attila. They know that cavalry is always stopped by killing horses.'

'I'm so sorry, Dio.'

'Aye, I know.'

They walked in silence to the vehicles and Heph embraced Philemon and Lenore and watched them quietly ease Boreas and the other two mounts into the back of one of the carriers. The driving teams were there, but they sensibly refrained from interfering. They knew all too well that they had transported eleven horses from Scotland and the fact that three of their carriers would now return empty spoke plainly enough of the destruction that must have been sown in the last few hours.

Agape guided Heph out of the circle of light and came close to him. 'Look after your team. Eat, wash, change. Then get yourselves back to Scotland. Hera will meet you at the other end.'

'What happens then?'

'I don't think anyone knows.'

She left him and he returned to Dio's side. 'There's only three bunks,' said his tall friend.

'We travel together. Find me some pillows and I'll sleep on the floor.'

In one of the other carriers, two of the driving team had been using the kitchenette and they emerged with steaming bowls of beans and sausages.

Heph placed a hand on Dio's arm. 'I'm truly sorry about Xanthos. And I'm sorry for all this loss.'

'It was pretty wild out there.'

'I don't think I gave the right commands, but you followed me anyway and, for that, I'm grateful.'

Dio smiled sadly. 'I'm learning that wherever you lead us, it seems to end with another dead King.'

Philemon and Dio ate hungrily, but Heph could not stomach the smell of the food and he handed his bowl back to one of the cooks, then began to unstrap his armour. To his surprise, his arms and torso were mottled with bruising, the base of his skull thumped and he had nicks and cuts on every piece of exposed flesh. Lenore took a couple of delicate mouthfuls of her beans, but her eyes never left Heph. Her thigh was heavily bandaged and she grimaced as she moved, but she smiled at him and in that moment he really loved her.

The remnants of the Companion Cavalry left the Field in a single horse carrier a little before ten in the evening and began their long drive across Europe. Heph arranged pillows against one of the horse stalls and reclined as comfortably as he could. They tended the horses. They talked. They ate. But mostly they just lay in silence and grieved for the departed and stewed over the terrible violence of this game they played.

Stopping three times to exercise the horses outside, the journey to Amsterdam took almost twenty hours. Once under the lights of Ijmuiden passenger terminal, they left the animals in the care of the driving team and took themselves off to a restaurant to fill up on pizzas and cold beer before their late evening departure. Their conversation was still muted, but the shock and adrenaline of the Battle had dissipated, leaving their bodies craving calories.

Eventually, they boarded the ferry and discovered that the interior boasted bistros, coffee bars and individual cabins with soft white king-size beds. Heph locked himself into his private space, stripped and showered for an age, before wrapping himself in a robe and lying on his bed, listening to the rumble of the engines as the ship departed.

He was drifting into unconsciousness when there was a sharp knock at the door. Shaking himself out of his daze, he padded over and unlocked it.

'You!' he exclaimed in consternation.

It was Agape, dressed in denim and leather, washed, made-up and scented with something far more floral than when he had last been with her.

'Change of plan,' she said, her eyes running down the length of his bathrobe. 'Get dressed and join me in the coffee snug on second deck.'

Ten minutes later, he found her wedged into a low-lit corner sofa, two flat whites and two amarettos on the table.

'That was my sister,' he said after he had settled.

'I guessed.'

'You guessed?' he blurted indignantly. 'Pray tell me, at what point did you *guess* that the skull-faced commander of the Black Cloaks was my sister?'

'At the parley with the Kings.'

That quieted him. 'You knew it was Morgan before the fighting even began?'

'I had an inkling when she spoke to you and then when she looked at me.'

'But she was masked and she'd done whatever the hell it was to her teeth.'

'I recognised her voice and then her eyes.'

Heph sat silent for long seconds, digesting this.

'Halvar once told me you two were close.'

Agape nodded. 'She was a very, very special friend. Olena, brightest sword of the Companions and my blood-sister.'

'So how the hell did she end up becoming that monster on the Field?'

'You'll have to ask Hera. She coordinated Morgan's disappearance and that's all I know. But I've always thought the best way to hide someone in the Pantheon is to hide them in plain sight. So I've long suspected Morgan was moved to another Palatinate.'

'What, she just waltzes in and becomes the head of the

Black Cloaks? Wouldn't Attila have had something to say about that?'

Agape inclined her head at a valid question. 'I can only assume powerful strings were pulled.'

They lapsed into reflection and then Heph said sadly, 'I don't think she was happy.'

'She died in your arms. She would have been happy at the end.'

'I miss her more than when I didn't know where she was.'

'So do I. She was a crazy, beautiful woman and she burnt so brightly. I pray she rests in peace.'

Heph felt tears threatening to drop at her words and so he reached for his coffee and drank deeply. When he finally replaced his cup, Agape was regarding him sternly.

'I have spoken with Zeus.'

'Is that why you're on this ferry?'

'We agreed it was important for me to confer with you before we dock at Newcastle.'

'Is he happy with his victory?'

'In confidence, I think he's as stunned as the rest of us and will need a few days to work out the ramifications with the rest of the Caelestia. We must await their conclusions, but technically, if I'm correct, I suspect he might now own six hundred Huns.'

Heph blanched. 'Bloody hell.'

'That could be quite a cavalry, Captain.'

'Well, we're not kitting that lot out in bronze and plumes, like you forced on Valhalla, that's for damn sure.'

Agape looked at him with interest. 'Spoken like a true leader.'

Heph grabbed his liqueur and slugged it without noticing her tone. 'So what's so important that you have to speak to me about?'

'Zeus is very clear on one thing. We have a King who fled from the enemy. No King in the history of the Pantheon has ever done that. We honour our sovereigns because their roles are to lead us through the Seasons and to face death on the Field of Battle with courage and equanimity. In return, we shed our blood to protect them. Alexander is a disgrace and cannot be permitted to continue.'

Heph rained hard eyes on her. 'If you're suggesting I make a Challenge, you can damn well forget it.'

'You're the glory of this Palatinate, the leader every Titan looks to. You're at the heart of every twist and turn and the troops see this. They sense your destiny is entwined with the gods and they will follow you. '

'In case you've forgotten, the only reason I'm not dead with a hundred Hun blades in me is because my sister sacrificed herself to keep me breathing. Maybe you can tell Zeus to bloody well let me come to terms with that!'

'You led two of your mounted Companions to protect an unworthy King and then you charged at two *hundred* Black Cloaks when you knew nothing of your sister. Every Titan considers that the single most courageous act they have ever witnessed.'

Heph groaned in frustration. 'It was battle-rage, Agape. You know that better than anyone. I wasn't thinking; I was just up to my eyeballs in blood mist. I'd make a useless tactician. You saw me send Nicanor's Phalanx off across the plain before I'd assessed the enemy. You told me yourself I was an impetuous fool.'

'Aye, you were. A damn fool. But you learn from your mistakes.'

Heph shook his head and closed his eyes. 'I can't do this, Agape. I just lost my sister and most of my Cavalry and I can't take this on. I'm sorry, no.'

It was the touch of her fingers that jerked his eyes open. She had leaned across the table to hold his hand. She had never touched him like this before and her fingers were so firm and warm and feminine and free of any hint of a scratch or a bruise or other mark from the Battle. He looked up into her eyes and swam in their depths.

'Don't make your sister's death meaningless,' she said with quiet ferocity. 'Morgan sacrificed her life for you and she killed her own King because she was so proud of you.'

'Proud?' Heph stuttered.

'That's what her look told me after you had announced you were the Captain of Companion Cavalry.'

'Her look?'

'Her eyes met mine and she said to me: *Thank you Agape, for taking care of my brother. He is glorious.*'

Heph sat speechless, the hairs on his scalp tingling.

'Keep making her proud, Hephaestion. Keep being glorious. Become the greatest Alexander.'

XXXIV

Heph returned to his cabin and collapsed on the bed, but there was caffeine in his veins now and sleep would not come. The engine rumbled from deep in the bowels of the ship and the cabin rolled gently with each swell. His mind drifted.

He could not rid himself of the image of his sister's face as she lay dying on the Field. The wildness of her eyes behind the skull. Her blade-sharp teeth with blood oozing through them to spill onto cheeks that seemed never to have seen the sun. It tore at him that he could not know what she had gone through or how she had arrived at Hortobágy at the head of a Hun army.

He supposed Morgan had always been the wilder sibling. He remembered the years on the Craigmillar estate when she had started to wear black and become unaccountably angry. She would disappear for nights on end and return with swaggering boys and an even more swaggering attitude. She had become tougher too. Confident, muscled, powerful. He would never be able to erase the image of her grabbing their mother and flinging her against the wall like a toy. The next morning, his mother had departed for a meeting and never returned. Somewhere deep in his brain, he had long ago locked away the suspicion that Morgan never got over this. The very last interaction between the two women had been a physical confrontation and he wondered how his sister had lived with the guilt.

For a while after their loss, Morgan had taken responsibility for her younger brother and had been there for him with support and money, but then she too had disappeared and he had been so certain the Pantheon had claimed her that he was exhilarated when Radspakr's Venarii party had come hunting for him on Fleshmarket Close and offered him a chance to join too. How long ago that all seemed now. He thought of his younger self pushing his limits in the training vaults of Valhalla with Halvar and Freyja, so convinced that he would see his sister after the Oath-Taking. What would he have thought if he had known she wasn't in the Horde, nor even in Scotland? That she was far away in eastern Europe transforming herself into Attila's most feared commander?

Heph screwed up his face in frustration because that was the bit that still made no sense. In little over two years, Morgan had risen from a friendless Titan outcast to lead the Huns' most ruthless horse warriors. How did someone move Palatinates and build a new martial reputation in so little time? But, then again, he himself had gone from a Thrall with no name in Valhalla to the Titans' most famous warrior in even less time.

He must interrogate Hera, he resolved. Every time he took another step towards understanding his sister's destiny, the winding trail pointed him back to the wife of Zeus.

They docked in Newcastle just after seven the next morning

under leaden skies and squalls that rinsed away memories of the bright heat of Hortobágy.

The three empty horse carriers switched south down the A1 and the single carrier with its three equine and four human passengers trundled north towards Alnwick and Berwick and the border. News had filtered through that Spyro and Melitta were doing well and this cheered them. The wounded had been transferred to the best private wards in Budapest and then, if strong enough, flown back to Pantheon hospitals in Scotland. The rest of the Titans had flown back as well and would already be returning to their homes for much needed rest and recuperation.

After two hours, the carrier approached Edinburgh and Heph recognised the prominent shape of Arthur's Seat on the horizon, but then the vehicle pulled off the A-road and wound through lanes to a large parking area with a spectacular view of Tantallon Castle and Bass Rock beyond. Dio arched his eyebrows at Heph and then leaned forward to tap the driver on the shoulder.

'These horses need to get back to their stables.'

'We had instructions to make a drop here, pal.'

'A drop?'

The man jerked a thumb over his shoulder. 'The Captain, there.'

Dio looked back to Heph. 'You know about this?'

Heph shrugged and pulled a face. 'When do I ever know anything? I just get passed around and talked at and told where to go. Seems every time I wake up, I don't know where I'm going to be by nightfall.'

They could see a Mercedes across the otherwise empty car park. Its door swung open and a man with silver hair stepped out, looking svelte and smart in a grey cashmere jumper and matching woollen overcoat.

'Who's that?' Lenore asked for everyone.

Heph shouldered his bag, exited the rear doors and walked across the blustery car park, conscious of several sets of eyes peering through the windscreen behind.

The man came towards him and held out a hand. 'Hephaestion. We have not had the opportunity to meet personally. I am known as Zeus.'

Heph took the hand. It was beautifully manicured and hairless. The man himself was in his late sixties, but retained smooth, handsome features and a full head of hair. 'It's an honour to meet you, my lord.'

Instead of a chauffeur, Zeus pointed Heph to the passenger door and sat back behind the wheel. They followed the carrier through the lanes, then overtook it on the main road and drove smoothly into the arms of the city.

Heph thought the Titan god would be full of praise and gratitude for his actions, but when the older man spoke his tone was flinty.

'Would you be good enough to tell me what exactly happened on that Field? Why did a Hun commander wheel her cavalry away from you and kill her King instead?'

'I don't know, my lord. Maybe there were issues between them.'

'Issues?'

'Hun politics. Perhaps she had been told she could replace Attila if he fell at the Battle.'

'By Kyzaghan?'

'You are probably better placed to answer that, my lord.'

Zeus drove in silence, perhaps considering this or maybe wondering at the lie.

'And what were you saying to her?'

'I was thanking her for saving your Palatinate,' Heph replied tartly. 'Without her actions, we'd all be Huns by now.'

'You seemed remarkably upset by her passing.'

'I wanted to help her. She was a hero, a sister-in-arms and I wanted to save her.' That, at least, was true.

Zeus turned off the ring road and took them north into the city, passing the Braids and on towards Morningside. He was obviously unimpressed with the answers he had received, but was not about to force the issue.

Heph decided to change the subject. 'So what happens now?'

'That, Hephaestion, is the question on everyone's lips. As you can imagine, there is uproar. My fellow lord, Ördög, is the second Caelestis to lose his Palatinate in as many months and he is not exactly sweetness and joy about it. There is a storm raging in Budapest and I imagine he will soon be on his way to Rome to demand an audience with Jupiter.

'There is also huge consternation amongst the Curiate and the wider Pantheon's backers. Many have lost fortunes on the actions at Hortobágy and they are convinced a conspiracy is afoot. Why else would a Hun officer turn on her King? Everyone who has lost money is convinced everyone else has made a killing by being in on the conspiracy. They clamour that Bleda must have been promised untold riches to strike Attila and that vast sums were wagered on this outcome by shady syndicates who have now made fortunes. It's a mess. No one trusts anyone.'

'I'm sorry to hear that. It wasn't exactly much fun for those of us who were doing the real killing on the Field.'

Zeus chose to ignore the remark and Heph realised he was in the company of a diplomat as well as a financier.

'It seems,' continued Zeus, 'after some earnest debate amongst the Caelestia, that I now own the Hun Palatinate, as well as Valhalla. Attila was killed by one of his own, but he was nevertheless killed by a sword in hand and that means his Palatinate must fall. At the time, his position on the Field was being attacked by our Companion Cavalry and our Hellenes, so the Caelestia has agreed that it is to our Titan Palatinate that the spoils of victory go.

'Next year, we will lead a hugely expanded force into the Twenty-First Raiding Season against Kyzaghan and his Sultanate in the second tier of a revised five-strong Pantheon structure, which sees the Kheshig and the Warring States below us in Tier Three and the Legion, of course, above us all.

'The detail within that plan is, naturally, unbelievably complex. I must work with Atilius and his central teams to determine *how* I oversee a Titan Palatinate that will have half its force in Hungary. We will need to consider the logistics of paying and providing for all these new troops and we must grapple with how we run Raiding and Blood Seasons against a Sultanate based in Istanbul.'

Heph brooded over this. He had been so focused on the deeply personal ramifications of the Battle that he had not considered the wider furore that must have blown through every outpost of the Pantheon, far and wide. He could perhaps see why Zeus was not in the mood for celebration.

They were crossing the greenery of Bruntsfield and ahead the Royal Mile rose into the rain-washed skies.

'In the shorter term,' continued Zeus, 'things are just as complex, especially the decisions and actions of the next few days. And that's why I decided to be your chauffeur this morning.' For the first time, he turned his head to examine Heph. 'I have need of you in Ephesus.'

'I had hoped I might go home to rest.'

XXXV

It was not unheard of for Jupiter to visit her Legion at their field camp deep in the beech forests of Mount Navegna, but it was a rare honour and one which had never before occurred without plenty of advance warning.

So, when her cortege of three Porsche Cayennes pulled up at the fifteen-foot wire fence with two thousand volts purring through it and the guards were told who sat in the back of the middle vehicle, a ripple of panic tore through the unit of Arma dei Carabinieri in their nearby control room. Urgent calls were placed to the main camp as the cortege was waved on along the final eight miles of woodland road to the southern gate in the camp's stockade.

First Spear raced to the nearest barrack block to haul out an honour guard of twelve and get them kitted as fast as possible. Cassia, Legate of the Second Cohort, was on duty that morning and she came striding out of the Principia, strapping on her helmet.

Caesar himself paced to the entrance of his villa, dressed in tunic and caliga sandals, biting on an apple. It was two days since they had all watched the feeds incredulously as the Battle at Hortobágy unfolded, and the news that his wife was about to arrive unannounced was something he had hoped to avoid.

Primus had the honour guard straightening themselves as the vehicles sped onto the parade ground and braked to a halt. The legionaries snapped to attention and Cassia raised her arm in salute. Jupiter emerged and nodded a response. Caesar knew he should go out to her, but he stayed put nonetheless. Let her come to him. It was a small, petty point, but it would infuriate her in front of the troops.

She wore a fine summer dress of cream linens and brocade, with golden sandals, outsize sunglasses and a small bag over one shoulder. She looked, he thought, as though she should be calling on the boutiques of Milan, not making an unexpected visit to the Legion's field camp.

'My dear, you must have had an early start. You should have informed me and I would have ensured you were not detained at the checkpoints.'

'It was no inconvenience. And my visit is, let's say, spontaneous.'

'My pleasure, of course. Can I offer you something to eat after your journey?'

'Coffee, nothing else.'

He wondered whether to lean in and give her a peck on the cheek, but she had not removed her sunglasses and he could sense the brittle angles of her posture and the tight lines of her jaw. The events at Hortobágy had set off explosions in every corner of the Pantheon and no doubt he was about to get the benefit of his wife's opinions.

'Come through,' he waved. 'We can sit by the fountain.'

'I have not come for a picnic in the sun.'

'Well then, perhaps the Principia would suit you better.' Caesar waved to First Spear. 'Have coffee brought to the HQ.'

Husband and wife walked together across the bright parade ground and into the shadows of the Principia. The sacellum chamber stood at the heart of the complex, lit only by small windows and home to the Eagle standards of Jupiter, and the First and Second Cohorts. Caesar showed her to a chair around the campaign table and she at last removed her sunglasses, while a servant brought a tray of crockery and a stove pot of coffee, then hurriedly departed.

'So, Marcella,' Caesar said in firmer tones, once they were alone. 'Would you mind telling me why you are here?'

He poured two coffees and she ferreted in her bag for her gold cigarette case and lit up. 'You know full well, Julian. Because of the shit-show in Hungary. We appear to have got ourselves into quite a mess.'

'Events were indeed somewhat surprising, but they achieved what we wanted. We said the Battle must only end with another dead King and another fallen Palatinate and that's what we got. At least they didn't fight themselves to an exhausted standstill with all three sovereigns still standing.'

'It seemed to my eyes that the fallen King should have been Alexander. He was exposed on the plain and seconds from being submerged by Hun cavalry. If not him, then Mehmed appeared equally close to peril. So, I keep asking myself, how did it come to be Attila who fell at the last, stabbed through the heart by one of his own Hun swords? I hoped you might be able to shed some light on it?'

Caesar seated himself opposite and took his time

answering. 'Looks to me as though Nikolas and Hakan came to some sort of agreement to ensure Mikhail was the loser.'

'Really?' Jupiter leaned towards him in mock credulity. 'What must they have agreed to entice the Huns to kill their own King? Is it really so easy to bribe a senior officer in another Palatinate?'

'Money can achieve anything; it's simply a matter of how much.'

'And yet, at the time, Nikolas and Hakan were extremely busy fighting each other. The Titan Phalanx had almost broken the Sultanate's Yaya square and the Janissary column was destroying the Companion lines. So much bloodshed. So many losses. At the exact same minute you say they had bribed the Huns to kill Attila.' She tapped ash from her cigarette. 'I suppose I've never been one to understand such complex military tactics.'

She was playing with him. He could tell from the barren wasteland of her tone and the way her words coiled around him. They argued often enough when they spent time together, but this was different. There was no heat to her anger. Instead it was implacably cold. She must have planned this conversation long before she arrived at the camp, but what did she want?

'Have you heard from any of them?' she asked unexpectedly.

'Have you?'

'They're *your* friends.'

'They are Caelestes, while I am a mere King.'

'Oh we've played that game enough, Julian. They were always your friends, the band of brothers you began all this with. Don't you feel anything for them? Raymond is dead and Mikhail is broken. He is a very angry man.'

'So you *have* heard from them?'

'I spoke briefly with him and, as you can imagine, I doubt he will go quietly. I suspect, Caesar, your Pantheon is in jeopardy.'

'Oh, it's *my* Pantheon now.'

'It was always yours. You created it.' She smiled thinly. 'I just rule it.'

He detested this. He stared at his coffee and she could see his jaw working as he tried to control his own temper. There were storm clouds around his eyes, as though he had not slept, as though he had spent nights alone in his villa pacing and fretting. As though, perhaps, he might even have shed tears.

And in that moment, she hated him. Truly, irreparably.

'I have watched the feeds several times,' she continued. This was an under-statement. She had watched them endlessly, feverishly, until her eyes could take no more. 'They do not make me think there was a deal between Caelestes, or even between Kings. If there was any pre-arranged agreement on that Field, the images suggest the parties involved were two officers. A Captain in the Titans and a Colonel in the Huns. They are clearly shown speaking together before the Hun dies. The Titan removed his helmet and the camera teams got their close-up. You must have seen it yourself.'

'I saw it.'

'So I am going to ask you one more time.' She kept her voice level because she had promised herself she would maintain a cool head for this encounter, even though her heart was pounding and her throat was so tight that she could barely force the words out. 'Why do you think a Hun and a Titan – two individuals who should have no way of identifying each other, nor any means to forge an agreement – nevertheless appeared to work in unison at the climax of the Battle?'

This was the question she had come all this way, unannounced, to hear her husband answer. He had one chance.

He blew it.

'There you go again, my dear, constructing conspiracies from thin air. Only a matter of a few weeks ago, you were certain Raymond had been despatched by a hired killer and you would be the next target. Now you're thinking our Pantheon troops are making deals behind our backs.' He tried to laugh the idea away. 'I saw only a brave Titan officer honour a fallen foe because her actions had saved his King. Such dignity in the midst of so much violence should be applauded.'

Marcella looked away and stared at the Eagle standards. She had never expected him to answer truthfully. Her husband had lived a life of such ridiculous privilege that he was forever blind to the hurt his actions caused others. Nevertheless, she felt a seam of deep, almost painful, disappointment. Perhaps there could have been a different outcome to this meeting. Perhaps he might actually have said and done something laudable. But no, he had stuck to his lies, just as he had stuck to them all these years.

Without taking her gaze from the Eagles, she said in a clear, confident tone, 'I am mobilising the Legion.'

'You're *what*?'

'Two Caelestes are gone. Two Palatinates destroyed. The entire Pantheon structure must adjust. And one individual man is at the heart of it all. One man, who rode onto a Field in Scotland with a cavalry which had not been formally revealed at the start of the Season and who killed a King. One man – one King Killer – who seemingly then turned the tide of a Hun attack and knelt beside his fallen foe with his helmet removed so that the world could see him, idolise him, fall in love with him. He is a mere Captain who has become the most famous warrior in the Pantheon and who is single-handedly making a mockery of us.'

'You can't just mobilise the Legion. We have no business in this. The Rules dictate—'

'Damn your Rules! I will not have my Legion sit by while this man – this *upstart* – rides roughshod over everything and makes this Palatinate a laughing stock.'

Caesar was crimson now, his words spluttering out. 'How dare you speak like that! The Rules dictate that a new structure is created. The Titans and the Sultanate will now oppose each other next year in Tier Two. They will face off in a Raiding Season, a Blood Season and then a Battle, as has been the Pantheon's way for the last two decades. The winner will meet us then – and *only* then – in a single fight at the finale of the year.'

'No, Julian. No.' Jupiter leapt to her feet and slammed the table so hard that it stunned him. 'Don't you understand, Julian? I *know*. I know all about your dirty little secret and now you've let it get so out of hand. Your darling King Killer is feted high and low. His presence has resulted in the fall of two Caelestes, the deaths of two Kings, and the storm that's ripping through our funding models. And you think our only response is to reorganise the Pantheon to fit around him?'

'You can't just—'

'Damn you, Julian. *Damn* you. Not only will the Legion mobilise, it will do so in seven days.'

'Don't be ridiculous. We cannot—'

'Seven days. We will meet this new Titan Palatinate, with its Vikings and Huns and King Killer, on a Field of Battle in one week. We will destroy them all and – most importantly – we will destroy *him*. Do you understand? We will destroy *him*, or this – you and me, the Pantheon, everything between us – it's over. Finished.'

'You're crazy, Marcella. You've let these conspiracy theories get to you. We will do no such thing. I forbid it.'

'Oh, you forbid it, do you? We'll see about that.'

She pulled her phone from her bag and hit a contact. Caesar was on his feet now too, but all he could do was stare incredulously, his chest heaving with an anger that had been pent up for so long.

A face appeared on the screen.

'Atilius. I am here with Caesar.'

She panned the phone so he could see them both.

'Ma'am,' the Praetor said uneasily.

'The Legion and the Titans will face each other on a Field of Battle in one week. You will make the necessary arrangements.'

'You will not,' snarled Caesar. 'I forbid it.'

'One week, ma'am?' Even on a phone screen, it was easy to see the Praetor's face blanch. 'I'm not sure that would be possible.'

'I didn't ask you for excuses. I require you to action my decision.'

'You will do no such thing, Atilius.'

'Ma'am, the logistics would be staggering.'

'Exactly,' Caesar agreed. 'It is a ludicrous proposal.'

'And the Curiate would have no time to place their wagers,' the Praetor added.

'This is not about money,' Jupiter countered, calmer than her husband. 'It has gone much deeper.'

'Of course it's about money, woman! This whole Game runs on money.'

'Ma'am, my lord Caesar is right. We must have the Curiate's support.'

'Atilius,' Jupiter said gravely.

'Ma'am?' The man looked trapped, desperate to be anywhere but on this call.

'Who is the Lord High Caelestis?'

'Don't listen to her, Praetor. This is *my* Pantheon. I am Caesar.'

'You are, ma'am.'

'Then you will do my bidding or face the consequences.'

Atilius took a deep breath and dropped his eyes from the camera. 'I will begin the arrangements, ma'am.'

'You fool!' Caesar shouted and threw up his arms in despair.

'Find a Field. Pay the landowners, sort the security.'

Caesar swore and collapsed back in his seat, his face creased with fury.

Atilius pretended he had not noticed. 'Do you have a location in mind, ma'am?'

'We can hold it in the forests near here.'

The Praetor nodded slowly, but his expression showed he was far from convinced.

'Spill it,' said Jupiter.

'Ma'am, if this is about honour and glory, rather than money, it might seem too stacked in your favour if you name a Field so close to Rome when notice is this tight. The more so because the Titans must coordinate not only their current troops, but a new Hun force still based outside Budapest. If you present the foe with such logistical challenges, your eventual victory will be all the more undermined in the eyes of our audiences.'

Jupiter considered this. She glanced at her husband, but his molten eyes were now fastened on a distant wall and were not going to budge.

'Are you suggesting Scotland?'

'If we can effectively coordinate the transportation of your Legion to Zeus' home soil, your feats on the Battle Field will be all the more glorious.'

'Very well. Identify a place as fast as possible. Pay whoever needs to be paid. Just sort it. The Legion will depart in five days. Keep me updated at all times.'

She cut the call and looked at her husband.

'You're making a huge mistake,' he said with quiet menace.

She extracted another cigarette and lit up, blowing smoke in his direction.

'I think it was you who made the huge mistake many years ago.'

XXXVI

Ephesus was quiet.

The commotion of the previous twenty-four hours had dwindled. The troops had returned, sorted their kit and been assigned leave. Weapons and armour had been collected for inspection, cleaning and recording. Administration launched into a flurry of registrations, resource reviews, hospital checks, payment protocols and formal reporting of logistics and transport provision. But that had all been completed by the time Heph stalked up to the changing areas and took a leisurely dip in the pool.

A few of Simmius' administrators floated around and a scattering of Heavies guarded the entrances, but otherwise, Heph had the place to himself. Zeus had told him to get some proper food inside him, then change and join him in the gardens on the top floor at midday. He swam a length of the pool as his mind wandered between memories of his sister, questions about how the horses might be settling back at their stables, and a growing unease that the darkness over Hortobágy at the end of the struggle had prevented him from checking if Calder was unhurt. His mind had been so preoccupied with one woman he loved, that he had failed to consider another.

Eventually, as time eased towards midday, he dried himself and discovered a red tunic and sandals waiting for him near the lockers. He dressed and made his way up to the gardens, where two of Nicanor's Heavies stood sentry by the doors.

'My lord, Hephaestion,' one of them said and placed a fist to his heart.

'Are you rested?'

The man pulled a face. 'I'll be ready for my bed.'

'It was quite an engagement out there, wasn't it?'

'I saw you speak with the Colonel before he marched us towards the Sultanate square.'

Heph reddened, wondering what the man thought of him encouraging Nicanor to advance across the open plain when they had not properly reconnoitred the foe.

'The Huns couldn't get near us and we broke those Yaya lines with ease,' the man continued. 'We were so close to Mehmed when the klaxon went. Almost took him down. It was a brilliant tactical decision, if I may say so, sir?'

Heph inclined his head and allowed a small smile. 'You may, thank you.'

The sentry stepped aside and opened the doors. 'Lord Zeus awaits you, as does the King.'

'The King? Alexander is here?'

'He is, sir.'

Heph walked into the gardens with the first warning signs tingling beneath his skull.

Scents assailed him. Rain pattered on the glass dome and humid warmth enveloped the greenery. Through the vines, he could see four figures waiting on the giant Star of Macedon mosaic: Zeus, Alexander, Simmius and Menes.

An odd mix. Heph's instincts whispered all the louder. They were dressed in Titan tunics like him and they had been sharing goblets of wine, which were now discarded on a stone table.

'Ah, Hephaestion,' said Zeus.

Alexander turned hate-filled eyes, rimmed with black from exhaustion and stress, towards him. His cheeks were scarlet, his jowls sallow cream. Menes kept his face averted, but Simmius watched the new arrival with unconcealed fascination, as though still not believing what he had seen on the feeds from Hortobágy.

'You are confident this is all we need?' Zeus asked Simmius.

'Yes, lord. As long as you are present and there are two further witnesses, we are formal.'

Heph kept his mouth shut and hovered a few yards from the others. He could see from their expressions that they had not gathered to exchange pleasantries.

'You bastard,' Alexander murmured at him. 'You've only been a Titan for one damn year.'

'Now, now,' said Zeus. 'We will maintain the decorum necessary on such a solemn occasion.'

'I might accept it if one of my senior officers stood there, but why should I do so when it is just this scrap of a lad, this Captain of eleven?'

'You will accept it,' replied Zeus with sudden zeal, 'because I have *already* accepted it.'

Sharp, visceral horror spasmed through Heph's chest. He realised suddenly why they were gathered and he knew he must say something to stop this stupidity. He had consented to nothing. He had asked for nothing. When Simmius began to speak, his words merely confirmed what Heph already knew.

'We have come together today in the presence of Lord Zeus, Caelestis of the Titan Palatinate, because Hephaestion, Captain of Companion Cavalry, has laid down a Challenge to Alexander, King of the Titan Palatinate. Lord Zeus has decreed this Challenge to be valid and acceptable and, thus, Alexander, King of the Titans, and Hephaestion, Captain of Companion Cavalry, will here and now contest this Challenge.'

Heph was so transfixed that he barely noticed Menes sidling up to him and murmuring, 'Now then, lad, let's not make a fuss. Zeus has decreed this, so you need to get your head around it.'

'But... but, I never...'

'I'll pretend I didn't hear that. The records say you've made a formal Challenge and we're not going to argue with that, are we?'

Menes looked him up and down, then said over his shoulder, 'He's ready, lord.'

Alexander's gaze had barely flinched from Heph. 'And when I win?'

'Then you will have earned the right to retain your crown,' confirmed Zeus. 'I will consider no further objections to your authority.'

Alexander weighed this. He was breathing hard and he ran a nervous tongue around his lips, but his glare was steady enough. 'Then let's get it done.'

Zeus signalled and Menes reached behind his belted

tunic and unsheathed two shortswords. He reversed them with casual dexterity, catching the points in his palms and proffering a hilt each to Heph and the King. Still in a daze, Heph accepted and held the blade up to inspect its edges.

He should be objecting. He should be discarding the weapon and refusing to have any part in this charade, but Agape's phrase was niggling at him. *Be the greatest Alexander.* If they had asked him to make a Challenge, he would have refused. If they had tried to sit him down to explain the politics, he would have waved them away. But now, like this, when no words had been wasted on persuasion, when no time had been permitted for consideration, when he stood with a blade facing a fat coward of a King who had no right to take the name of the greatest general in history, he felt his bile rise and his blood pump and his grip on the hilt tighten.

They had brought him to the edge of the precipice without fanfare or prelude and now he must take the leap of faith or fall forever.

'My lord King, are you ready?' Simmius asked.

Alexander stood like a bull in the centre of the floor, his belly rising and falling, the sword held casually in one big paw. 'I am.'

'And Hephaestion, are you ready?'

No, he thought, *of course I'm not. I'm exhausted from a Battle of three armies on the plains of Hungary. I'm broken by the loss of many brave riders who trained with me in the foothills of the Ochils. I'm shattered from cradling my long-lost sister as she died in my arms. So, no, I'm not bloody ready.*

'I am,' he said.

And with a speed that belied his weight, the King of the Titans came at him.

Where is the fool?

Skarde pressed the bell again and followed it up with another furious volley of thumps on the door. *Check your monitor, you imbecile.*

He had been loath to call ahead. Kustaa would have asked too many questions about why he was returning and whether he had indeed contacted Valerius and succeeded in securing a conversation with Jupiter. Much better to arrive unannounced and do what he had to do with the minimum of fuss.

But it had never occurred to him that the house might be empty.

Where could the bloody Thane be? The man held the God Killer in his custody, so surely he would sit tight and do nothing stupid. Him and that damn woman, Aurora, who had got herself caught up in it all. Skarde still did not rightly know who she was or how she had become involved, but it was her poor luck because he now had his orders from Jupiter. Aurora's last thought would be to curse herself for ever meeting Skarde.

Except that she didn't seem to be where she was supposed to be.

He stepped back from the door and gave it a critical examination. It was the original entrance to the grand property. Old, solid, damn hard to break down without creating a lot of noise. *Why the hell aren't they answering?*

He tried to think rationally. They had nowhere else to go

or, at least, that's what Kustaa had led him to believe. He supposed they must make the occasional excursion to get food and essentials, but surely only one of them would do that. Skarde had stolen Kustaa's car, so any trip would have to be on foot, and no further than to the local village shop. So where could they be?

A chill blossomed across his shoulders. What if Atilius had already sent his teams to requisition the house? Kustaa had said he feared this. He was no longer a Thane of Valhalla and the house was Pantheon property. Could they have come and found the damn kid and taken them all away?

Christ! Skarde knew he had been absent much longer than he had planned, but no one could build in contingency to cover the Lord High Caelestis herself deciding to throw him in her cells for a week and have her muscle boys give him a daily kicking.

There was movement and Jupiter's Praetorian appeared from the side of the house, shrugging. 'No sign of movement in the lower windows,' she said.

She was the most impressive woman Skarde had ever met. At least six foot two and broad as a horse. If she had spent her career in an office, her heft would have run to fat, but Skarde knew the movement of muscle well enough. She had greying hair, cut short like a boy's, and had been wearing the same stretch jeans and loose coat since they had landed at Edinburgh and picked up Kustaa's Mercedes AMG in the long-stay car park. Her only adornments were two gold stud earrings, one through her left ear and one through her right nostril. Domna, she had called herself in a tone that had brooked no questions when first introductions had been made, but that was as personal as they had got.

He had sat next to her on the plane and then again in the car, and his mind had gone to very dark places. The things he could do to a woman of such strength. The things they could fight over, tooth and nail.

But he had to rein back his instincts. He was under Jupiter's orders and the presence of this Praetorian had been a condition of the agreement. If he still yearned for a place in the Pantheon, if he still believed he could forge a new role in Jupiter's Legion, he must carry out her wishes and kill the four targets. When the task was completed and Jupiter's attention had wandered to other things, perhaps he and this glorious Praetorian could play for real.

'Maybe they're hiding,' Domna suggested.

'He's got a monitor. He'd see it was me outside.'

'Then maybe he doesn't trust you.'

He knew she was toying with him, so he swallowed an angry response. 'Well, I guess we're going to have to lose our element of surprise.'

He pulled out Kustaa's phone and rang the number for Aurora.

'Yes?' came the woman's voice tentatively down the line after several rings.

'It's me. Put him on.'

There were a few seconds of muffled exchanges and then Kustaa spoke: 'Who is this?'

'It's Skarde, you idiot. Where the hell are you?'

'Why are you asking?'

'Because I'm standing outside your front door.'

More muffled words.

'What do you want?'

'What do I want?' Skarde was getting angry. 'I'm back

with orders from Jupiter, what the hell do you think? She wants us to bring the boy to her.'

'That won't be possible.'

'Why not?'

'Because we're not there.'

Skarde pressed two fingers into his eyeballs to physically restrain himself from yelling abuse down the phone. 'I know that. Where the hell are you?'

'I decided we needed to take him somewhere more secure.'

'So tell me where that is and I'll come and we'll talk and then we'll take him to Jupiter and claim our reward.'

'It's not that simple.'

'Why not?'

'Because we've travelled a long way.'

Skarde held his breath and stared at the Praetorian, forcing himself to remain calm. 'Just tell me where and I'll come to you.'

There was such a long silence that he thought he had lost the connection.

'Hello? Are you still there?'

'Yes, I'm here. But I'm not yet ready to tell you where we are.'

'Why the hell not?'

'Because I wasn't expecting your call and I need some time to think about it.'

'Kustaa, I swear, if you start pissing about, I'll not be responsible for my actions. While you've been sitting on your arse doing fuck all, I've had an audience with Jupiter and I've negotiated places of honour for us both in her Legion, as long as we give her the boy. Do you understand?'

'I hear you, but I'm not ready to tell you our location.'

'Christ, you idiot! Jupiter didn't say we could just bring him to her when we felt like it. She's not the type to let people do things at their leisure.'

'That's your problem, Skarde. When I've thought this through, I will make contact and propose where and when we meet. And that's an end to it.'

Skarde was shaking with rage. He was so close to hurling the phone against the door, but he caught the look in the Praetorian's eyes and forced himself to calm down.

'Okay, have it your way. In the meantime, perhaps you can do me a different favour. I assume your duties as Thane included oversight of Palatinate accommodation?'

'It did, but I have no access to records now.'

'Can you recall the address of one former Viking called Calder?'

There was another pause, pregnant with suspicion. 'Why?'

'That's Jupiter's business, not yours. Can you or can you not recall it?'

'As a matter of coincidence, I do know this one. She asked Sveinn for a change of address just before the Battle at Knoydart and it was one of his final instructions to me.'

'Tell me.'

Kustaa gave him the address and he repeated it aloud so the Praetorian would remember the details too. 'Hermitage Gardens, right.'

'We'll speak again in due course, Skarde.'

'You're damn well right, we will.'

He cut the line and scowled at the Praetorian. 'Bastard's run for cover.'

'Then we will need to flush him out.'

'Aye, indeed. But first we have another fish to catch. A prize I've been waiting to claim for a long time.'

XXXVII

Alexander crossed the six paces between them in a flash and the needle point of his shortsword struck faster than a cobra.

Heph had no time to drop into a fighting stance and parry. Instincts kicked in and he simply threw himself to one side. He felt the blade snatch the edge of his tunic and pass harmlessly. The King was overextended and unbalanced and if the blood song of conflict had been pumping through Heph's veins, he would have struck without thought. But the fight was only seconds old and his movements were still sluggish. He retreated and permitted his opponent to right himself and prepare again.

Now Alexander lowered his sword arm and hoped to entice Heph to take the offensive. It was a risky strategy, but he could see that his opponent was still in shock from the suddenness of the situation and there was never a better time to take advantage in a duel than when your adversary's fighting senses were not yet warmed. Seduce the fool into a laboured assault and then strike. If not the death blow, then a flesh wound would suffice. Draw first blood. Weaken him early.

He made a play of looking away and winking at Menes,

but even this would not draw Heph, so he abandoned the ploy and decided that fast, violent assault was the best response. With an explosion of movement, he closed the gap again and thrust high at his opponent's throat. Heph barely registered the danger, but some subconscious part of his brain brought his blade up to deflect the King's sword.

The man had reckoned for this though and he kept coming, his weight bearing into his lighter adversary. Heph found himself going backwards, his sandals scrabbling for purchase on the mosaic and failing to stay with the momentum of his upper body. He went down hard, the impact punching the air from his lungs. Alexander was over him and his blade came inexorably again, seeking Heph's ribs, hoping to skewer his heart to the floor.

Somehow, Heph rolled, but not fast enough to avoid the strike. Livid white-hot pain seared through him as steel sliced the edge of his left bicep and tore into the muscle of his back. A cry broke from his lips, but the impact had not stalled his movement. As Alexander reared to stab again, Heph kept rolling until he had the space to scramble to his feet. The fire of the wound burned through him. Blood smeared the floor and ran warm beneath his tunic.

The King growled in triumph at the sight and came at him again, but now there was nothing sluggish about his opponent. Heph could feel the fighting rage calling him. The tang of blood was in his nostrils. Adrenaline flooded him. His lungs burned and his brain coalesced around the most basic of instincts. Kill to survive. Fight to live. Take blood and keep taking it until there is nothing more.

This time, as Alexander thrust, Heph swatted the attack aside and stepped forward with his own lightning strike.

The blade should have buried itself in the King's ample gut, promising him a long, awful death, but somehow Alexander saw it and used his momentum to shoulder into Heph's open flank and force the weapon aside. It sliced tunic and skin, but left nothing more than a scratch.

With a bellow, the big man's free hand grabbed at Heph's own tunic and he swung his extended sword arm to bludgeon the pommel against the side of Heph's head. Sparks exploded in Heph's vision and he was momentarily stunned by the blow. His knees gave way and he collapsed, but this movement saved his head from a second punch. Alexander missed and overbalanced. His bulk dropped onto his kneeling opponent and for precious moments, both fighters sprawled clumsily in unison.

The sweat stink of his adversary engulfed Heph and his stomach roiled. Spluttering, he pushed himself free and struggled upright. His left arm was hanging heavy and the heat of his wound was cooling to an indescribably heavy throb. He took several long breaths and raised his sword arm. Alexander had got himself onto one knee and was steadying himself to stand, but he was wheezing uncontrollably and spittle hung in a fine bead from his open mouth.

Now Heph could see fear in the man's tight, piggy eyes. Not the terror that comes when a warrior knows he is beaten, rather a shifting confusion that something else is amiss.

The King clambered to his feet, took gulps of air and then pointed his blade again and came at Hephaestion. Iron rang as they clashed. Heph had to call on all his new Titan training to remember not to swing with his blade. Valhalla's longswords had been designed to hack at flesh and mail, but these shorter blades were all about the stab. The two fighters thrust and parried, first high, then low.

Despite his wound, Heph felt his feet responding and he began to dance across the floor. Speed, however, had deserted the King. His bulk weighed on him more than ever. He grunted with exertion each time he attacked and stepped away to suck oxygen into his lungs. Spittle still oozed from his lips and his eyes darted with fear.

Something was not as it should be. Heph could sense it. His own wound was the more grievous and he had laid no real hits on his foe, so Alexander should be in the ascendancy, buoyed by the blood still leaking from the younger man and confident in his own strength and experience. But instead, the King was slowing and keeping back from Heph's reach whenever movements allowed. His breathing was coming faster and faster, his brow beading with sweat.

He swung furiously at Heph as though he were a bothersome wasp, carving the air once and then a second time, even though Heph could step away with ease. He attempted a charge and a stab, but there was none of the killer momentum now and Heph bobbed out of reach. Alexander paused and wiped a fist across his chin, and his eyes flitted towards Zeus. He steadied himself again, focused on Heph and came at him with hateful fury. Blades sang once more and this time Heph found he had the strength to hold his opponent's attack at bay.

The King was weakening.

Heph disengaged and examined the man. His wheezing was becoming convulsive, his face boiling red. His arms were loose, the sword's point drooping towards the floor.

His gaze kept leaving Heph and shifting between Zeus and Simmius, shocked and accusatory.

Heph too turned dissenting eyes on Zeus. 'I will not fight an ill man.'

'The Challenge has begun,' replied Simmius. 'One of you must end it.'

A groan broke from Alexander and he summoned every ounce of strength to raise his sword, but the blade wobbled like his jowls and Heph felt no need even to bring his own weapon up. He stood silently, sword by his side, watching the King. Alexander did not have the stamina to maintain his fighting posture for long. His blade drooped again and he closed his eyes in an attempt to stop the gardens spinning. He forced himself to steady and for a moment he seemed recovered, then his knees buckled and he crumbled into a heap on the floor.

No one else moved. Heph wanted to go to him and offer his hand to help his adversary rise, but he could not yet trust the iron still gripped in the King's fist. The three spectators did nothing. It was as if Alexander's unexplained collapse was of no consequence. The King was twisting on the floor, an arm reaching towards the stone table where the discarded goblets of wine had been placed.

'You poisoned him!' Heph blurted, in a moment of clarity, and then tossed his sword on the floor. 'Well, you know where you can stick your bloody Challenge. I will not kill a man who has been incapacitated.'

Simmius looked to Zeus and Zeus glanced at Menes. The new Colonel of Light Infantry paced over to Heph and picked up the fallen sword. Heph thought he was going to attempt to persuade him otherwise and offer him the hilt again, but instead Menes swung away and, before Heph could react, thrust the blade so hard beneath Alexander's ribcage that it buried itself in the layer of fat right up to its cross-guard. Alexander jerked upright, heaved a vast gasp of pain and surprise, then started to tremble. He choked once and vomited blood down his front. He tried to lift one hand to grasp at the implement embedded in him, but he did not have the strength to hold his weight with the other arm. He sank back, emitted a single long bubbling hiss and died.

There was silence.

'The Challenge is complete,' stated Simmius, as though concluding a meeting.

'What?' barked Heph, turning on him. 'You forced me to fight a man you had already poisoned!'

'The poison alone would not have killed him. It needed a blade to do the job.'

'But why? How could you do such a thing?'

'To ensure you won.'

Heph had no words to respond. He shook his head in disbelief and ran a hand through his hair.

'And for a while there,' said Menes, 'we wondered if even that would be enough. He damn near had you.'

'Menes, for three years that man held your own position as Colonel of Lights. He was your commander. When he was crowned, he promoted you. How could you turn on him like that?'

It was Zeus who answered in a tone which cut through the debate. 'Because he fled from the enemy.'

Heph turned his attention to the Caelestis, but the words had punctured his anger.

Zeus continued. 'This King ran away on the Field of Battle, in front of the entire watching Pantheon – not just from the enemy, but from the desperate plight of his own forces. Do you think for one second that we could have allowed him to win this fight?'

'Hephaestion,' Simmius spoke. 'Challenge or no Challenge, our troops would never again have accepted this man as their sovereign. When he ran, he signed his own death warrant.'

'By rights, he should have died on the blades of Bleda's Black Cloaks,' rumbled Menes.

'But he didn't,' Heph said emphatically, with anger rising in his veins.

'Indeed,' interceded Zeus. 'The Fates determined otherwise. So we had to complete the deed ourselves.'

Heph shook his head again and lapsed into silence. He still could not believe he had come through the horror and violence of the Battle, only to be required to participate in a blood fight. Emotions slunk out of him like a deflated balloon and his shoulders sank as exhaustion hit and the pain of his wound came roaring back.

Simmius saw him grimace and waved impatiently towards the doors of the gardens, where the two sentries had their faces pressed against the glass. 'Get a medic up here immediately. And don't you breathe a word of this to anyone or I'll have you flayed alive.'

Zeus rose from his seat and approached Heph. Gently he reached out and placed a hand on his shoulder. He waited until Heph raised his downcast face. 'I will not call you Hephaestion again. You are now far more than that.'

'What if I don't want it?' Heph challenged through teeth gritted from the pain.

Zeus smiled. 'Many months ago, my wife told me of her breakfast meeting with you. Of the man who spoke so passionately about ancient military matters and the wonders of cavalry. I watched you nurture your mounted unit, demand of them, inspire them. And then I saw the beauty of your charge on the Field in Knoydart and I knew I now owned something – some*one* – very special. Your actions at Hortobágy only confirmed this opinion as not one, not two, but three Palatinates – Titan, Viking and Hun – looked upon you at the finale as their new God of War. Oh, I know you want it. You've always wanted it.

'So, I salute you. Alexander of Macedon – High King of the Titans, Commander of Companions, Protector of Pella, Persepolis, Ephesus and Thebes, Lord of the Sky-Gods, Captain of Companion Cavalry, General of Hellenes and Huns, Killer of Kings. Rest and recover, and then go and claim your army.'

PART FOUR

KING

XXXVIII

L ana could not stomach cooking.

She sprawled on one of the mismatched chairs around the dining table in Freyja's kitchen and stared glumly at the pots and ingredients she had put out on the island before her bath. She always called it Freyja's kitchen. Force of habit. It was hers now, but she took no pleasure in that formality.

When she had finally arrived back at the house, she had determined that she must be disciplined and active, otherwise her brain would shut down and the demons would come screeching back. She knew she must get some decent food inside her – a good Thai curry perhaps – and she had gathered everything she would need on the kitchen surface, then gone to fill the tub. But as she had lain amongst the bubbles, the memories returned and her body numbed.

She could not countenance why she wasn't dead, nor even wounded. Her cuts stung like crazy when she had first sunk into the hot water, just as her deep aches eased a fraction in the warmth. But how could she be this unscathed? The struggles in Hortobágy had been intense and so many of her troops had forsaken their lives for the fun of inconceivably rich voyeurs, hacked and sliced and run through by sharpened steel, their corpses abandoned to the auspices of the *libitinarii*. Indeed, by now, they were probably just ash – and that thought made her wilt.

She dried herself mechanically, pulled on a tracksuit and returned to the kitchen. Through the glass doors, the light was just beginning to fade. The squalls had blown over and the remaining clouds were black against a pale rose sky. She ignored the curry ingredients and instead buttered herself a slice of bread, which had been defrosting while she bathed, and sliced a hunk of cheese that still looked edible after a week in the fridge. She chewed and tried to force the food down, but her taste buds had deserted her and her throat moaned at being forced to swallow.

She was assailed by emotions she could not compute. Shock was the big one. The kind of delayed shock that only comes in the quiet moments after action and enervates body and mind. Guilt was there too. Repugnance at what she had done to others and what she had witnessed. Shame that she lived and was lucky enough to see this sunset, when so many on all sides of that Field were not. Anger too. Loathing for the people who benefited from watching so much violence, and actually enriched themselves by it.

And there was one more. Abhorrence. Disgust for the fat, useless prick called Alexander and his whole Palatinate, and disgust for herself and her fellow Vikings for ever allowing themselves to be cowed by them. Alexander had been convinced that his new Hellenic Regiment had deserted their position and fled from the fury of the Huns. Some of the Titan officers had attempted to disabuse him of those views, but he had been deaf to everything except his own interpretation of events. He was incensed that he had been caught running away from the onslaught of the Janissaries and his only response had been even more dogmatic and autocratic than ever.

He had not rested until weapons, armour and hoplons had been removed from every Hellene and they had been left with nothing but their tunics and boots. He had them marched from the Field in a bedraggled column and then forced them to wait hours through the night while meagre food was supplied, before being loaded onto buses. While the other Titan units returned to Scotland in planes, Alexander had ensured that the Hellenes endured a long, uncomfortable journey back across Europe by road, still in their tunics, still barely washed, the interiors of each vehicle stinking of blood and dirt and sweat.

So, yes, abhorrence and disgust for Alexander and a refuelled hatred for the Titans. She had sworn to herself on the coaches and again on the slow walk back to Morningside and once more in her bath that she would never again allow that Palatinate to control her and would never again put her body on the line for them. It had been a shared resolution too. She could see it in the black glances and mutterings of Ingvar and Stigr, the stone-hard glare of Ake and the sporadic eruptions of Bjarke. These Vikings were done with it all. They would never again pull on the bronze armour of their conquerors, no matter what retribution the Pantheon meted out.

Then there was something else – a feeling that had surged through every pore of her as the struggle reached its climax and which still lay heavy somewhere in her ribcage. *Dread* was probably the best word to describe it. Utter, immeasurable panic at the sight of Tyler driving his horse towards the oncoming Huns. She had run headlong from the trees, shrieking as she sprinted towards him, so desperate to get to him before the foe engulfed him, so terrified of losing him. She had lain in her bath and tried forlornly to understand those feelings.

Tyler. Her thoughts coalesced around him. They had not spoken since she had walked away from him at the top of Dublin Street, but his words that day were scrawled indelibly across her memories, and perhaps across her heart. How could he say such things? How could he talk of love, of shared futures, when the Pantheon had cut them apart as cleanly as any sword strike? She had thought she could contain his words, box them up and put them somewhere out of reach, but her own emotions were less easy to ignore. She had tried to focus on the preparations for the Battle and the logistics of getting to Hungary, but she had watched him trot to meet the Kings before the start of conflict and felt her heart quicken.

Once the struggle began, a calmness had settled over her and a clarity. She could see how the Battle was unfolding and understood what they must do and how she must lead her Hellenes. War had arrived in her veins and detached her from every other thought. She had led her Hellenes into the onslaught and they had followed willingly. God knows how they had decimated the Sipahi. The awesome might of that mounted charge had been like nothing she could ever have imagined, the power as those horses plunged into the reeds after them. She had lost count of how many animals she had killed. She had cut and torn at anything that wore the silver armour, and she had not stopped until Ake's arms came around her and Ake's voice told her it was over.

Her warrior senses had returned as they ran back to the

main fight and she had led the counterattack on the flank of the Janissaries. The Hellenes had fallen on Mehmed's vaunted soldiers and their onslaught had tipped the balance. Companion and Hellene, peltast and Band, had finally stopped the Janissary momentum.

Yet, in that same moment, her vision had filled with the sight of Tyler – Hephaestion – charging the Black Cloaks, and suddenly nothing else had mattered. She had experienced a similar helpless, overwhelming terror only once before in her life and that was during the agonising months of her daughter's fight with cancer. She had believed she would never feel such emotions again and now, as she sat cradling a mug of herbal tea and staring at the bread and cheese her stomach could not tolerate, she did not know how to come to terms with this.

Outside, there was just a vein of pink sky left above the trees at the bottom of the garden. It was May and the city centre was humming with tourists and energy, but out here darkness still lay heavy on the leafy suburbs and brought stillness and peace. She was about to rise and throw the bread in the bin, when she caught the briefest of movements against the dying light. She turned and peered through the bifold doors.

Once, she would have remained behind the protection of the glass and pulled the blinds, but she was a swordmaiden now and shadows did not frighten her. She clicked the doors and stepped out into the warm night.

'Hello?' she said. 'You'd better show yourself.'

Nothing. Not a rustle.

There were voices somewhere on one of the further roads and the hum of a plane far up amongst the stars, but absolute silence in her garden. Her warrior instincts chattered, but then gradually began to settle. This was Morningside, not Hortobágy. There were no Huns beneath the trees, no Janissaries amongst the shrubs.

Stupid, Lana. Relax and rest.

She turned back to the doors.

The impact into her spine was so sudden and silent that she had no chance to cry or brace herself. She fell like a stone and hit the ground with such force that the air was driven from her lungs. Before she could even comprehend what was happening, a woman's hand came under her and grabbed her mouth, then hauled her bodily back up. Another arm wrapped itself around her chest, pinning her with clinical precision. She began to squirm, but she knew instinctively that she was in the grip of someone consummate in such arts. The arms did not budge. The clasp was iron.

And then, a vision of horror.

A second figure emerged from the night in front of her. Bruised and brutal and grinning from ear to ear.

My god no, please, no.

Skarde.

XXXIX

Heph spent the rest of the day stuck in the Ephesus clinic under the auspices of several medics. The unit treated injuries too minor for the main Pantheon wards and the medics reassured him the wound was of little consequence – a neat blade cut through the deltoid muscle of his left shoulder and on into the teres muscle on his upper back – but the pain felt major enough to him.

They lay him on his front, sterilised the gashes, stitched and bandaged them and jabbed him with painkillers, all the time calling him *lord* and treating him as a sovereign, and it maddened him because he needed time and space to get his head around the ramifications of the fight. Zeus had departed as soon as the Challenge was over. Simmius floated in and out to confer with the medics and eye their patient. Faintly Heph wondered who had been dispatched to the gardens to clean the bloodied floor and haul away the corpse of the last Alexander.

Eventually he fell under the influence of the drugs and drifted in and out of consciousness. When he came back to his senses, he was alone, but he had been moved onto his side and the clock on the clinic wall said twenty forty-two, which meant he had been horizontal for six hours.

Grimacing, he forced himself up, yanked a canula out of his hand, and shuffled barefoot to the main changing areas, where he found his street clothes still in the locker where he had hung them before the Challenge. Screwing up his face in pain, he dressed and exited to Reception.

'Get me a car,' he said tersely to the man on duty.

He had expected resistance, but the man simply bowed and said, 'My lord, your car awaits you in its usual spot.'

Heph frowned, but refused to engage further, so he took himself carefully down the flights of stairs and out to the car park behind the hostel. The cloud-studded sky was still bright and, for a moment, it shocked him. The Pantheon embraced the dark winter months. The Twentieth Year should have finished several weeks ago, the troops given leave and the strongholds closed for the Interregnum, but now it was May and the air was scented with summer and Zeus had forbidden anyone to depart the city until the Caelestia had agreed a way forward.

A BMW was parked by the steps and Heph smiled to see Stanek behind the wheel.

'To the stables, my lord?'

'No, to my apartment in the West End. I need some time to rest.'

When Heph was finally alone in his penthouse lodgings, he broke open a bottle of Talisker and perched on one of the cream sofas, staring out of the vast windows as dusk finally began to slink across the city. He knew he needed to eat, but the drugs and the whisky were a bad partnership. Nothing in the damn world was going to get him upright again that night. With a small gasp of pain, he slumped back against the cushions and dropped into sleep.

He was woken by a chime from his mobile in the bedroom where he had left it before departing for Hungary. Morning was streaming through the windows and his back had stiffened during the night. He moaned from the pain of his wound and forced himself to the bedroom.

'What?' he hissed through gritted teeth.

'My lord.' It was Simmius. 'The medics were intending to change your bandaging last night.'

'I'm fine,' he lied.

'Where are you?'

'At my apartment. Does it matter? I thought perhaps I could actually be left alone for a while.'

'Yes, well, you had a visitor to Ephesus last night, sent here by Atilius. When we couldn't find you, I had her taken to your stables in Perthshire where I assumed you had gone. So I hope Diogenes has made her welcome.'

'Who is it?'

Simmius paused. 'It might be best for you to get over there and see for yourself. You'll be surprised, my lord. I know I was.'

Heph cut the line and swore. He desperately wanted to shower, but wondered how to accomplish this without getting his bandaging soaked. Beneath the pain, he was also conscious that he was starving. Irritably, he punched another number.

'Stanek, where are you?'

'Outside, my lord.'

'Outside?'

'It's the job of the King's driver to be on call at all times.'

Heph's anger dissipated. 'Have you slept?'

'Surprisingly comfortably, lord. I'm used to it.'

'Well, er, I need to go to the stables.'

'Of course, my lord. I've got some bacon rolls that may still be warm. Thought you might need one?'

'You're a saviour, Stanek. I'll be down.'

The food was cold by the time Heph had washed at the sink and dressed, but he didn't care. He munched delightedly on two bacon baps as Stanek drove them over the Forth in soft morning sunlight. It took them an hour to round the Ochils, descend Gleneagles and delve into the rolling countryside of lowland Perthshire and it was mid-morning by the time they turned up the drive to the farmhouse.

Dio was outside waiting for them and he opened the rear door and gave an awkward bow. 'My lord, Alexander.'

'Don't you start,' Heph said sharply. 'News travels fast.'

Dio inclined his head. 'Especially when it's brought to us by a truly unexpected visitor.'

'So I hear.'

'Seems Atilius sent her to meet with Alexander at Ephesus and she thought she was meeting the fat one who fled on the Field. But that particular one, she was informed, is now *indisposed* and she should instead direct her attentions to the man called Hephaestion. It seems the King Killer is now the King.'

Heph shrugged sheepishly. 'I'm sorry you had to learn that way, my friend.'

'A Challenge?'

Heph nodded. 'And I've the wounds to prove it.'

'Bloody hell,' Dio whistled. 'Your Pantheon career is somewhat meteoric, if you don't mind me saying, my lord.'

'Don't call me that.'

'Well, you're not Heph anymore.'

'Then think of something else, just not *lord*.'

Dio's eyebrows came together. 'Alexander is a mouthful and you're sure not an Al.'

Heph sighed. 'Who's this visitor?'

'You'd better come and see. We fed her last night and then she bedded down with the horses. She seemed happy enough with their company.'

The two friends began to walk across the field to the stables.

'How are the others?' Heph asked softly.

'Lenore and Philemon are in the farmhouse and excited to see you. Spyro and Melitta are doing okay and should be with us soon.'

'Thank god for that.' Heph stopped abruptly and turned to Dio. 'Have you heard from Calder?'

'Not a whisper. But I had Simmius check the casualty lists and she's not on them.'

'So she's okay?'

'It would seem so.'

Heph nodded grimly and continued towards the stables.

'Hey,' called Dio. 'Xander.'

'What?'

'Xander. I think it suits you.'

Heph considered this and then smiled weakly. 'Okay, Xander it is. Just as long as you don't call me *lord*.'

Dio shrugged. 'Everyone else will.'

Xander did not recognise the woman waiting for him in the stables.

She had been sitting on a hay bale examining the horses,

but she stood when he entered and dipped her head. A foot shorter than him, she was nevertheless sturdily built, with broad shoulders and a confident stance. Her hair was tousled and boyish, but her face had at least a decade on him and was creased and weathered by a life outdoors. She examined him with the professional interest of a soldier.

'My lord,' she said in accented English. 'I had expected to meet with a different Alexander.'

'So I understand. And who, may I ask, are you?'

'Ellac, Colonel of the Second Horn.'

Xander stopped in his tracks and air leaked from his lungs. 'Ellac? The one, they say, who killed Bleda?'

'She was a traitor, my lord. She killed her King, so I led my Horn against her. It does not matter who held the blade that killed her.'

Xander broke his gaze and steadied himself by looking at Boreas in his stall. The stallion tossed his head and stared back at him.

'So what are you doing in my stables, Ellac of the Second Horn?'

'The Praetor sent me to meet my new King and to receive my orders from you, lord. Ördög's Palatinate is no more. Attila is dead. Bleda too. Uptar of the First Horn is lying in the Pantheon wards with a broken leg. So I am the most senior representative of your new Hun forces.'

Xander reached for one of the stalls to lean on, pain rippling through his left shoulder. 'But the Battle was only days ago. I've been King for less than twenty-four hours. Why have you come so soon?'

'The Praetor said it was urgent. None of our forces have yet been stood down. We remain in our camps, ready for orders. It seems the Caelestia are holding the Twentieth Year open until they have discussed what happened at Hortobágy.'

'You're still in your camps? You haven't gone home?'

'No, my lord. We are stationed with our horses. We lost many on the Field, but there are still five hundred and twenty of us.'

'Five hundred and twenty Huns,' Xander mused.

'Not Huns, lord. We're Titans now.'

'So what am I supposed to do with you?'

'Dress us in bronze if you want. Give us armour and helmets and plumes like you.'

Xander glanced at Dio, who was waiting by the door. 'No,' he said slowly. 'I don't want that.'

They were silent for several moments and then Ellac indicated towards the stalls. 'These are all the horses you have?'

'Aye,' spoke up Dio. 'Just the three left.'

'And five riders,' added Xander.

'It is not enough for a King,' Ellac said simply.

Xander knew she was right, but he was tired of the conversation. He longed to devote his attentions to Boreas, to step into his stall and feel the texture of his coat and the warmth of his flanks.

Dio could read his friend's expression and beckoned their guest. 'Come, Ellac. We'll give the King a few moments alone with his horses.'

Xander spent the next thirty minutes at peace with the three beasts, stroking each of them and listening to their movements. The scent of the hay filled his lungs and the warm spring sunshine flooded through the windows. He was numbed by the speed of events and his wound still growled whenever he moved, but at least these wonderful horses failed to change.

Eventually, regretfully, he pulled himself from them and wandered back to the farmhouse, where Lenore and Philemon beamed to see him. They shared a lunch of flatbreads and soup, and Ellac ate quietly with them. Then Dio said they would give the horses some exercise and she joined them readily, keen to see the stallions in action.

Xander took himself away with Dio's laptop and found a distant room. There he spent the afternoon researching Alexander the Great. He studied maps of his campaigns and his empire, which stretched from Macedon to the Indus Valley. He read again about the major battles at Granicus, Issus, Gaugamela, Bactra and Hydaspes. He gauged the ancient king's battle tactics. The movements and decisions that had won him victories against far superior forces. He sought out articles on how Alexander had administered his empire, how he had treated the conquered peoples.

And then he sat staring out of the windows at the hills and thinking what the great Lord of Asia meant to him now, and how he – Xander – should act. He would not be like the other Alexanders he had known, men who had not deserved to hold such a name. He must act like his original namesake. He would be fair to the conquered Palatinates and honour their customs.

And on the Field of Battle, he would lead from the front, not loiter behind flags at the rear. He would be a lord of war. Like Caesar. Caesar had always been a King who marched at the head of his Legion and the man was respected for it throughout the Pantheon.

Later, as his team groomed and fed the horses, and his eyes were glazing over with all the new information, his mobile jolted him alert.

It was Zeus and he sounded far from happy.

'It seems that you are not going to have a quiet start to your reign. Forget about an Interregnum. Forget about easing into the Twenty-First Year. Our Lord Jupiter has decided the Twentieth isn't finished yet.'

'What does that mean?'

'She has decreed that we face the Legion in six days' time.'

'What?'

'I spent most of last night online with the remaining Caelestes and there's all hell breaking loose. Jupiter is adamant that she will not have her Legion continue to stand uselessly in the wings while we have destroyed two Palatinates. In her opinion, our exploits on two Fields of Battle have made us the undisputed challengers to the Legion and she demands we face her troops before the Twentieth Year is complete.'

Xander's jaw hung loose. 'But it's ridiculous. We're only just recovering from Hortobágy and counting our losses. You must stamp on this madness.'

'I've tried, but the news has already been shared with the Curiate and their syndicates. Money is in play already; the first bets are being recorded. Nothing can stop the momentum once wagers are live. Get back to Edinburgh and brief your officers. Atilius and Simmius will handle all the logistics of getting the troops ready, including the Huns.'

'I don't understand—'

'Jupiter's sending her Legion here.'

'To Scotland?'

'Atilius is still working on the location of the Field, but you can be assured we will be meeting Caesar somewhere in the north.'

Xander was floundering with all the implications.

'But... but it's against every Rule in the Pantheon. Jupiter can't just select a rival and call a Battle.'

'Forget about the Rules. Two Palatinates have disintegrated in one Season. The Caelestia are broken and the Curiate are baying for blood. The Rules have gone, Alexander. It's personal now.'

Xander briefed Dio, then made a spontaneous decision to wave Ellac into the car and get in beside her as Stanek took them back to the city. In the chaos of the final moments at Hortobágy, he could never know whether she had personally wielded the blade that killed his sister, but he was a King now and he needed the allegiance of the Huns.

In blunt sentences, he told her of Jupiter's demands and asked her to work with Atilius and Simmius to oversee the transportation of her Hun army to Scotland. She took the news with wordless implacability and asked simply, 'Are we to be Titans?'

'Why would I force you to be Titans? The real Alexander may have forged his empire by breaking every opponent on the battlefield, but he held on to it by honouring his conquered peoples and adopting their customs. Your strength lies in who you are. Stand with me on the Field as Huns and use the skills of the steppe warriors to help me defeat Caesar.'

Her brows knitted at this. 'You are asking me and not compelling?'

'I suspect the Pantheon will compel you, but I am asking you, as one soldier to another, stand with my Lion banner and lead your Horns against the Legion.'

She fell silent and they were deep into the suburbs of Edinburgh before she spoke again. 'You will need your own royal cavalry, my liege.'

Xander harrumphed. 'There's no time for that.'

'Can Diogenes source more stallions?'

'In five days? Perhaps, if he works fast with Simmius, but Zeus would need to agree the expenditure because new horses are ten Credits each.'

'But *replacement* horses are not.'

'What are you suggesting?'

'For each Titan horse you can source, I will relinquish a pony. That avoids expenditure.'

'And who will ride these new Titan mounts?'

'I will make a selection from my Huns. We ride bareback and stirrup-less like you; we carry small shields and spears like you. The skills are much the same.'

'But you ride steppe ponies which are half the size of the Titan stallions.'

'We also live in modern Hungary, where the majority of us ride other breeds for pleasure when we are not on Pantheon duty.'

Xander toyed with this answer and then reached for his phone. 'Okay, I'll get Diogenes on it right away.'

'Can he source a hundred?'

'A hundred!'

Ellac leaned towards him and held his gaze. 'You are

Alexander, the King who conquered all of Asia at the head of his mighty Companion Cavalry. If you can source a hundred horses in five days, a hundred helmets, a hundred sets of armour, a hundred hoplons and a hundred spears, I will find you your cavalry.'

XXXX

'Who is this?' Menes queried indignantly when the Titan officers gathered in the Ephesus War Room.

'This,' answered Xander, staring down the man's belligerence, 'is Ellac, Colonel of the Second Horn. And she attends this Council as the nominated commander of my Hun cavalry.'

The new King examined his officers. Nicanor, Menes and Parmenion were bandaged, cut and bruised, and looked as bone-tired as he felt. Only Agape seemed untouched by violence and sat silently on one of the wooden seats, waiting for him to take the central place.

'Where is Calder?' Xander demanded of Simmius.

'As you requested, lord, I sent word that her attendance was required, but I've received no response.'

'*I* command the Hellenes,' blustered Menes.

'Not any more, you don't,' Xander responded.

'What? I am Colonel of Lights.'

'Indeed you are and you will continue to command the Companion infantry and have oversight of Parmenion's peltasts and Agape's Band. But the Hellenic regiment now reports directly to me and, as such, I expect their leading officer to attend this meeting.'

'They have no officers. They are basic hoplites, all of them.'

'And that was our mistake.' Xander turned from Menes in a gesture that was regal enough to stop the man's protestations, and the smallest of smiles fluttered across Agape's lips.

'Get someone to find Calder,' he continued irritably and flung an arm towards Simmius, 'but we can't afford to wait.'

The Adjutant sent a message on his iPad, then came to join the others in the ring of seats.

Xander took his place and peered around at his command team. There had not even been time to introduce himself properly as their new King, but they waited on his words as though he had been their sovereign for years.

'In five days,' he declared, 'we will stand on a Field somewhere in north Scotland and look across the divide at a thousand soldiers of Rome. It is something we could never have countenanced, even just a few weeks ago.'

'The timescale is ridiculous,' rumbled Nicanor. 'We'll not be ready.'

'We'll have to be. Simmius is deep into the logistics and our Titans remain on standby in the city.'

'Our Titans,' Nicanor retorted, 'are exhausted and bloodied and only just recovering from a Battle in Hungary.'

'Then we must ask them to find new strength. All they need to do is make sure they're ready to be transported when the time is right. Simmius, what can you tell us?'

'My lord, I have sent messages to all our troops summoning them to gather in their respective strongholds after this meeting, so that we may brief them more fully.

They should be arriving as we speak. As for the location of the Field, Atilius is still working on this. Once he has confirmed, we will be in a position to move. Coaches and trains are requisitioned. Supplies are prepared. Weapons and armour are being packed.'

'As soon as we receive even the vaguest information about location, I want us to go,' Xander interrupted. 'The quicker we're back in the Highlands again, the faster we will harden into a battle-ready force.'

'What of the Huns?' Parmenion said, glancing at Ellac.

'We will be ready,' she replied.

'Can you transport your horses in such time?'

'For over a decade we have faced the Sultanate in Tier Two and every other year we have taken our cavalry to the wilds of Turkey to wage Battle. We know how to transport our ponies.'

'Indeed,' agreed Simmius. 'We have all the necessary trailers on standby. Most of the troops will be flown. It will take at least three days to have the horses in Scotland, but we can focus on getting this done once we know the location of the Field.'

'Don't wait for that, man,' Xander urged. 'We already know it's somewhere north of here, so get the horses on the road across Europe immediately.'

Ellac nodded in agreement. 'I will work with the Adjutant, my lord. We'll have them here.'

'And what of the Legion?' Agape spoke up.

'They have no cavalry,' Simmius replied. 'So they are all booked on private flights into Inverness. They will be arriving in two days.'

'And where do they go from there?'

'Atilius is organising field camps in suitably unobserved terrain.'

'So where are those?' Xander demanded.

'I don't have that information, lord.'

'Well, damn well find it. If Atilius takes them north, west or south from Inverness, it will surely give us a clue about his plans for the Field.'

Simmius bowed his head and Xander sighed in exasperation. 'Agape,' he said, turning to his most experienced officer, 'what do we know about the Legion?'

The Band's captain gathered her thoughts. 'They are the largest, most resourced Palatinate and they have never been defeated. They number twelve hundred veteran Legionaries, marshalled into Centuries of eighty. There are six Centuries in a Cohort, and Caesar commands two Cohorts. Legate Flavius leads the First and Legate Cassia the Second. They are both hugely experienced and clever tacticians.

'The final two hundred troops are the Imperial Praetorian Guard, Caesar's personal bodyguard and amongst the best units in the Pantheon. They are commanded by Augustus, a Prefect who styles himself more like an emperor.'

'We've rubbed shoulders,' said Xander ruefully, remembering getting a beating on Palatine Hill while the golden bastard watched.

'The strength of the Legion is not in the individual fighting skills of each Legionary, but in their armour, their weapons and their military organisation. We all know what a Roman Legionary looks like. They are clad in good steel armour, much tougher than our own bronze, and also more mobile because it is constructed from bands that are riveted together and which therefore move with the body beneath.

'Their scutum shields are oblong and curved, protecting the body from shoulder to knee, but only three-foot wide, thus allowing troops to march in closer-packed formations than we can with our hoplons. While we use a vertical handle and strap to lock our hoplons to our forearms, the Romans have a single horizontal hold on their scutums, clasped overhand, so the shield can be brought up very fast or punched like a huge knuckleduster.

'Their swords are short like ours and used in a similar fashion to stab and twist, rather than hack. These blades, however, are not iron. They are high-carbon steel and they will go through mail.'

'What about our breastplates?' Menes asked.

'It's never been properly tested, but I sure wouldn't want to take a direct stab from one.'

There were glances around the circle, but Agape forged onwards.

'The other primary weapon of the Legion is the pilum spear. Four foot of ashwood and two foot of thin iron. They use this mostly as an aerial missile, approaching and throwing from behind their scutums, then driving home the attack with their swords.'

'Not much different from the tactics of my peltasts,' observed Parmenion.

'Indeed. But whereas each one of our companies specialises in a different skill – your peltasts with their javelins, our Companions with their dories and swords, the Phalanx with their sarissas – every Legionary is trained in all these techniques. They can move seamlessly from tight testudo "tortoise" formation, bristling with pilum points like our Phalanx, to open-line approaches with precisely sequenced spear throwing. When they close on their foe, their scutums create an impregnable shield wall and they are drilled in the stab and twist of the battle-line. As soon as a front-ranker is exhausted, he or she steps back to the right and is replaced seamlessly from the left by someone from the second rank.'

Menes swore dismissively. 'If it's a shield fight they want, my Companions will give it to them.'

'And such a fight may decide the outcome of the whole Battle.'

'How will they be organised on the Field?' asked Xander.

'I do not know and this is what makes them so formidable. They will likely bring three Eagle standards to the fight. One will be Jupiter's own, and the other two represent the First and Second Cohort. Flavius and Cassia may stand close to these, but not necessarily. You will recognise the Praetorians by their plumes like ours. The Legionaries in the Cohorts do not bear plumes, except their Centurions, who wear a traverse crest.'

Xander shifted his attention to the newest member of his command team. 'Ellac, can you offer any insights from your clashes with the Legion?'

The Hun considered his question. 'The Cohorts that the Captain speaks of are unimportant. They will not come at us as two Cohorts, they will attack as twelve Centuries. Twelve units of eighty troops each, which can operate independently. They will shift from closed-order, to marching column, to attack-line and shieldwall as events dictate. They have spent almost twenty years facing the armour of Mehmed's Janissaries and the speed of my Huns, so they know how to break an infantry attack and how to keep cavalry at bay.

My ponies have been unable to break their walls of pilums, even when we have attacked in number. In short, I think they know every trick in the book.'

The Titan officers considered her words glumly.

'What are their weaknesses?' Xander asked.

Ellac pursed her lips. 'Tactically, I can think of few, but there are perhaps two liabilities of a more personal nature. The first is Caesar himself. He considers himself the most important soldier in the Pantheon and he sets a glorious example by leading from the front. Expect to find him in the battle-line, not hiding behind his Eagles.'

'So he's a target?' Xander said.

Agape smiled thinly at him. 'Are you thinking of adding to your tally of sovereign deaths?'

'If he's in the battle-line, then he's a clear target. In 331 BC, Alexander overcame hugely superior numbers at the battle of Issus by focusing on killing King Darius. He did not achieve his objective, but he did force Darius to flee the field and the day was won. So brief your troops that if anyone gets near Caesar, then cut him down. Sword, spear – this time it doesn't matter. Just take him down.'

There were nods at this.

'And the second weakness?' Parmenion asked.

'Prefect Augustus,' Ellac replied. 'The man does his own thing in the midst of Battle. He's a glory-seeker, not minded to stick to agreed formations and never content to be overshadowed by Caesar. He might just do something that surprises his own side as much as it does us.'

The Council digested this and Xander thought how good it would be to meet Augustus again in a settling of scores.

Finally, he raised himself from his reverie. 'Thank you,

Colonel. We will deliberate on this information and gather on the Field much better prepared. Any other observations?'

Nicanor sighed. 'I never once believed I would cross blades with the Legion. Twelve hundred is an army like none other in the Pantheon.'

Xander turned to him. 'Just a few short weeks ago, we were a Palatinate of barely a hundred and forty waiting to face King Sveinn in Knoydart, and the Legion's numbers would have seemed overwhelming. But since then, we have been swelled by Blood Credits, Vikings and Huns alike, and our own headcount is nearing nine hundred. We are also a force to be feared.'

'Caesar will be quaking in his boots,' said Menes acidly.

'Yes, perhaps he is.' Xander looked to Simmius. 'Adjutant, are the troops gathered?'

'They should be, lord. Usual places. Nicanor's Heavies here in Ephesus. The Companions in Persepolis. Peltasts at Thebes. Band in Pella. And the Hellenes down in the Tunnels of New Alexandria.'

'Good, then we shall disperse to our units. Brief them on everything you have heard today and prepare them to move north. Time is precious. Use every moment to plan your movements on the Field. We will only have once chance against the Legion.'

Nicanor, Parmenion, Menes and Agape rose and bowed to him, then left the chamber.

'Ellac,' Xander said, 'Go with Simmius and review the logistics for getting your troops to these shores as fast as possible.'

She dipped her head and stood to depart with the

Adjutant, but another thought came to Xander. 'You still think a hundred, Colonel?'

'Yes, lord.'

He frowned with uncertainty, then nodded and waved a finger at Simmius. 'Can you find us a hundred more stallions?'

'In five days, lord?'

'Call in every favour you're owed. Twist every arm. Just get them here and I'll sort it with Zeus.'

Simmius looked shell-shocked, but he pulled himself together. 'I'll try, my lord.'

'And a hundred new sets of armour. I intend to come before Caesar with a cavalry worthy of a King.'

XXXXI

Xander paced up the Royal Mile at speed.

It was eight-thirty in the evening and the daylight and the crowds still took him by surprise. During the dark winter Conflict Hours of normal Seasons, it was so much easier to morph into the steely warriors that the Pantheon demanded, but now, when the city brimmed with summer life, it was disconcerting. One moment, within the walls of Ephesus, he was king of all he surveyed. The next, dressed in civvies and surrounded by tour groups, al fresco diners, evening shoppers, theatre-goers, and every language under the sinking sun, he was just another non-descript guy going about his business, unnoticed and uninteresting.

He reached the Tron Kirk, then turned left down Blair Street, which ran below South Bridge, towards the South Gate of what had once been Valhalla. He descended the steps to the small iron door plastered with graffiti and heard the buzzer release the lock, but he paused and peered back up to street level to wait for a moment when the bustle of nearby pedestrians eased, then shouldered through and quickly closed it behind him.

The Titan Gatekeeper made to say something to him, but he strode straight past and hurried up the Tunnel towards the main Hall. He was angry that Calder had not shown up to the officers' briefing, but there was also a seam of worry in his gut. He had barely laid eyes on her since they had stood together on Dublin Street and spoken of love, and no one else had any hard information about her whereabouts since the Battle.

Damn her. Well, he would make the whole lot of them listen to what he had to say now.

He strode into the Hall and stopped dead. It was empty except for two Titan sentries.

'Where the hell are the Hellenes?'

'My lord?'

'The Hellenes, they were summoned here.'

The Heavies looked blank and Xander swore. He spun on his heels and marched back to the South Gate.

'Where are the Hellenes?' he demanded again when he saw the Gatekeeper.

'My lord, no one has arrived, but you should see this on the monitor.'

Xander entered the small office and the Heavy pointed at one of the screens, which showed a figure standing with his back to the East Gate on Market Street. 'He's been there for at least thirty minutes and I recognise his face. I think he's one of them.'

Xander nodded grimly. 'He is indeed.'

'My lord, Menes decided the Hellenes should only use that Gate and he's had their kit moved to the Eastern Armouries.'

'So our friend here knows where to stand to intercept them all?'

'Yes, my lord.'

'I'll pay him a little visit.'

Xander strode back to the Hall and into the East Tunnel without a glance at the two sentries. He reached the East Gate in the back of one of the Market Street vaults and pointed to it. 'Open up.'

The door buzzed and he shoved through into the thickening dusk. Birds were deep into their evening chorus and the scent of fried food hung in the warm air.

'So at least one of you made it,' the King said.

The man was just a couple of paces away, staring down the street, and he swung round at Xander's voice.

'Heph!' he said in shock, his thin features nervous and pale.

'Not Heph anymore. Alexander.'

The man's eyes bulged in consternation. 'You? You're…'

'The new King of the Titans. The other one departed unexpectedly.'

'But…'

'I think you mean, *but, my lord…* And when I summon the Hellenes to gather in these Halls, I expect them to come.'

The man swallowed and looked at his feet, then raised his head with more defiance in his eyes.

Xander stepped to him. 'We've come a long way since I first saw your ugly face in the Nineteenth Armatura. You almost killed me before the *Sine Missione* and you almost killed Calder in the castle on the final Raid Night and I won't forget that. So don't give me any of your arrogant bullshit, Ulf. I am your King now and you had better damn well accept that.'

Ulf bottled what he had been about to say.

Xander pressed his forehead into Ulf's. 'Have you been turning around every Hellene when they arrive?'

'Just the few that came.'

'What about the rest?'

'Bjarke messaged them.'

'Messaged them!'

'Of course.' Some of his natural belligerence returned. 'You don't think we haven't been swapping numbers and communicating since we became prisoners in your Palatinate.'

Xander pulled his face away and studied him. 'Bjarke messaged all the Hellenes and told them to disobey a direct summons to attend a briefing tonight? And he sent you to dissuade any who didn't get the message?'

'You're catching on.'

Xander balled his fists. 'I am your King, Ulf. I should have you executed.'

Ulf sneered. 'You're not the King of Valhalla. You and your Palatinate can go to hell.'

Xander had to control the anger seething through his blood. 'Is that what Bjarke told you?'

'It's what we all agreed after Hortobágy, when that fat King you've replaced marched us away like prisoners. We fought with valour on that Field. We destroyed the Sipahi cavalry before they could crush your precious Companions into tiny pieces. And we did it despite all the injustices, all the insults. We stood our ground dressed in your bronze armour, holding your damn shields, and we still broke the might of their charge.'

Ulf glared at him and for just a moment, the two men could have been back in the ruined warehouse where they had first met. On that night two years ago, Punnr had whispered to Ulf, '*Is that all you got?*' and the rivals had almost torn shreds off each other.

'So you are refusing to fight for my Palatinate?'

Ulf's black eyes sparked in defiance. 'Aye. We are Vikings and we will die Vikings.'

'Well you'll have your wish as soon as the Pantheon authorities find out. They'll execute the lot of you, don't you get that? The Caelestes don't muck around. They're not going to allow an entire conquered Palatinate to dictate terms. They will send Vigiles to each of your houses and they will have you killed.'

'Then we will die with honour.'

Xander cursed and stared up to where the last of the sun's rays were illuminating Calton Hill. 'Is that what Bjarke thinks too? Though he's not man enough to come here and tell me himself? Instead, he sends you to do his dirty work.'

'It's a group decision.'

'And what about Calder? Does she agree with this?'

Ulf paused and his expression faltered. 'I don't know.'

Xander stepped in to him again. 'What do you mean? Where's Housecarl Calder?'

'I haven't heard from her. Nor has Bjarke. She returned with us after the Battle, but I don't know where she is now.'

Xander prodded a finger in Ulf's chest. 'Are you telling me the truth?'

Ulf looked ready to hit him, but then relented. 'Aye, I am.'

Xander was silent as he considered this, then his eyes focused on something else. 'You've not been shaving.'

Ulf had never mastered the art of growing a beard, but a few weedy bristles were sprouting on his chin and upper lip.

'Vikings don't shave,' he replied defiantly.

Xander nodded slowly. 'Nor should they.'

He stepped away again and stood contemplating the other man.

'Ulf, what if I told you to keep growing your beard? What if I said that when you next come to the Armouries, they will be filled with chainmail and iron vambraces and battle-axes and longswords?'

'I'd say you're playing games.'

'Not so. Ulf, I am the new Alexander and I have the power to dictate what I want in my Palatinate. Cleitus is gone. I killed him. Tell that to Bjarke. And tell him that I still honour him as the Jarl of Hammer Regiment.'

'What are you saying?'

'That my Palatinate is home to Viking and Hun and Titan alike. I will raise Valhalla again. In five days, we must face Caesars's Legion on a Field here in Scotland, not some foreign place we know nothing about. Here, in the Highlands.'

Ulf gawped at him. 'Caesar is coming here?'

'Damn right, he is. Him and twelve hundred Romans. And I need you and Bjarke and Calder and Ingvar and Ake and Stigr and every single Viking to be there with me. Wolf, Hammer, Storm and Raven, your banners returned, the Triple Horn flying beside the Lion of Macedon.'

Ulf stared wide-eyed at him. 'Is that an order?'

Xander wanted to yell that of course it was a bloody order, but he sucked in a deep breath and stopped himself. 'No,' he said as calmly as he could. 'But if you don't turn up when you're summoned to travel to the north, the Pantheon authorities will recognise your insubordination and they will destroy you, have no doubt about that. So tell Bjarke that I, Alexander, ask him to bring Valhalla to the transport when word comes from Atilius and then to travel north. There you will find your mail and weapons and banners, and you will once again be resurrected as Valhalla. As long as you are present on the Field, the Pantheon authorities will not notice your insubordination. What Valhalla chooses to do at that point, however, I leave to Bjarke and Calder to decide.'

Ulf eyed him suspiciously. 'You are not ordering us to fight for the Titans?'

'I am asking the brave warriors of Valhalla to recognise that they were fairly beaten on the Field in Knoydart and they now owe their allegiance to this Palatinate. But I am also admitting that they have been treated unfairly and dishonourably by my predecessor. Gather in five days in your regiments and litters, face the lines of Rome, and decide your own fates. That is what I ask, so tell that to Bjarke and Calder.'

Ulf nodded. 'I will.'

'Go then. You will receive alerts on your phones when you are supposed to gather for the transport.'

Ulf made to turn away, but Xander's voice stopped him.

'Think on it, Ulf. Better to die in glory on a field of battle, than to die in secrecy at the hands of the Vigiles. Go and raise Valhalla for the mother of all fights.'

XXXXII

'Where the hell are you, Kustaa?'

'Where are *you*?'

'Pulled up with the bridges in front of us, like you told us!'

Skarde was sitting at the wheel of Kustaa's Mercedes AMG, parked in a layby above South Queensferry with a glorious view of the three floodlit bridges spanning the Forth. Behind him, he could see the Praetorian's bulk in his mirror and next to her sat Calder, bound and gagged, with a hood on top of her fair hair, ready to be yanked over her eyes when they didn't want her to witness their movements.

They had spent twenty-four hours in her house, raiding her kitchen for food and pacing like caged tigers while they waited for Kustaa to provide directions. Skarde had been wide-eyed when he found the gym and training pells in the cellar, no doubt wishing there was time to draw blades and get joyously physical with his captive.

'Did you find the woman called Calder?' asked the Thane down the phone.

'I did.'

'Did you hurt her?'

Skarde took a deep breath to control his temper. Every

time he conversed with this idiot, he ended up wanting to kill someone. 'I gave her Jupiter's message as I was tasked and now I need to come to you, so we can both accompany Oliver on his journey to the High Caelestis.'

Skarde did not notice, but at the mention of Oliver, Calder's eyes trained on the back of his head and every fibre in her body tensed. The Praetorian next to her, however, did notice. She glanced at her captive, so fragile and beguiling, and made a mental note that this Oliver boy meant something to her. She nudged an elbow into the slim arm pressed against her as a quiet warning to behave.

'Okay,' Kustaa said down the phone. 'Come north.'

'How far?'

'Inverness.'

'Will you be there?'

'No, but when you get there, I'll give you further instructions.'

Skarde cut the line and gunned the motor. 'I swear,' he said aloud without thinking, 'I'm going to take such pleasure in murdering that Thane when we finally meet again.'

Next to her, the Praetorian once more felt the captive tense and Domna thought what a loose-mouthed fool this Skarde was. The man believed he was so special, so dangerously valuable, but he was street trash really. Worthless.

No one would cry for him when he was gone.

'Are your Praetorians ready?'

Marcella walked with her son across the lush lawns towards the helipad where his ride waited to take him to Rome airport.

'Of course. They will fly in three hours and everything had better be organised in Scotland for our arrival. I've no wish to spend one moment longer than I must in that awful country. You should have insisted we fought the Battle here.'

'The optics are much better if we destroy the Titans in their own backyard.'

Fabian harrumphed, but accepted the point.

The chopper was warming up and its rotors jostled the shrubbery. Marcella took her son's arm and pulled him round to face her.

'I have no doubt that our Legion will win a fine victory in Scotland and will re-establish our pre-eminence.'

'There was never any doubt in that, Mother,' Fabian interjected.

'Indeed, there was not. But I want to impress upon you something more before you leave.' She gazed into her son's eyes, gauging his strength and his ambition. 'There is one man whose deeds and reputation in these last few weeks have made him the most famous soldier in the Pantheon. He outshines even you, my darling. Even the great and glorious Augustus cannot eclipse the King Killer. My sources tell me Zeus has gone further and made him King of the Titans. The man is now Alexander himself.'

Fabian tensed at this news and his eyes fired.

'Destroy him, my son. Do not leave the Field while he is still standing. His star must die, so that yours can shine once more. The brightest in the firmament.'

'Stop there, where I can see you,' Kustaa shouted, his silhouette just discernible in a faintly lit window above.

The little party halted midway across an ancient bridge and Skarde bent to pluck a stone from the ground and sling it over the parapet into the water of a loch. It was a necessary action to stop him yelling blue murder at the Thane and he gritted his teeth as he listened to the plop of the missile. It had been raining since leaving Inverness and it was still raining when they abandoned the car at the end of the road and hiked the next mile along a slippery, muddy forest track. Skarde was saturated, cold, hungry and dangerously livid.

'What the hell kind of joke is this, Kustaa? What is this place?'

There had been precious little light filtering through the heavy clouds all day and the gloom had become so thick along the track that Skarde had felt obliged to switch on his phone's torch. As they had finally broken free of the trees, a scene had opened before them which seemed unchanged in several centuries. The ground had dropped away to the shores of a loch winding sinuously between the flanks of the surrounding mountains. Set back against the darkening waters was a small castle planted on an islet a couple of hundred yards from the shore and connected by an old stone bridge. An outer wall ran around the perimeter of the islet, containing a turreted keep and a single outbuilding. It was perhaps too generous to call it a castle, more likely an ancient clan tower to defend against marauding neighbours.

'I trust you with the custody of the God Killer in Fife, I travel to Rome for an audience with Jupiter herself and when I return you lead me on a bloody wild-goose chase to a castle in the middle of nowhere. What are you playing at, pal?'

'This seemed a safer place for such a precious captive.'

'Well, open up, you. We're soaked.'

'Not until you tell me who you have with you, because I expected you alone.'

'I've brought the woman we spoke about.'

'Housecarl Calder? Why? What is she to us?'

'She is of interest to Jupiter and that's all you need to know. Get that door open.'

'And the other one?'

'Her name is Domna. She is one of Jupiter's personal Praetorians.'

Domna stood silently behind Calder, one big hand gripping the Housecarl's bound arms. Rain ran in rivulets from her short hair, but she seemed unconcerned. She listened to the interaction, while her eyes roved over the castle, weighing its impregnability, assessing its strength.

'You brought a *Praetorian* here?' Kustaa shouted incredulously. 'What madness is that?'

Calder recalled the plump Thane with his curly hair, so very different from his vulpine predecessor, and she wondered what chain of events had brought him to this lonely tower on a forgotten loch, to argue with Skarde in the rain and the last light of day.

'She is here to oversee the safe passage of the God Killer back to Rome, by order of Jupiter, so enough of the questions and let us in.'

Kustaa spoke with an unseen person behind him, then retorted, 'Just you and the Housecarl. The Praetorian can shelter in the outbuilding, but she does not enter this keep.'

'You have the boy?'

'Of course. He's locked up comfortably enough.'

Skarde looked back at Domna with murder glistening in his eyes. She shrugged and passed Calder to him. 'Can you do it alone?'

'Aye. It's just that idiot and his lady friend, although she might have a gun. Leave it to me and I'll find an opportunity.'

Calder's skin crawled as she felt Skarde take hold of her arm. 'Come on, my pretty. Let's make ourselves more comfortable.'

'If you hurt Oliver,' she hissed, 'I'll kill you.'

Skarde glanced at her, surprised by the steel in her tone. 'We'll see about that,' he growled and led her across the bridge and under the arch into a puddled courtyard. Domna followed and then waited near the outbuilding while the other two approached the keep.

Kustaa was still leaning out of the window above, watching their every move.

'Open the damn door,' Skarde snarled as the rain bounced off his upturned face.

Bolts were heaved back and the door creaked open. Light danced out to play on the cobbles.

Skarde had expected to see Aurora, but instead a much larger figure stepped outside and inspected them. Dressed in a long woollen tunic and heavy boots, the man had the appearance of a monk with his cropped greying hair and aquiline features, but he was a head taller than Skarde and the hands beneath the folds of his tunic were thick and strong. On his belt were fixed a bunch of large keys.

'Who the hell are you?' Skarde demanded, taken aback by this new presence.

The man did not respond and continued to examine them with serious, doleful eyes.

'We call him the Custodian,' Kustaa called down. 'He looks after this place. He doesn't say much, but he also doesn't tolerate any unpleasantries. So you play it easy, Skarde, you hear me?'

The Custodian stepped wordlessly to one side to let them pass and Calder felt his eyes on her as Skarde steered her through the door and into a firelit interior. They entered a large room with a flagstone floor and vaulted ceiling. Flames spluttered in a large hearth, adding their flickering light to the lamps on each wall. The room spanned the whole of the ground floor and in the far corner spiral stairs wound up to higher floors and also down to subterranean depths. A sturdy oak table sat in the centre of the room, with other pieces of furniture of considerable antiquity spread around the perimeter. Drapes hung either side of the window and one wall was covered by a faded tapestry depicting warriors hunting stags. Above the hearth several long swords were displayed, similar to those Calder had handled many times in Valhalla. Save for the electric lamps, she thought the place might not have changed since the first clan chieftains had called it home.

A woman in her fifties with a dishevelled blonde bob, greying at the temple, was standing beside the table holding a pistol. She looked anxious and just about ready to use the thing. The Custodian bolted the door and then stood covering the exit. Calder was shrewd enough to know Skarde had planned violence the moment he encountered Kustaa after their long tortuous journey north, but she could also sense that now he was uncertain what to do. The presence of the figure by the door had perplexed him.

Kustaa bustled down the spiral stairs and stepped

cautiously over to the hearth, keeping a good distance from Skarde and ensuring he did not block the woman's line of fire. He took in Calder's bound hands, then nodded a curt welcome to her.

'I am surprised to see you again, Thegn. I'm sorry you are caught up in this.'

'You have the boy?' Skarde demanded, giving his captive no chance to respond.

'He is detained upstairs.'

'Show me.'

'Really, that's not necessary.'

'Show me.'

Kustaa ensured the woman kept her weapon trained on the pair, then hurried back up.

'Oliver!' Calder gasped when Kustaa returned with the young teen in front of him.

'Lana!' Oliver cried and made to dash towards her, but Kustaa grabbed his arm and tugged him back.

He looked thin, Calder thought. Much thinner and paler than when she had last laid eyes on him. But he was also taller, more muscular, with the gangly limbs of an adolescent. His hair was curly and unkempt, his jumper and jeans in need of a thorough wash. Blotches circled his eyes and fear lay deep beneath the fresh glitter of hope in his gaze.

'Are you okay?'

He shot a glance at her bound hands and nodded. 'Is it just you?'

'For now, yes. But don't worry, it won't be long.'

Skarde dug his nails into her arm and stared hard at the other woman. 'Are you going to put that gun away, Aurora?' he asked in a tone dripping poison.

Aurora checked with Kustaa and he nodded. Carefully she slipped the weapon into a pocket. 'Don't do anything stupid, Skarde. I don't need much of an excuse to use this.'

Skarde smirked and forced Calder into one of the upright chairs around the table. 'Why have you led me to this place, Thane?'

'It seemed a much more secure location for our God Killer. There's only one way in and one way out. We can observe the approaches to the bridge. And, best of all, no one seems to know it exists.'

'So how do you?'

'This is Valhalla property. A lonely fortress used by Odin and Sveinn on discreet occasions in Seasons past, but kept a closely guarded secret amongst a very few individuals. As Thane, I had oversight of all the Palatinate records and I was permitted access to the information about this place.'

'Hey, you,' Skarde sneered at the Custodian. 'Hasn't anyone told you Valhalla has fallen? No one's paying your salary anymore, pal.'

The tall figure made no sign that he had even heard Skarde and Kustaa spoke instead.

'Our friend here is paid by the Pantheon, not the Palatinate. But I believe he would remain at his post regardless of any remuneration. He has overseen this place for two decades and he feels a certain loyalty to it.'

Skarde laughed hollowly, but refrained from responding. Calder watched him glance around the room again and knew he was calculating if he could take them all down, but then he seemed to accept the current imbalance of forces and began to unbutton his coat.

'I'm wet and starving, Thane. Do you have a change of clothes?'

'Just more tunics, like our friend.'

'Then get me one – and probably one for her too. And food, damn you. Two nights you made us sleep in the car, two bloody nights of waiting on you. By rights I should break your neck, but I'll settle for something to eat.'

Kustaa pulled Oliver back towards the stairs. 'Get back up there, lad. We'll bring you some food shortly too.'

Oliver stared imploringly at Calder, but stayed silent as he was shepherded towards the steps.

'Do you have somewhere for her?' Skarde demanded, pointing at Calder. 'She's a swordmaiden, so I'm not trusting her with so much as a sniff of freedom.'

'There's only the one room habitable upstairs, so it'll have to be the cells below. The Custodian will escort her.'

The man approached Calder, but Skarde stepped forward and blocked him. 'Make sure you lock her up nice and tight, you understand, pal? She's got a temper on her.'

The Custodian regarded him with disdain, then eased past him and took Calder gently by the arm and led her towards the steps.

Calder mouthed silent reassurance to Oliver, then the lad went up, while she was taken down into the shadows beneath.

XXXXIII

Xander stood in the head beams of four executive coaches that had pulled up on the Castle Esplanade at the top of the Mile.

If anyone had sought his opinion, he would have said it seemed a damn public place for the Titans to be boarding their transport for the coming Battle. Despite the rain glistening on the cobbles and the lateness of the hour, he could still make out a crowd of curious bystanders leaning on the barrier at the entrance to the Esplanade, which the authorities had been persuaded to drop to stop these camera-toting tourists getting any closer. Above him, the castle's walls and turrets and battlements were spot-lit, and on all sides the city itself twinkled and hummed beneath the wet night.

The location of the Field had been confirmed by Atilius that afternoon. Somewhere called Abernethy in the heart of the Cairngorm massif, south of Inverness. The name meant nothing to Xander, but Parmenion had spoken of thousands of hectares of Caledonian pine forest, which Xander thought sounded far from ideal habitat to unleash five hundred horse soldiers. No one knew how Atilius had sorted such a location in just a matter of days, but some said the landowner was a national wildlife charity, no doubt grateful for a vast donation heading their way, while others suggested the land might even be part of the Royal estate surrounding Balmoral. Xander smiled at this, but if anyone could buy the nation's royalty, it was probably the Pantheon.

The good news was that the Cairngorms were little more than two hours from Edinburgh and Xander was thankful for this. No one wanted a tortuous journey to the deep wilds of the far north and he had genuinely feared the logistics of getting massed cavalry to one of the remote islands. So two hours up the A9 was just fine with him, although he suspected that the land around Royal Deeside under the balmy skies of spring could be teeming with outdoor enthusiasts. Well, that was Atilius' problem. No doubt he had the resources to seal off every route into the Field, but did he have the time?

The Titans were arriving on the Esplanade in dribs and drabs, which was good because this did not overly arouse the curiosity of the onlookers, who were mostly focusing their lenses on the castle's night-time finery. Dressed in civvies and shouldering rucksacks, the warriors of Macedon resembled a large group of visitors taking a journey at an unusual hour. He watched them board the coaches, depositing phones and wallets and watches into boxes provided on each front seat. Nicanor and Parmenion stood beside one vehicle, hands in pockets, conversing softly. Agape floated in and out of the shadows.

His mind wandered to the opposite end of the Mile, down near the Palace of Holyrood, where another five coaches *should* be loading with occupants, but he had no way of knowing. He had decided he must leave Bjarke and Calder and Ulf and all the other Vikings to make their own decisions about this Battle. He had warned Ulf of the consequences of a no-show, but he could only surmise how Ulf had reported their conversation back to the Jarl and Housecarl.

Standing on the Esplanade now, he wondered if he had made a huge mistake by giving Valhalla such autonomy. What if the fools did not come? What if the coaches at Holyrood waited this very minute, empty and forlorn?

His mobile's vibration scattered his fears and it was Zeus' voice in the receiver.

'Are you almost ready to depart?'

'We are, my lord.'

'And the others?'

'Diogenes is on route from the stables with our mounts and the rest of the Companion Cavalry. Ellac says the Huns are coming up the A1 from Newcastle in a huge procession of horse carriers and coaches. Valhalla are boarding as we speak.'

This last was a wild assumption, but what else could he say?

'And I can confirm,' Zeus added, 'that your new horses are being ferried all the way to the Inverness docks and will come south from there in the morning.'

'Thank you, my lord.'

'Don't thank me, thank my wife. She and Simmius have been calling in every favour to get you a hundred rideable stallions. Truth be told, she's an equine fanatic and she's been rather enjoying the challenge. She seems to have a lot of faith in you and your cavalry.'

'I am indebted to her, lord.'

Zeus harrumphed and then went silent for a moment. 'Listen, Alexander, I wish I did, but I don't have much fresh advice for you. We are all in shock about this situation. There is huge unrest amongst the remaining Caelestia and even greater furore and distrust amongst our speculating supporters. Jupiter has used her power to eviscerate the Rules and by doing so she is dismantling the very bones of the Pantheon. We have already stood on two Fields this Season and, by right, nothing more should be demanded of us until the Twenty-First Year next winter, but Jupiter thinks otherwise.'

'We'll get through it, lord. Nothing can be as daunting as walking onto Hortobágy Plain to face *two* foe both of whose numbers far outstripped anything we could boast.'

'You speak well. Perhaps you should say such words to the troops in the hours before conflict. It also bodes well that no King needs to die this time. For more than a decade, the Legion has waged an end of year Battle with one of either the Huns or the Sultanate and no sovereign has ever fallen. There is no reason for this to be any different.'

He paused again and Xander could sense the Titan god thinking. 'Alexander, hear these words. Jupiter is angry. Cold and furious in a way I've never known her. She has demanded this Battle to make a point. Your actions over the last few weeks and the continued success of this Palatinate, have stung her. The Legion has always been the most glorious force in the Pantheon and she resents her thunder being stolen by us.

'This forthcoming conflict is once more supposed to be limited to one Battle Hour and hostilities should end when the klaxon sounds, but Jupiter wants her pound of flesh, I can feel it in my bones. And the most likely target for her wrath is you, Alexander. The King Killer turned King. The most famous soldier in the Pantheon. If she can have your scalp during this Battle, she will take it with glee.'

'I hear you, lord.'

'So stay behind our banners. Resist the urge to lead from the front. You've done enough charging about on that damn horse of yours at Knoydart and Hortobágy. Get through this one unscathed. *Live*, Alexander. That is the best riposte you can give to the likes of Jupiter.'

They bade their farewells and Xander strode over to the coaches.

'Are we ready?' he asked Agape, who was waiting for him.

'All accounted for.'

He had not shared with her his fears about Valhalla. That was a burden he must bear alone.

'Then let's get this journey underway.'

Agape glanced up at the sky. 'The forecast is pretty awful for the next few days.'

Xander grinned and reached out to grip her shoulder. 'Well, we wouldn't want those sun-loving Roman boys and girls to come all the way over here and not get a proper Scottish welcome.'

Calder had feared the worst when the Custodian led her down to the castle's cells. She had imagined a black dungeon, dripping and cold, scurrying with rats, but in fact the cell he unlocked was clean and lit by a single electric lamp. The ancient stone had been whitewashed and the floor tiled. There was a chair, a table and a slim bed with a double blanket. In one corner was a wash basin and a toilet, and these could be screened off by a curtain. High above the toilet was a small window, and opposite the bed, a door stood ajar, leading to another room, which was unlit.

She perched on the bed as the man untied her bonds and placed a tunic and a pair of sandals next to her. Then he departed and locked her in. Rubbing her wrists to ease the circulation, Calder walked over to the open door and peered into the adjacent room. It was utterly dark and seemed to have no window and no obvious light switch, so she closed the door.

Listening to ensure no one was coming down the stairs, she began to undress and used the hand towel by the wash basin to dry herself before slipping on the tunic and sandals. Then she climbed onto the toilet and managed to peek out of the window. It was set at ground height and she could see across the courtyard. Night had arrived and there was a light coming from the outbuilding where she spotted Domna's shadow moving about. She heard footsteps and the Custodian walked across the yard, hunched slightly against the rain. He was carrying a tray of food and he deposited this at the door to Domna's temporary residence, then retreated. Calder watched as the big Praetorian stepped into the night and crouched to retrieve the tray, then disappeared back into the shelter again.

Calder dropped down from the toilet and went to study the lock on her cell. It was sturdy enough and she quickly gave up any hope of escape that way. She sank onto her cot and listened to the constant hiss of the rain and the murmured voices above. A little later there was movement outside her door and then a key turned and the Custodian appeared with a tray. He left it on her table and departed without a glance. There was a bowl of steaming stew, a hunk of buttered bread and a mug of tea. The smell of the stew was divine and hunger rolled in her gut. She sat at the chair and worked studiously through every morsel, then cradled her tea and let the night extend.

Sometime later the lamp dimmed as she lay on her cot. She was still listening to the movements and voices above, but exhaustion crept up on her and the next thing she became aware of was the sound of her door unlocking again. Dull morning light filtered through the window as the Custodian entered with a new tray of food for breakfast. He placed a bowl of porridge on her table and she was about to rise and accept it, when he did something unexpected.

He took a second bowl and opened the door into the darkened room. She watched as he placed the bowl on the floor a few feet into the shadows, then backed carefully out and closed the door. This time he paused to look at her and then uttered the first words she had heard him speak.

'Don't worry about him.'

He bent to retrieve her used crockery from the night before and left, locking the outer door behind him.

Calder perched on her bed and stared at the side door, her heart pounding.

Someone was in there.

Someone else shared her cell.

XXXXIV

Diogenes gripped Xander's hand with a warm smile. 'Welcome to paradise, my King.'

The rain came waltzing across the vast landscape in flurry after flurry. *Paradise* was not a word he would have used himself, but he had to admit there was something breathtaking about their surroundings.

The coaches had dropped them at the very end point of the tarmac road and the Titan regiments had hiked for an hour through the wet. Unlike the muddy wilderness of Knoydart, this had been on well-made tracks, built for off-road vehicles to manage the estate and conserve the wildlife. Where Knoydart had been barren, this huge glen was overflowing with purple heather and juniper, and studded with the most beautiful trees he had ever seen. In the distance, a wide river wound lazily to the west and beyond that the ground rose to meet a wall of mountains. Even through the deluge, Xander was sure their summits shone bright.

'Is that snow on those tops in May?'

Dio smiled. 'Aye. That's the Cairngorm Plateau, the only truly alpine landscape in Britain. Ben MacDui's up there somewhere, second highest peak in Scotland.'

'I take it you agree with the choice of Field.'

'Time will tell if it has military merits, but I can't deny the place makes my Highland heart sing.'

Xander studied the trees. 'This isn't like a normal forest; they're all spaced out.'

'Aye, they're ancient Caledonian pines, even though they look more like giant oaks. They tend to grow more widely dispersed and this encourages the juniper and heather between them. It's a forest, but not like any other.'

Xander eyed it shrewdly. 'Nowhere to hide.'

'Not amongst the trees themselves, but the land rolls a lot between here and the river could conceal more than you think.'

'What about this heather?' Xander mused, kicking at some that reached to his knees by the edge of the track. 'Will it hinder horses?'

'Not in itself, but if we move fast we risk not seeing holes and rocks and other obstacles.'

Xander chewed his lip grimly. He had a Palatinate with five hundred horses, while the Legion boasted none. Moving fast was the one thing he wanted to do.

Behind him, a camp had been erected and the Titans were breaking themselves into units and getting out of the rain. There was a large mess tent releasing delicious scents and a second that Dio said would be Xander's command tent, but there was little else of homely cheer under the sodden skies.

'It's not much, I'm afraid,' said Dio.

'It'll do. We're not here to enjoy the accommodation. What about *our* team?'

Dio's brow furrowed. 'The first twenty of the new horses

have already arrived from Inverness. As always, they're beauties and good temperaments, but no provision's been made for them in this weather. The rain will ruin their hay, so all of them – including our four – are still in their trailers.'

'You got the carriers down here?'

'Most of the way. They're back up the track and off to the right.'

'I don't want them kept in their stalls. Damn Atilius. He knows we have horses.'

'I guess he couldn't sort everything in the time he had. Lenore's mounted up already and gone to see if she can find alternative stabling.'

'Good for her.'

'There's another thing you should know. The Hellenes' tents have been pitched way over there beyond that rise.' Dio pointed west. 'The camp teams said the order came from you.'

'I agreed they could be separate.' Xander looked at his friend and weighed up saying more. 'And I promised them that if they come, they won't be Hellenes.'

'*If* they come? They have a choice?'

'If they come, the banners flying over their tents will be Raven, Wolf, Storm, Hammer and the Triple Horn.'

Dio stared at him, his bald head slick with the rain. Then he broke into a huge grin. 'Spoken like a true Alexander.'

'Except it might all backfire. Has there been any sign of movement in their camp?'

Dio shrugged. 'The track they'd use branches off someway back. Let's take a look.'

The two men cut across the heather, lifting their feet to

avoid tripping. Xander thought perhaps the rain was easing, or maybe he was just so wet that he no longer noticed. They climbed the rise and stood between a copse of the giant pinewoods, staring down at an empty camp.

'Shit,' Xander said quietly.

'They may be delayed on the road.'

Xander did not reply. Instead, he looked south towards the mountains. 'Has the Legion graced us with its presence?'

'I've seen nothing, but the camp teams say the Roman tents are being erected somewhere by the river.'

Xander squinted into the distance. 'They haven't come in through here?'

'There are other routes from the west.'

He pondered a landscape where nothing moved and wondered how twelve hundred Legionaries could just disappear.

'Heads up,' said Dio.

Xander turned and gratitude surged through his veins. There were figures on the path towards the empty camp. They came in groups, drawn out along the route, but as the two men watched, more and more came into view.

The pair strode down the slope and set a course to intersect the column. Xander recognised the bulk of Bjarke near the front. His blond tresses might have been shorn, but he still had the bearing of a Jarl. Xander waved and the lead group stopped, though none returned the gesture.

'You've come,' Xander smiled when they got in hailing distance.

'Aye,' Bjarke called back. 'But only on the condition that what Ulf told us proves true.'

Xander and Dio reached the track and faced their old comrades. 'Your camp is just down there. You'll find crates containing new banners of Valhalla and all your armour and weapons. I will have mess teams sent over to get food on the go.'

Bjarke rumbled in his throat. Stubble coated his chin where he had stopped shaving several days ago, but it would be years before he could braid a glorious Viking beard once more.

'How many have come?' Xander asked.

'All except one.'

'And which individual has decided to be so defiant.'

Bjarke gave him a long assessing stare. 'Housecarl Calder.'

The energy that had propelled Xander down the slope tiptoed away. *Lana. Not you. Surely not you.*

'Did she say why?' His voice sounded husky, but Bjarke did not notice.

'We've had no communication from her in a week. If she's gone, I think she's really gone.'

Dio and Xander looked at each other. There would be role-calls before the Battle commenced, numbers judiciously counted and identities checked so the *libitinarii* would find it easier to sort the dead from the living when the violence ceased. Soon enough, she would be missed and the Pantheon would send its squads to locate her.

Xander steeled himself and turned back to Bjarke. 'Thank you for coming. Get yourself in the dry. My promise to Ulf stands. When the klaxon sounds, Valhalla is free to do what you see fit.'

Bjarke nodded, heaved his bag onto his shoulder and

strode on towards the tents. Xander and Dio stood back to let the column pass. A horse nickered behind them and they turned to see Lenore approaching, her sodden hair plastered over her shoulders.

'I've found somewhere that might be suitable stabling.'

'Show us.'

'It's a way off, so I suggest we ride.'

'I was looking for a reason to see Boreas.'

Calder spent much of the morning perched on her cot, staring at the door into the next room and listening for any sound.

At one point, Skarde came down the stairs to check on her. She curled herself up at the far end of the bed and glared at him guardedly. She could see he was agitated. Obviously he had not yet found a way to wreak the violence he had planned on Kustaa and Aurora, and his eyes twitched like a cornered rat.

'That's it, girl,' he growled. 'You stay nice and tight in here and I'll see to you later.'

He glanced around her cell, then retreated and locked her in once more.

The morning stretched and the rain at last eased, although she could still hear drips somewhere deep within the stonework. She dreaded the thought of spending a second night in the cell when someone – or something – could come through the side door at any moment, so she pushed herself off her cot and tiptoed to the door to listen. Nothing stirred. Her heart in her mouth, she twisted the handle and pulled the door open. Light from her own cell filtered into the darkness, but not enough to illuminate the far corners.

'Hello?' she said. 'Is someone there?'

She could see the bowl of porridge on the floor, cold and untouched.

'If anyone's there, make yourself known.'

Nothing. Absolute silence, but her nostrils flared at the stale air. It was heavy with the odour of another body, with the breath of another being.

She strained her eyes, but the room refused to reveal its secrets and eventually her fear got the better of her and she closed the door firmly and shoved the table and chair up against it.

Disconsolately, she slunk back to her cot.

It must have been an hour later, when something happened upstairs.

There was a shout, a thump and single gunshot.

Calder sprang to the door of her cell and her mind flooded with worry for Oliver. There was another shout and a tussle, followed by the sound of furniture moving.

Then footsteps rushed down the stairs and the key was thrust into the lock.

It was Skarde, fury scrawled over his face and a knife clutched in his hand.

'Get over there!' he shouted and pushed her towards the cot. For an awful moment, she believed he was going to try to rape her again, but then he forced her hands behind her and bound them once more with a length of cord. 'Upstairs, now.'

He hauled her up the spiral steps and into the main room.

The fire had gone out and a cold breeze jostled through the open door from the courtyard. The Custodian loomed in one corner and Kustaa was kneeling by the hearth. On the other side of the table, Aurora was lying on the floor. She was alive and moving, but her blonde hair was matted with blood. Above her stood Domna, holding one of the swords that had been hanging above the fireplace. Of Oliver, there was no sign.

'Get over there,' Skarde muttered and manhandled Calder into one of the chairs.

He looked around at the other occupants, his knife held ready, then paced to Aurora and picked up the gun by her side. He emptied the remaining bullets, walked to the door and hurled the weapon into a far corner of the courtyard, then bolted the door closed.

'Right, at last. Our little gathering has gone on too long. Let's get this done the old-fashioned way, Domna.'

The Praetorian nodded and bent to prop Aurora up against one of the chairs.

'We need evidence,' Domna said in matter-of-fact tones.

Skarde reached into his tunic pocket and pulled out Kustaa's phone, which he had been using since he confiscated it from the house in Fife. 'I'll video.'

He fussed with the screen, then turned abruptly on the Custodian and pointed a finger at him. 'This is none of your business, pal, you understand? We're following orders, Pantheon orders from the very top, so you keep your nose out of it. You got that? One move and my friend here will run you through.'

The tall man showed no emotion and simply waited for events to unfold.

'Okay,' said Skarde, looking back to Domna. 'We finish this and then we get out of here.'

He raised the phone and tapped record, and Domna stepped astride Aurora with her sword arm pulled back to strike.

And in that moment, there was a pounding on the door.

XXXXV

'The lights are on,' said Dio, stepping back and squinting up at the building as the rain rallied.

'What a place,' Xander said for the second time. 'Who would live here? There's not even a road in.'

They had walked their mounts across the old stone bridge and left them with Lenore in the limited shelter under the arch. She had shown them the outbuilding she had spotted earlier and they had dipped their heads in and agreed it was a good place for the beasts, at least for one night.

'Come on,' Xander urged irritably under his breath, but the door remained steadfastly closed.

'I thought I saw the door open when we were on the bridge,' said Dio, 'but it could have been a trick of the rain.'

Xander cursed and leaned forward to rap hard on the door once more.

Inside the tower, the arrival of these unexpected visitors had sparked a series of wordless aggressive movements.

Skarde flung an arm around Calder's throat and brought his knife to her ear, then pushed her into a corner adjacent to the door. Domna grabbed Aurora by the hair and dragged her behind a large sideboard. Kustaa flapped backwards and forwards, his eyes on stalks, then finally bounded up the spiral staircase and crouched just out of sight. Only the Custodian remained still.

'Get rid of them,' hissed Skarde.

Without acknowledging Skarde's command, the tall man approached the door and pulled back the bolts.

'Bingo,' said Dio, and the two men waited for the door to creak open.

Xander had been about to speak, but his words dissipated at the sight of the figure. He had never seen someone so tall, but the man's dimensions were only part of the surprise. He was dressed in the robes of a medieval monk, great keys hanging from a belt of rope. His grey hair was cut almost to nothing, exaggerating his long, angular face. The eyes that regarded the two visitors revealed not a scrap of emotion.

'Er, good day.' Xander found his voice. 'We're sorry to disturb you. We've been caught in this storm and we're hoping we could shelter our horses in your outbuilding for the rest of the day and perhaps the night as well.'

The man said nothing, but his eyes shifted to take in Lenore under the arch.

'It's just the three of us at the moment,' continued Xander, following the man's gaze. 'But we have another twenty horses with us, all in need of dry fodder. Your building seems large enough to house them all.'

He glanced at Dio as his words still elicited no response.

'We can pay,' said Dio. 'And we wouldn't disturb you.'

They could just make out the well-furnished interior and

both were thinking how nice it would be to step inside out of the elements, but the man regarded them in silence.

'Yes,' agreed Xander. 'We'll stay in the outbuilding and not get in your way. We have our own supplies and we'll be gone at first light.'

At last the man nodded and raised a finger to point to the outbuilding.

'Thank you,' said Xander. 'We're obliged to you. We'll fetch the other horses.'

They turned away from the tower, both pulling faces, and jogged across the puddled cobbles to Lenore.

Behind them, the door closed once more and the bolts scraped across.

'I said get rid of them, not give them a bed for the night!' Skarde spat.

The Custodian ignored him and walked silently off to the castle kitchen. Kustaa reappeared and descended the stairs, wide-eyed and utterly confused. 'What do we do?'

Domna stood and exchanged a silent look with Skarde. Evidently, the idiot Thane had not realised she had been seconds from killing Aurora before the interruption, and the next victim would have been him.

'We delay?' she checked quietly.

'Aye,' replied Skarde in exasperation. 'We wait, at least until we have a better idea what those bastards are doing here and what they're up to.'

A groan came from Aurora's prone form behind the Praetorian.

'Is she going to cause us trouble?' Skarde demanded.

'She's in a mess, but I'll keep her quiet.'

'Okay.' Skarde still had Calder by the throat. 'Kustaa, check on the kid. Make sure he can't cause a scene. And you, my darling,' he whispered in Calder's ear, 'it looks as though we're going to have to postpone our little play.'

With these words, he dragged her across the room and back down the steps to her cell. His gaze took in the small window above the toilet and he swore. 'Can't have you tapping on that for help, now can we.'

Still keeping his grip on her, he kicked the table and chair out of the way of the adjoining door, then shoved it open and peered into the dark. 'This will do you. Scream all you want; no one will hear.'

He used the knife to slice her bonds, then pushed her forward. 'See you tomorrow, my dear. Those bastards said they'd be gone by dawn and then we can finish our business.'

He slammed the door shut and pushed the furniture back.

Calder was abandoned in the pitch dark.

Two storeys above, Oliver leaned against the glass panes and peered down at the figures in the outbuilding.

The window had long ago rusted itself solid and no amount of effort over the last few days had resulted in him managing to open it. Raindrops continued to spatter against it, making it impossible to see down to the outbuilding in any detail. He only knew that these people had not been welcomed by Kustaa or Aurora or Skarde – and that made them his friends.

He rapped on the window and hollered, but rain

was hissing across the loch and rushing through the old gutters and they could not hear him. He kept waving and banging, and he thought one of the figures came out into the courtyard and looked up at him.

He must do something. He stared around the room and spotted his empty porridge bowl. He grabbed it and prepared to throw it against the old panes, but at that moment, Kustaa barged into the room and saw him.

'Don't!' the Thane shouted, and ran at him.

Too late. Oliver hurled the bowl at the window, but his aim had been hurried and it crashed against the stone edge of the window, shattering into pieces, but not breaking the glass.

'You runt!' Kustaa rasped and barged into Oliver, knocking him onto his bed.

They tussled on the mattress and Oliver managed to squirm from under the fatter man and wrestle himself up. Kustaa had underestimated his captive. This young man had spent a year in the Valhalla Schola. He had learned to fight the hard way and he sent a fist into the side of the Thane's head, knocking him almost senseless, then stretched his fingers around his throat and squeezed.

Fury exploded through Oliver. This bastard had held him prisoner for almost a month, kept him locked in the house in Fife, bound him whenever he took a trip to the bathroom, threatened him, forced him into the boot of a car for hours and hours, and never allowed him into the fresh air except to march him along a track to his lonely castle. *So die, you bastard. Die, right now.*

A shape loomed in the corner of his vision. He had just a

moment to recognise the Praetorian and then a huge blow knocked him into oblivion.

Calder's terror froze her to the spot where Skarde had left her.

The room was so dark that she could not even see her own hands and all she could think about was the presence of the other prisoner. She could smell him. She could feel his eyes on her – so much more habituated to this lightless space.

She must control her fear and tell herself she was a swordmaiden of Valhalla, unafraid of the dark. She took a ragged breath and tried to focus. One thing was clear: when Skarde had pulled her into the corner upstairs and the Custodian had opened the door, she had recognised the voice of the man outside. Only the gods knew how he came to be there, but Tyler was on the threshold of their lonely tower and now he was still out there across the courtyard, sheltering from the storm in the outbuilding. She cursed herself for not crying out when she'd had the chance. Skarde had held a knife to her throat, but he intended to kill her soon anyway, of that she was sure. She should have shouted to Tyler. It might have been the last sound she ever made, but it might have helped Oliver.

The memory of this missed opportunity put steel in her belly and she stared into the black nothingness.

'Hello, sir,' she said tentatively. 'Are you there? Are you chained?'

There was no answer and no sound. Holding her hands before her, she walked forwards, heart in her throat, until her knees bumped into a cot and her hands felt the cold stone of the wall above. Her fear blossomed again as she lowered her hands to touch the bedding, but there was no shape beneath. She felt for the wall again and inched along it, utterly convinced she would walk right into the prisoner, but she came to the corner and continued along the next wall.

After several awful minutes, she had traced the entire perimeter of the room and walked several lengths up and down the middle, and not heard a single rustle or felt anything except stone. She found her way back to the door and pushed at it, but Skarde had ensured the furniture would not budge.

Sightless and forlorn, she stood still and forced her brain to think, and then a new realisation came to her.

When Skarde had come for her and dragged her upstairs, he had not locked the cell door behind him.

If there really had been a captive in this room, he was now somewhere else in the castle.

XXXXVI

It was mid-afternoon when Lenore returned with the new horses.

They came in a line behind her across the bridge and each carried a human on its back.

'What is this?' Dio exclaimed, pacing out to meet her.

'Ellac was true to her word,' Lenore grinned. 'The first of a hundred Huns who have volunteered to ride these mounts and to wear our armour. The rest are still on their way to the main camp, but will arrive before dark.'

'Just in time,' said Xander, coming from the outbuilding.

He examined the warriors as they dropped from their beasts. They were an equal mix of men and woman, skin darkened by the elements on the Hungarian Plain, hair matted and unkempt, bodies unwashed, eyes diamond hard, dressed in an assortment of dirty civvies, and the cheeks of the men pocked with scars and burns to stop their beards from growing.

They were a terrible sight to behold, but Xander loved them.

He was Alexander and this was his Companion Cavalry.

Each new arrival carried a large backpack and Lenore slung a further two down to Dio and Xander. Inside were sets of armour and rations. Strapped to each horse was a shortsword, a helmet and a sack of hay and oats, and clasped in the grip of every rider was a lance.

They led the horses into the shelter and set about spreading hay along the back wall where it was driest. Dio found buckets stacked in one corner and oversaw the distribution of oats and more hay for the animals to feed. The new arrivals each found their own square metre of floorspace and laid out their armour and rations, and Xander was pleased to see them set about cleaning and buffing the armour as though they had owned the war gear for many Seasons.

Evening settled over the valley. The rain relented and an occasional patch of purple sky winked between the clouds. As the group was settling on thin blankets and grimly reviewing their cold rations of beans and breads, Xander was surprised to see the tall man walk over from the tower to check on them. He stood in the entrance and watched them in silence, oblivious to the twenty faces peering back at him. His eyes ran over the armour and helmets, and then his gaze settled on Xander.

'You are Pantheon?'

Xander was so surprised to hear him speak that he said yes before he could stop himself. The man nodded slowly, then turned without another word and retreated to the castle.

'Sociable bastard,' Dio remarked.

Lenore was looking at Xander. 'Strange that he asked that, don't you think?'

'I do.' Xander looked out at the black bulk of the castle. 'And I'm beginning to wonder if this place is more than it seems. Even though the selection of this Field was an almighty rush, Atilius would have ensured his teams checked the area and they're not going to miss a castle on a loch. So why no Vigiles or security patrols?'

'Well, whatever else this place might be,' growled Dio, 'It's surely the worst hotel I've ever stayed in. A man shouldn't go to war on a cold stomach.'

As if in response, the door of the tower opened again and light spilled across the courtyard. The man returned bearing a large cauldron and a lantern. This time he entered their shelter and placed the cauldron amongst them. Inside, it was stacked with firewood and tinder.

'Pantheon,' he said once again.

'Thank you,' said Xander.

When he was gone, they set about building the fire and lighting the tinder with the lantern. After much coaxing, the flames caught and Xander sat back and watched as Dio collected every warrior's ration of beans and poured them into the cauldron. He added some water and then wedged the pot onto the wood, and soon the place was filled with warmth and the sweet scent of dinner.

Just as they were preparing to eat, there came the sound of more hooves on the bridge and two riders trotted into the courtyard.

Lenore beamed at Xander. 'I thought I wouldn't tell you and spoil the surprise.'

Xander strode outside. The riders jumped down and he laughed in delight. Spyro and Melitta had been released from the Pantheon wards and were back with them. He embraced them and then stepped back for Dio to hug them too.

'We've brought more rations,' Spyro grinned and Dio roared with delight.

Together they ate and tended the horses, and beyond their ring of firelight, night settled across Abernethy.

Alone in the darkened upper room of the tower, Skarde squatted by the window and stared down at the glow from the outbuilding.

He had seen the new riders arrive, and now that the rain had eased he could catch glimpses of detail through the open door. Firelight glinted on iron and bronze and Skarde's blood ran cold. This was no passing group of horse trekkers. He knew weapons when he saw them.

He dropped down the stairs to the main room, where Domna had pulled one of the chairs over to the door and sat with the sword on her lap, silently declaring that anyone who wished to leave would have to go through her first. Kustaa hovered by the hearth. Oliver had been bound and pushed into a chair after his attack on the Thane, but they had since relented and released his wrists. Aurora still lay beside the sideboard, groaning as she fell in and out of consciousness.

'They're armed,' Skarde declared.

'I thought as much,' replied Domna.

'They are Pantheon,' said the Custodian from his place beside the door to the kitchens.

Every eye turned to him.

'What on earth are they doing here?' Kustaa gasped.

Domna shrugged. 'I thought perhaps you might tell us.'

'Me?'

'You said this place belongs to Valhalla.'

'Yes, but no one knows about it, and because of the fall of Valhalla it will take time for anyone in the Titan Palatinate to notice its existence on the property records.'

'They are Titans,' said the Custodian.

'Titans!' Kustaa exclaimed. 'How have they found this castle so soon?'

Skarde clenched his fists. He knew only too well that he had fled from the victorious Titans at Knoydart and would have been recorded as absent without permission. If they found him, they would kill him.

He approached Domna and said softly, 'As soon as they leave at first light, we do what we came to do and then we get out of here.'

The Praetorian nodded. 'Agreed.'

XXXXVII

When the first stirrings of light crept across the loch, slowly revealing the distant shoreline and the hulks of the mountains, the Companions mounted up in silence.

They had eaten an early breakfast of bread and cheese, washed down with a little wine brought by Spyro and Melitta. They had groomed and fed the horses and helped each other into their war gear. For the Huns, this was the first time they had worn Titan bronze and it took them time to fit it and admire each other. Xander worried that it was foolish to introduce them to a new way of fighting on the day of a Grand Battle, but they mounted their bareback stallions confidently enough and gripped the lances and hoplons as though they had carried them for years.

The first rain was starting again, but as Xander led Boreas from the shelter and inspected the column, a shiver of pride ran down his spine. Just a short time ago, these men and women had been his foe. They might even have been amongst his sister's Black Cloaks, charging down the slope at him. Yet now, in their white tunics, bronze breastplates, plumed helmets and scarlet cloaks, they looked as glorious as anything on this dull colourless morning. When they reached the main camp, there would be eighty more waiting for them and a further four hundred Huns under Ellac's command.

Xander now led the cavalry he had dreamed about when he first breakfasted with Hera in the dining room of the Balmoral Hotel, and today he would lead them against the Legion and show Caesar that he faced a truly worthy foe.

Unseen above him, Skarde hunched against the window and watched the column prepare to move out. He could not begin to understand why there was a unit of Titan cavalry outside this remote castle, but he was damned well not going to hang around for long to find out. Coiled like a hyena, he waited for them to depart so he could spring into action downstairs.

The Titan commander was directly below him. The man raised his lance and the column began to trot under the arch. The commander waited until they were all through and then followed at the rear. As he reached the arch, he turned his horse and squinted back at the tower. The man was helmeted, but something about his figure, his confidence, his armour, coalesced in Skarde's brain and he sucked in his breath.

The King Killer.

The King Killer was in the courtyard below him. The man Jupiter wanted more than anything else.

The rider wheeled his horse and disappeared under the arch. In the same moment, Skarde bounded out of the upper room and down the stairs.

'The King Killer! We had him in our grasp.'

Domna inclined her head. 'And now he leads a column of twenty armed warriors, so there's not much we can do about it.'

'But imagine Jupiter's pleasure if we could get to him.'

'There's no chance.'

Skarde stared wild-eyed around him. 'We do what we have to now,' he murmured at her. 'We get it done and then we follow the column. Maybe there will be one chance to get to him.'

Domna rose. 'Then fetch the girl.'

Calder was perched on the bunk of the unknown prisoner when Skarde came for her. Her eyes had become accustomed enough to the dark to make out the walls and the outline of the door, and she was startled by the light from the other cell when Skarde flung open the door.

Instantly, Calder knew this was it. There would be no more preamble. As he strode towards her, she threw herself at him, fists balling and flying at his face. She smashed him in the eye and whacked the side of his skull, then got a knee into his stomach before he roared and slammed her backwards into the wall. Oxygen hissed out of her lungs and he thrust a hand around her throat and raised her off the ground.

'That's it, you little bitch, you fight me.'

For a second, he was tempted to do it right there, while they were pressed together in the dark. A final hurrah before the blood flowed. But then he relented, grabbed her in a headlock and once more dragged her upstairs.

As the pair appeared, Oliver leapt from his chair and charged at them. 'Don't you hurt her, you bastard!'

He rushed into Skarde and grappled with him, tugging at his hair and kicking. Skarde swore murderously, crooked his free arm and smashed his elbow into Oliver's face. The boy fell like a stone and collapsed on the floor, senseless.

'What's happening?' Kustaa cried, his eyes wide with confusion.

'Shut up,' Skarde snarled and then jerked a finger at the Custodian who still hovered by the kitchens. 'You keep out of this, you freak. This is none of your business.'

Aurora moaned and tried to shift from beside the sideboard. Domna strode over and shoved her sword into the woman's belly, as one might spear a hunk of beef. Blood burst from Aurora's mouth as she raised her head in shock. For a heartbeat, her ragged greying blonde hairdo trembled and then she collapsed, lifeless.

Kustaa's mouth opened and closed, followed by a long wail. 'This is not right. What have you done? We should be taking the boy to Jupiter.'

'Change of plan,' Skarde spat.

Domna advanced on the Thane and Kustaa backed against the wall, flapping his hands. 'Stop his madness! We have the God Killer; we can sell him to Jupiter.'

'She doesn't want him,' Skarde said.

Kustaa's eyes fluttered to Skarde in shock, then flew back to the Praetorian and her bloodied blade.

'No, wait, there must be another...'

Domna killed him with a single clinical strike through the ribs. She held him wedged against the wall for a long second, then dragged the steel out and watched him sink into a lump on the floor.

'You have your phone?' she demanded of Skarde.

'Hold this one,' he said and hauled Calder over to the Praetorian. Domna grabbed her arms and pinned them behind her, then Skarde released his grip around her throat.

He ferreted around in his robe and pulled out the phone, then leaned over each corpse and photographed them.

Once he was satisfied with the images, he turned back to Calder and pulled the knife from his belt. 'And now it's our time, my dear.'

He was interrupted by the solemn voice of the Custodian. 'You should not have come to Erebus.'

Skarde gaped at him. 'What did you say?'

'You are not welcome in Erebus.'

Skarde's face paled, then flushed crimson. He rushed to the Custodian and grabbed him by the front of his robe. 'How dare you say that, you bastard! This is not Erebus.'

'This is Erebus.'

'Erebus is heat and dust and stink, you liar!' Skarde screamed the words up into the Custodian's face. 'I should know.'

For a moment it seemed the man would say no more. Then he looked down at Skarde and said slowly, 'The Pantheon has more than one Erebus.'

Skarde's chest heaved and he looked on the brink of thrusting his knife into the other man. 'You lie.'

The Custodian continued calmly, as if they were having a debate about the weather. 'This is Erebus IV. It was a Pantheon prison for two decades, but is seldom needed now.'

Slowly, his eyes fixed on the Custodian, Skarde released his grip and stumbled backwards. He seemed lost. He broke his gaze and stared around the room as if he had forgotten where he was. Finally, his focus fell on Calder once more and a heavy stillness came over him.

At last, he gave a sad smile. 'Well, what a place for our last waltz, you and I. It's been so long since I first had you. You were young then, so innocent, but I wanted you to struggle and I wanted you to fight and you didn't, so it was over too soon.'

'You took that innocence,' Calder croaked. 'You raped me when I was barely a woman and I knew nothing of the Pantheon, nothing of bloodshed, or violence, or war. You took all that innocence from me, all that life, all those possibilities.'

Skarde smirked. 'Well now you can show me what you've learned.' He made to approach her and then a thought stopped him. 'In fact, this might be more fun if we just use our hands.'

He turned away to the table and discarded his knife.

Before he could look back, he felt thick arms come around his own and pin him. He shouted in surprise and went to wrench himself free, but the grip was iron.

'What the—?' He twisted his head and glimpsed his assailant. 'Domna! What the hell are you playing at? Get off me!'

The Praetorian spun him round to face Calder. 'Do it,' she said evenly.

Calder stared at her in astonishment.

'Do it now.'

Calder's gaze shifted to the livid, snarling features of the man she had hated for so long. The man who had destroyed the woman she had once been. And she understood.

She stepped to the table and picked up the knife.

Skarde saw her movement and swore at her. 'You bitch! Don't you—!'

She stabbed him in the gut so hard the blade drove into him up to the hilt. He gasped and his eyes bulged.

She wrenched it out and stabbed a second time. He yelled, but his throat was already choking with liquid. Again, she drove the knife. And again. She thrust into him, just as he had once thrust into her. And with each stab she felt him dying. Blood flew, an explosion of scarlet on her arms, her chest, her face.

Once more she buried the weapon and this time she knew he went. The evil spark that had been his life was finally extinguished.

With a cry, she dragged the blade out and flung it on the floor. The Praetorian grunted and thrust Skarde's body across the room, where it hit a chair and collapsed.

There was silence, save for Calder's ragged breathing.

She stared at the corpse until she was certain he had gone, then she looked at her bloodied hands. A vision floated before her – the face of her daughter, Amelia. For a moment, her daughter watched her with such soft love and then the image faded, and with it went a heaviness which had lain inside Lana Cameron for so many years.

Her mind returned to the room and the iron-stink of blood, but there was a new light in her soul and she barely noticed the horror around her.

She turned to the Praetorian and tried to smile. 'Thank you.'

But the words died on her lips.

Domna had her sword held in front of her and her expression was implacable.

Calder frowned. 'You are still going to kill me?'

'My orders are from Jupiter.'

'But, why...?'

'A man like that needed to die at your hands.'

Calder braced herself and backed away. She looked imploringly at the Custodian, but he stood motionless, letting events play out. The Praetorian advanced and prepared to skewer her.

Then Domna's eyes went to something behind Calder, to a figure standing on the spiral stairs, and her mouth opened in shock. 'Who are—?'

She never finished her question. She had forgotten the other occupant in the room.

Oliver came from behind with the knife Calder had discarded. He took the Praetorian in her left side, spearing the blade hard through her kidney and deeper into the mass of organs above. She grunted in surprise, swivelled on him and grabbed his shoulder with her free hand, but she could not raise her weapon. The sword clattered to the floor and she stared at him in astonishment, then released his shoulder and sank to her knees. She gave a single spasm, fell to her side and lay still.

Oliver dropped the knife and tottered slowly to Calder. She opened her arms and he collapsed into them and they clung to each other.

Around them lay four bodies. Blood coated the antique furniture and the ancient stones. Tears of relief cascaded down Oliver's cheeks and Calder held him tight.

She glanced at the silent Custodian, then turned to look at the spot on the stairs where Domna had stared in such surprise.

A man stood there, leaning his weight against the wall in case his legs gave way. His body was wasted, his chest no more than a ribcage. His feet were bare and blackened. His hair was long and rank, his beard hanging limply to his collar bones. But his eyes looked at Calder with a strength the rest of him did not possess.

And she recognised those eyes.

She sighed in understanding. 'Freyja told me to look to Erebus.'

XXXXVIII

'In Portmahomack we have a saying about the weather,' announced Dio through gritted teeth. 'It's either raining or it's about to rain.'

'I'd take *about to rain* any day,' murmured Lenore.

Two bedraggled armies were hunched against the elements, helmets drooping, shoulders rounded, eyes down, grimly enduring the wind and wet that swept across Abernethy.

Xander sat on Boreas at the centre of his troops, his cloak rippling across his shoulders. He had briefly toyed with changing the name of his horse to Bucephalus, Alexander's trusted mount on his campaigns across Asia and perhaps the most famous animal in the ancient world, but in the end he had decided against it. Boreas was Boreas and that was just the way it was.

Behind him, the Companion Cavalry was drawn up in twelve rows of eight. To his right was Nicanor and the Phalanx. To his left, Menes and the Companion infantry, then Parmenion's peltasts. He had stationed the Huns on both flanks, the First Horn on the right and the Second on the left, while the Black Cloaks lurked in the rear. He led a weary army. So many carried wounds from Knoydart and Hortobágy. Arms were bruised and scratched, faces drawn and subdued. Xander's own injury still throbbed. He could swing his arm feely enough, but every time he stretched his back the movement made him grimace.

Earlier, Ellac had sheltered with him under a giant pinewood and briefed him more on her experience of facing the Legion and her words had held little comfort. Hun arrows were less efficient against Roman steel armour and their horses were only useful if a Century splintered from its military precision. However, she had never faced the Legion alongside allied infantry and the Huns had all seen how Mehmed's square had been broken by the Phalanx at Hortobágy.

'Use us with your sarissa lines,' she had said. 'They can be the ram that punches the hole and we will be the sea that floods in and sinks the ship.'

Above Xander's head could be heard the whine of an occasional drone, though they were barely visible in the murk and most would be grounded in these conditions.

'I hate to think of the quality of the footage,' remarked Spyro.

'They've mobile film crews on the flanks,' said Dio, 'but it's still going to be messy.'

Xander didn't care about the cameras, but he *was* worried that he could not see the foe properly. Caesar's troops were out there, no doubt. They had all heard the trumpet calls and seen the dark masses that moved onto various high points about six hundred yards south across the heather, but it was impossible to count the different Centuries or discern their formations. Even now, suited and bladed, minutes from the klaxon, the Legion was still a mystery.

Valhalla had not come onto the Field that morning. Disappointment and frustration fizzled in Xander's gut, but he would not speak of it. He had welcomed them as Vikings, returned their arms and armour, rejuvenated their banners, honoured their customs, and still they would not rise for him. Well, damn them to hell. He would do this without them.

'Company,' warned Dio, his face sheathed in bronze.

Sure enough, from the sodden murk came a single rider, walking his or her horse steadily towards the heart of the Titans.

'I thought the Legion had no mounted troops,' said Melitta.

'They don't,' answered Lenore.

Xander stared at the figure and realisation dawned on him. 'My god, it's Caesar.'

Spyro forced a grin. 'Sensible chap is surrendering already.'

Xander ignored him and heeled Boreas forward. The wind whipped and water ran from his helmet onto the back of his neck and slunk beneath his armour. He sensed spirited drone operators fighting to bring their babies down through the clouds in a desperate attempt to capture this meeting for the watching Curiate, because these would be the money shots. Caesar Imperator and the King Killer, face to face. The words before the war.

Boreas high-stepped across the heather and Xander stared at the man approaching. His helmet was gold and silver, his plume white ostrich feathers. He wore a golden breastplate shaped like a human torso, with a scarlet scarf to stop the rim of the armour chafing his neck. His tunic beneath was spotless white, his hobnailed boots gold-painted leather. He carried no scutum shield and no lance, only a silver-sheathed gladius sword at his hip, and Xander guessed that the Roman King would abandon his horse once conflict began and lead his Legion on foot.

The man's face was mostly hidden by an eye-mask, mandatory throughout the Pantheon, and the one detail that spoiled the otherwise perfect resurrection of a Roman emperor in military apparel. Xander, however, could still make out a long aquiline nose and smooth jutting chin, as well as the sinewy, bony limbs of an older man who prided himself on his fitness.

'Welcome to Scotland,' Xander said as he halted Boreas and watched the Roman advance the last few yards.

'I had not planned on being here,' came the sour response.

His accent was English, home-county diction, with a splash of east-coast American commonly found in many globe-trotting financiers.

'And I,' replied Xander, matching the man's cool tone, 'had not planned on fighting three Battles in one Season.'

Caesar harrumphed at this. 'None of us is master of our destiny. We do what our Pantheon owners dictate.'

'Even you?'

'Even me.' Xander could feel Caesar's eyes glint at him from behind the mask. 'You are young to be a King.'

'Six weeks ago, I was still a captain of just seven horse soldiers. Events have been stacking up at speed.'

'I've followed your exploits with a keen eye and I will admit your actions have been impressive. The first man to bury a blade in a King. The *only* one to charge single-handedly at several hundred Black Cloaks.'

'I did not charge alone. I had two equally impressive soldiers at my shoulders and they are back there now, awaiting your Legionaries.'

Caesar smiled thinly. 'They will not be disappointed.' His gaze shifted to take in what he could of the lines through the rain. 'I had expected an army of Titans, but I believe I see Huns on your flanks.'

'My conquered Palatinates remain free to wage war in their own ways and under their own banners.'

'Young *and* wise. You have the makings of a King who will be remembered. Perhaps we will face each other on future Fields.'

'Let's take them one at a time.'

Caesar laughed and nodded. 'Well said. Nothing matters except the Battle to come. So where are your Vikings? I have heard so much about them, but I do not see them.'

'On a battlefield, surprise is everything.'

Xander had gone one step too far with his smooth replies and Caesar bit back. 'So is experience and you would do well to remember that, lad.'

Xander dipped his helmet. 'My lord.'

Caesar's displeasure blew away on the wind as fast as it had come. 'They call you the King Killer,' he said more ruminatively. 'Two dead sovereigns in two fights. Do you intend to kill me?'

'If I must, lord, though I would do so with a heavy heart.'

'Why?'

'Because I believe you are a good King and a brave one, who leads from the front. And I also understand you created this Pantheon that we are each a part of.'

'That was a long time ago.' The Roman peered around

him, no doubt thinking of the bloodshed to come across this extraordinary glen. 'And sometimes I wonder if I created a monster. Good men and women will die today. Some will die in glory, but others will be trampled into the mud and will fade from us unnoticed amongst the slime and the blood and the piss. All for the entertainment of a few thousand bastards who have never held a blade, never stood on a battlefield, yet think they have the right to own our lives.'

'I thought you created the Pantheon for just such entertainment.'

'I created the Pantheon,' Caesar responded hotly, 'to resurrect the glorious warrior races of old, to witness them once more called to war. The money and the wagers were only ever a means to an end.'

'In my opinion, lord,' Xander said humbly. 'You did not create a monster. Your Pantheon has a place in this world and it means something, not only to those who belong to it, but to many others whose lives it brightens. God knows, I spent my youth dreaming about it.'

Caesar was silent. He deliberated upon the words and drank in the sight of the young man before him, then he raised his hands and unclipped his helmet.

'Lord?' Xander said in warning, nodding to the skies.

'I think they know what we look like by now.'

The King removed his helmet and Xander looked into a face that seemed the perfect fit for a modern Caesar Imperator. Startling blue eyes, the remains of a good head of fair hair, a patrician nose and the gaunt cheeks of an aesthete. He was handsome. The kind of man who might quieten a boardroom and animate an army.

Tentatively, Xander reached up and eased off his own bronze helmet. The Macedon helm covered the whole face, except for deep-set eye holes and a slit between the cheek-guards, so Caesar was seeing him properly for the first time. The older King studied him, running his eyes over every detail in serious, steadfast silence.

When he finally spoke, it was with words that jolted Xander.

'I am sorry about your sister.'

'How do you know about her?'

'Your words at Hortobágy were captured on the feeds.'

'No one else has managed to do that.'

'I have my methods.'

Xander was unconvinced, but he held his tongue.

Caesar was toying with his next words, formulating them. 'I grieved for you both.'

'You *grieved* for us? Why?'

'Because it was a glorious act of love and family loyalty. She chose to sacrifice her King for her brother, and I honour that.'

Xander had no response to this.

The two men sat their horses in the pouring rain and looked at each other.

'Fight well today, Alexander,' Caesar said eventually. 'Show your sister that her sacrifice was worthwhile. Show her that when all is said and done, family is the most important thing we have.'

'My family are all gone.'

The older King's eyes were pools. 'Then honour their memories.'

The pair were silent again, oblivious of the two armies that awaited them.

At last, almost regretfully, Caesar broke his gaze. 'To war then.'

They replaced their helms.

'To war,' Xander echoed.

Caesar turned his horse into the storm. 'Lead your armies with glory, Alexander of Macedon. Today we make history.'

Xander had never faced an army so silent.

At Hortobágy, the Huns had shrieked and the Janissaries had sung their marching songs. At Knoydart, the Titans had yelled their commands and the Vikings had roared to their gods. But here in Abernethy, the klaxon's blare had been followed by a series of Legion trumpet calls communicating orders, but not a single Roman voice was raised.

A mass of them was coming now. He could hear the clink of their armour and the tramp of their feet, but the rain made it hard to pick out the detail. There must be at least four Centuries, more than three hundred Legionaries, marching wordlessly towards the heart of his lines, but the other units were just shadows in the murk.

He could feel Nicanor's eyes on him. The colonel was straining at the leash to be at them and he was probably right. Caesar was starting with his own steel punch and it might be best to meet like with like. Those four Centuries would be double the number in the Phalanx, but while the Romans might bristle with six-foot pilums, they had never experienced the impact of eighteen-foot sarissas.

The distance was closing and Xander could make them out better now. They came in lines of twenty, perhaps fifteen deep. He shifted and looked at his Phalanx readied in ten rows of twelve, sarissas held at the vertical, and he remembered Ellac's words. *Punch the hole and we'll flood the ship.*

He signalled to Nicanor and the big man raised an arm and roared commands. The first three rows of sarissas lowered to the horizontal and were slotted into their slings, then the whole Phalanx rippled and stepped forward. A cheer rose from the Companions and Xander's spine tingled as the sound was joined by the whoop of four hundred Huns.

The Heavies marched grimly past his position and stamped out across the heather. So much for scouting and probing and testing each other first. There would be no feints, no skirmishes, no arrow storms. Both Kings were aware of the single Battle Hour and had opted to land their big blows immediately, so the armies strained to witness this encounter of the heavyweights.

There were more trumpets and Nicanor's bellows came back across the sodden landscape. Xander squinted through the rain at the vague masses of the other Legion units, and his stomach stirred with unease, because the plan seemed too simple. He looked to his left and signalled to Ellac. Nicanor would smash a bloody rift through those Romans, of that there was little doubt. They would counter by bending around his exposed flanks and by sending more Centuries to stab at his sides. They in turn would expose their own flanks to Xander's lines, so he would release the First and Second Horns to pour onto them. Heavies and Hun in tandem, just as Ellac had advised.

But it seemed too obvious.

Where are you, Caesar, and what are you going to do?

Halvar the Rock.

Halvar, the great bear of a man, the true Housecarl of Wolf Regiment. How could he be reduced to this?

Together, Calder and Oliver helped him limp out of Erebus IV. Each of them took a bony arm and placed it around their neck, then levered him across the courtyard and onto the bridge, but it was painfully slow. He bore the indignity in silence, though his breathing was laboured and his features set in a grimace.

Calder had stripped Domna of her coat and then struggled to get it on Halvar. Once, he would have filled it, but now it enveloped him. She had sent Oliver to get his own coat and to find the clothing she had arrived in, then quickly returned to her own cell to change. The Custodian had brought boots for Halvar's feet, but it was the one small helpful contribution he had made throughout all the violence and killing, and she could barely look at him.

They left without a backward glance, although she knew he stood by the door. The bodies were still scattered around the interior and she wondered if he would clear them himself or contact the Pantheon authorities. She suspected the Custodian of Erebus IV had seen many grisly things in his time and he would file the experience away in his memory without emotion and continue his wordless routine.

Oliver panted on the other side of the Housecarl and strained to take his weight. *Such a courageous, amazing, special lad*, she thought, *who had grown up too fast*. She feared what he must have been through since the loss of his parents and his own abduction, and she wondered what strange currents had washed him up at this lost castle in the clutches of Kustaa and Skarde.

They paused to rest at the end of the bridge and she looked with a sinking heart at the muddy track disappearing into the forest. She had searched Skarde's clothing for any sign of the key to the car he had brought her in, but to no avail. It was parked somewhere off the track about a mile up, but without a key the three of them would have to walk out of this glen or perish trying.

Halvar shifted from where he had been leaning against the stonework of the bridge and Oliver caught him before he toppled.

'Have you rested enough?' Calder asked.

'Aye,' Halvar croaked. It was the first word to break his lips.

She took him again under an arm and together the trio trudged up the track with heads bowed to the rain.

'Brace!' Nicanor yelled.

The Romans were only yards away now, and the front ranks of Heavies gripped their sarissas with both hands and hunkered behind the scalloped shields attached to their forward shoulders. Behind them, the remaining ranks still held their long weapons aloft, waiting to lower them when gaps appeared in the lines.

So close now. The wall of sarissas reached for their victims.

Then the first three ranks of the Legionaries abruptly

shifted from their march, pulled their pilum spears back
and hurled them. It was an endlessly practiced drill and
their volley was precise and low across the helmets of the
closest Heavies. Sixty pilums arced into the faces of the rows
behind, taking them utterly by surprise. Most bounced
harmlessly off bronze helmets, but others sunk into necks
and arms, and the steady cohesion of the Phalanx stuttered
as Heavies stumbled and vertical sarissas dropped. The
front ranks continued their drive unimpeded and gaps
opened between the rows.

Now it was the turn of the Romans to experience a new
enemy. Those who had thrown their pilums had drawn
their steel shortswords, but these were useless when their
Titan foes were still five yards away. The sarissa points
hit them. Some Legionaries tried to brace and block with
their scutums, but they were pushed backwards. Others
dodged the first points, only to be struck by those of the
second and third rank Heavies. Heads were twisted. Necks
disintegrated. Jaws collapsed in bloody messes.

Nicanor bent into the task. Around him, his Heavies
thrust and retracted, then thrust again, all the time stepping
forward. It was grisly, hard, meat-grinder work, made all
the more challenging when they began stepping over the
first bodies. Each time their boots came down, they did not
know if the squelching mess beneath them was a field of
heather and mud, or blood and bone.

But the Romans were learning fast. More pilums flew at
them from the rear ranks, clanging against bronze helmets
and seeking soft flesh. It did not slow the Titan momentum,
but it made them keep their heads down and stumble all
the more. Nicanor had never seen foe hold their shields as

these Legionaries did. Instead of having them attached to their forearms as basic defence, they gripped them in their left hands. One man in the centre with the transverse plume of a Centurion, held his scutum out and punched it straight into an oncoming sarissa. The Titan weapon broke through it, but the man then shoved his scutum away from him and diverted the spearpoint. Then he let go of his shield and dropped to his knees beneath the sarissa, still clutching his shortsword. Others saw him and quickly followed his example. One by one, they punched the sarissas, forced them wide and released, then crouched and drove underneath.

'Watch below!' roared Nicanor, but his front ranks could not protect themselves while they clutched such unwieldy weapons with both hands.

Roman swords struck into groins and thighs, seeking the soft flesh above bronze grieves. Titans shrieked as their femoral arteries were impaled and their vitals stabbed, and they began to collapse in blood-spouting heaps. The momentum of the Phalanx stalled. Nicanor shoved his sarissa once more into a distant Roman target, then just had time to drop it and draw his sword as he saw another Roman helmet coming at him from below. He stabbed the woman as she rose to thrust at him and then kicked her backwards to withdraw his blade from her torso. He was pleased to see his iron sword had broken her steel armour, but his stab had been strong and he had still felt momentary resistance. His Heavies must fight hard to break these Romans.

There were cries of warning from the flanks and he rose high to peer across helmets. More Legionaries were advancing, a Century on each side. They came fast, but still in close military order, with their pilums ready to prod at the exposed outside ranks of Heavies. His troops did what they could to angle their sarissas and lower them to face these new attacks, but they could never swing them around ninety-degrees and the Romans came in fast under the long poles, jabbing with their pilums, then drawing their shortswords.

Titan cohesion collapsed. Those on the flanks dropped their sarissas and reached for their own swords. Those further in stood uselessly holding their sarissas at the vertical and watching the carnage unfold.

And then there came a new rhythm in the mud beneath their boots.

The pounding of hooves.

Zeus gripped the edge of the desk and gaped at the screen in front of him.

He had wondered about travelling north with his Palatinate, but in the end decided to stay put in his residence near Edinburgh. Outside, the gardens rose in manicured terraces, magnificent with spring colour. Raindrops pattered lightly on the window panes, though it was nothing compared to the elements pounding down on his army in Abernethy.

'My Heavies,' he moaned. 'Caesar's Cohorts are destroying my Phalanx.'

Hera sat next to him. She had dismissed the staff for the afternoon and prepared baked halloumi and mango snacks, as well as loukoumades – honey dough balls – but none of the food had been touched. She sipped a glass of Muscat and studied her husband.

'We should never have been facing the Legion,' he sighed, not taking his eyes from the screen. 'Only two months ago we were happy enough in our place beside Valhalla, vying for the spoils of Tier Three. Then you hatch a madcap scheme to buy horses and our worlds haven't stopped spinning since. I should never have allowed any of this to happen. Odin might still be alive and Jupiter would not have demanded this Battle.'

'None of us could have foreseen the chain of events that has unfurled with such alacrity.'

'But we should have stopped them nonetheless. We should have known we were never ready to face Caesar's Legion. Good men and women will die today because we could not control the forces we released. We should have stood up to Jupiter. Told her this Battle was a demand too far.'

Hera looked at the Phalanx fighting for its survival.

'Much can still happen during this Battle Hour, so have faith, my dear. The outcome may surprise you.'

XXXXIX

Xander had watched the disintegration of the Phalanx and the coming of the new Centuries from the sides, just as predicted. He also saw the exposed flanks of these new arrivals and the chaos of the struggle. Infantry formation had broken down and, into chaos, cavalry could come.

What he could not see was what the rest of the Legion was up to and once more he cursed bitterly at the Highland weather. He glanced across to Ellac and saw her staring back. She wanted him to let her go, to let her rush the outside Centuries, but he hated not knowing what Caesar was planning.

'You're going to have to do something,' Dio warned from behind. 'Or are we just sitting this one out?'

Xander crinkled his nose in irritation, but accepted the realism of his friend's words. He looked back to Ellac and waved a fist.

Go.

She raised her sword and signalled the advance. On both sides, he felt and heard her troops take up the order. Ponies snorted, cries broke from lips, and the First and Second Horns surged forward. Almost three hundred warriors, broken into two huge sections, stampeded full tilt across the sodden heather, weaving around the occasional giant pinewood as sinuous as serpents.

So many, Xander thought. In one simple motion of his fist, he had released three hundred souls and now there was no calling them back. They galloped without heed of further orders or military formation. They bayed and howled and tore towards the Centuries, and Xander wondered what he had done. They were lost to him now. Over half his Palatinate was out there on the Field and only the gods knew where this fight would end.

He could feel the Black Cloaks behind him, wanting to be released as well, filled with the scent of blood on the air, but he must hold them. He must play his hand carefully, keep his remaining cards close until he knew what the hell he was supposed to do.

At one hundred and fifty yards, the Huns let go of their reins and raised their composite bows. The first volley tore into the flanks of the Centuries on both sides of the Phalanx. The second took them with even more precision. Romans fell. Shafts broke through steel armour, splintered scutums. Some Legionaries bravely stood their ground, but their lines were already broken and were angled towards the Phalanx instead of this new threat coming at them so fast.

The Huns screeched with glee, released a third volley, then shouldered their bows. Three hundred blades were drawn from horse-leather scabbards and each warrior selected a Roman quarry. Whereas the meeting of the Phalanx and the first Centuries had been like the coming together of two armoured walls, the Huns arrived like a wave across a stony beach. They flowed into and around the broken flanks of the outer Centuries, stabbing down at raised faces, kicking out at scutums, steering their ponies into human obstacles, then surging on to the next one.

For precious moments they seemed unstoppable. Ranks of Romans disappeared beneath them and the Huns crowded and competed to claim the most kills. But gradually – just as that wave on a stony beach always relents – the momentum of Ellac's troops faltered and they could only twist and turn on the spot as pilums thrust at horseflesh. They became so crowded together that most of them could not even reach out to strike a foe and could only jostle and whoop amongst their fellow Huns.

Then their howls became cries of pain as new volleys of pilums flew through the air and buried themselves with alacrity into torsos covered only in hardened leather and legs wrapped only in linen. The Huns' skull-masks were also no protection from these projectiles. Steel punctured black hoods and cracked bone. New Centuries came from both flanks, another eighty troops on both sides, marching in military precision with walls of scutums and swords.

Ellac tried to rally her troops, but half of them were on the opposite side of the Phalanx and even those around her were in no condition to respond to commands. Their outflanking manoeuvre had been outflanked. She could glimpse the Eagle banners beyond and knew that Flavius had held back his First Cohort until the Huns were fully engaged, then sent two Centuries to the aid of Cassia's Second Cohort.

The Roman shield walls broke into them and steel

stabbed again and again at horseflesh, bringing down the ponies first, then impaling the riders. Ellac chopped and hacked and kicked, desperately keeping her pony away from the bloodied pilums coming for her.

The plan had gone awry and she had been outplayed. She screeched and drove her blade into the throat of a young Legionary, even as she felt her pony jolt and shiver as a pilum found its heart.

They had been walking for almost a mile, but Calder and Oliver were exhausted by their burden.

The rain had turned the track into a myriad of earthy streams that soaked their boots and threatened to upend them with every step they took. Although Halvar forced himself to keep placing one foot in front of the other, his head sagged more heavily and he seemed on the edge of consciousness.

Calder spied a boulder beneath the trees and steered them to it. Carefully, they seated the Housecarl and then released his arms. Oliver straightened and rolled his neck with a quiet grimace of pain.

'We can't go on like this,' Calder decided aloud. 'There's no telling how long this path is or how far we must travel before we find help.'

'You go,' said Oliver firmly. 'I'll wait with the Housecarl.'

Calder weighed his proposal, glancing at the sodden skies.

'I don't know how long I'll be.'

'Be as long as you have to; it's our only option.'

'I'll return before dark, with or without help. If we must, we'll turn back to the castle for the night.'

Oliver's gaze was firm as steel. 'I'm not going back there. I'll spend a dozen nights in this forest if I have to, but I'm never going back there.'

Calder nodded her understanding and crouched to look at Halvar. His head was sagging, but his eyes met hers clearly enough.

'I'll find help,' she said. 'I'll come back and get you both.'

He rumbled his agreement and she reached out and fastened the zip of Domna's coat tighter around his throat. Then she straightened and was about to bid them farewell, when Oliver tensed and pointed silently up the track. She followed his finger and saw three figures walking towards them. They were hunched against the rain, but in the same instant they spotted the group by the boulder and bounded into the trees out of sight.

'Shit,' blurted Oliver, aghast. 'I won't let anyone take me back there.'

Calder reached out to him. 'I know. Be strong.'

Steeling herself, she stepped out to the middle of the track and held her head up into the rain. 'Who goes there?'

The silence extended. Just the tinkle of streams and the slosh of sodden trees.

Then a female voice came from the woods. 'Who are you?'

Calder considered her reply. There had been something unusual about the three figures. Their coats had not looked like the type worn by hikers or estate workers; they had been long and loose, more like cloaks. She thought of Tyler's voice outside the castle and the sight of the Companion Cavalry leaving that morning.

'I am Calder, Housecarl of Raven Company in the Horde of Valhalla.'

There was a long pause and then the three figures emerged from the trees and the lead one walked forwards and threw back her hood with a smile.

It was a face she recognised from her old Raven Company.

It was Sassa.

Xander watched open-mouthed at the carnage in front of him.

He had been so proud of his new combined Palatinate and so trusting of Ellac's advice and experience. He had seen the sense in waiting until Legion discipline broke down in the heat of battle and then releasing the Huns, but the rain had stopped him seeing the full extent of the Roman numbers and he had sent them too soon.

More than that, though, he realised there was one soldier on the Field with such strategic experience that it dwarfed all the combined advice of his own Council of War. The man with the white plume. The man who had started the whole Pantheon and led his lines for twenty years. Somewhere out there in the rain, Caesar played his pieces.

'Where the hell did they come from?' Dio said, bringing his horse next to Boreas.

'They must have marched up the edges of the glen and waited until I'd committed Ellac's Horns.'

'We'd have seen them easily enough without this damn rain.'

'But that's just it. Without this damn rain, they wouldn't have been sent up the edges. They'd have decided on a different strategy. Caesar's adapting his moves to the conditions, whereas we're stuck with plans we agreed long before we even lined up.'

Dio saw the sense in this. 'So we need to adapt as well. Is it time for us to move? You have a hundred-strong heavy cavalry now. We could break right through that mess.'

'That's the issue. It's just a mess out there. Titan, Hun and Roman all in one huge struggle. We can't charge into that. We'd be breaking our own troops as much as Caesar's.'

Lenore steered her mount to the other side of Boreas. 'So where is Caesar? They say he leads from the front, so he must be preparing to do something.'

Xander peered hard at the surging chaos. 'How many Centuries do you see? I released Ellac because I thought most of them were already engaged, but I fear I've been foolish. Each Century is so autonomous and so effective that there seem to be more of them involved than there really are.'

Dio mused. 'Well, at least four were combined for the first advance against the Heavies. At eighty troops apiece, that would make over three hundred, which seems about right. Then another two closed on Nicanor's flanks as we expected, so you sent Ellac to break them up.'

'But then at least another two have closed on her,' interjected Lenore. 'So there's a minimum of eight Centuries engaged as we speak.'

'Christ,' Xander cursed. 'That means there could be another four still out there and I've seen no Praetorian plumes. Where the hell is that bastard, Augustus?'

'We could ride around the whole fight and go find him?' suggested Dio.

'I want to *see* my target before I commit the Cavalry. And if I let the Black Cloaks go, I'll never get them back.'

'So, do we stick or do we play?'

Xander chewed his lips, then heeled Boreas and steered him around Dio's mount. 'Wait here.'

Xander trotted along the front of his lines. He could feel the eyes of his Companion Cavalry and the Black Cloaks on him and Menes shouted at him when he crossed in front of the bronze ranks of Companion infantry.

'Are we just going to spectate?'

'Hold fast,' Xander spat over his shoulder and kept trotting.

He reined up by Parmenion and his peltasts.

'Where's Agape?'

Parmenion pointed with his javelin beyond his troops. 'There, on the far edge.'

Xander made his way to her and steered Boreas to a halt.

He leaned down and asked softly, 'What do I do?'

She had tied her blue hair into a braided rope that hung beneath her helm like an ornately embroidered centrepiece running down her blue cloak. 'Caesar's been watching each of your moves.'

'But he shouldn't be able to see any clearer than we can.'

'He studied our lines while you talked. He will have seen the Phalanx at our centre and the Horns on our flanks, and guessed what you had planned.'

Xander shook his head at the foolishness of once again allowing a King to get so close to his formations before the Battle klaxon even sounded.

'So what should I do?'

Agape stared out at the carnage unfolding on the sodden landscape. 'He has four more Centuries and the Praetorians still in reserve. We need to tempt him to commit those, so we can see where they are.'

'So, do I advance the Cavalry?'

'No. Your Cavalry is what Caesar fears. He has nothing to counter heavy horse. You must not lead them until you can see your target clearly and you know your objective.'

'Then what? Menes and his hoplites?'

Agape nodded slowly. 'Aye. Send him down this left-hand side in spear formation, with Parmenion and me embedded within. If Caesar doesn't react, we can march right around the fight and come in on his Centuries from behind. He won't allow that, but nor can he attempt another flanking manoeuvre with you holding your Cavalry back. He knows you can break any Centuries which do that.'

'So?'

'So he'll have to meet us head on, shield line to shield line, hoplites against Legionaries. Then it will all be about how many Centuries he commits. If we can make him throw most of them at us, then you can send the Black Cloaks around his rear or punch with your Cavalry. But you *must* wait until the critical moment.'

'The critical moment,' Xander repeated. 'Always that damn critical moment.'

He ran his eyes over her elite Sacred Band, then nodded his rain-drenched helmet. 'God speed, Agape.'

'We are almost halfway through the Battle Hour,' she replied. 'What you do over the next thirty minutes will determine this fight.'

He turned Boreas and cantered back to Menes.

'Ready your ranks, Colonel. Advance in spear formation down the left flank and make space for Parmenion and Agape's Band. They will be joining you. I will cover the right.'

Menes saluted and roared his hoplites into formation, as Xander returned to his mounted troops.

'Decision made,' said Dio.

Xander reined in ahead of his Cavalry and turned once more to the struggle further up the glen. 'Time to tease him out.'

Buffeted by wind and rain, the drone footage was appalling, but Zeus had seen the collapse of the Hun attack and he railed at the screen.

'This is preposterous! Caesar has too many Centuries. Light cavalry can do nothing against his disciplined ranks, we all know that. It doesn't matter what Alexander throws at him; he will always have the numbers to counter.'

'My love, I don't think—'

Zeus banged the desk. 'No, Hera, don't give me more false hope. Don't you understand? We've allowed everything to unravel too far. Jupiter wants this Palatinate destroyed. She wants our regiments crushed and Alexander, the King Killer, torn apart by her Legionaries. She intends to take everything from us, don't you see?'

'I see that she is angry.'

'She has taken the extraordinary events of this Season very personally and I don't know why. Maybe Odin's death shook her. Maybe our success has hurt her pride. Perhaps she fears she is losing control of the Pantheon. Whatever it is, she intends to devastate our Titan Palatinate on this Field and leave us with nothing.'

Hera deliberated her next words while she waited for his anger subside. Then she put down her wine glass and took both his hands in hers.

'I need to tell you something.'

'Not now you don't. I must watch the feeds.'

He tried to pull his hands away, but she tightened her grip.

'I have a story to tell you.'

L

Agape ran onto the Field, heather catching at her greaves and sodden mud pools sucking her boots deeper.

Around her, the rest of her blue-cloaked Sacred Band ran too, and around them Parmenion's peltasts, clutching a handful of javelins each, and around them the sixty-strong ranks of Companion infantry in spear formation with Menes at the apex. The rain came even harder, sluicing down their plumes, soaking beneath armour and washing across hoplons. Their cloaks were saturated and weighed heavy on their shoulders. Their helms made it difficult to see anything more than the trooper in front. But still they ran because speed and surprise were everything.

She had told Menes to skirt the raging struggle in the centre of the Field where Ellac's Huns were entrapped and Nicanor's Phalanx was crumbling. To rush to help would simply mean they too would become trapped as Caesar swung in fresh Centuries. They were, after all, only sixty Companions, fifty peltasts and twenty Band, while somewhere in the murk behind it all, Caesar still held in reserve over three hundred Legionaries and two hundred Praetorians.

So surprise was the only card the Titans could play.

Hoplites cursed as they slipped. Armour clanked. Hoplons knocked. Somewhere on their left, Vigiles accelerated across the terrain in 4x4 vehicles, desperately trying to keep pace with this mass of infantry so they could bring their cameras to bear.

Menes drove the pace from the front. Agape had no love for the man, but he was a hard bastard in a fight and she was pleased he was on her side. She had expected some of the Romans in the main struggle to break off and challenge the Titan infantry as it passed, but the Centuries were so disciplined that they only responded to trumpets or the bellowed commands of their Centurions. So the Titans progressed unhindered and as the glen opened before them, suddenly they spied through the murk a mass of waiting troopers and the Eagle standard of the First Cohort of Flavius.

Menes let rip a cry of defiance and the Titans charged.

Agape saw Menes hurl himself into the Legionaries and break through the first rank of scutums. The rest of the Companions followed and their angled bronze spear formation flattened out against the enemy until it became a classic shield-line struggle between Titan and Roman. Hoplons and scutums punched at each other. Iron and steel shortswords stabbed under and over. Blood spilled on bronze and Imperial red.

'Cover!' yelled Agape. A coordinated volley of pilums flew over the shield-lines and came arcing towards peltasts and her Band. She just managed to get her hoplon up before she felt the impacts all around. Mostly the projectiles clanked off helmets and cuirasses, but there were cries of pain as well, especially from the peltasts in their thinner fish-scale armour.

But the Titans were ready to answer back. Parmenion yelled his peltasts into order and Agape crouched as they threw their own volley of javelins. They each held another two in their free hand and so they grabbed the next one, stepped back and threw again. Now there were Roman cries beyond the shield-lines and gaps appeared amongst the steel helmets.

The front ranks of both sides were deep in the rhythm of their blood fight. After the shock of the charge and the first impact, their training and discipline had kicked in. Roman and Titan shield-lines strove to get the upper hand. Shove forward, stab, retract, step forward again. But beneath the discipline, it was a snarling, cursing, heaving, eye-to-eye fight and the killing was close and personal.

Menes was hitting and stabbing with such momentum that he was getting deeper and deeper into the enemy lines. Parmenion's troops lurked behind the Companions, ready to prod with their last javelin whenever a scrap of Roman flesh appeared between the bronze wall. Agape had planned to add her Band's weight to the struggle, but now she saw how quickly this would waste them. Instead, her eyes were drawn through the rain and haze to a prize worth claiming and she signalled to Kyriacos. With a wave, he gathered the Band and they followed as she rounded the inside of the shield-lines and bounded through the puddles towards Flavius and his Eagle standard.

He saw her with only seconds to spare and drew his sword, hollering at the standard bearer to retreat and signalling frantically for another Century of Legionaries to advance and protect the Eagle. But she was on him so fast. They had met before at formal Palatinate Gatherings where they had exchanged respectful pleasantries between two hardened and experienced servants of the Pantheon and now their eyes met again for the briefest of heartbeats, just long enough to acknowledge each other and for Flavius to recognise the coming of his own death. Her blade took him in the gut beneath his silver armour before he even had time to parry and as she extracted it, he sank to his knees in the mud, looked once up at her and then collapsed.

Kyriacos was on the standard bearer. He cut him with a precise thrust, then grabbed the Eagle as it tottered towards the mud and held it up jubilantly while the Band cheered. It was a precious moment of exhilaration amongst the bloodshed, a moment to grin and slap shoulders.

Then the clank of armour came to them and another Century stamped out of the haze with their pilums levelled and Agape cursed because there never seemed to be an end to these Romans. She marshalled her Sacred Band and they gathered in a ring of bronze around the Eagle of the First Cohort. Their blue cloaks and blue plumes marked them as the Pantheon's most elite unit and as Agape braced for impact, she swore they would sell their lives so dearly that this struggle at the heart of the Battle would be watched and rewatched and celebrated for Seasons to come.

'You've come!' barked Bjarke as he strode towards the new arrivals. 'Why didn't you show up in the capital?'

'I was otherwise engaged,' replied Calder grimly. 'What's going on here?'

It had been Sten and Geir who had been scouting the terrain with Sassa. They had been overjoyed to come across their Raven Housecarl, and after a few surprised stares at the strange man slumped on the rock, they had carried him for ten minutes through the trees to a clearing where the rest of Valhalla loitered.

Calder peered around her. The Horde had obviously been in the middle of a group argument because expressions were strained and petulant. To her shock, she realised they were wearing Viking mail and Viking furs.

'What has happened? Why are you here?'

'You don't know?' exclaimed Bjarke in surprise. 'Alexander is leading his Titans and his new Huns against the Legion.'

'Against Caesar's Legion?'

Bjarke waved an arm. 'Right over there, as we speak.'

Calder thought of the Cavalry at the castle and it finally made sense.

'And he permitted you to fight as Vikings instead of Hellenes?'

'He had no choice,' Bjarke spat.

'So what are you doing here?'

Another voice carried across the clearing in response. 'Having a lively difference of opinion.'

Ingvar lumbered over. 'It was agreed that we would travel to this Field with the Titans, so that the Pantheon authorities cannot accuse us of absconding, but we owe Alexander nothing. He might have given us back our mail and our axes and our banners, but he's still a bastard Titan and we will not bleed for him or any one of them.'

'So you're sitting this one out while they take on the Legion?'

Ingvar spat angrily and Bjarke scowled at him.

'What is your opinion?' Calder asked the Jarl.

'We are the Horde resurrected and I say we fight.'

There was a fallen pine on the edge of the clearing and Sassa's Ravens helped the man to seat himself. Calder turned her back on the argument and ran caring eyes over both her charges. She knew she should get them to safety and give them a chance to recuperate. Her own experiences at the hands of Skarde and Domna were nothing compared to what these two had endured. She wondered if Halvar had been kept in that castle for the whole year since she had last laid eyes on him on the island before the Grand Battle of the Nineteenth Season. From the state of him, she suspected he had. And she could not even begin to imagine what Oliver must have been through.

But there was someone else pulling at her heartstrings.

Skarde was dead. Not just dead, but killed by her own hand, and something about this knowledge had lifted a vast weight from her shoulders and finally – incredibly – freed her soul. Now her heart ached for someone new, in ways she could never have believed.

As if to corroborate her thoughts, Oliver strode to her and whispered sternly, 'What about Tyler? He's one of those Titans and he needs our help.'

The lad was right and she knew it.

She turned back to Bjarke and Ingvar. 'You stand in your

war gear, but natter like old housewives while others fight for glory?'

Both men scowled awkwardly and shot each other black looks.

'We are Vikings,' continued Calder, her voice louder so it carried around the clearing. 'I don't care about that fat bastard Alexander, but I do care about the stories we still have to write and the legends we still have to forge as the Horde of Valhalla.'

There was a murmur of agreement from the crowd.

'Fat Alexander is dead,' said Ingvar above the noise. 'The one called Hephaestion is the new King of the Titans.'

'Hephaestion?' Calder felt her insides roll. 'He is Alexander now?'

'Aye, it was him who gave us back our war gear. And to think he was once just Punnr the Weakling.'

'Punnr?' The question came from a new voice, a croaky, weak, tired voice.

'Aye,' answered Ingvar, looking to the man on the tree. 'And what's it to you, stranger?'

The man grunted with discomfort, but used his hands to push himself upright. Oliver stepped in to help him, but he waved him away. 'What's it to me, you ask? What's it to me that Ingvar, Lord of the Berserkers, skulks in this wood and will not raise his axe against Caesar Imperator and his Legion?'

Ingvar stared at the man.

Bjarke edged closer and squinted at him too. 'Halvar?' he said softly.

'Halvar?' Ingvar repeated. 'Halvar the Rock?'

The man nodded, 'Aye, though not such a rock these days.'

'Halvar!' Bjarke bellowed and Calder had to stop him bounding forward to grab at him.

The name was taken up around the clearing. 'Halvar! Halvar!'

Fists were raised and Vikings whooped and cheered.

For a moment Halvar faltered and Oliver caught him. The Housecarl nodded his thanks and placed a hand on the lad's shoulder to steady himself. Then he looked around at the beaming faces and mustered his voice. 'And I never believed I would witness the day when the Horde shied from a fight! That is Caesar out there! Raise your banners. Take up your shields and your blades, and go give him a proper Valhalla welcome to Scotland!'

The clearing exploded in cheering. Ingvar beamed and slapped Bjarke with a wild laugh.

'Gather your weapons,' bellowed the Jarl. 'We go to war.' Then he turned back to Calder. 'We have your war gear here as well. It was all brought from Edinburgh.'

'I must see to Halvar and the lad.'

'No,' said Halvar. 'You must go. You have a Palatinate to lead. I will be fine with young Oliver.'

Calder looked uncertainly at Bjarke and the big Jarl inclined his head. 'Housecarl Calder, it is your Horde now. We follow you.'

She reached up and squeezed his shoulder. 'Then so be it. Show me to my mail.'

'Our tents are just ahead,' said Sassa to Halvar. 'You can rest there and get food.'

Halvar waved irritably. 'Go.'

Calder gave Oliver a hug, then followed Bjarke and the rest of Valhalla out of the clearing.

The quiet returned until it was just the rain beating incessantly.

'Can you make it to the camp if you lean on my shoulder?' asked Oliver.

Halvar smiled painfully. 'Aye, I think we can manage that together.'

He rested his arm once more around Oliver and they walked carefully across the grass.

'Tyler said so many great things about you,' said Oliver.

Halvar laughed weakly. 'Did he now? And how did our Tyler know you?'

'I was his neighbour and I helped him with the clues to the Assets in the Nineteenth Raiding Season. But then I was taken away and initiated into the Valhalla Schola. I was supposed to join the Horde, but then the Titans closed the Schola and threw out most of the new intake. I was saved by a girl called Meghan.' Oliver lapsed into silence as his heart quickened at the use of Meghan's name and he realised just how much she meant to him. With an intake of breath, he forced himself to continue. 'But then I lost her again and now I don't know where to go or what to do. I don't belong to anything anymore.'

'Well that's where you're wrong, lad. You're Pantheon now, whether you like it or not. You're one of us and we look after our own. So you and I are going to get strong again, and then we'll find your girl, Meghan, and we'll take care of you both. You have my promise on that.'

For the first time since he had lost his parents, since he

had killed Odin and since he had been imprisoned by Kustaa and Skarde, Oliver Muir pulled back his lips and smiled.

'God damn them!' Xander shouted in fury. 'God damn them all!'

He had lost control of the Black Cloaks.

They had been straining behind him ever since Ellac had led her Horns into the fray and as the minutes of the Battle Hour ticked away, they had become so wired with expectation that their murmurs were an audible hum of impatience and even their ponies stamped and whinnied in exasperation.

Then something had set them off, but only the gods knew what. Perhaps the sight of their fellow Huns trapped in the chaos, or the bronze Companion ranks loping away into the haze to crash into the foe, while they themselves sat on their ponies at the very rear, waiting and waiting for this new Titan King to give the signal. It probably only took one fool to let the excitement go to his or her head and to kick their heels. One idiot accelerating from the pack and then the whole damn lot broke free.

They flew down the left flank of the Field towards the point where Menes and his Companions were in a blood fight with the Centuries of the First Cohort, a mass of skull-faced, black-clad shrieking riders intent on claiming scalps. They might be able to round the fighting and lay into the Centuries from the wings, but the Black Cloaks were light cavalry and could do little against coordinated infantry.

Xander swore blue murder until he realised his own

Companion Cavalry were watching their new King and his demeanour was hardly inspiring confidence. He forced himself to quieten and watched the last of the Black Cloaks disappear into the rain and mist.

'Just us then,' commented Dio and this made Xander seethe again because he had promised himself he would be a King like Caesar who led from the front. A King like the true Alexander himself, who sped across the battlefields of ancient Asia to lead his cavalry into the heat of the fight.

So why was he, Xander, still sitting in the same spot at the rear of the Field where he had been when the klaxon first sounded? There were less than twenty minutes remaining before the klaxon called an end to hostilities and the feeds would show the new Alexander, with his glorious hundred-strong Companion cavalry, still loitering at the back with no one to attack and nothing to do. *Wait until the critical moment*, Agape had said. Christ, he might as well have stayed in Edinburgh.

'So, do we follow them?' Spyro demanded from behind.

'There's too much going on out there,' Dio responded. 'Huns everywhere. They'd get in the way and break our momentum.'

'And we can't charge at what we can't see,' added Xander irritably, and he glared at the low-slung clouds, praying for a break in the elements.

'My lord,' said Lenore, but he was lost in his thoughts. 'My lord,' she said again more forcefully.

'What?'

'Something's coming.'

This had his attention. 'Where?'

'On the right flank. Look, movement. Far right.'

All eyes turned and sure enough, a dark mass was approaching through the murk.

'Who is it?' Spyro asked aloud.

'Whoever it is,' Dio replied, 'They've come from really wide again.'

'How is it,' said Xander, 'that we're the Palatinate with all the horses, but we're not the ones making use of all this space?'

'They're turning,' warned Lenore. 'Coming into the centre.'

Eyes strained.

Individual figures began to materialise. Armour. Plumes. For a moment they thought it was the Companions come full circle, but they were on the opposite flank of the Field.

'Praetorians!' shouted Dio.

Praetorians. The Imperial Guard of the Legion marched through the rain and angled back into the centre. They came in a wedge, ten abreast, twenty ranks deep, scutums protecting front and flanks, pilums at the vertical, and at their head was a single shining figure, crimson plume, crimson cloak, encased in golden armour.

Xander sucked in his breath as he remembered the man who watched him being beaten on Palatine Hill and the voice that had dripped with arrogance.

'Augustus, Prince of the Pantheon,' he said sarcastically.

'What a pretty boy,' Dio added.

'What's he doing?' asked Lenore. 'Isn't he going to steer them into the side of the Phalanx? He could close around Nicanor and destroy him.'

'Men like Augustus aren't interested in Nicanor. He's coming for us.'

Lenore glanced at Xander. 'You mean, he's coming for you.'

'Kill the King,' said Dio.

'Kill the King,' repeated Xander. 'Prepare the troops.'

'We can't charge them,' Dio protested.

'We bloody well can. I'm not letting that bastard march right up here unchallenged.'

'They're in tight wedge formation, shields and spears a wall on each side. Our horses won't charge that.'

'Well, they must. This is the critical moment!'

Dio glared at him and said firmly, but softly, 'Xander, my friend. You know the horses won't hit that. They'll split or stop or throw us and then we'll be sitting ducks.'

'That's Augustus out there and he thinks he's something special. He's walking straight at us bold as you like and I'm damn well not letting him come any further. We're *heavy* cavalry, Dio. Five abreast, full gallop. We'll smash them.'

'No we won't. They're twenty ranks deep.'

But Xander refused to listen.

'Form them up, Spyro. Five abreast. We're going to punch these Praetorians into the next life.'

Commands were passed through the ranks and stallions snorted and whinnied as they were manoeuvred into column. Xander raised his spear and the rain lashed its iron point.

'My lord,' said Dio earnestly. 'This is a mistake.'

'It's also the critical moment of the Battle, Horsemaster, and Kings do not watch idly while such moments pass them by.'

He made to dig his heels into Boreas, but Lenore's voice arrested his movement.

'They're changing formation.'

Sure enough, without a pause in their momentum, the Praetorians suddenly blossomed outwards. The ranks behind jogged forward and fell into step beside the front lines. Now they were arranged in rows of twenty-five and only eight ranks deep. Still, they came marching directly for the Companion Cavalry.

Augustus strode a pace ahead and he raised his pilum towards Xander and his voice carried across the open space.

'I see you, King Killer! Hiding at the back. Watching while your soldiers die. Hoping the Battle Hour will end. But there's still time and now I'm coming for you. Behold my Praetorian Guard!'

'I see you too, Golden Prick!' Xander yelled back.

'Why have they done that?' Dio asked quietly. 'They were invincible in their wedge, so why open up in line like that when they're facing heavy cavalry?'

'Just eight ranks deep now,' Xander said, turning his attention to his Horsemaster. 'Are you more confident we can break them?'

'I'm still far from sure any horse would carry through a charge against that sort of shieldwall, but they're a damn sight thinner than they were.'

Xander remembered the demonstrations he had witnessed with the Kheshig in Mongolia. *Smash through them, then turn and kill at leisure.*

'Enough deliberation,' he said with finality. 'We're going to blow that bastard away.'

Once more he raised his spear. 'Companions!'

He looked left at Lenore and Spyro, then right at Dio. 'It's time for glory.'

He clicked his tongue at Boreas and dug his heels. 'Let's go, boy. At last, you can run.'

Alexander moved out. Diogenes, Lenore, Spyro, Melitta and Philemon rode in line behind him. Then the rest of the Companion Cavalry followed in twenty ranks of five.

The horses picked up speed, slowly at first because of the treacherous ground, but steadily they shifted from trot to canter. Boreas ran ahead and he realised his master was going to let him free, so he stretched gleefully into a gallop and the charge was on.

Spray flew from plumes. Sodden cloaks stretched out behind them. Spears levelled.

Around the world, rich syndicates stared at their screens, jaws slack, champagne forgotten. Over the Seasons, they had witnessed the might of the Legion. They had watched the wild charges of the Huns and the implacable marches of the Janissaries. But they had never seen anything like this.

Alexander's Companion Cavalry in full flight towards the Imperial Praetorian Guard.

This was it. This was the moment the Pantheon had waiting two decades to see.

Rain lashed through Xander's eyeholes, almost blinding him. His legs could barely find purchase against Boreas' flanks, they were so wet. His cloak flapped like a vast sail, dragging at his shoulders. He could feel his horse stagger as his hooves caught soft ground.

But nothing stopped their momentum. They tore across the ground and Xander could hear the thunder and jangle of his Cavalry behind. Elation surged through him as the sheer wonder of the attack took hold and the blood-lust claimed him. There was Augustus through the rain. The Praetorians had halted, but the man was still out in front of his Guard, golden and arrogant. Xander aimed his lance directly at him and urged Boreas even faster.

The Cavalry rushed straight for the heart of the Legion's lines and Boreas did not falter. They were moments from impact.

And then the Romans changed the game.

Augustus lunged to one side and at the same moment his entire Praetorian Guard opened up down the middle. All eight ranks splintered apart, throwing themselves in a single disciplined action to right and left.

Xander was so shocked, he barely had time to think of reining Boreas. The wonder of the charge was still flowing through his horse and the animal kept galloping with delight to see the open ground ahead. Behind him, Dio cursed wildly, but Xander knew his Cavalry was still coming. They flew between the Praetorians, who were turning their scutums inwards, as though they were an honour guard lining the route for the Titans.

Within moments, Xander was through the Roman ranks and thinking he must slow Boreas and turn him back to attack them from behind, but before he could do anything, he felt his horse make its own decision to brake. Boreas had sensed something ahead. Something he did not want to charge. Xander was almost thrown by the sudden change of speed and he had to grab his mount's neck. He heard shouts behind as other horses broke from their gallop too and swerved or reared.

Regaining control, Xander managed to bring Boreas to a trot and peer ahead through the rain. Then he saw what had spooked his horse. Directly before them was another huge mass of Romans. Their scutum shields were locked into an impregnable wall, their pilum spears readied, and standing at their centre was a figure in gold and white, ostrich feathers gracing his helm.

Caesar had set his trap.

Jupiter stood alone amongst her monitors, the blinds drawn to keep out the Mediterranean sun.

Despite the poor visibility on the feeds, she could see her husband leading his Cohorts against the Titan Cavalry and she could see her son in his glorious golden armour closing off any escape route for the Macedon foe.

And there was the King Killer, caught in the middle.

Nowhere to run now, boy. Nowhere to hide.

Jupiter's hands tightened into fists and her nails dug into her palms.

You've been his dirty little secret all these years and you will pay with your life.

LI

Xander hauled on Boreas' reins and steered him round. Behind him, his vaunted Companion Cavalry was in disarray. The horses had broken from the column and were wheeling away or circling on the spot, snorting and kicking. They were as shocked as their riders to have discovered Caesar's Centuries blocking their charge and to have braked so hard. Companions had fallen. Others were desperately attempting to get control of their beasts. Lenore and Dio and Spyro turned their mounts alongside Xander and weighed the options.

The Praetorians were already plugging the escape route back. Their ranks slammed shut once more and the wings curled around the outside of the mounted troops. Trumpets sounded behind and Caesar's Centuries moved forward and, just like the Praetorians, broke from ten abreast to twenty. They knew the Cavalry had no space to regain momentum and there would be no more glorious charges, so they did not need depth of ranks.

Some of the riders managed to break away, but most were quickly circled and then the first volleys of pilums flew.

'Cover!' yelled Spyro and shields came up, but shafts still buried themselves in horseflesh and human limbs. Stallions screamed in shock and pain. Some bolted and threw their riders as they tore around the ring of scutum shields. Romans stepped out of line and speared those Companions who fell. Trumpets peeled again and the circle began to close, one stride at a time. Anything they encountered was jabbed with a pilum or struck with a shortsword. Titans attempted to use their mounted height to spear down at their attackers, but it meant bringing each horse into range of the pilums and the Romans grimly killed the beasts first. So the Cavalry could do nothing except shuffle backwards into a tighter and tighter mass.

'We have to break out!' Dio shouted to his King. 'We stay, we die.'

Xander forced Boreas back through the seething crowd to better view the Praetorian lines. They were still only eight ranks deep, and he thought it might be possible to spearhead a way through. It only needed a small break and then the sheer weight of horseflesh would prise it further open. But the Praetorians were Rome's best troops. Big, heavy soldiers, deeply proud of their status, and together they were a finely tuned killing machine. Not a single crack appeared between their crimson and gold scutums, while their pilums were held overarm so they could jab across the rim of their shields. They moved in unison – a step, a strike, a roar and then repeated.

Only Augustus stood apart. He was one pace ahead of the scutum wall and Xander realised the man might be an arrogant prick, but he was undoubtedly a fine soldier. He held his scutum brazenly to one side and scythed with his gladius blade, slicing any living being who came within a yard. For a heartbeat, Xander wanted to push Boreas through the remaining Cavalry and have a go at the bastard himself, but he knew it was a fool's idea. He was a King now and his troops looked to him for leadership. He could not allow a personal vendetta to cloud his judgement, not when ploughing towards the Praetorian ranks would mean certain death.

He urged Boreas around again and stared south through the rain, trying to judge where Caesar's Centuries were weakest. Other horses were jostling him. Rumps and hooves banged together, stallions bit at each other. Then more pilums rained down and the curses turned to screams.

Dio had sworn he would stay close to his King, but the melee had forced him away. Xander could see him attempting to control his terrified mount. Lenore was beyond him and her horse went down and she disappeared beneath the chaos. Spyro's horse reared, but the man clung on and controlled it, then he heeled it straight for the scutum perimeter. The stallion took several mighty strides, but refused to charge the foe and instead spun round and kicked them with its rear hooves. The wall caved in and blood misted Roman armour. Spyro wrenched his mount into the gap and more Companions joined him. For a moment Xander thought the brave trooper from the Band had found a way out and he heeled Boreas towards the fight, but even as he did so he realised the Legionaries in the rear ranks had no intention of buckling. They swamped into the gap Spyro had created, stabbing at him, killing his horse and hauling him down. Xander yelled despairingly and urged Boreas onwards.

But then came the most terrible moment of all.

'Does the name Maitland mean anything to you?'

'Of course it does,' Zeus answered his wife irritably without taking his eyes from the screen. 'It was the name of the traitor, Olena, who led Timanthes and his Companions into a trap in the Eighteenth. You know I tried every avenue to unearth her, but she disappeared.'

'And did you know it is also the surname of our new Alexander?'

This question turned her husband from the feeds.

'Alexander is also Maitland?'

'He's Olena's brother.'

'What?' Zeus exclaimed. 'The Pantheon does not permit siblings.'

'The Rules do indeed seem clear on that point.'

'He changed sides from Valhalla and surrendered on the Battle beach.'

'Yes, he was not supposed to do that, but fate has a way of throwing up the unexpected.'

Zeus pulled his hands indignantly away from his wife's hold. 'Just what the hell have you been up to?'

Hera picked her words. 'There was one other who also shared that surname, a person who was very special to me.'

Zeus dredged his memory and then his eyes widened. 'Rebecca?'

Hera nodded. 'Rebecca Maitland, my dear friend.'

'But she was killed in a hit and run almost a decade ago.'

'Leaving a daughter and a son.'

Zeus gaped at his wife. 'Why didn't you tell me?'

'It seemed information best not carried by a Caelestis.'

Huns were swarming all over the Battle feeds, but Zeus seemed to have forgotten about the action in Abernethy. 'Are they... are they his?'

'Yes.'

'My god.' Zeus' eyes glazed as he thought back to those early years of the Pantheon. Rebecca had joined as a finance assistant in Julian's London offices and her looks had obviously caught his eye. He had inducted her into the Pantheon's administration and promoted her to his private Legion team, thus ensuring she was amongst his retinue at the Caelestes parties. Soon she became a face well known to the other gods.

'She was such a spark of energy,' Hera reminisced, as though reading her husband's thoughts. 'Beautiful, fun, exhilarating. Everyone loved her – except, of course, Marcella.'

'In my opinion, Marcella did an admirable job of averting her eyes whenever her husband became entranced with another woman. He may have lavished wealth and influence on his wife, but that does not mean he treated her well.'

'She has lived a privileged enough life,' Hera snapped. 'And she ensured a power-base for that awful son of hers.'

'So... did she know about the children?'

'No. If she did, she would have destroyed them. But something happened to make Rebecca flee to Edinburgh. Perhaps Marcella decided this particular affair had been going on far too long, or maybe Julian himself ended it. Whatever the reason, she brought the children north – and when Odin started suggesting you should relocate your

Palatinate to Edinburgh, I was keen on the idea because it meant I could be closer to her.'

Zeus pondered this for several moments. 'Did Marcella kill her?'

'I've often wondered, but I'll never know. The accident was never solved and it may simply have been a careless driver.'

'So you looked after Rebecca's children?'

'As much as I could, in a low-profile way without them knowing. I kept their bank accounts topped up, ensured social services were active, built contacts with their schools. But Caesar became more and more convinced that he could keep a better eye on them by quietly inducting them into the Pantheon. He briefed Atilius and asked me if I would bring the elder one – Morgan – into our Titan Palatinate.'

Zeus puffed his cheeks out. 'Didn't you think I had a right to know?'

'Marcella had become Jupiter by that time and it seemed to me you had enough difficulties in dealing with the Lord High Caelestis without bearing such an explosive personal secret. Caesar thought his daughter could mature unobtrusively in our Palatinate and he could watch over her from afar.'

'Well, his plan didn't go quite so smoothly.'

Hera inclined her head. 'Morgan was always a wild one. Timanthes rather liked the spirit in her and fast-tracked her to become his second-in-command of the Companions, but no one could ever have foreseen she would get caught up in her own wild love affair with a Viking and betray us.'

Zeus glared at his wife. 'At that point, you should have

confessed all to me and we would have dealt with her accordingly.'

'Perhaps I should. But I had promised Rebecca I would always look after her children and Caesar was desperate to save his daughter. He travelled in secret up to Edinburgh and together we got her out of the city, although I never knew what he did with her after that until the actions of Bleda at Hortobágy.'

'That was *Morgan*?'

'Caesar must have called in a favour from Ördög and, of course, Atilius was helping pull the levers. I would never have recognised the woman Morgan became in the Huns, not until the moment she changed the direction of her charge and I saw the images of Bleda and Hephaestion whispering together. I think, perhaps, the shock of learning she was Caesar's daughter drove her to greater extremes.'

'And what of Hephaestion?'

'His name is Tyler. Despite Morgan's treachery, Caesar was even more adamant that he wanted his son inducted into the Pantheon. He was convinced he could better watch and shape his younger child from within our structure. And, probably like most proud fathers, he wanted his son to experience his father's work and perhaps, one day, even inherit it.'

'But you did not induct him into our Palatinate.'

'After the mess with Morgan, it had to be Valhalla.'

'Was Odin in on the secret?'

'No one in Valhalla knew. This time we did it legitimately. Atilius ensured Tyler was on the list of names for the Venarii to recruit and we thought he would train as a Thrall and swear his Oath to the Horde without commotion. But it seems he was too loose with his tongue. He suspected his sister's disappearance had something to do with the Pantheon and he started asking questions of Radspakr. Eventually it got to Odin's ear and the whole situation must have become too hot for Tyler, so he took the one escape option open to him. He ran across the beach at the Battle of the Nineteenth Blood Season and surrendered to Agape. I will admit that I needed to bring both her and Simmius into some of these secrets, so they are aware that he is Morgan's brother, though not the link to Caesar.'

Zeus shook his head in wonder. 'Might I suggest your decision to encourage Tyler to build a Cavalry did little to help him stay under the radar.'

Hera smiled weakly. 'Perhaps I was foolish. He impressed me so much and I got caught up in the dream.'

'And now Caesar's son is Alexander of Macedon, King of our Palatinate.' Zeus puffed out his cheeks again and then he looked hard at Hera as a new thought took hold. 'Does Jupiter know? Is that why her Legion advances against us as we speak?'

'I can't answer, my dear. I really can't. There is no reason she should have found out, but perhaps a little bird has whispered our secrets to her and this huge Battle is her vengeful reply.'

They both turned their attention back to the feeds where bloody bedlam was consuming the Field.

'If she does know,' Hera said quietly, 'she won't allow Alexander to leave the Field alive.'

'And what of Caesar?' Zeus pondered open-mouthed. 'He fights his own son.'

LII

Xander did not see the projectile, but he felt the mighty frame of Boreas quiver beneath him.

A great shiver ran down the stallion's spine and the horse tossed his head in shock, emitting a deep rumbling snort. He bucked his neck and took another step forward, but then leaned so far to one side that Xander almost slid off.

'Hey, boy, come on. Are you okay?'

Boreas righted himself and took another pace forward, then whinnied and went down hard on his front knees. Xander grabbed hold of the mane to stop himself from collapsing over the top of his horse's head.

'Boreas! No, Boreas. Stay with me, boy!'

Xander tried to urge him upright again and the stallion turned his head just enough for one chocolate eye to stare back at his rider, then he collapsed heavily on his flank and the King of the Titans slammed into the mud. He lost his grip on his spear and his helm was clouted round so he could see nothing. The weight of the horse trapped his left leg and all he could do was flounder in the darkness of his helmet, feeling the vibrations of pain sweeping through

Boreas and hearing the roars and cries and thumps of the violence above.

In moments, a Roman would see the King of the Titans exposed and defenceless as a baby and would stride in and shove steel through Xander's neck. And that would be the end of his journey. The end of the game. To die in the mud, lost to his friends.

Then somewhere over it all, he thought he caught a new sound. A wave of howls like the howls of wolves. Blood-surging cries that did not belong to the disciplined silence of the Roman lines. Heathen cries.

And the smallest spark of hope kindled in Xander.

The Horde of Valhalla strode onto the Field at Abernethy in the dying minutes of the Battle Hour and were faced with a sea of Praetorian backs.

From their position between giant pinewoods on the eastern flank, the rain made it impossible to comprehend the drama of the full Battle, but they could see clearly enough the action closest to them. Alexander's Companion Cavalry must have charged Caesar's Centuries and become ensnared when the Praetorian Guard of Augustus closed a trap behind them. Now the Cavalry jostled and heaved and spasmed in the very centre of a vast ring of steel, which was closing on them one pace at a time, jabbing and killing, intent on destruction. Horses reared and screamed. Red-plumed riders fell beneath the crush. Volleys of pilums flew into the melee and Praetorian blades misted with blood.

Calder watched the violence with an implacable calmness. She was dressed in her chainmail, a shield on her arm and a spear in her hand, her iron helmet glistening in the wet. On either side of her she sensed her Horde vibrating with adrenaline. They had organised themselves into their Wolf, Raven, Hammer and Storm companies and held the Triple Horn banner aloft, but she knew there was no time for tactics and plans. These next minutes would simply be about surprise, momentum and battle-rage.

'Praetorians,' Bjarke hissed next to her.

'Your chance to carve into the best,' she said.

'I never thought I would see the day.'

She looked left and right. Ake and Stigr stood ready at the head of the Wolf litters. Ingvar was goading his Berserkers into a steaming, artery-popping frenzy. Estrid, Sten, Geir and Sassa were poised beneath the Raven banner.

Every eye waited for her.

She raised her spear high and screamed into the rain, 'Valhalla!'

Carried on a wave of roars, a hundred Vikings rushed across the soaking ground and tore into the Legion.

Praetorians turned in shock at the noise. They were in the back ranks and had been expecting an easy final few minutes of the Battle. Instead, they were faced by a raging, bellowing heathen army.

Calder used her momentum to smash into the first Romans. She left her spear embedded in one and unsheathed her longsword. Bjarke swung his axe just yards from her and she felt hot, bright Praetorian blood spray across her neck and hands. The Legionaries were tough, experienced soldiers, but they were dumbfounded by Valhalla's attack and all around her, she felt the Roman ranks buckle.

Desperately, Xander reached for his leg and hauled at it, but it would not move. Boreas was still breathing and kicking, but the weight of his body pinned Xander. Something kicked his helmet hard and for a moment he saw nothing but sparks. There was fighting over him. He could hear the curses and feel boots knocking him as they tried to find purchase on the slippery ground. He sensed a blade thrust into the mud next to him and wondered if an unseen foe had just stabbed at him.

He forced his torso upright and wrenched his helmet back in place. The Battle came back to him. Rain and mud and blood. Bodies struggling. Iron and steel hacking. Hooves kicking. Poor, dear Boreas, raising his head and dropping it again. Xander pulled at his leg, but it was no use. It would not budge.

Then someone grabbed his cloak, wrapped it around their wrist and hauled him backwards. His leg sprung from the weight of Boreas and he was dragged unceremoniously across the trampled heather, his armour banging and his shield torn from his arm. The grip on his cloak was released and for startled seconds he panted up at the heavens.

Summoning his last strength, he struggled upright and spun to see who had pulled him free.

A figure in white and gold stood before him, scutum abandoned, gladius sword held casually by his side. The ostrich feathers were dirtied and bent, but the gold muscled cuirass still glistened.

Caesar Imperator.

The King of the Legion waited for Xander to right himself and gave him space to draw his own blade.

Then nodded in respect and raised his weapon.

The final Battle of the Twentieth Year reached its climax.

Ellac had fought with abandon since her pony perished beneath her, but she was never going to escape the flanking manoeuvre of the Legion. They punctured her with pilums as they closed around her Huns and harvested their lives.

Nicanor had been battling since the very start of the Hour and he had nothing left to give. His shoulder-shield was splintered and his sarissa long gone. Gore coated his cuirass, blood ran from a deep gash in his thigh and his lungs rattled beneath his armour. His precious Phalanx lay wrecked and those Heavies who still lived were deep in their own isolated struggles. He died surrounded by jostling Legionaries, steel piercing his side and his shoulder and his hip, and his last images were of Roman feet as he sank into the mud.

Menes too died amongst Romans. He had ploughed so far into their lines that he had lost touch with his own Companion shieldwall. Blades bounced off his cuirass and clanged on his helm, but a Legionary from further back had time enough to aim his pilum properly and ram two foot of iron through his throat. The force thrust his head up high enough to stare momentarily at the Eagle of the Second Cohort behind the rows of steel helmets, then his vision blackened and Menes knew no more.

The Praetorians taunted Ingvar before they killed him.

They knew his swinging axe was certain death for anyone in its path, so they backed away in a circle and let him spin in wild abandon. But each time the huge blade swept round, the Romans took it in turns to step in behind it and thrust a pilum point into Ingvar's kidneys. Finally, like a great bull elephant, he felt his strength escape and he stumbled to one knee. The axe bit into the ground and would not rise with him again. The Praetorians danced in close and finished him in a blur of jabs.

Ake was shoulder to shoulder with Stigr, howling her insults and scything her longsword when she was hamstrung by a low blow from behind. She collapsed onto Stigr and he grabbed her and held her so that he could look into her startled eyes. Her body jolted against him and he felt steel break through her and prick his abdomen. She tensed and stared wild-eyed at him. Then her delicate features broke into a single mad grin and she left this world.

Ulf was in the mud. He had tripped on a body and collapsed below the stabbing frenzy of the Praetorian battle-line. A Roman foot stamped on him, then stepped over as the soldier tried to find better purchase on the ground. For a moment it seemed as though Ulf had been forgotten and he lay between the boots and the trampled heather and abandoned weapons and cooling corpses. Anger bubbled in him. Outrage that his journey in the Pantheon should be this short. Years he had spent in the Valhalla Schola as a *lost child*, always training and hardening himself to become someone more respected in the Horde. But it had all gone awry when that bastard Punnr had changed Palatinates, then destroyed Valhalla and now, as King of the Titans, he had pitched them into an unwinnable fight on this godforsaken

Field against Caesar's Legion. It was not supposed to end like this. But even as he raged, Praetorian eyes inevitably spied him on the ground and Praetorian blades came for him. Two years. That was all the time he had spent in the Pantheon proper. And he would not see another Season.

It was First Spear who came for Agape beside the Eagle of the First Cohort. She recognised his Centurion's plume, but not his senior rank. They fought hard, both determined to be the one owning the Eagle when the klaxon sounded. Around her, the Band was diminishing. They might be the best swordsmen and maidens in the Pantheon, but twenty of them could not hold against a Century of Romans.

For perhaps the first time in her life, Agape felt true exhaustion and the searing sting of flesh wounds, but she refused to give ground to this grizzled Centurion. He punched her with his scutum and she was taken backwards, but she dug her heels into the mud and spun under his sword thrust, then raked her own blade across his groin. She heard him grunt and falter and she called upon her last resources to wheel past him and cut into the small of his back. As First Spear collapsed, she took a moment to stare around the rain-lashed Field at the carnage unfolding.

When would the klaxon sound? So many lives must already be lost and so many more would flicker away in these fading moments. But *she* would stand. Agape, greatest of the Pantheon's warriors, would live to see this Battle end.

'My thanks,' gasped Xander as he eyed Caesar Imperator. 'You could have killed me while I was pinned beneath my horse.'

Around them, chaos reigned.

Caesar's eyes widened in surprise behind his mask.

'Why would I kill *you*?' he protested. 'You are the most glorious soldier I have ever witnessed.'

Xander did not know how to respond. He held his sword ready and Caesar still gripped his own, but the older man showed no inclination to attack. Xander wondered if it was a trick and he side-stepped warily, drawing Caesar in a circle.

'But I am your enemy King. If you kill me, you can take over my Palatinate. Those are the Rules.'

Caesar seemed genuinely amused by this idea. 'My lord, Alexander, I am already at the very top of the Pantheon structure. What good is your Palatinate to me?'

'So why do we fight? Why all this death and misery, all this reaping of lives, if you don't want to win?'

'Because, my son, is this not the most glorious and beautiful thing? Here on this Field in Scotland, we have resurrected Roman, Greek, Hun and Viking. Never in history have these warrior races faced each other like this. It is why I first dreamed of the Pantheon and why I still love it. But I am aging now. I cannot be Imperator forever. The Pantheon needs a new prince. A leader every soldier from every Palatinate can look to in wonder.'

Xander peered at the man before him and tried to compute his words. Everywhere good people were killing each other, but this man spoke of glory and beauty.

'So you will not fight me?'

Caesar smiled sadly and lowered his blade. 'No, I will not fight you. Not now, with just seconds to go before the klaxon. You are too precious for that.'

'*Precious!* What's that supposed to mean?'

'It means you're the future, Tyler. You're *my* future.'

Time stopped for Xander. The roar of the Battle quietened. The tang of blood and earth and rot eased. His sword arm dropped limply and he stared at the other King.

'How do you know my name?'

Caesar was about to answer when his eyes shifted over Xander's shoulder. The world came back to Xander and he spun just in time to see Augustus leaping the corpse of a horse and bounding straight for him. The golden bastard had his blade arm drawn back ready to strike like a cobra and Xander's own weapon still hung limply by his side. One more pace, one more split second, and Augustus would skewer the upstart King of the Titans and that would be an end of it. There was nothing Xander could do except ready himself for the coming of death.

But in the same moment, Caesar stepped beside him and drove his sword so hard into the gut of his onrushing stepson that the blade sunk up to the hilt and the point shattered spine and pelvic bone. Augustus was stopped in his tracks with his own sword just inches from Xander's chest. He hung there like a puppet on Caesar's blade and his lips drew back in a rictus of pain beneath his golden helmet. The eyes behind his mask were wide with shock, desperately trying to understand what had just happened.

He was Fabian. Son of Jupiter and heir apparent to the Pantheon. He was supposed to have a life ahead of untold riches and power and privilege.

So how could he be standing in this sodden, muddy, miserable field in Scotland with the steel of his stepfather's sword sticking through his broken spine?

He tried to speak, but only blood came from his mouth. He wanted to curse the man he had always detested and to spit on the upstart King of the Titans, but his body would not obey him. His legs had already gone and he was only upright because his stepfather still held him impaled.

With a final surge of hatred, he lunged towards the object of his loathing and sliced the man's throat with the tip of his sword.

Then Fabian's energy deserted him, his sight clouded, and the last thing he knew was the cold clammy caress of the earth.

Diogenes was down.

His stallion had been hit by a thrown pilum and it reared so violently that even his enviable equestrian skills could not stop him from slipping backwards and hitting the earth hard. He convulsed as the air was expelled from his lungs and he lost his grip on his spear. He levered himself half up and was attempting to bring his shield round towards the advancing Legionaries, when a hoof cracked into his helmet and he blacked out.

It must have been only seconds that he was lost to the world, but when the sounds and the smells of the Battle came back to him, he realised there were Roman boots around him and Roman blades above. With a wild cry he lunged for his sheathed longsword, but the movement sharpened the attention of his foe. Someone shouted and stamped on his arm before he could grab the hilt of his blade. Someone else came above him and jerked a pilum back ready to plunge it through his cuirass.

It was the moment of his death and he roared defiance.

But the pilum never came.

There was a flurry of violence above him. Another boot stood on his chest, lighter than the others. Blood spattered from the heavens. There was a groan and a body fell heavily next to him. Then the boot was gone and in its place was a hand, delicate and warm, pulling him up.

He clambered to his feet and looked down at the iron-helmed face of his Viking friend.

'Calder!' he gasped. 'You came.'

'Where is the King?'

Dio unsheathed his blade and pointed. 'I got separated from him. He's over there.'

'Then follow me.'

Xander held Caesar.

The Imperator had collapsed into his arms with blood leaking from his torn throat. Xander lowered him to the ground and cradled his head. He wanted to remove the King's helmet, but the clip was too close to the ragged wound, so Xander tore his own helmet off and leaned close to the other man, so that their eyes could meet.

Caesar gurgled as he tried to speak.

'Don't,' cautioned Xander. 'Don't tire yourself.'

Somewhere above him, he was aware of figures around him. Friends defending him, raging hard to protect him while he knelt over the fallen Imperator.

Caesar grimaced and attempted to speak again. He raised a hand and one finger touched Xander's cheek delicately, as though tracing the line of his jaw.

'You are...' Caesar's teeth clenched in pain and his eyes closed. Then he forced them open once last time and peered longingly into Xander's eyes.

'...my heir. My future.'

The wail of the klaxon broke across Abernethy.

Helmetless, Xander rose and stared unseeing at the slaughter. Limbs contorted. Horses shrieked. Humans cried. The Highland air stank of blood and the rain kept plastering his hair to his scalp.

Someone was near him. They were removing their helmet.

He tried to focus.

Iron mail. Viking mail. Skin so pale. Eyes deep and wide and far more caring than they should be in this place of death. A rope of blonde hair over her shoulder.

She opened her arms and a tumult of emotions poured from him. He collapsed towards her and she enclosed him and pressed him to her and held him so tight.

Not even knowing why, he cried into her neck.

Epilogue

Agape was waiting for her outside Pella, wearing sandals and a floral summer dress.

'I've never set foot in a Titan stronghold before, if you don't include the abomination that was New Alexandria.'

Agape pulled a face and held the door open for her to enter. 'I'm not sure we can call this a stronghold anymore.'

She led her up flights of stairs to the wide loft space five storeys above Brodie's Close, where ladders still rose to hatches in the ceiling.

'What do I call you?' asked the taller woman.

'Lana, I suppose. No Pantheon names now.'

'No, indeed. And I am Kinsley.'

They shook hands hesitantly. Kinsley had padding beneath her dress and there were plasters on her hands and stitching on her calves. She pointed to the hatches. 'He's up there.'

Lana raised her head and imagined the Sacred Band flowing out onto the rooftops on Conflict Nights. 'Are you joining us?'

Kinsley smiled. 'No. I think he needs you to himself.'

She watched as Lana climbed a ladder, pushed open the skylight and hauled herself through, then Kinsley walked slowly back to her small office and continued sorting her belongings.

Lana raised herself cautiously upright and looked around at the city humming below. The clock on the Balmoral was nearing ten, but dusk was only just settling in these last days of May. The evening was warm and muggy, and the streets still filled with life. Laughter reached her. Vehicles revved and tooted. The scent of food and alcohol drifted on the currents and clouds hung solemnly above, pregnant with rain, but hesitant to spoil the revelry.

She stole across the slanted roof towards the edge that looked down on Lawnmarket and the Royal Mile. Hands out to clasp the stonework, she rounded a chimney stack and there he was, perched on a parapet, legs folded, peering at the final blushes of sunset on the Castle. She approached quietly and was almost upon him before he jolted round in surprise, then relaxed and smiled.

'You found me.'

'With a little help from Kinsley.'

Gingerly, she lowered herself next to him and curled her legs under her. 'Wow, what a view.'

'It's pretty special, isn't it?'

Lana did not answer immediately. She let the lights and the buildings and the sky seep into her, then said, 'I've spent so much time embracing violence and horror that I've forgotten to see the beauty in things.'

Tyler sighed. 'I'm still not sure I can. There's been too much loss and I can't accept it yet.'

It was a week since the Twentieth Year had formally ended and events were still raw. They had both lost friends and colleagues, while others lay in tortuous pain in Pantheon wards. Boreas was gone. Spyro too. Lenore might never walk again. Mighty Bjarke was attached to drips.

'I keep asking myself, was all that suffering because of me? If I hadn't kept pushing the limits, taking gambles, playing war games, would more of them be alive now? If I'd not even joined Valhalla in the first place, if I'd told Radspakr to go fuck himself that night on Fleshmarket Close, would the bloodshed have been less?'

Lana reached for his hand and squeezed it. 'You weren't to know.'

He laughed emptily. 'You mean I wasn't to know I was the son of Caesar? No, I suppose not. That was a little chestnut learned at the climax of Abernethy, then confirmed by Hera and Zeus last night. Seems the Maitlands were one hell of a dysfunctional family.'

He quietened and she felt his fingers curl around hers and squeeze back.

'I miss my sister. Christ knows what she must have gone through to transform herself into that monster, and yet, despite it all, when I needed her most, she sacrificed everything for me. She wheeled a whole army, changed the course of a Battle, killed her King – and all to protect me, her little brother.'

He ran out of words and they sat in heavy silence, looking towards the Castle.

'How was Zeus?' Calder asked eventually, feeling it best to move him to easier ground.

He sighed and shifted. 'He and Hera fed and watered me – or tried to – and plied me with compliments. They are desperate for me to lead a new Pantheon.'

'A new one? Is the old one already dead?'

'Well, Jupiter is gone. When Caesar fell from a sword strike, she lost her Palatinate and her position on the Caelestia.'

'I hate to think of her fury, but she deserves it.'

'She watched her son and her husband kill each other. I don't know what emotions are boiling through her, but I wouldn't wish that on anyone. In the end, all her power could not prevent such tragedy.'

Lana let him settle again, then said, 'So all that's left is the Kheshig, the Warring States, the Sultanate and one enormous Titan Palatinate.'

'There's nothing left. The old Pantheon is unworkable. Gone. But Zeus says there are many avaricious eyes that will jump at the chance to rebuild it. The concept of the Pantheon will never die because there is too much money to be made. Others will claim it. Others even less savoury than the likes of Odin. There are rogue states, political movements, criminal enterprises, who would leap at the chance to create their own Palatinate, not just for the money, but for the profile and prestige. They've been banging at the doors for years, but could never get a foothold. Now, suddenly, it's open season.'

'And Zeus wants you to lead this new era?'

'He says the only way to stop these repugnant forces is for us to claim the space first. He has the contacts to create a new Caelestia and to finance new Palatinates, but he can't do it without me. Alexander of Macedon, Killer of Kings, the most famous warrior in the old Pantheon, and son of Caesar.' Tyler harrumphed. 'What a ridiculous set of titles. Most of the time I still feel more like Punnr the Weakling.'

He turned to her and saw she was cold in her shirt, so

he struggled out of his jacket, grimacing at his old wound, and wrapped it around her shoulders. She smiled and leaned into his warmth. The clouds were lowering and they could feel a change coming on the air.

'You always said the Pantheon was a force for good,' she mused. 'People dreamed about it, looked up to it. It was something exhilarating in this dreary world.'

'Are you suggesting I should do as Zeus wants?'

She straightened and looked into his eyes. 'Good heavens, that wasn't meant as an opinion. My voice means nothing in all this.'

'But that's where you're so wrong, Lana.' He took her hands in his again and held them to his heart. 'Your voice is the most important one of all.'

'How can you say that?'

'Because the last time we were together in this city, I told you that whatever I do next, I want it to be with you. Because I love you, Lana. In all this craziness, that's about the only thing I'm certain of.'

She blossomed at these words and felt her heart quicken. She leaned in and planted the lightest of kisses on his lips.

'Let's get out of here,' he said, taken up in the moment. 'Let's go somewhere far away from this place.'

'Where have you in mind?'

'I thought perhaps north.'

She laughed incredulously. 'North! I think I've had my fill of that.'

He smiled too. 'Forbes has an amazing house. You should see the waters of the Dornoch under a summer sun. And there's a girl up there called Beatrice I'd love you to meet.'

'I hope her favourite food is hay.'

He grinned, but then grew serious and held her attention. 'I mean it. Time to think. Time to recuperate. Time beyond the Pantheon.'

She nodded at this. 'Time to be the real us.'

'Time to be the real us.'

A thin rain stole from the Forth, sullying the city, smearing its bright lights.

Author's Note

Dear Reader,

So we come to the end and I want to thank you for being with me on this extraordinary journey. I must admit that there have been many occasions when I haven't known the route, nor the length, nor even the challenges which have awaited us, but eventually we discovered a firm enough path and followed Tyler and Lana and Forbes from the winding Closes of Edinburgh to the bloody climax in Abernethy.

Like most journeys, when I sat down many moons ago to write the first book in the series – *The Wolf Mile* – I could picture my eventual destination, as well as the key staging points along the way, but the intricate details of the passing scenery and the moments which would slow me, trip me, even panic me, only revealed themselves as each new corner was navigated.

I always wanted the series to end with Tyler and Lana together on the rooftops above the Royal Mile, just as it had begun with Timanthes at similar heights, and it felt appropriate for the final sentence in the Pantheon to be the same as the very first one. Likewise, I always knew where Morgan was and how she would be revealed, and Tyler's relationship with Caesar was set in stone from the start.

But so much of the rest of the story has come to life only as I progressed. Sub-plots ran off in directions which cried out to be followed. Characters developed whom I had never properly considered. Oliver was one of these. At the beginning of *The Wolf Mile*, he was simply supposed to be a device for better introducing Tyler to the reader. The young neighbour, full of wonder for the new arrival in the flat opposite. Not for a moment did I realise the ordeals I would subject this youngster to – bereavement, kidnapping, bullying. Nor did I understand his hidden strengths, how he would rise with a howl of vengeance and kill a god. Similarly, Aurora was a bit-part player who ended up with a star turn.

And what of all the other characters who joined us on our journey? So many arrived unexpectedly and then stayed for the ride – Lenore, Ellac, Kustaa, Geir, Hera, Ake, Belgutei. None of them were with us at the start and yet I'm so glad they were waiting for us along the path.

So, I hope you have enjoyed the adventures of this Pantheon cast just as much as I've loved bringing them to life. Strangely, I feel little for those I killed along the way, but I am bereft at the need to say goodbye to those who walked every step with us. They have been my inspiration and my close companions for several years, and it is very hard to hug them and let them go.

But there are new stories to be told now. New characters to journey with, though I do not yet know their names or their plans.

Perhaps, one day, the Pantheon will come roaring back. This world is, after all, too greedy, too merciless and too bloody to turn its attentions from the Palatinates for long.

If you'd like to connect, please visit:
cfbarrington.com
Facebook – @BarringtonCFAuthor
Twitter – @barrington_cf
Instagram – @cfbarrington_notwriting

Thank you again for your company.

C.F. Barrington

Acknowledgements

Over the course of the Pantheon series, many people have given me their support, advice and expertise, and most of these have been mentioned in the acknowledgements of at least one of my earlier books.

On this occasion, therefore, I want to highlight just a few key individuals who have made such a critical difference to my writing career:

First and foremost, Laura Macdougall of United Agents, who discovered me amongst her huge pile of submissions and believed in the potential of the Pantheon. Only through her focus and tenacity did the script for *The Wolf Mile* ever see the light of day and come to the attention of publishers. I am indebted to her.

Next on the list is Hannah Smith. Although she has moved on to pastures new, Hannah was commissioning editor for Aries Fiction at Head of Zeus when Laura approached her with *The Wolf Mile* and she decided to sign me on a three-book contract. Thank you, Hannah. You make dreams come true.

Peyton Stableford has been my publishing editor for the latter half of the Pantheon series and I love working with her. Not only is she fantastic at keeping me to schedule and dealing with the entire publication process, she is also such a champion for the Pantheon. Her enthusiasm fuels my motivation and I often find myself writing a scene and thinking 'Peyton's going to love this bit…'!

My gratitude to the marketing and design teams at Head of Zeus. I've loved all the covers and promotion. All four books have recently been given brand new cover images and I think they are perfect. Indeed, the image on the front of *The Bone Fields* was first designed when I was only halfway through the writing and it inspired me so much that I decided the climactic scenes must include a lonely castle on a loch. Without the HoZ design team, these scenes would never have been created.

A big thank you to Lydia Mason, who has worked on many of the structural and copy edits for the series. Your passion for the Pantheon and your critical analysis has helped make each draft so much better.

I am very grateful to Angie Crawford and all the staff at Waterstones Scotland for deciding to stock the Pantheon series. Visiting your stores across Scotland, from Inverness to Dumfries, signing books, giving talks and meeting all the welcoming teams has been utterly amazing for a new author.

Then there's my Sacred Band, who have all helped shape my belief in my writing in their different ways. Some through boundless enthusiasm; some through creative input; and others through getting me away from my desk and onto the hills! Mike Dougan, Mark Clay, Dave Follett, Howard Sims and David Robinson.

Finally, love and thanks to my parents – who nurtured my

passion for storytelling – and to Jackie – who has supported me through thick and thin and always believed in me.

Oh, and then there's Albert – who has done everything possible to stop me writing by wagging his tail and begging me to get out there for another run!